A PINEGROVE FD NOVEL

LIBBY KAY

The characters and events in this book are fictitious. Any similarity to real persons, living or dead, places, or events is coincidental and not intended by the author.

If you purchase this book without a cover you should be aware that this book may have been stolen property and reported as "unsold and destroyed" to the publisher. In such case the author has not received any payment for this "stripped book."

Old Flames
Copyright © 2025 Libby Kay
All rights reserved.

ISBN: (ebook) 978-1-964636-52-8
(print) 978-1-964636-54-2

Inkspell Publishing
207 Moonglow Circle #101
Murrells Inlet, SC 29576

Edited By Yezanira Venecia
Cover art By Emily's World By Design

All Rights Reserved. No part of this book may be used, including but not limited to, the training of or use by artificial intelligence, or reproduced in any manner whatsoever without written permission, except in the case of brief quotations embodied in critical articles and reviews. This book, or parts thereof, may not be reproduced in any form without permission. The copying, scanning, uploading, and distribution of this book via the internet or via any other means without the permission of the publisher is illegal and punishable by law. Please purchase only authorized electronic or print editions, and do not participate in or encourage piracy of copyrighted materials. Your support of the author's rights is appreciated.

DEDICATION

For Kathleen.
Much like Jessie, you're the best sister
anyone could ask for.

LIBBY KAY

PROLOGUE

10 Years Earlier

"Did you finish all the Moscato?" Jessie asked, reaching blindly and pawing around in the dark. Seconds later, she smacked Malcolm straight in the face.

"Oof," he exhaled, smothering a smile as he handed her the nearly empty wine bottle. It was ghastly stuff, sweeter than his nana's sweet tea, and left the chemical taste of grapes in his mouth, but he'd do anything for Jessie Mays.

Always had, always would.

"I'm thinking you should switch to water, JJ," he suggested, unscrewing a fresh bottle and jostling it overhead. Grabbing the wine cork, he tucked it into his pocket. Not necessarily the most comfortable position, he was propped on his elbows, with Jessie's head nestled on his lap. The whole damn meadow could burst into flames, and he'd be tempted to stay exactly where they were; two souls sharing the same air. *And a really awful bottle of vino ...*

Jessie, completely undeterred, blew raspberries before downing the last of the wine. She covered her mouth as she belched, the sound echoing in the empty space. Fireflies flitted around them, their lights providing the perfect romantic atmosphere—despite his girl's sound effects.

High school graduation had been that afternoon. While their classmates were at various parties getting drunk on their daddy's vodka or their momma's schnapps, Malcolm and Jessie had stolen a bottle of wine from her mother's stash and headed out to the meadows of a local farm, Hog Hollow.

What used to be a large farm and plantation had turned into a smaller, more workable farm with acres of meadowland and pine groves stretching out in every direction. Their small town had lots of better places to find trouble and embrace teenage drama, so very few kids ventured to the fields. Malcolm and Jessie had discovered the space the year before, desperate for a spot to just be.

Not to say they didn't get up to a fair bit of trouble, but most of their time in the meadow was spent doing this ... laying with their faces toward the night sky, searching for answers in the stars. And any place that he and Jessie could claim as their own held a special spot in his heart.

Sometimes, Malcolm would point out constellations he remembered from their astronomy class, and it was no different today. "Isn't that the Big Dipper?" he asked, knowing damn well it wasn't.

Jessie scoffed. "I may be drunk, but that's clearly Orion's belt." Her words slurred, her breath tickling his skin.

Malcolm inched closer and whispered, "Did you know it was originally called Orion's Fanny Pack?"

Jessie burst out laughing, rolling onto her side and poking Malcolm in the ribs. "Like hell it was," she said through another round of giggles. He would do anything to warrant a laugh from JJ; it was like taking a deep breath after being underwater—life-affirming.

"Water, Jessica June Mays, or else I'm telling your momma about the pilfered wine. We can discuss Orion's fashion choices later." Malcolm did his best to channel his father's sternness, but he sounded mostly smitten.

Jessie sighed, finally taking the water and chugging a

third in one go. "Pfft. Pilfered, look at you, College Boy." She winked to soften the dig, her blue eyes sparkling in the dim lighting.

Malcolm swept a lock of reddish-brown hair off her forehead, clearing the view to her lovely profile. "You can still join me," he offered, his voice low and tentative. "That acceptance letter hasn't expired."

He held his breath, knowing already the answer was a big fat *no*.

"Malcolm," Jessie warned, suddenly sounding more sober than she was. She angled her head to meet his gaze. "You know I have to try this. Please don't follow my parents' lead. It would be nice for someone to support my plan." She hesitated a moment and sighed. "Even Trevor's giving me guff. I don't know why everyone is on my case."

Her older brother Trevor was a good friend of Malcolm's, and he knew how much Trevor struggled with his sister leaving. The Mays clan was a tight-knit family of four, so surely their only daughter and sister moving away would sting. Growing up an only child, Malcolm understood all too well how it felt to be in a small family. There were invisible ties that could feel both comforting and cloying.

"I do support your plan, but that doesn't mean I won't miss you." His finger traced down her cheek to her neck, committing the path to memory. He was intimately acquainted with every inch of his girl, but he couldn't keep his hands away.

When his fingers reached her shoulder, she covered his hand with her own. "I love you, Malcolm. Me joining the Peace Corps doesn't change that."

"I love you, too." He dipped his head and pecked her lips before pulling back and staring up at the sky. Blinking away tears, he focused on finding the constellations, hopeful they could point him toward safer topics of conversation ... and a heart that wasn't splitting in half.

"My first tour is just six months, so I'll be home by

Christmas. It'll be like I'm at college, and we'll see each other over breaks." Linking their fingers together, she brought their joined hands to her lips. "Leaving Pinegrove doesn't mean I'm leaving you," she urged, but Malcolm didn't answer.

His eyes roamed the stars, his heart beating an urgent rhythm. Jessie Mays had been the girl of his dreams since he arrived in town four years prior. His father was an engineer, sent to rural Georgia for the project of a lifetime. His mother's acting career had cooled, and she'd welcomed the change of scenery. At the time, Malcolm had whined about leaving everything he knew in Atlanta behind. Those arguments ended quickly that first day of high school when a certain brunette lent him a pencil in algebra class, and his world flipped upside down.

Within a month of meeting, the pair were joined at the hip. They were high school sweethearts, always expected at family functions, school dances, and community events like the fireworks festival. Malcolm had foolishly hoped their coupledom would continue after graduation, but Jessie had other ideas.

"I know, JJ." The lie melted bitterly on his tongue. Jessie dreamed of travel, wanted to see the world and help her fellow man. Malcolm was a homebody who loved their small town and the roots they'd planted. Despite his youth, he wanted those roots to grow into a life, a family, a future.

"You'll see, nothing will change." Jessie seemed to be reminding herself as much as Malcolm. Squeezing her hand, he swallowed past the lump in his throat.

"I trust you." He blinked away a tear as it slid down his cheek, dissecting his somber expression in half.

"I'll write all the time; you'll be sick of hearing from me." Jessie laughed, but it sounded like it was under water. After a few sniffles, she sat up and wiped at her face.

"JJ," Malcolm whispered her nickname, pulling her to his chest, "we'll figure it out. I love you."

"Love you more, and I mean it, dammit." She coughed

into his T-shirt, soaking the fabric with her tears. "I know no one thinks high school romances go anywhere, but we'll prove them all wrong."

Covering the back of her head with his hand, Malcolm cradled Jessie against him, rocking them in time to the crickets' chirping. In the distance he heard the sounds of animals in the barn and hushed voices. It could be classmates saying goodbye to their high school years, or it could be the farm owners. Either way, Malcolm wasn't keen on getting caught.

Despite not wanting the night to end, they needed to get home. Much like a ticking clock, the thudding of his heart reminded him that their time was drawing to a close. Because regardless of what Jessie promised, Malcolm knew the truth.

Not all love stories had a happy ending ...

*

"Daddy," Jessie whined, hands thrust on her hips. "It would be nice if you backed me up, please." She tapped her foot in time to her racing heartbeat.

Her father rested on the doorjamb to her bedroom, arms crossed over his chest. His usual jovial expression was pinched as he frowned at the luggage on her bed. "Forgive me," he started, letting out a sigh that nearly blew the curtains. "I'm a sad to see my little girl leave."

Jessie picked up a stack of tank tops, waving them wildly in the air. "You've known about this for weeks, and if all you're going to do is cry and mope, I'll call Malcolm."

"Hush up now," her mother warned, joining her husband and resting a hand on his shoulder. "Forgive your daddy and I for hating that our only daughter would rather live south of the equator than in lovely Pinegrove with us."

"Not again, Momma," Jessie warned, balling up a pair of cargo shorts and shoving them with too much force into her duffle bag. "I'll be home at Christmas. You won't even miss me, I promise."

"Ha!" Her mother, Daisy, snorted. "I'm sure you're right, sugar. I'll hardly notice that my eighteen-year-old has fled across the globe to stop world hunger." Her father snickered, earning a glare from his wife. "Not you, too, Nick. Back me up here."

Nick rubbed his face, stepping into the room and flopping down on the corner of the bed. He took his time folding a stack of T-shirts, lining them up carefully next to her suitcase. "I'm incredibly proud of you, June Bug." His praise came out soft, and Jessie had to strain to hear it. "But," he added, clearing his throat, "that doesn't mean I won't miss you something awful. It isn't easy watching you leave, no matter how much good I know you'll do."

Having been the stoic fire chief in Pinegrove since Jessie was old enough to tie her own shoes, she wasn't used to seeing her daddy this upset. Bottom lip trembling, she closed the distance and wrapped her father in a fierce hug.

How could she possibly explain to her parents that she had to try this? She had to leave the safety of her small hometown. This itch to travel wasn't what her friends were doing this summer, palling around Europe and staying in hostels while they drank beer and ate their weight in tapas and cheese. Jessie wanted to see the real world, to go where the tourists didn't, and make her mark.

She'd always struggled with her place in Pinegrove. Never one of the pretty, popular girls, she'd fumbled her way through school, never making lasting friendships. Jessie had always been tight with her brother, but they were older now. Trevor was at the academy preparing to follow in their father's footsteps. Daisy wanted nothing more than for her daughter to stay home, marry Malcolm, and fill the town with their offspring. *For a progressive woman, her mother still had old-fashioned ideas ...*

Jessie opened her mouth to explain herself, or at least attempt to, when the doorbell rang. Daisy sighed, patting her damp cheeks. "I'll get it. It's probably Malcolm."

There was no doubt her boyfriend was at the other side of the door, and that didn't help Jessie's roiling belly. For all her muster to go, she hated leaving Malcolm behind most of all. Her parents would be fine in the end. Parents were meant to raise children and set them free, right? But Malcolm, her sweetheart boyfriend, was a walking marshmallow, always soft and tender. She didn't want to hurt him, but she didn't know how to avoid it either.

Nick pushed himself to standing. In the distance, they both heard Daisy greeting Malcolm, but they didn't join them. "June Bug, listen to me." Her father's voice didn't waver, despite his trembling bottom lip. "You're going to do amazing things, I have no doubt. There's greatness in you, but remember you always have a place here." He pointed at his feet, hand quivering.

He pulled her to him, resting his chin on top of her head. Jessie let out a sob, unable to stop the waterworks. He shook around her, and she squeezed until she feared they'd both pop like balloons at the county fair. Reluctantly, her father stepped back. "Take your time with Malcolm. We don't have to leave for Atlanta for another hour."

Take her time ... if only.

"Thanks, Daddy," she breathed, frantically swiping away more tears as Malcolm approached.

Malcolm stood awkwardly in the doorway, nodding at her father as he made his exit. His hands were shoved into the pockets of his shorts, his gorgeous brown eyes downcast and red-rimmed. His dark skin was ashen, jaw tense. "Hey, JJ," he said, unable to look up. He'd recently gotten a haircut, his riot of black curls tamed into waves. It made him look older, like a different person. She hated this small reminder that his life was moving forward already.

"Hey," she whispered, falling onto the bed with a huff. "Damnit, this is depressing." Her exhale left in a whoosh, but she didn't bother hiding the tears as they slid down her cheeks.

Malcolm glanced over his shoulder, ensuring the coast

was clear before joining her on the bed. Even though they'd been dating for years, they both respected house rules and left the bedroom door open. Easing himself down onto the mattress, he snatched her hand and pulled it toward his chest, cradling it like a precious treasure. "You know what wouldn't be depressing?" he asked, voice barely audible.

Jessie knew what he was going to say, and she begged him to stop. The last thing they needed was a repeat of their last round of fights. It was impossible not to be sad when one of them was leaving. Jessie understood they'd only be delaying the inevitable. Malcolm left for college in three weeks, and she'd be alone anyway. All she was doing was beating fate to the punch.

"Don't," she warned, pulling her hand free and sweeping a short curl off his forehead. His skin was smooth and cool under her touch, despite the summer heat outside. "Please don't, Malcolm. You know I have to go."

Slowly, he shook his head. "You really don't, JJ. You can come with me to school and we can—"

But Jessie didn't have the fight in her anymore. She slid her hand down to cover his mouth, her own lips quivering. "I need to try this. You know I do. I've never felt like I fit in, and I want to see if I can find out who I am. Please, you have to let me go."

Hand falling down to her lap, Jessie squeezed her eyes shut, unwilling to watch his face crumple. Beside her, she heard the rumble in Malcolm's chest as he struggled to collect himself. "But I love you, JJ. Doesn't that matter?"

She hated him in this moment, for poking at the hole in her plan. Her desire for self-discovery had one flaw—that she was leaving the love of her life behind. These days, Jessie clung to the old adage of *If you love someone, set them free...*

Right now, she clung to Malcolm, turning to face him until he wrapped her against him. He pressed a kiss to her temple, his lips whispering terms of endearment meant only for her. "I love you so much, and I'll be back." She repeated the promise over and over again until her parents knocked on the door.

"Sorry, kids," her father said, actually sounding remorseful. "We need to get ready for the airport."

Malcolm helped her father carry out her luggage, swiping at the tears on his cheeks when he didn't think anyone was looking. Once her parents were in the front seats, she tugged him to the side of the driveway and repeated the mantra she'd been saying since she accepted her first position with the Peace Corps. "I love you, and I'll write every day."

Jessie kissed Malcolm goodbye, telling herself she wasn't making a mistake, telling herself she wasn't walking away from the best man on earth.

LIBBY KAY

CHAPTER ONE

Present day

Malcolm "Smithy" Smith had been a firefighter and EMT for nearly a decade. The job was tailor-made for him: the perfect mix of excitement, planning, and variety. Nothing compared to the rush he got when he raced off to a scene—the danger was always lurking, but it wasn't front of mind.

It was rewarding. It was challenging. It was everything.

"Yo, Smithy!" Javier "Javi" Ortiz called from the opposite side of the bullpen.

"Yeah, Ortiz?" Malcolm asked, not looking up from the report he was typing up. He and his buddy were part of an arson investigation that was heating up—pun unfortunately intended. A series of fires had sprung up all over Pinegrove, from residential developments to the retail district. Their captain, an inept man who got the job through nepotism, hadn't given the investigation the support it deserved. Scott Hastings was a tool, but Malcolm never skirted a commanding officer. Even morons like Hastings …

Javi walked over to Malcolm's desk, leaning against it

and yawning. His dark hair was slicked back and perfectly styled, a feat for anyone who wore a helmet on the job. "I've been thinking …" he said, scratching his jaw.

"That'd be a first," Malcolm quipped. Javi discreetly flipped him the bird before snatching a peanut butter cup off Malcolm's desk. "Hey," he argued, but it was too late. Javi had already unwrapped the candy and popped it in his mouth.

"Maybe next time you'll be nicer, man." Javi winked, lips covered in peanut butter.

Malcolm went back to his typing, hoping Javi would take the hint. No such luck. "Other than stealing my snacks, you need something, Ortiz?"

Javi tipped his head back and forth in thought. After swallowing his stolen snack, he said, "I've been looking at the accelerants used, and I think …" but he didn't get to finish his thought, because the alarm sounded.

Five-alarm fire called in, Warehouse District. EMTs requested.

Dispatch blared through the speakers, the team already on their way to the garage and jumping into their gear. Malcolm's heart rate kicked up, but only a little. He was ready as he slid behind the wheel of the ambulance. Tiffany Maxwell, one of the rookies, was hot on his heels.

A young mother of two, Maxwell was no-nonsense. She made it perfectly clear she was one of the guys, and she'd happily punch anyone in the nuts who disagreed. He'd never admit this to Javi, but she was Malcolm's favorite partner.

"Ready, Smithy?" she asked as she buckled in, helmet smothering her sandy hair.

Malcolm shot her a thumbs-up as he switched on the sirens and turned onto the main road. It was evening, and fortunately most of the rush hour traffic had died down. *Or as much rush hour traffic as Pinegrove, Georgia, got with less than ten thousand residents.*

Maxwell chatted with dispatch as Malcolm sped to the Warehouse District. Even before they arrived, Malcolm had a feeling this fire was tied to the series of arsons they were investigating. It was too suspicious and too coincidental, but he'd worry about the logistics later. Right now, he needed to get to the scene. Hopefully he and Javi could talk to Hastings about their investigation before the end of their shift.

Parking the ambulance on the curb, he radioed the main truck that he and Maxwell were ready to attend to the injured. "I'll check the south perimeter," Maxwell said as she hopped out and jogged away, her bunker gear clattering with each step.

Malcolm went to work getting the gurney ready, all the while listening to chatter on the intercom. A few moments later, Javi and Trevor arrived. "Smithy!" Trevor barked, running up in his gear. His voice was muffled through his helmet.

"Maxwell went south. I'm going to join her out the back."

It was the last thing Malcolm said before he ran into the fire, flames licking up the walls, smoke billowing all around him. He scanned the space, fortunately not finding anyone else. Using his flashlight, he swept it across the room, but the smoke was thick.

Creaking and groaning echoed around him, and Malcolm was careful of his steps as he paced into the second room. Again, no one was in sight as he continued into a far corner. Just as soon as he stepped through a doorway, a loud crashing sound reverberated, a chunk of ceiling crashing at his feet. Singed wood and crumbling drywall added dust to the smoke, making visibility nearly impossible.

Malcolm licked his lips, pulse skyrocketing, about to call out to the crew when a log-like structure fell directly on Malcolm, pinning him to the floor. The force knocked the wind from his lungs, but he didn't panic yet. He was in his gear, his team knew where he was. They were all prepared; it would be fine.

For the first few minutes, no one came. Blinking through the smoke and tears, Malcolm struggled to slow his breathing, fought to keep his cool. Yet, the minutes ticked by and help didn't arrive. This warehouse was in a remote part of town, but that didn't mean there weren't other lives to save. He knew his crew was doing their job.

Their job, his job. It was the biggest joy of his life. Of course, there was something else that brought him joy, and he'd give anything to see Jessie one more time. If this was the end, that would be the bigger tragedy, not being able to say goodbye. Not being able to hear her laugh, to feel her in his arms …

The very last thing Malcolm thought about as he closed his eyes was his girl, her warm smile welcoming him to rest. As the smoke wafted around him, he reached out with his free hand, eager to get a touch of her smooth skin. He only hoped she knew how much he missed her, how much he still loved her.

As another chunk of ceiling fell at his feet, faint voices approached Malcolm's prone form. "He's over here," yelled Javi, urgency coating his hoarse cries. "Smithy's over here!"

"Are you sure? I don't see his reflective gear!" Trevor called out, stomping around a pile of debris.

Malcolm closed his eyes and smiled, reassured that his friends were here at the end. He also took comfort knowing that Trevor would take care of Jessie; she was his little sister after all. She would be okay, he mused as he passed out from the pain.

She had to be.

*

Jessie Mays had been working for the Peace Corps for nearly a decade. She'd always loved the comradery of her coworkers, the selflessness they shared while serving. But she also loved the variety. Depending on the location, she could be working with kids and teachers on educational initiatives, building houses and schools, or helping towns struggling with critical water shortages. There was always something new, always something different.

Currently she was stationed in South America on an agricultural mission. She was tasked with helping a village start over after a devastating series of fires. Forests and farmland had been demolished by Mother Nature, and Jessie was part of a team to support the farmers.

When she first arrived, Jessie couldn't help but see the parallels to her and Malcolm's jobs. As she walked through fields of soot, she thought about Malcolm—and her brother and their father before—who put out fires like this for a living. They put their lives in danger constantly to ensure their neighbors were safe. It was noble, and it fit her ex to a tee.

Jessie strode out of her tent, clipboard under her arm and slathered in sunscreen and bug spray. Ahead her supervisor, Noel, spoke with one of the farmers about crop placement.

Noel was older than Jessie by about ten years. He'd been working for the Peace Corps since he graduated high school, and he showed no signs of changing careers. He was what Jessie aspired to be, management with more of a say on his projects.

After shaking hands with the farmer, Noel turned to Jessie. "There you are, Jessie. I was chatting with Gael, and we're debating between sugar cane and beans for this plot of land. I'd love to pick your brain over breakfast."

Noel strode ahead, toward their series of tents. His blonde hair was tucked under a Panama hat, his fair skin bronze from the sun. Jessie's own skin had turned a golden caramel color, bringing her freckles out in force. She'd learned to keep her hair shorter during her missions, and it was currently hidden beneath a bandana.

Once they were inside, Noel kicked out a chair and motioned for Jessie to join him. She eagerly slid into her seat, placing her clipboard on the table. Fingers trembling, she tucked them under her legs until Noel met her gaze. She'd been hungry for an opportunity to lead more ventures, and she prayed her boss was about to deliver good news.

"You want some coffee or anything?" he asked, reaching across the table for a carafe of coffee. Jessie nodded and he poured them two cups. The best part of this particular assignment was this coffee; grown and roasted mere miles from where they sat, it was rich and flavorful. Not the stuff she'd usually add a vat of cream and sugar to. This was mellow and smooth, the perfect wake-up call.

When she knew her hands wouldn't shake, Jessie picked up her cup and sipped while Noel updated her on the project. "As you know," he said, opening up a folder and shuffling around papers. "We expect to wrap up this project within the month. Then we'll all have a break back in the states before we can apply for our next placements."

Jessie nodded, sipping her coffee and hoping she could blame her bouncing foot on caffeine jitters. "Yes, sir."

Noel smiled, chuckling as he clicked his pen. "C'mon, Jessie. You can call me Noel. I've been your supervisor for years now, and we're beyond the formalities."

"Yes, sir. I mean, Noel!" she practically shouted, her cheeks flaming.

He downed his coffee in two long gulps, placing the mug on the table and sliding it to the side. "I wanted to talk to you about a potential opportunity. There are no guarantees anything I'm about to say will get approved, but I thought we should talk."

"Okay." Jessie's voice was barely a whisper. Her heart galloped in her ribcage, and she feared if she spoke again it would either be a yelp or a scream. Nerves on fire, her pulse pounded; this could be the big break she'd been waiting for. "You think there's a promotion opportunity?"

"I do," Noel answered, handing her a sheet of paper with a job description. "Again, I need to stress that nothing is even official. We have to see what happens with budgets and the board, but there should be at least two opportunities to lead teams next year."

"Really? Two opportunities?" she parroted, not believing her ears. Supervisory roles did not come up often, and when they did, it was usually one position that had already been earmarked for someone with connections.

Adjusting his hat, Noel leaned back in his seat. "I've been very impressed with you for a while, Jessie. You're dedicated, you're fearless, and you lead by example. What you've been doing with Gael and his farmers has been inspiring. You really know your agriculture."

Jessie nearly fainted right out of her seat. While she took pride in what she did, she knew she wasn't alone in that skill. With enough time and guidance, almost anyone could learn the basics of farming. Not to mention, Noel didn't hand out compliments freely. If he was saying she did a good job, she believed him.

"Thank you, s … Noel." She cleared her throat. "What do I need to do to be considered for this?" Pointing at the job description, her hand shook like a leaf.

"Right now, exactly what you're doing. I've been keeping notes in your employee file, and I'll be happy to share them should you choose to apply." He inched closer and added in a hushed tone, "And remember, this isn't official yet, so I'd appreciate if you didn't publicize until we know more."

Jessie's head bobbed in agreement, her grin overtaking her face. This was her shot, this was what she'd been working for all these years—an opportunity to lead a team, but also have more control over her placements.

Noel got up, pushed his chair in, and collected his papers. "Grab some grub and meet me in the west fields with the team in about thirty. Thanks for chatting, Jessie."

As soon as her supervisor was gone, Jessie sprang to her feet and did a little happy dance around the table. Her body vibrated, and she couldn't stand still. This conversation alone had given her a confidence boost she hadn't realized was missing.

Granted, she understood that she did a good job. She'd seen the results of her work, the people she'd helped, the communities that were reborn. This current assignment had been her favorite, because it gave her the opportunity to work with animals and crops.

Jessie had never been a good student, eager to avoid making plans for college and a desk job. She'd always thrived outdoors, getting her hands dirty, the sun beating down on her. While her brother aced his tests and asked for extra credit, she'd turn in half-completed homework assignments and barely managed to show up to take the SAT, let alone excel at it.

When the time had come to start looking at colleges, her high school guidance counselor was quick to suggest other career paths. Trade schools, the military, and even beauty school were suggested. Jessie had gestured at her cut-off denim shorts and crooked ponytail and quickly nixed that latter suggestion. *Although her momma would have loved to have a girly girl...*

During a quiet night in her room with Google, Jessie had found links to the Peace Corps, and the rest was history. It took nearly a year of applications and talking her parents—and Malcolm—into it, but she never regretted her decision.

Well, that wasn't entirely true. Sometimes she did. Like when it was late at night in the South American jungles and her only company was a lizard and her soggy sleeping bag. Or that one time in the deserts of West Africa when she stared up at the stars all alone, no one by her side to point out constellations and make up stories about their origins.

She missed Malcolm, every day. But she wasn't sure what to do about it.

Instead of wallowing, Jessie shoved a granola bar in her pocket and strode out into the sunshine for another day on the farm. She was eager to work with Gael and his team on planting for their future.

She could worry about her own future at another time.

CHAPTER TWO

"Jessica, it's Momma."

That was the moment Jessie knew something was terribly wrong. The last time her mother used her given name was when she called about her father's death. It was a sudden heart attack; a moment in time that broke her heart and trashed her hope in the future. If Nick Mays was gone, she had no reason to stay anywhere near the great state of Georgia. Life simply didn't make sense without her daddy.

"Noel, I need to take this," Jessie said, her hand clamped over the team's shared satellite phone. Out here in the wilds, cell service was spotty at best. Most phone calls sounded like they came through cotton wool, but it was better than nothing.

Her boss waved her into the rear of the tent and closed the canvas flap to provide the illusion of privacy. She exhaled and squeezed the phone before talking to her mother.

"Momma? Is it Trevor?" Sweat pooled under her arms as she waited for her mother's reply, her mind whirling with prayers of good news, despite her mother's quivering voice.

She often feared a call like this would come. Even

though she grew up surrounded by firefighters, and the risks they took, she'd operated under the misconception that the flames and smoke would never touch her family.

"No, sugar. Trevor will be fine."

A whoosh of air escaped her as Jessie sagged against the folding chair in the makeshift office. The card table in front of her was piled high with paperwork and a laptop that was three years beyond its replacement date. Ah, the joys of working for a nonprofit in a third-world country.

"That's good, I'm glad Trev's okay." Jessie wiped sweat off her brow, her eyes unfocused. "What happened?"

There was muffled conversation on the other line until her mother finally responded with, "There was a fire."

The hairs on the back of Jessie's neck rose the longer her mother spoke. "But Trev's okay?"

"He has some smoke inhalation and bumps and bruises, but he'll recover. Whitney is taking care of him."

"Who's Whitney?" Jessie asked, leaning forward. A fly buzzed around her face, but she couldn't bother to swat at it. This phone call was distracting enough.

Her mother chuckled, the first happy sound she'd made this whole phone call. "She's your brother's new girlfriend, an absolute doll. You're going to love her."

"So you're calling to tell me about Trevor's love life?" While not necessarily a boring topic, she was happy to learn her brother had moved on from his horrid ex-fiancée. Yet it didn't explain her mother's urgent tone. Noel had sprinted out of the management tent when the phone rang, gaze searching for her as she wrapped up a conversation with a colleague.

Her mother cleared her throat, and Jessie pinched the bridge of her nose. Something was clearly up, and she needed answers before she had a panic attack in the middle of the jungle. "Momma, what is going on?"

"It's Malcolm." Two words—maximum impact.

Jessie bolted to her feet, pacing back and forth around the cramped tent. In her haste to move, she kicked over an empty canteen. "What about Malcolm?" The question nearly choked her.

"He was there, sugar, at the scene. They got him out before the building collapsed, but he's not in good shape."

"What do you mean, not in good shape?" Her voice sounded funny to her own ears, like she was stuck in a tunnel.

"He's in ICU. He's got a couple broken bones, smoke inhalation, and a possible head injury. He is doing better; he was in a medically induced coma until the swelling went down in his skull."

"Holy shit!" Jessie exclaimed, falling to her knees with a thud. Her head tipped forward as she gasped for breath. "Is he going to …" She couldn't force herself to utter the words, to bring the thought that Malcolm Smith wouldn't be on this earth. She'd lost so much with her father's passing, she couldn't lose Malcolm, too.

"They don't know yet," her mother said, voice dripping with fatigue. "I wanted you to know, in case …" but she thankfully left that sentence unfinished.

"I'm coming home."

"Sugar, that's not why I'm calling. I only wanted you to know." Daisy hesitated a moment and added, "I think he'd want you to know what happened."

She believed her mother, knew she wouldn't want Jessie to waste what little free cash she had flying across the globe on a whim. But this was Malcolm, and she couldn't live with herself if she wasn't by his side.

"I'm getting on the next flight out of here. I'll text when I land. Can you pick me up in Atlanta?"

"Sugar, you know I will. But don't jump to conclusions. I'll keep you posted on Malcolm's condition."

Jessie sighed, her chin dipping down to her chest. "Momma, I'm coming home. I missed Daddy's heart attack. I can't live with myself if I don't get to see Malcolm."

Daisy was quiet, save for the din in the background. When she spoke again, her voice sounded normal, filled with determination and support. "You text me your flight details, and I'll be there in Atlanta."

"Love you, Momma."

"Love you more, sugar." Her mother disconnected first, leaving Jessie alone with her thoughts and a crushing sense of dread.

"Is everything all right, Jessie?" Noel asked, joining her in the tent.

It was hard to believe that a couple days ago they were discussing her future career plans, and now she was about to take leave before the project was complete.

"There's a situation back home," she said, running a hand down her face. Her eyes felt gritty, her mouth dry.

Noel raised an eyebrow. "It's serious?"

"Yes, sir," she said, not bothering with being casual. "My brother and friend were in a fire at work, and they're both in the hospital." *Technically not the whole truth, but Jessie would worry about that later.*

Back when her father passed, Noel had been very supportive. He gave her extended bereavement and ensured she made it home to grieve and be with family. The trouble now was, he didn't seem as keen to offer her escape. Gone were the damp eyes and sullen expression. In its place were a set jaw and bored demeanor.

"That's terrible. I hope they'll recover soon." Noel blinked, holding out his hand for the satellite phone.

The pair of them stared at each other, the only sounds that of the ruckus outside the tent. The team was working on building an irrigation system, and the hammering echoed through Jessie's skull.

"I need to take some leave, please. After everything that happened with my dad, I need to be with family." She pulled her bandana off, fluffing her hair with her fingers. Fidgeting had been a nervous habit from childhood, but in this instant she found it comforting.

Noel tucked the phone into the pocket of his cargo shorts, grimacing at the ground. "Of course, you're free to go home. But Jessie"—his words faltered as he collected himself—"I'm about to put your name in for one of those promotions. If you leave now, before we can finish our work on these farms, I can't promise it will help your application."

Jessie rocked back on her heels, her gut churning. "But my ..." She couldn't find her words. The situation was impossible: the choice between seeing Malcolm and her brother and potentially moving forward in her career. How on earth was she supposed to choose?

Sighing, Noel rested his hands on his hips. In the dim light of the tent, he looked older, more worn out. Jessie could relate. "I don't mean to sound insensitive, but we both know these opportunities don't come along very often."

"I know," she said, her voice a pained whisper. "But, sir, I won't be able to live with myself if something happens. I'll have to take my chances." Jessie squared her shoulders, meeting her supervisor's gaze with her chin held high. "I appreciate you putting in a good word, but I need to see my family." *She needed to see Malcolm more than her next breath ...*

Noel nodded, holding the tent flap open for her to exit. "Then I hope everything goes well back home. Keep me posted on your return." He patted his pocket where the phone rested, and all Jessie could do was nod.

Sprinting to her tent, Jessie threw her meager belongings in her duffle. She hadn't even looked for flights yet, but she had to do something productive or she'd crumple to the ground. It took her a couple hours, but she found a flight that left the following evening. As she bid farewell to the crew, she said a prayer that she wasn't making the biggest mistake of her life. Yet even if she was, she knew Malcolm was worth it.

*

Pinegrove had the best fire department in Georgia, hands down. Despite years of razzing each other and causing trouble on the job, when the rubber hit the road, this crew had each other's backs. That's why when Malcolm finally opened his eyes in the ICU, he knew he wasn't dead. His brothers and sisters in arms wouldn't allow it.

"Son, it's Chief Warren." The reassuring baritone of his boss eased a tiny bit of Malcolm's nerves. He blinked under the fluorescent lighting, his throat scratchy and raw as steak tartare.

"Ch …chief?" Malcolm leaned forward, coughing as his body shook with the effort of trying to say one word. His esophagus burned like he'd drunk battery acid, bile rising up. His stomach tensed as he gasped for air.

"Shhh," Chief urged, resting a hand on his shoulder to keep him still. "Let me get you some water." A moment later, a paper cup was thrust under Malcolm's sight line. "Slow sips," Chief instructed. "I pressed the button for one of the nurses."

In the time it took Malcolm to have one sip of water, a team of nurses barged into the cramped room. "Mr. Smith, it's good to see you awake," the senior nurse said as she strode over to his bedside. Chief Warren jumped to his feet and stepped into a corner as the other two nurses checked the machines by his bed and jotted down notes in an iPad.

The youngest nurse leaned over Malcolm, pulling back his eyelids and flashing a pen light in his face. "Can you tell me your name and birthday, please?" she asked coldly.

"My what?" he asked, turning his face away and coughing into his pillow. His lungs burned with every exhale, and he realized he couldn't bring his left hand to his mouth. Wiggling his limbs, he discovered one of his legs was in an air cast, dangling from a support in the ceiling. His left arm was also wrapped, so heavy he could hardly lift it from the mattress.

Panic surged through his veins as Malcolm strained against the nurse's touch. "What happened to me?" He screwed his eyes shut, desperate to remember what brought him here. Obviously it was something on the job, but his mind was blank.

"Can you give him a minute, please?" Chief Warren asked, stepping back to Malcolm's side. "He just woke up."

"What happened to me?" This time, Malcolm addressed his question to his superior officer.

"There was a fire, son, in the warehouse district. Everyone made it out okay, but you took the brunt of the injuries." Chief's eyes were tired, dark smudges marring his face. His voice sounded strained, but from more than fatigue. "You're going to be fine, isn't that right, Nurse Hopkins?"

The older nurse nodded, ushering the other nurses to the doorway. "You will, Mr. Smith. But I do need to collect some samples and run more tests to determine if there's been any brain damage."

Malcolm's skin paled at the mention of brain damage. "Are you serious?" He blinked, trying in vain to remember the last thing that happened. He remembered being at the station shooting the shit with Javi, Trevor, and the rest of the A shift. After that, it's a haze of shadows.

"Chief Warren, if you can wait in the hallway, I'd like a little privacy with my patient."

Always a rule follower, Chief nodded and carefully patted Malcolm's shoulder. "I'll be right outside. Your parents are coming down from Tennessee later today, but I'm not leaving until they arrive." He rubbed a hand over his jaw. "Trevor, Javi, and Maxwell are chomping at the bit to visit. As soon as you're ready, the whole damn station wants to see you." Chief paused a moment and chuckled. "Hell, I think half of Pinegrove wants to stop by and check on you."

Malcolm smiled, but the movement made him grimace. Every muscle in his body felt strained and exhausted, like he'd been dragged over a mile of hot coals. *Well, maybe he had?*

After chatting with the chief for another moment, Malcolm's heavy eyes finally closed. As he drifted back to sleep, he thought about his parents' impending visit. Yes, he wanted to see them. Even though he was pushing thirty, he still wanted a little TLC from his folks. The problem was, nothing was ever little with his mother.

Growing up in Atlanta, he'd been used to her being gone during filming season. She was the star on a cable soap opera in the early '00s, *Atlanta Hearts,* which left Malcolm alone with his father, and more often his own thoughts. Being absent as long as she was, when Estelle was back in their family home, she was the Queen Bee, dictating what everyone did and overwhelming Malcolm with attention. He hadn't realized how much she could smother him until tastes changed and cable soaps were no longer a draw.

When the show went under just before Malcolm entered high school, everyone agreed it was time to move to a quieter part of the Peach State, at least until his mother could figure out her next move. His father's career afforded him the flexibility to live anywhere, and they'd chosen the little hamlet of Pinegrove. The rest, as they say, was history.

The next twenty-four hours were a blur of nameless doctors and nurses and his parents. Javi, Trevor, and Maxwell visited, each wearing anxious—and almost guilty— expressions. Malcolm didn't want any pity. Their job dealt with risk every day, and sometimes the odds weren't in their favor. However, there was a visitor who brought news that nearly sent Malcolm catapulting off the bed—injuries be damned.

Daisy entered with his team, hanging close to Chief. It was public knowledge that the pair had been courting, and Malcolm was thrilled to see both of them smiling ... and living ... again. "I hear your parents are coming soon," Daisy said, filling up his water cup and unwrapping a fresh straw.

"Yes, ma'am," Malcolm said, striving to keep his tone light. He wasn't used to this many people fussing over him.

"Well, speaking of visitors." She licked her lips, her gaze snagging his. "I spoke with Jessie, and she's coming home for a visit."

"JJ's coming home?" His question was laced with hope and a tinge of fear. Perhaps all the medications he was on sent him into a tailspin—or maybe he was hallucinating this whole encounter.

Daisy steadied the cup of water under his chin and waggled the straw, urging him to stay hydrated. "Yes, sugar, she'll be here in a few days."

Malcolm didn't remember a damned thing after Daisy's news. The hospital could have imploded and he wouldn't have noticed. All he could think about was the fact that JJ was coming home. Granted, Daisy said it was for a visit, but he'd take any scrap of his girl he could. Maybe it was having a warehouse fall on him, but Malcolm needed to see her, needed to feel her and hold her as close as he could.

Yet, before his girl would arrive, the other woman in his life was due in Pinegrove. Every time he opened his eyes, Malcolm braced for the piercing tone of his mother's voice. Before he was ready, his parents invaded the relative quiet of the ICU.

"Malcolm, baby!" Estelle wailed as she glided into his room. Better dressed for a night on the town, she was clad in a sundress and heels that skittered on the floor. "How are you?" she asked, her manicured fingers already combing through his hair.

Malcolm winced, her nails snagging on a stitch below his hairline. "Ouch," he hissed as he forced a smile.

"Baby, what hurts?" Estelle crumpled onto his bedside like she was auditioning for a role on Broadway, her free hand fluttering over her heart.

"Estelle, please," his father said behind her, attempting to get her into a chair. "Give the boy some air."

While his mother was the emotional heart of their family of three, his father was the brain and spine. For as dramatic as Estelle loved to be—and as a retired actress it was in her blood—his engineering father, Craig, was the polar opposite. His even gaze swept up and down his son's broken body, lips pressed in a firm line.

"How are you feeling?" He carefully took his wife's jacket and hung it over the foot of the bed. Pulling another chair closer, he took a seat and waited for Malcolm's reply.

"Umm, I'm okay?" It came out as a question because Malcolm had no answers. All he knew was he was in pain and wanted to be anywhere but in a hospital. Fatigue weighed him down, and keeping his eyes open was a chore. He yearned for a measly night in his own home, in his own bed, but apparently he wasn't going anywhere yet—especially alone.

"The doctors said you broke your arm and leg, and your lungs were damaged!" Estelle fanned herself with Malcolm's chart. Craig patted her back and pulled a paper fan from her handbag, swapping out the two. He carefully hung the clipboard back, glancing at the cover sheet and wincing.

Estelle flipped open the fan with a flourish, the movement jangling the tennis bracelets on her arm. In an instant, she'd turned into a modern-day Scarlett O'Hara.

Craig cleared his throat. "They also said you didn't suffer a concussion and would likely be discharged by the end of the week. You'll need physical therapy, but overall you dodged a bullet."

"That's good," Malcolm said as he rested his head back and pinched his eyes shut.

Apparently the notion of him resting was a step too far, as Estelle leapt to her feet and cried out, "Baby, are you okay?"

Malcolm winced at the shrill tone in her voice. "Mom, please. I'm resting my eyes."

"Estelle, do we need to go back to the hotel?" Craig's tone suggested this wasn't their first attempt visiting their only child.

His mother blew her nose into a lacy handkerchief and shook her head. "I'm fine. Hush up." She winked to soften the blow and his father chuckled.

"You rest up, son. I'm going to look for some coffee."

Craig dipped down and muttered something in his wife's ear, but she flapped a hand to dismiss him.

Malcolm listened as his father's measured footsteps disappeared down the hallway. It could have been the fire, the medications, or the general exhaustion, but Malcolm was already half asleep. Fortunately, Estelle took the hint and quietly hummed a tune he remembered from childhood.

As his eyelids closed, he thought of the last time he'd seen Jessie. It had been ages ago, during a rare visit back to Pinegrove. In typical fashion, they'd spent the first half of her trip together, acting as if the years hadn't marched on. Then when it came time to download her boarding pass, they'd begun fighting. Right now, he couldn't remember the details, simply the hollow feeling that crippled him when she crammed her belongings into her duffle and disappeared—yet again.

It had been a decade since their official breakup, but that didn't mean the pair didn't make reconciliation an Olympic sport. All it took was a visit to Pinegrove, and Malcolm crawled back to Jessie every single time. Apparently resistance when it came to JJ was futile, as all he needed to hear was his name on her lips and he was a simp.

But none of the past mattered now, because Jessie was on her way back to him.

He may be laid up in the ICU, but Malcolm would have a dozen burning buildings collapse on him if it meant he got even one hour with his girl. Because despite what JJ thought, she was still his top priority.

Now he just needed to get out of this hospital and show her.

LIBBY KAY

CHAPTER THREE

"Sugar, I'm driving as fast as I can." Daisy huffed, merging into the fast lane as her daughter fidgeted in the passenger's seat. "And you know how I feel about backseat driving."

The warning look Daisy shot Jessie had her toes curling in her sneakers. "Yes, ma'am."

"Why don't you tell me about your journey? That oughta distract you plenty." Narrowly avoiding a semi in the middle lane, Daisy sped around him and settled into the right lane again. Jessie surreptitiously checked the speedometer and saw she was going five miles over the speed limit. For her mother, that was tantamount to a NASCAR race.

Jessie leaned back in the seat and sighed. "Not too much to tell. I was glad there weren't any delays."

That was a lie—there was plenty to tell.

While packing up her duffle at the Peace Corps headquarters, she broke down when a local asked why she was so upset. As soon as she'd mentioned Malcolm's name, the dam burst and she'd soaked the poor woman's shirt with tears. She'd admitted things to this stranger she'd dare not speak in Pinegrove. Her lingering feelings for Malcolm, her fears over leaving home again, and most importantly, the possibility that following her heart home could cost Jessie her dream job. *Yeah, there was certainly a lot to tell.*

In the taxi that took her to the airport, she broke down again when the driver turned on the radio to an American station that played pop songs from the 2010s. "Love Me Like You Do" by Ellie Goulding had played, and she'd nearly wept herself dry. That had been the first song they danced to at their senior prom, the scent of cheap body spray and floral corsages heavy in the air. If she concentrated, Jessie could still feel the polyester blend of her lacey dress, the pinch of her mother's heels that never quite fit right.

When she thought she'd finally pulled herself together, Jessie arrived at her connecting airport in Mexico City. She found a corner with an electrical outlet and charged her phone. While scanning her social media feeds for updates, she realized she'd missed Malcolm's birthday. That had never happened in all their years of friendship, dating, and breakups. No matter what, they each made an effort to cheer the other up on their special days. The realization had her crying so hard, she lost her breakfast in the airport restroom.

Earlier that year, Malcolm had sent her a care package brimming with beloved Southern treats. There was a box of pralines from her favorite local shop, as well as roasted pecans and peanuts from the nut shop. But the item that warmed her heart and nearly broke her resolve was the T-shirt from that year's fireworks festival. The soft cotton was butter under her fingertips, and when she brought it to her nose, it smelled like Malcolm: warm and woodsy.

She wore the shirt now, huddled in her mother's car as the skyline of Atlanta disappeared behind them. She smoothed her hand down the fabric as she composed herself, another wave of emotion barreling toward her.

"I spoke with Estelle before I left Pinegrove," her mother said, attention briefly flashing to her daughter. "She said that Malcolm is sitting up and eating now."

"Does Estelle know I'm coming?" Jessie snatched Daisy's right arm, fingers digging into tender skin. "Was she upset?"

The car jerked slightly as Daisy corrected, chastising her daughter. "Sugar, if you can't calm down, I'm pulling over and stuffing you in the trunk. I mean it."

Jessie jerked her hands back and shoved them under her legs, her feet bouncing anxiously. "Sorry," she muttered.

"As I was saying"—her mother smirked—"Malcolm is doing better every day, but prepare yourself for the bandages and such. I love Estelle, but she nearly caused a riot when she first saw her son. And to answer your other question, she's delighted you're coming home. You know the Smiths love you like kin."

"I'm coming to visit," Jessie corrected. While she left her post faster than she ever had before, she intended on going back. There was still work to do, people to help, and a town to rebuild. She couldn't step away now, could she?

Daisy frowned but rallied quickly. "Right, to visit. Either way, she's excited to see you, and I'm sure Malcolm will be, too."

It was impossible to miss the tension in her mother's gaze, and Jessie swallowed a lump in her throat. *Malcolm's wasn't the only heart that broke when she left ...*

"Yeah," Jessie said with a nod, squeezing her eyes shut as a tear slid down her cheek.

What had gotten into her? She usually wasn't such a crybaby, but apparently, she was today. *It was probably the jet lag ...*

Malcolm was important to her, always would be, but that didn't mean she was ready to come home and put down roots. For the last decade, Jessie had honed her life into a series of adventures around the globe. Cabin building in the Amazon Delta, farming in the deserts of Western Africa, and rebuilding a community in Southeast Asia after one of the worst cyclones in modern history. These were the things that brought her to life ... mostly.

There was also a crooked grin that belonged to a sweet-hearted man with dark curls and eyes the color of her favorite candy bar. She couldn't pretend she didn't love Malcolm, but she wouldn't set herself up for a life of heartbreak like her momma had. Jessie watched her mother fall apart when Daddy died, and she wouldn't allow that life for herself. *Would she?*

Somewhere between the exit for Columbus and a pit stop outside southern Atlanta, they arrived in Pinegrove. Daisy nudged Jessie awake when she'd parked in the hospital lot. "Sugar, we're here."

Jessie flew up right, steadying herself on the dashboard. "We're at the hospital?" She blinked, adjusting to the harsh light of a Georgia summer. *They always hit a little different.*

Daisy turned off the car, dropped her keys into her purse, and hummed. "I still think we could have swung home for a bit. You don't want to ... you know?" She mimicked showering and putting on makeup, going so far as to make sound effects of rushing water.

"Momma, I need to see him." Unwilling to argue, Jessie flung the passenger's side door open and stomped into the Southern heat. She turned to close the door, catching her reflection and wincing. "Maybe we should have gone home," she muttered, jogging around the car to catch up to her mother.

Daisy was better dressed for a hospital visit in a pair of capri pants and a matching blouse. Her graying hair was brushed off her face, a pair of kitten heels clacked as she headed toward the entrance. By stark comparison, her daughter wore a rumpled T-shirt and leggings, her hair not seeing a brush since the Mexico City airport.

When they approached the reception desk, they were given visitor badges and instructions on where to find the ICU. "There's a limit on how many people can be in an ICU room at the same time, so please follow the nurse's orders," the receptionist said.

"Thank you," Daisy replied, carefully clipping her badge to her top. Jessie clasped it in her hands and dashed for the elevators. "Slow down, sugar! I'm in my late fifties, I don't run anymore."

Jessie thumbed at the up-arrow button until the doors finally slid open. Once both women were inside, Jessie checked her reflection in the elevator doors and winced. "Do you happen to have—?"

"Something in my bag of tricks to make you look human? Yes." Daisy held up a finger, rummaging in her purse with her free hand. She retrieved a travel hair brush, a tube of lip gloss, and a compact. "Here," she said, shoving everything into Jessie's waiting hands.

"Thanks." Jessie sighed, combing her tangled waves into shape before pinching color into her cheeks and swiping on lip gloss. While Jessie's back was turned, Daisy spritzed her with some perfume.

The elevator dinged their arrival, and before Jessie could find the nurse's station, Estelle had found them. "Aren't you a sight for sore eyes, my girl!" Estelle exclaimed, pulling Jessie into a hug that took the air from her lungs. "I am so glad to see you."

Craig approached, a tray of coffees in his hands. "Perfect timing. I thought I'd stock up on caffeine for the lot of us. Jessie, how are you?"

Jessie unfolded herself from Estelle's hug, offering a lame wave to Malcolm's father. "I'm fine." She cleared her throat, willing her mouth to form words. "How is he?"

Around them echoed the beeps and shrill alarms of the ICU. The room in front of them had a man who looked like he'd already met his maker, the heart monitor beeping as slow as molasses in January. Down the hall, a woman in a hospital gown was being wheeled by a pair of nurses, her cough deep and racking.

Malcolm shouldn't be here. He should be driving the

ambulance and saving people, not lying broken in a hospital bed. Her eyes misted over as Jessie waited for Estelle and Daisy to share their greetings.

Finally, she couldn't take it anymore. "Can I see him?"

Estelle blinked, probably appalled by her lack of manners. The aging starlet was a stickler for the decorum that came with being a Southern Belle. Jessie had never had those skills or manners, yet the other woman always adored her.

"Of course, honey."

Before she could stop herself, Jessie blurted, "And he wants to see me?"

Craig coughed into his fist. "You could say that."

Estelle patted Jessie's shoulder, her eyes shining. "You go on back, room 112."

"Thank you!"

Less than a minute later, Jessie stood at the threshold to Malcolm's room. She didn't hear voices inside, just more beeping. She ran her clammy hands down the front of her shirt, knowing it did nothing to calm her or make her look less disheveled.

After pushing the door open, she stepped inside a nearly empty room. Chairs had clearly been rearranged a few times, with jackets piled on one, flowers resting on both nightstands. The air was chilly, the industrial AC running overtime.

Malcolm was asleep, mouth slightly open. One of his legs was wrapped and hung from the ceiling, and one of his arms was bandaged and braced. She had feared he'd been covered in burns, but she only saw a few small bandages marring his gorgeous dark skin. Her fingers ached to touch him, to feel his warmth, to catalog every injury.

Since he was sleeping, Jessie took in her fill of Malcolm. Beyond his injuries, he looked lean and strong. The arm that wasn't wrapped still had a firm bicep peeking out from behind his hospital gown. His hair was longer than the last time she'd seen him, but she wasn't complaining. Malcolm's hair was always soft between her fingers, and the longer he let his curls grow, the more she could play with it. Many a quiet evening was spent with Jessie's fingers in the corkscrews, making sound effects as she massaged his scalp. She leaned forward, dying for one swipe through those dark curls …

Malcolm's eyes fluttered open, just as her hand hung over his head. His normally bright, clear gaze was clouded over and tired. "JJ?" he croaked, one side of his lips quirking up into a grin.

"Hey," she said, inching closer. She dropped her hand, resting her elbows on the side of the mattress, holding her breath until he spoke again.

"You came." The two words slid out on another smile, and it was obvious he was on some powerful pain meds. "You came," he repeated.

Jessie pressed her hands together. If they touched, she didn't know if she'd ever be able to leave this man's side again. "Yeah," she replied, the queen of one-word answers.

Malcolm's hand, and the only one not covered in bandages and sensors, pawed around blindly toward her, his expression pinched. "Where are you?" he asked, voice strained.

"I'm here," she said, taking his hand, squeezing it harder than she probably should. Mindlessly, her thumb traced over his knuckles, wincing at the dry, cracked skin. Despite his current state, zings of electricity shot through her, every nerve ending on fire from touching him.

"It's better than it looks," he urged as he raised her hand. He tried to bring their joined hands to his mouth, but he only made it halfway before crying out in pain and letting go. The machines by his bedside clanged and lit up like Christmas trees.

"Mr. Smith," one of the nurses ground out his name as she marched up to the machine and stabbed a few buttons. "What did we say about overdoing it?"

Jessie couldn't hold her tongue. "It's my fault. I

shouldn't have come." She rose to her feet, tripping over a chair leg.

Malcolm scowled. "JJ, don't go." He panted as he got a better placement on the bed. "It's always rough when I wake up. Stay."

"I'm not going anywhere, I ..."

But Jessie didn't know what else to say, because she hadn't thought beyond this moment. She hadn't thought beyond what would happen when she clapped eyes on him, could prove he was breathing and alive. She hadn't thought about how her senses heightened around Malcolm. The light was brighter, the air crisp, each sound reverberating against her eardrums. Malcolm made everything better, and that was a foolish thing to forget.

The nurse clicked a few more buttons and the room fell silent. "Get some rest, Mr. Smith," the nurse ordered, offering Jessie her own personal glare. *Great.*

"I'll rest, JJ," Malcolm said, his tone sharper than she'd expect, "but I need you to be here when I wake up."

"Aren't we bossy? The ICU brings out your grumpy side ..." Her words died on her tongue as she watched his chuckle turn into a flinch. "I'm sorry. I'll shut up."

Malcolm moved his head slightly, the best he could do given his current state. "Don't shut up, and don't go." He waggled his good hand until she took it again. This time his grip was certain. "Please, JJ."

If she closed her eyes, they were back in the meadow, fireflies dancing overhead and the air thick with the scent of flowers. Holding Malcolm's hand was an anchor, keeping Jessie from falling apart.

And that was that. Jessie could rarely say no to Malcolm on a good day, and today was certainly not a good day. "I'm here," she whispered, leaning down and pressing her lips to his forehead. His curls were matted to his sweaty skin, but she didn't care. He looked beautiful, perfect—alive.

Beneath it all, he was still Malcolm.

All she could think as she watched Malcolm drift back

to sleep was, *How was she going to walk away this time?*

LIBBY KAY

CHAPTER FOUR

It could have been the drugs, it could have been the pain, but Malcolm knew Jessie was here. Despite the strong smell of his own sweat, disinfectant, and his mother's cloying perfume, he was pretty certain Jessie's vanilla scent permeated through to his soul.

"JJ?" he asked, mouth as dry as cotton. He struggled to open his eyes, only to find his mother's worried face hovering over his.

"Baby, it's Mom!" she announced an inch from his ear. Malcolm grimaced, an alarm sounded on the wall, and Craig was there in an instant to pull her back to her seat.

"Darling, please take a seat. You hovering over the boy like a UFO isn't helping."

"UFO? How dare you, Craig?" She fluffed her blonde hair before frowning at her son. "Are you all right?"

Malcolm rolled his eyes, head falling onto the pillow. "Never ... better," he ground out when a nurse was back shining a flashlight in his eyes.

"Mr. Smith, can you answer a few questions for me?"

"Where's JJ?" he asked, ignoring the nurse's attempts at helping him. He was so tired of being pampered, prodded, and poked. All he wanted was five minutes alone with Jessie.

The nurse pursed her lips. "Answer my questions first, Mr. Smith. Can you tell me your first name and birthday, please?"

Malcolm went through a tedious slew of questions that seemed too easy, even for an ICU patient. After reciting the current president, his birthday, names of his parents, and his profession, he was given what he really wanted: Jessie's whereabouts.

"She's in the cafeteria," Estelle said when the nurse left. "Poor girl hadn't had anything to eat since the airport."

Malcolm pressed the button to adjust the bed, bringing himself up a few inches until he could see without craning his sore neck. "How long have I been out?"

Craig folded up the newspaper he was reading and rested it on his lap. "Give or take, a few hours. Jessie came with Daisy, but Daisy left about an hour ago. Javi and Trevor are due by soon, and I think Trevor will take Jessie back home."

Back home. Those two words made Malcolm feel like a million bucks.

Malcolm opened his mouth to ask more questions, but the familiar sounds of his friends and coworkers echoed around the room. "Smithy! You're awake!" Javi clapped his hands as he stalked up to Malcolm's bedside.

He reached out to touch him, but Estelle was faster. "Don't!" She screeched. Her acting training kicking in as she projected her voice so loud, they likely heard it at the Alabama border. "Javi, please. He's still so tender."

Javi held his hands up, backing up until he walked into Trevor. "Oof," the other man said, sidestepping before Javi took off his toes. "Watch the feet and take a seat, goober." Trevor kicked out a chair for Javi as Craig steered Estelle from the room.

"Why don't we let the boys have a few minutes? We can check on Jessie."

Trevor nodded, shaking Craig's hand as he passed. "Send my sister up when she's done binging on all the Jell-

O."

Malcolm's parents waved before closing the door and leaving the three firefighters alone. "How you feeling? You scared the shit out of us, Smithy," Javi admitted, leaning forward in his chair. "I'm not kidding, we're all still talking about it."

Trevor nodded, face pulled down in a scowl. "It's a night I'd certainly like to forget." He raised his hand to scratch his chin, and Malcolm noticed a cluster of bandages.

"You okay, Trev? I thought by now you'd be free of those wraps."

Trevor flapped a hand, dismissing Malcolm's concern. "It's nothing. Frankly, I feel fine, but between Whitney and Momma's hovering, I might go insane."

Javi snorted. "Yeah right. I'm sure you're devastated that your girlfriend is all over you. Poor Trev." He made a lewd gesture, and Trevor tossed a spare pillow at his head. Javi dodged it in time, cackling.

Malcolm snorted, savoring the brief moment of normalcy. Unfortunately Javi's shenanigans caused a coughing fit that lasted an eternity. Trevor got him water while Javi looked on with concern. "You're sure you don't need a nurse or anything? There are a few cuties out there, and I wouldn't mind finding you the best." He winked, and Malcolm managed to flip him off with his good hand.

"You're in the ICU and you're still trolling for girls."

Javi splayed a hand over his heart. "I'm *visiting* the ICU. You know if I were a patient I'd already have everyone's phone numbers."

"Of this I have no doubt," Jessie agreed from the doorway, striding in with a tray of cups and a paper bag. She dropped her bounty on the end table before turning to her brother.

Trevor enveloped her in a hug, pulling her off the floor. Her sneakered feet dangled in the air. "Jessie, it's so good to see you," he said into her neck.

"Why don't you knuckleheads stay out of trouble, huh?

My delicate heart can only take so much." She smiled when Trevor released her, but Malcolm didn't miss the dark circles under her eyes.

Javi snagged his coffee and a donut from the bag, eating it in two bites while Jessie walked over to Malcolm. "How are you feeling?" she asked, voice low.

"Like I ran a marathon in the center of the sun," he joked, coughing as he adjusted his position to see everyone.

"When did the doc say you can leave?" Javi asked through a mouthful of donut, powdered sugar dusting his lips.

"Hopefully soon," Malcolm said. "I have no idea what things will look like with physical therapy, but they mentioned me getting a walking cast." He gestured to his leg, which was suspended from the ceiling.

Malcolm had both the benefit and the curse of being in the medical field. In addition to being a trained firefighter, he was also an EMT. Even through his drug-induced haze, he knew his recovery was not going to be quick or painless. He likely had months of PT and rest ahead of him, which was tantamount to a death sentence.

He was an active guy, from keeping busy at the job to working out and training for marathons. He kept in shape and was often the first person ready when a call came. Speed was his trademark, but now the effort of reaching out for his cup of water zapped what little energy he had.

Yawning, Malcolm collapsed back into the pillow. Despite that two-hour nap he just had, his body was ready for another one. "Can you hand me that water, JJ?"

Jessie was there, cup at his lips, helping him take little sips as the burn in his throat subsided. "Good job," she cooed. "I asked the nurses, and they said you can have some Jell-O later if you're hungry."

"You mean you didn't eat it all?" Trevor asked, earning an eye roll from his sister.

"Real nice, Trev. I spent ten hours on a plane, and you know I can't find Jell-O anywhere else."

Javi collected the empty coffee cups and stacked everything on the tray. "I'm going to find a trash can, and maybe a date for Friday night. Smithy, I'll be back tomorrow. Let me know if you need anything, brother."

"Thanks for coming," Malcolm said, his eyes already drifting closed.

Trevor rose, dusting powdered sugar from his hands. "I'll walk Javi out." Pointing to Jessie, he added, "I'll meet you down the hall by the elevators. I'm taking you to Momma's." Jessie opened her mouth to protest, but her brother cut her off. "You need to shower, and judging from how you're slumped over, you could use a nap as much as Smithy. This is non-negotiable."

"I can see why they promoted you to captain," Jessie replied, hands on hips.

Trevor smirked. "Damn straight, don't you forget it." He stepped forward, carefully resting his hand on Malcolm's cast. "Rest up, Smithy. We'll be ready whenever you are, okay? I spoke with the chief, and he has some ideas for light duty once you're released."

Malcolm nodded, but he hated the idea of light duty. Light duty meant grunt work and time staring at spreadsheets on a computer. But he knew now wasn't the time to argue, so he kept his trap shut.

Once Trevor and Javi left, Jessie sat on the edge of the bed. Pulling his good hand closer, she pressed a gentle kiss on his knuckles. "I'll be back tomorrow, but you call me if you need anything."

"You'll come back?" Malcolm asked, knowing it was a dumb question. Of course she'd be back. She'd hardly leave her post just to come eat Jell-O in the Pinegrove Hospital. *Although if it was lime Jell-O with pears, he knew she would have made the trip.*

"Yes, Malcolm. I'm here for a little while."

A little while. Three words, maximum impact.

That was the thing with Jessie, their time together always had an expiration date. He never knew if a visit would last for days, weeks, months, or forever. His throat closed up as emotions threatened to choke him. He would not blubber in the ICU, he was a grown ass man.

"See you tomorrow," he croaked, blinking rapidly and hoping against hope she didn't see how upset he truly was.

"Rest up," she said over her shoulder as she padded away, lips pursed. *Was she struggling as much as he was?*

Several hours later, Malcolm woke in a dark room. His parents were both asleep in their chairs, a new nurse hovered over his IV, checking fluids. "Hello," she whispered. "I'm Nan, I'm covering the night shift. Can I get you anything?"

He tried to answer, but a cough came out instead. The hacking sound woke his mother, who was at his side and fussing over him like he was a newborn foal. "Baby, it's okay." She ruffled his hair, nearly knocking poor Nan onto her bottom.

"Ma'am, can I have one more moment with my patient?" Her professional tone melted into pure ecstasy when she recognized his mother. "Oh my Lord!" Nan rubbed her eyes, blinking in shock as she registered who his mother was. "Are you Estelle Winters from *Atlanta Hearts*?!" She clasped her hands over her mouth to stop from squealing.

Estelle loved these interactions—and since Netflix picked up the show, streaming brought her a whole new generation of fans. Her maiden name of Winters was her stage name, so it made sense the nurse wouldn't have made the connection right away.

"Yes, honey. I am Estelle Winters." She lowered her voice and winked. "But let's keep that between us. I don't want anything getting in the way of my son's care." That was an outright lie, as Estelle loved nothing more than discussing the show that made her a star. Fortunately though, she also loved her son and wouldn't let the moment run away from her.

Nan crossed her heart with a trembling finger. "I won't say a word, Ms. Winters."

"Thank you," Estelle said magnanimously. "But would you like an autograph?"

Nan gasped, shoving her hands in her scrubs pocket and retrieving a crumpled piece of paper. "Would you? This is such a thrill. I used to watch your show with my momma religiously. When you fell from the skyscraper in the season seven finale, I literally cried."

"Aren't you a doll?" Estelle scrawled her loopy signature. "Thanks for taking such good care of my son."

"You're very welcome!" Nan sighed with delight. "Oh my gosh, wow."

The fangirling session came to an abrupt end when one of the doctors strode in with an iPad. "Mr. Smith," he greeted without looking up. "You did well for your first night outside of ICU. We can start looking at discharge options soon."

"That's good news," Craig replied from his perch in the corner of the room.

Estelle joined her husband, grasping his hand for support. "How long do you think he'll have to stay in the hospital?"

The doctor clacked away on the tablet another moment without answering. "That depends on what type of care Mr. Smith will have at home. He'll require some physical therapy, but that can happen with visiting nurses. He will need some assistance once we switch him to a walking cast, but either way, he won't be able to live alone for a couple weeks. There are bandages to change, wounds to inspect that he can't reach in his current state. The head injury was ruled out, but it's mostly keeping Mr. Smith comfortable and off his feet."

"We'll be here," his mother urged, and Malcolm wanted to fall back into a coma. He loved his parents, truly, but the worst thing about his recovery would be needing their help. He wasn't a kid anymore, damn it.

Jessie's face flashed in his mind before he could blink her away. She'd take excellent care of him, he had no doubt.

"Can we figure out logistics tomorrow?" Malcolm asked, eager to join the conversation about his own care.

The doctor nodded, finally meeting Malcolm's eye. "Yes, Mr. Smith. We certainly can. I believe Nan is bringing up something for you to eat, but we'll talk more in the morning. Rest up, everyone." And with that, he was gone.

Malcolm endured his bland supper before crumpling back into a dreamless sleep. The next time he opened his eyes, his girl was back, "JJ," he whispered.

"Hey," she said, voice coated in sleep. "I hope I didn't drool on your bed." She wiped at her face. "Your parents went to the hotel to get showered, and I didn't realize I dozed off." There were pillow creases on her cheeks, her hair mussed.

"Thanks for coming back," he said, meaning every word.

"Don't thank me yet, all I've done is sleep."

Malcolm shook his head, pain coursing down his neck. "Don't sell yourself short, JJ. You're here, and I appreciate it."

Jessie's face softened. "I couldn't stay away, Malcolm. I know we're ..." She trailed off, still unable to catalog their current relationship.

He would gladly offer her suggestions on what they were ... *soulmates, lovers, best friends,* the list went on indefinitely.

Instead of scaring her, he said, "We're fine."

Jessie nodded, swiping a lock of hair off his forehead. "We are, and you will be soon."

"Okay, Nurse Mays."

Jessie chuckled. "You joke, but I want to help. Let me take care of you."

"What?" Malcolm cursed the heart monitor that betrayed his reaction to her offer. It beeped and clanged so loud, he wanted to yank the sensor off his chest.

Jessie licked her lips. "If you're up for it, I offered to help your parents when you get discharged."

"If I'm up for it?" Malcolm snorted. "JJ, I'd love your help."

He would more than love it. Malcolm's mind went wild with all the possibilities. Sponge baths, nightly cuddles, and stolen kisses came to mind. As if reading his thoughts, she swatted his arm.

"Ouch," he hissed, and she immediately apologized.

"Sorry, sorry! But you know that this means medical help. I'm not fulfilling your sexy nurse fantasy."

"Are you sure?" He pouted, knowing full well the only thing he could do physically right then was kiss her senseless ... which actually didn't sound like a bad idea.

"Yoohoo, we're back!" his mother announced, effectively killing the moment. "Oh good, Jessie's here. Did she tell you the good news?"

"I was in the middle of it," she said, turning to greet both his parents with quick hugs. Now that she was standing, he saw she'd changed into a pair of cut-off denim overalls with a pink T-shirt. Jessie always wore pink, a hue he'd come to love more than any other. Pink meant Jessie's rosy cheeks when she laughed too hard or he said something sweet. Pink was the color of the flowers he used to bring her on dates, the color of his favorite dress of hers ... the list went on.

And here he was getting a little too excited in a hospital bed surrounded by his parents and half the medical professionals of Pinegrove. "Mom, can JJ and I have another minute?"

"But we just got here." His mother frowned.

"Estelle, we haven't even had coffee. The boy is fine. Let's get breakfast." Craig took his wife's elbow and directed her out into the hallway.

"We'll be back in a jiffy!" she called out to no one in particular.

"Why do I have a feeling nursing you back to health is going to be an ordeal?" Jessie asked, her hands on her hips.

"Because it'll be chaos," Malcolm said, his smile growing the longer he looked at Jessie.

His girl was back in his life, and no matter how long she stayed, Malcolm was going to be a happy man.

LIBBY KAY

CHAPTER FIVE

Nine years ago

Jessie's whole body trembled as she boarded the plane home for the first time in six months. This had been the longest she'd been away from Pinegrove, and she simultaneously ached to see her family and Malcolm, but also itched to get her next placement.

She'd met amazing people, experienced different cultures—both from the other workers and volunteers and from the locals—and she'd already learned so much about herself. There were certain things, certain routines, she'd quickly left behind when forced to share cramped quarters with relative strangers.

As she hefted her duffle bag off the luggage carousel in Atlanta, she heard the familiar baritone of her father's voice. "June Bug!" Her nickname cut through the din of the airport, and Jessie's knees nearly buckled with relief.

"Daddy!" she shouted, bounding toward him, her arms already open.

They embraced in the middle of other travelers eager to continue or end their journeys. If Jessie listened carefully, she could hear Bing Crosby wishing everyone a white Christmas overhead. "Merry Christmas," Nick said, smacking a kiss to the top of her head.

"Merry Christmas," she replied into his chest, tears welling. No matter how old you were, sometimes you needed a hug from your dad, especially during the holidays.

"Our guy's got us double-parked out front, so we better hurry." He pulled back, reaching out to take her bag.

"Trev's here?" Jessie asked, following quickly on her dad's heels.

Without turning around, he said, "No, Malcolm."

Jessie's feet skittered to a halt, causing a young mother with a stroller to bump into her. Even being surrounded by holiday cheer, the other woman muttered some very un-Bing-approved greetings as she navigated around her.

Nick realized Jessie was no longer following him and stopped, a sullen expression crossing his face. "Oh hell." He sighed, shoulders slumping. "You two aren't together anymore?"

Jessie opened her mouth a few times, the personification of a goldfish. "No, we are," she said, voice low. "I guess I thought I wouldn't see him until he came back from college."

Malcolm and she had shared letters and emails as often as the time difference and their hectic schedules allowed. She knew they'd see each other on this trip; hell, she yearned for one glimpse of his smile, but being back now felt different. A part of Jessie feared they wouldn't feel that spark, that the combination of time and space had been too much for their young love story.

Finally, Nick relaxed. "He got home yesterday, called right away to ask when you landed. Momma and Trev are busy with baking and wrapping, so we thought we'd have a little road trip." He hitched a thumb over his shoulder. "We were even going to stop at Bojangles for you."

Jessie covered her rumbling stomach, the thought of fried chicken and a biscuit making her mouth water. "That sounds amazing," she groaned.

"Then we're good? Because if you need me to ..." Her father looked around the crowded airport, as if there was a department next to the baggage claim to store the object of your muddled affections.

Holding up her hand, Jessie politely stopped her father's ramblings. "Daddy, we're good. It's just a lot, you know?" She nibbled her bottom lip, eyes downcast at the tiled floor. "I miss him, and I love him, and I don't want to hurt him."

"Oh, June Bug." Closing the distance, he wrapped an arm around Jessie. "Anyone with eyes can see you kids are crazy about each other. I understand it's been hard with the distance, but you're home now. Things will settle back down. Your momma and I were the same way—young love is fickle and fire at the same time."

Not realizing the emotional bomb he'd detonated, Nick picked up her bag and strode toward the exit. Jessie swallowed down the lump in her throat, fantasies of fried chicken sandwiches curdling her stomach. Her father thought she was done with the Peace Corps, just like Malcolm had assumed.

There wasn't time for Jessie to spiral, because as soon as they stepped into the Georgia sun, she saw him, leaning against her father's pickup with his arms crossed over his broad chest, gaze trained on the exit. Any doubt she had about seeing him evaporated as their eyes locked, his smile taking over his handsome face.

Uncaring about the pickup double-parked behind him, Malcolm sprinted toward her, ready to tackle her to the ground. "JJ!" He was breathless when they met each other, no hesitation before he picked her up and spun her around like they were starring in a romcom. "JJ," he repeated, peppering her neck with kisses as she giggled, feet dangling in the air like a rag doll.

Allowing them a moment, Nick took her bag and tossed it in the back of the truck. Jessie was idly aware of the holiday masses milling around them, but her world had narrowed down to Malcolm.

"You're here." Jessie breathed in his citrus, woodsy scent, pressing kisses to his cheeks before finally meeting his lips. Their first few kisses were frantic, staccato pecks until they found their rhythm again.

Malcolm's tongue darted out, parting her lips and earning a sound she really shouldn't be making in public, let alone within sight of her father. Jessie's hold on Malcolm tightened, pulling him as close as she could with her purse—and rapidly beating heart—between them.

"I missed you," he muttered in between kisses, fingers digging into her hips.

"I missed you, too," she agreed, reluctantly pulling back. She blinked, taking him in up close. The first semester at college had given him leaner cheeks, longer hair, and a scattering of stubble over his jawline. She liked it—a lot.

Behind them, Nick tooted the horn and stuck his head out the window. "You kids can continue the reunion on the road." He cleared his throat, and added, "Maybe not the full reunion." He flushed and dipped his head back inside, causing both Malcolm and Jessie to burst out laughing.

"C'mon," Malcolm said, taking her hand and leading the way. "I don't know if your daddy told you, but we've got fried chicken in our immediate future."

The drive home was one of Jessie's favorite holiday memories. Nick stopped at the first Bojangles they passed, ordering more than three people should consume in one week, let alone one day. He turned on the holiday station on the radio, offering the backseat to Jessie and Malcolm for their fried feast.

The three of them laughed, caught up on the last six months of their lives, and finally sang a very off-key rendition of "The Twelve Days of Christmas" as they crossed into the Pinegrove city limits. Nick took the scenic way home, driving through Main Street where the shops were decorated with greenery and a million twinkling lights.

Malcolm held her hand the entire time, only letting go to eat his sandwich and tuck a receipt into his pocket. "Merry Christmas, JJ," he whispered, peppering her with Cajun-scented kisses.

Their bubble burst as they pulled into the driveway. Jessie spotted a familiar car. "Your parents are here?" she asked, shooting a look to Malcolm.

His head fell back and he muttered a few choice words. "Easy, son," her father teased. "That language isn't appropriate this close to the Lord's birthday." He winked in the rearview mirror before throwing the truck in park.

Jessie's sneakered feet hadn't even hit the pavement before Estelle and Daisy burst through the front door, Craig and Trevor following at a more leisurely pace behind them. "Jessica June, you get your fanny over here," Daisy ordered, closing the distance in three strides. The air left Jessie's lungs in a woosh as Estelle joined the fray.

"My goodness, honey. Aren't you a sight for sore eyes?" Her Chanel perfume was both cloying and comforting, and also a stark contrast to Daisy's cozy vanilla scent. Where Estelle's aroma came from an expensive bottle from a high-end department store, her mother's scent came from warm kitchens where memories were baked and savored.

Trevor helped their father with her bag as Craig cleared his throat. "Good heavens, Estelle. The cameras are off, and this poor girl probably needs some Oxygen. Cut!" He made a slashing motion with his hand, earning an elbow in the side from his theatrical wife.

"Hush up. Can't a girl be excited?"

Malcolm scrubbed a hand down his face. "Mom, there's excited, and then there's scene stealing."

Nick and Trevor returned, their new basset hound puppy, Gus, yapping around their ankles. Saving everyone from an Estelle rant, Trevor stepped up and pulled Jessie in for a quick hug. "Welcome home, goober," he whispered into her ear before dropping his arms and gesturing to the hound dog. "I don't believe you've met the newest addition to the Mays clan."

If Jessie thought she'd fallen in insta-love with Malcolm all those years ago, it had nothing on the emotions clogging her throat at the small dog before her. He had huge, sad eyes and a pair of ears that dragged on the ground. He sat back on his rump and offered a few woofs before she fell to her knees and nestled him to her heart. "Oh my Lord," she breathed.

Daisy snickered. "I knew you'd love him." Turning to Estelle, Daisy said, "We weren't even in the market for a dog, but when Nick heard about the fire at the dog breeders outside of town, we had to check out the little guy."

Estelle and Craig made their excuses to leave, although Malcolm gladly accepted Daisy's offer to stay for dinner. When the meal was done, dishes were cleared, and her parents and Trevor were occupied, Malcolm shrugged on his jacket. "You must be exhausted," he said, covering his own yawn with the back of his hand.

Truthfully, Jessie needed a shower, a dozen hours of sleep, and another helping of her mother's gumbo—and maybe a few Gussy cuddles—but she couldn't say goodbye to Malcolm now. "Nah, I've got a second wind." She winked, and Malcolm beamed.

He shoved his hands in his pockets, rocking back on his heels. "You want to go for a little stargazing?" he asked, voice tinged with hesitation.

Jessie closed the distance, getting on tiptoe to kiss Malcolm chastely on the lips. "Give me five minutes, and I'll meet you at your car."

Less than twenty minutes later, the pair was back on the grounds of Hog Hollow, strolling through the meadow hand-in-hand. Despite the chill in the air, Malcom's hand was warm in her grip, anchoring her to the moment. Unlike their visits during the summer, the Georgia winter had chased the bugs away. All that surrounded them was open fields and a sky full of stars.

Always the planner, Malcolm had brought a blanket along, which he gingerly placed on the ground. He sat down, pulling Jessie into his lap. She leaned back, resting her head on his shoulder. It was a cloudless night, the sky clear and bright. Countless stars twinkled, each sparkling just for them.

"What's that one up there?" she asked, pointing to a cluster of stars over the barn.

Scoffing, Malcolm squeezed her middle. "That's easy. That's the seven cousins."

Jessie was incredulous. "Isn't it the seven sisters?" She wiggled back into his hold, squirming when he tickled her sides.

"No, ma'am, it's actually more of a family reunion. Atlas wanted to protect all his favorite cousins in the sky. That one on the left is Harry, and the one all the way over there is Jerry." His voice cracked the longer his nonsense story continued.

As their laughter subsided, Jessie melted more into Malcolm's hold. No matter where she went, nothing ever felt like being with Malcolm. Yet sometimes, like right now, the ease of their relationship scared her. Weren't first loves supposed to flame out like the stars above them?

Shaking away the fear, Jessie confessed, "I missed you." Her admission floated into the night, carried away on the wind.

Malcolm nuzzled her neck, causing goosebumps to erupt from her hairline to her belly. "Missed you more, JJ. I'm so glad you're home." Against her will, Jessie's body tensed. Attuned to her body, Malcolm stopped his trail of kisses above her collarbone. "JJ?" he asked.

"Only for holidays," she said carefully, voice even despite the roiling happening in her ribcage. "I get my new assignment right after the new year."

Malcolm's body went rigid, and suddenly it was like she was sitting in an uncomfortable chair and not in her boyfriend's lap. "But I thought you were going to stay, maybe find a job until the next semester starts?"

Jessie pivoted so she could snatch his gaze. "I never said that," she accused, raising an eyebrow. "Who told you that?"

Malcolm swallowed, his Adam's apple bobbing. "Your parents. On the drive to the airport, Nick said they were getting your room ready and ..."

And Jessie had heard enough. She pulled free of Malcolm's hold, stumbling to her feet. "I'm not ready to come back permanently. I'm just getting started! I've still got so much to see, so much to do. College isn't for me, you know that. I feel like, like I fit. I can't explain how it's different, but it is." Her eyes pleaded with him to understand.

But Malcolm didn't understand. It was clear from the set of his jaw, the frown marring his handsome face. "Let's get you back," he said as he pushed to his feet, kicking the blanket into a ball before tucking it under his arm. There was no handholding on the long slog back to the car.

Jessie struggled to meet his stride, nearly tripping over a rock. "Malcolm, come on," she groaned, snaking his elbow. "Can't we talk about this?"

She was horrified when the first tear slid down his cheek. Bottom lip trembling, Malcolm shook his head. "I guess we're done talking, JJ. Sounds like you made up your mind."

The drive back to her parents' place was painfully silent. Jessie toyed with the hem of her shorts, posture stiff. Malcolm hadn't bothered turning on the radio. There were no Christmas carols, no conversations of the constellations, just a horrible silence that made her ears ring.

As soon as Malcolm parked in the driveway, he leaned over to open the glovebox. "I was going to wait and give this to you on Christmas, but maybe I should do it now." He thrust a small box out, dropping it into her waiting palm.

Bile crept up Jessie's throat as she studied the small box—a ring box. "Malcolm," his name escaped on a whisper.

He scoffed. "Don't worry, Jessie. It's not what you think."

At the mention of her name, the lack of her nickname, she jerked her head to stare at his sullen profile. His jaw clenched, eyes pinched. Finally, she couldn't look any longer. Carefully, she opened the box, gasping at the ring inside. It was a silver band studded with tiny gemstone stars the color of the rainbow. "It's beautiful."

"It's a promise ring," he admitted, still unable to face her. "I saw it and thought of you." He sighed and added, "Of us." Before she could say anything, he soldiered on. "I love you, and I wanted to give you something special. I can't say I'll wait around forever. I feel pathetic enough already. But you know where to find me when you're ready."

Jessie pressed the box to her chest. "Malcolm, please. You're not—"

He gripped the steering wheel, the leather protesting in his hold. "It's okay. It's not the first time I misread the situation. Enjoy the holidays with your folks. I think it's best if I don't come over for Christmas."

"What?" Jessie was incredulous.

"It's sending the wrong message." *To him or her family? She couldn't tell.*

"Malcolm." Jessie rested a hand over his, which was as cold as ice, and he still wouldn't look at her. "Why can't you be excited for me? I'm finally doing my own thing. I'm not ready to come home."

"Message received," he said through clenched teeth. "All I want is for you to be happy." Finally, he turned to face her, but she wished he hadn't. Never had she seen her happy-go-lucky boyfriend look this stricken, this hurt. "Go see the world, and if you wear this, think of me." He leaned over, kissing her cheek. "Goodbye, Jessie."

Jessie couldn't remember much after that, it was as if her brain was saving her from herself. The next week went by in a blur of tinsel, ham, cookies, and family. By the time her boss called with the details of her next placement in West

Africa, she was already packed and ready to leave Pinegrove. While stuffing her duffle, she pretended she hadn't noticed the way the light leeched from Malcolm's eyes at her declaration. She also pretended her stomach didn't twist in knots when she told her parents she wouldn't be home for Easter, that she'd likely miss Trevor's graduation from the academy.

But this was what she wanted, what she needed to do. Jessie's purpose hadn't been written in the stars like her daddy and Trevor's, and even Malcolm's and his folks'. She never clambered out of bed with a goal in mind. All Jessie knew was that her feet itched to travel, her hands burned to create, and her heart ached to help people.

Daisy drove Jessie to the airport in Atlanta, her lips pressed in a line, eyes red. "I'll call as soon as I get set up, Momma." Jessie forced some cheer in her voice.

Reaching out, her mother patted her knee, never taking her eyes off the road. "I know you will, sugar."

By the time they arrived at the airport, Jessie begged Daisy not to park and come inside. "It'll be faster for both of us this way." Jessie flung the door open and bounded onto the sidewalk, throat closing the longer it took to say goodbye. "I love you, Momma."

"I love you, too, sugar," Daisy cooed, rubbing her hands up and down her daughter's back. "You be safe and go save the world, you hear?"

Jessie grudgingly pulled back, swiping at her damp cheeks. "Will do." Turning on her heels, she sprinted inside the airport, swallowed up by the crowd before she had the chance to look over her shoulder at her mother's somber expression. "I'm doing the right thing," she told herself as she checked in at the departures counter.

"I'm doing the right thing," she said again as she slid into her seat an hour later, wedged between a traveling salesman and a young backpacker. Before she stored her carry-on, she took out the ring box and slid the ring on her finger, a talisman to keep her centered.

When she landed in Liberia, Jessie knew she had done the right thing, eagerly tossing her gear into her bunk and meeting the new team. Everyone seemed nice, and there was even a cute boy with brown eyes who reminded her of another set of chocolate eyes. For a while, she barely thought of Malcolm, but it was only for a little bit. At the end of the day, she missed stargazing, silly jokes, and warm laughter that wrapped around her like butter on a biscuit.

She missed Malcolm.

*

Malcolm shoved his textbooks into his backpack and stomped out of his dorm toward his biology class. For the last two weeks, he'd been a combination of angry, depressed, and anxious. Considering he was usually a walking ball of sunshine, it was really starting to piss him off. JJ wasn't going to change her mind, ring or no ring.

Despite everything they'd been through, despite falling right back into each other's arms, his girl—correction, ex—had hopped a plane as soon as he asked her to stay, as soon as he asked her to choose *him*.

Now the only thing Malcolm could focus on were his classes and the grades that would surely start to slip at this rate. He needed to get his shit together, and fast.

Footfalls faltering, Malcolm tripped over a crack in the sidewalk. In an effort to overcorrect, Malcolm fell headlong into a tall girl with braids and her own heavy backpack. "Ooof," she exhaled as she landed in the grass, the books in her arms scattering all around them.

"I'm so sorry," Malcolm apologized as he quickly collected her fallen books. He held out his hand for her, helping her to her feet before handing the books back.

"Steady there, cowboy," she teased, hiking up her bag and tucking her books under her arm. She flashed a grin, one filled with cheerfulness and straight teeth. Malcolm almost forgot what happy people looked like. "Aren't you in Dr. Brennan's bio class?" she asked.

Malcolm blinked, racking his brain to see if he knew this girl. "Uh, yeah."

Tilting her head, she offered, "We can walk over together. That is, if you promise not to bowl me over again." She winked, and Malcolm was charmed.

"Yeah, sounds good." They took a few steps before he remembered his manners. "I'm Malcolm ..."

"Smith, I know." She looked over her shoulder as she paced ahead. "I'm Talia Saunders."

"Ahh," he said, realizing she was the girl who sat in front of him in class. Now that he'd shaken the ghost of JJ away, he remembered staring at the back of her head for the last semester. "Right. Sorry, Talia."

Talia jogged ahead when they reached their building, kicking the door open and breezing through before another cluster of students got in her way. "You can stop apologizing. I'm glad I wasn't carrying anything breakable."

When they arrived in the classroom, they took their seats. Dr. Brennan walked in, pulling out his notes for class. "Settle down, everyone, it's time to pick our lab partners for the rest of the semester." As the professor droned on, Talia turned around and mouthed, *Want to partner?*

He flashed her a thumbs-up, pleased he'd made a new friend.

Over the next three months, Malcolm and Talia went from lab partners to friends to something more. They weren't quite official, but they were certainly spending a lot of time together.

Talia was great, a good time and even a bit of fun. But her laugh wasn't JJ's laugh, her wit wasn't nearly as sharp. When they kissed that first time, Malcolm nearly winced at the lack of chemistry between them. Hell, there was more chemistry on the pages of their textbooks.

It was time to face facts: He wasn't over JJ yet. And Lord, he didn't know when he would be. He knew it wasn't fair to Talia, but Malcolm tried his best to find that spark, find a connection worth keeping.

On a particular blah Wednesday afternoon, they lounged in his dorm room while his roommate was out. "You know," Talia said, closing her textbook and scooting closer to Malcolm on the bed. The mattress dipped with her weight, as she nibbled her bottom lip. "The semester is over in a couple weeks, and we haven't discussed our summer plans."

"What do you mean?" Malcolm asked, because he really hadn't thought much about summer beyond his desire to avoid all the memories of JJ that hung heavy in Pinegrove like the morning fog.

Talia nudged him. "Malcolm, c'mon. I live in Atlanta, and Pinegrove is only like an hour away. Are we going to keep seeing each other or what?"

"Or what?" Malcolm asked, heat crawling up his neck. Deep in the pit of his stomach, he knew what this was—it was what he did to JJ every time they spoke of the future. Poor Talia was making plans, and Malcolm was planning his exit. *How did JJ do this every time?*

Blinking at him, Talia took a long breath. "You know what I think?" she asked in a tone that did not give anything away. Malcolm could only shake his head as she sprang to her feet. "I think, we should cut our losses."

"What?"

"Don't 'what' me, Malcolm. We've been dating for months, and I feel like I barely know you. We never make big plans, you never open up about your feelings, and all I know about your family is that your mom is Estelle Winters. And this." She waved a hand toward his bulletin board. There was a scattering of photos of his family and friends. One lone picture of him and Talia was tacked in the corner, a souvenir from a campus mixer they'd attended the month before. "In your whole room, this is the only sign we're a couple."

Malcolm cupped the back of his neck, suddenly needing to catch his breath. Talia wasn't wrong, and that's why he couldn't argue with her. Malcolm hadn't wanted to open up, because as soon as he started talking about his feelings, JJ would come back and consume his thoughts.

"Talia, I'm not really a photo kind of guy." The statement sounded lame to his own ears, and Talia rolled her eyes.

She stabbed her index finger on the board, causing their photo to come loose and flutter to the floor. Before she could collect it, a cluster of other photos fell free. In his haste to bury his feelings for JJ, he'd tacked his picture of Talia and some takeout menus over them. As if hiding pictures could erase nearly five years of loving another woman.

Both Talia and Malcolm watched in horror as the photos of him and JJ fluttered to the floor. There was their senior prom picture, JJ looking radiant in pink. Another photo from the Pinegrove Fireworks Festival, their lips tinged blue from a cotton candy binge. And finally, the most damning picture of all was a shot of them kissing by the Christmas tree. Trevor had taken the photo right before their fateful trip to the farm, where she broke his heart for the last time.

Talia moved faster than Malcolm, scooping up the photos and thrusting them into his hands. "Not really a photo kind of guy?" she repeated, hurt dripping from every word. "I have never seen you smile like this with me. Why are you hiding these photos? Who is this girl?" She glared, unblinking at him while he struggled to find his words. "You know what, I'm outta here." She snatched her purse from his bed and spun on her heel. "Please don't call me, and please don't insult either of us by saying you want me back. I can be a grown-up while we finish bio lab finals, but I'm serious, Malcolm. We're done."

And with that, Malcolm's first attempt at dating in a post-JJ world went up in smoke. That first summer back in Pinegrove was daunting to say the least, but all wasn't lost. Nick had bumped into Malcolm at the grocery store, and the pair struck up a conversation on Malcolm's plans for the summer. In a matter of minutes, he'd convinced Malcolm to volunteer with Trevor at the fire station. Turned out those biology classes were a strong foundation for getting EMT certified, and maybe even becoming a firefighter.

It was the first time in ages that Malcolm found a purpose and, more importantly, a purpose that didn't involve JJ. Yet for as much progress as he made at the station and with his career planning, he couldn't forget about his girl.

On the nights he wanted to be closer to JJ, he'd drive out Hog Hollow and plod out to the meadow, collapsing into the grass to stare up at the stars. He told himself JJ was doing the same thing halfway across the globe. And maybe, just maybe, she was missing him, too.

A guy could dream, right?

LIBBY KAY

CHAPTER SIX

Present Day

Jessie was used to Estelle and Craig, their dynamic and in particular the former's flair for the dramatic. So it was no surprise that it took an hour to go over the discharge process. Nan, who had become everyone's favorite nurse and PT specialist, kept a professional smile in place as Estelle asked more and more questions. By the time they were finished, poor Malcolm looked ready to throttle his mother.

"And you're sure Malcolm will make a full recovery?" Estelle nibbled on her manicure, expression as pinched as her Botox injections allowed. Craig patted her shoulder, his expression far less grim.

Fortunately for all involved, Malcolm took after his daddy. The patriarch of the Smith clan had a cool head, wicked wit, and the ability to handle crises well. Those were the qualities that made Malcolm such a terrific EMT and firefighter. They were also the qualities that Jessie had fallen in love with all those years ago …

Pulled back into the moment, the PT specialist Tim, a

young man with a shock of red hair and freckles, turned toward Jessie and Estelle. "Now, physical therapy will be key in Malcolm's recovery. We should be able to do mainly at-home exercises, given Malcolm's age and fitness level. Who will be in charge of Malcolm's care overall?"

Both women held their hands up and said, "I am." This earned a chuckle from Tim, an eye roll from Craig, and a snort from Malcolm. Unfortunately the snort turned into a sneeze, which led to a full-on coughing fit. Estelle wasn't faster than Jessie, who made it to his side with his water cup at the ready.

"Remember, slow sips," she ordered, resting on her haunches. Malcolm nodded, his fingers covering hers as he drank. Despite being in a stuffy hospital room surrounded by people, she shivered.

Craig stepped closer, draping his arm around his wife's shoulder. In a tone that left no room for argument, he said, "We will be staying nearby Malcolm's place, but Jessie will be there overnight."

There was something about the way that he said it that caused Jessie to flinch. It sounded so untoward, but then again it was also the truth. She'd made the decision to be there for him, for a variety of reasons. Their relationship status might be as murky as the swamp at the border to Pinegrove, but it was also important to her. This man had been her rock for years, and she wasn't about to let him suffer under his mother's good intentions. *There was a fine line between mothering and smothering ...*

Tim made a note on his clipboard and turned to Nan. "I've said my piece. What do you have for the patient and his care team?" He turned to Jessie, handing her a stack of papers. "This goes over everything in detail, but my email is on there as well. You let me know if you run into any questions."

"Thanks," Jessie said, folding the notes and shoving them into her purse.

Nan handed her another stack of papers, her expression

firm. "Now my list is a little different. If you notice any of the symptoms listed in red on page one, you call 911. If you notice any of the symptoms in yellow, get Malcolm back here ASAP. Otherwise, you can call the main line here with questions."

The hospital staff left, and Malcolm wiggled in his wheelchair. He'd been given an air cast for his left leg, and it was propped up straight. His arm was bandaged to his side to keep it immobile, and already the bruises were starting to fade. Jessie was pleased to see signs of the man she knew shining through.

"Who's driving me out of here?" he asked, clearly impatient to get moving.

Estelle nearly elbowed Jessie out of the way. "I've got it!" she shouted, spinning Malcolm around too quickly and hitting his foot on the doorjamb.

Malcolm's head fell back as he yelped in pain. "Mom, please!" He reached for his foot but winced when he moved his bad arm. Were he not in agony, his attempts at gymnastics would be hilarious.

Craig took over, politely shoving Estelle out of the way. "We'll meet you in the lobby. Jessie has the situation well in hand." As he walked past Jessie, he patted her shoulder. Lowering his voice, he added, "I apologize for Dale Earnhardt Jr. over there. You know she's trying to help."

Jessie simply nodded. "See you downstairs."

Malcolm sighed, coming back to himself. "I love that woman," he started, chest already rumbling with a laugh.

"But she should not have let them kill off her character in *Atlanta Hearts*? She's got enough drama left in her for a spin-off series and at least two movies." She winked to soften the dig, but Malcolm didn't seem to care.

"Thank you," he said, tone more serious. He blinked up at her with nothing but appreciation in his chocolate gaze.

Jessie lifted an eyebrow. "I haven't done anything yet."

Malcolm snatched her hand, pulling until she went back to her knees and was eye-level with him. "You know that's not true. You've literally flown across the globe to be here, and now you're spending your leave helping me—saving me from suffocating under my parents. That's far from nothing."

"You're welcome, but you're going to be fine," she said, throat closing as a single tear fell. Suddenly, the seriousness of the whole situation slammed home. Jessie vowed to get Malcolm back on his feet, with minimal drama.

"Shh," he cooed, letting go to swipe the tear away. She leaned into his touch, her heart hammering for more reasons than concerns over his recovery. "JJ, I'm here. Okay? I'm talking and breathing and, frankly, that's more than I thought I'd get." She sniffled, but Malcolm soldiered on. "I have a feeling some Vitamin JJ is all I need."

"Your jokes are still terrible," she teased, dabbing at her eyes with the back of her free hand.

"Meh, it'll give me something else to work on during recovery." He chuckled, his lungs struggling with the effort. "Although right now, all I want is a nap in my own bed."

Jessie kissed his palm before resting his hand in his lap. "Your momma said she changed the sheets and spruced up the place. As soon as we get you home, you'll be in dreamland."

Malcolm frowned. "Spruced up? That means she's put scented candles everywhere and thrown out the junk food."

"Then it's a good thing I'll be there to smuggle in nachos from The Pecan Pit when they go back to their hotel." Jessie laughed as she pushed the wheelchair to the elevator bank. "Javi said they do DoorDash now."

A slew of nurses and staff waved as they passed, Malcolm dipping his head in embarrassment. "Gosh, I hate being the center of attention."

Jessie belly laughed. "Then you're in for a real long recovery until your parents go back to Tennessee."

"Don't remind me," Malcolm lamented.

When the elevator opened into the lobby, they were greeted to a sight that brought a fresh round of tears to both of their eyes.

Trevor, Javi, Chief Warren, Daisy, and a slew of other firemen cheered and held signs and balloons offering their congratulations and wishes for a fast recovery. "Smithy!" Javi cheered, dashing over and offering his friend a fist bump. "It's good to see you out of that bed."

Malcolm's lips quirked. "A saying I don't think you've used too often."

Always the ladies' man and not one to shy away from the truth, Javi barked out a laugh and clapped Malcolm on the shoulder. "Man, I've missed you."

Wincing at the contact, Trevor came to the rescue. "Javi, knock it out. Let the man get home and recuperate before you beat him up."

The rest of his teammates surrounded Malcolm as Trevor pulled Jessie aside. "This is so nice," she said, giving her brother a one-armed hug. "I know he misses y'all and the station."

Trevor let out a sigh, his own voice still hoarse. "Trust me, Jessie, we miss him, too." Glancing over his shoulder, he confirmed no one was eavesdropping. "Do you have everything you need to help Smithy? I can come over and—"

Jessie held up a hand to stop him. "Thank you for offering. I will likely need help soon, but right now he wants to get home." She lowered her voice. "Plus, I think what will be really helpful is if we can distract Estelle. You know how she can be."

Nodding, Trevor sucked his teeth. "I'll talk with Momma, and we'll figure something out. Maybe she can join that slutty book club everyone is in?"

Jessie was incredulous. "There's a slutty book club and no one has invited me yet?"

Javi joined them, throwing an arm around her shoulder. "They're a real hoot. You should join us."

"Of course you're a member of the slutty book club, Javi."

"Member? I'm hoping to become the group leader." Javi waggled his eyebrows, earning a playful gut punch from Trevor.

"Easy, Javi, you know that's Momma's pride and joy."

Flapping her hands to get back on topic, Jessie said, "I don't need to think about our mother reading porn." She made a gagging sound while Javi protested.

"You'll see Jessie, this is high-end stuff."

Jessie scoffed, but offered Javi a quick hug. "If you say so." Turning to her brother, she said, "Thanks, Trev." She pulled him into a real hug before heading back toward the crowd. "Listen up, Pinegrove FD!" she shouted, earning everyone's attention. "I'm taking Lieutenant Smith home to start his recovery, but my very helpful brother will send you an email for meal signups. While I can play nurse, I cannot play chef."

Everyone chuckled and offered their final wishes before leaving Malcolm alone with his parents and Jessie. "Ready to head home for your first nap of the day?" Jessie asked, steering Malcolm out into the sunshine.

Craig took her keys and pulled up Daisy's car, which Jessie was grateful to borrow. One of the problems of not living full-time in the States meant she didn't have her own car or place. As she and Craig loaded up Malcolm—and Estelle sobbed behind them—Jessie wondered what her life back in Pinegrove would look like *if* she had her own things, her own space.

Would her place be shared with Malcolm? Would the lack of obstacles have paved the way for a smooth happily ever after, or were they always doomed to live parallel lives? She shoved those questions away and focused on getting Malcolm home.

Once his son was buckled in, Craig carefully closed the door, knocking his knuckles on the top of the car. "We're going to go back to the hotel and find some lunch. Do you mind if we come by with dinner around five o'clock?" Craig asked, stepping back and waving at Malcolm, who already looked exhausted.

"That sounds perfect," Jessie said, shooting a thumbs-up.

"See you in a few hours," Craig said over his shoulder, nearly dragging Estelle along.

"A few hours that will feel like seconds." Malcolm sighed as Jessie slid behind the wheel. "I'm currently stuck in this position, but I plan on hugging you to death once we're home," he promised, sending a shiver surging through her. "I can't thank you enough for helping out."

Jessie faced Malcolm, his eyes sparkling in the sunlight pouring through the windshield. It was the first time since her return that he looked nearly like himself. Despite the terrible bedhead, his curls were still there, his dimples popping as he smiled. There was a paleness taking over his dark skin, but he still looked ludicrously handsome. She had to clear her throat twice before finding her words. "I'm happy to help. I'm only sorry you need it."

Lifting his bandaged arm, Malcolm quipped, "It's barely a scratch."

Jessie howled with laughter. "Oh yeah, tough guy. I forget buildings fall on you all the time."

"I mean, I don't want to brag." With his good hand, he patted her knee, his palm pressing into her, anchoring him in place.

On the short ride back to Malcolm's place, Jessie's hands slipped off the steering wheel approximately a million times. She was sweating like a tart in church and couldn't calm down. They were mere moments away from being in Malcolm's place, alone.

When she pulled into his driveway, Jessie threw the car in park. She had been with Malcolm when he bought the condo, and they had spent a lot of time celebrating in the new space—with and without clothing. If she closed her eyes, she'd hear the ghosts of their previous selves, laughing and reveling in their time together.

However, it was her last visit that stuck out in her mind's

eye. The last time they'd had a really big fight. The topic wasn't new, but the passion behind it certainly was. As if reading her mind, Malcolm was abnormally quiet. He stared sightlessly outside. Jessie wished she knew how to fill this silence.

Deciding practicality was best, Jessie asked, "What's the garage code? That's probably the easiest way to get you inside without using steps," she asked.

A slight flush crept up his neck. "Oh." His voice barely a whisper, he said, "It's uh, still your birthday."

Jessie's face turned the color of raspberry jam. "Oh," she breathed, their eyes locked on each other. *This doesn't mean anything*, her brain chanted, all the while her treacherous heart pounded in her rib cage. *He never changed it!*

Malcolm blinked, fumbling with the doorknob. "Might as well start the fun," he said, fighting with the handle.

"I'll help." She stopped his exit with a hand to his forearm. Even though he'd spent a week in the hospital on a diet of liquids and crackers, Malcolm was still fit. Cords of muscle tensed under her grip and Jessie had to remind herself that she was here to help, not grope him.

"Sit still, Mr. Patient. I'll be right back."

She hopped out of the car, opened the garage door, and met Malcolm at his door with a walker. "You heard what Tim said," she started, making sure Malcolm's feet were on the ground before helping him up. "You only need to use this thing until you're steady on your feet."

"Why do I feel like I'm on my way to the early bird special and The Pecan Pit?" Malcolm grumbled, but he managed to stand still once she'd shut the car door.

"Look at you, standing there like a big boy." She giggled at his eye roll and walked with him to the door.

As soon as they crossed the threshold, Malcolm's worst fears were realized. The house smelled like a Bath and Body Works exploded, with competing scents of vanilla, citrus, spice, and lilies. "My eyes are going to melt before I make it to bed," he coughed, slowly walking through his kitchen.

Jessie found plug-ins on their walk to the bedroom, and she pulled each out and planned to toss them in the trash before Estelle returned. "I'm on it," she promised.

Ten minutes later, Malcolm had used the bathroom on his own—a victory for all involved—and had collapsed onto the bed. Jessie helped him under the covers, careful of his bandages and casts.

"Oh my God," he purred as he melted into the pillow. "I never realized how great this bed was." He made some animalistic sounds that raised the hair on her arms.

Cupping the back of her neck, Jessie groaned. "I'm pretty familiar with the amazingness of that bed."

Malcolm stopped his writhing, eyes flashing to her. "JJ," he warned, eyebrow lifting.

"Haha." She laughed, although it sounded maniacal to her own ears. "Don't listen to me." She grabbed the nearest pillow, fluffing it before tucking it under his head. She smoothed back his matted curls, savoring the feel of his warmth.

Malcolm rested his palm on her cheek, eyes focused on her freckles. "You're an angel, JJ. I wouldn't have made it this far without you."

Never one to be comfortable with moments of vulnerability, Jessie snorted. "Oh yeah, I highly doubt your dad could have stolen those air fresheners so quickly and made inappropriate comments."

"I mean it." Malcolm's tone was urgent, despite his sagging eyelids. He was seconds away from passing out, and Jessie welcomed the reprieve from her own racing thoughts.

"Shhh, get some rest."

Malcolm's eyes fluttered closed, a small smile tugging his lips. "Thanks for coming home, JJ." It was the last thing he said before sleep finally took hold.

Jessie didn't move for a while after that. Too lost in memories of the past, she stayed by Malcolm's side until the light shifted in the room and her belly grumbled. Malcolm's parents were due back soon, and she needed to take care of a few things before they arrived. *Like burying those air fresheners in the bottom of the trash can ...*

Her confused heart would have to wait. Malcolm needed her, and she wouldn't let him down this time.

CHAPTER SEVEN

Malcolm woke to the sound of hushed whispers and the heavenly smell of his favorite food: chili.

Yes, it was a firefighter cliché to love chili as much as he did, but he wasn't going to fight it. Spicy or mild, vegetarian or meaty, he could not get enough. Ever.

"I don't see why I can't go in there and wake him up, Craig." His mother's stage whisper nearly had him cackling. It could be her training as an actress or her prerogative as his mother, but Estelle could project her voice from Tybee Island to New Orleans on one lungful of air.

"Estelle." His father's exacerbated tone proved this wasn't their first argument of the day. "I love you, darling, but, please, let's give the boy a little privacy. Jessie will make sure he's up and ready for dinner. Why don't you get the drinks together? I packed that chardonnay you like. Hmm?"

Brilliant play on his father's part; his mother never met a white wine she didn't love. "Fine, for now. But I want to help him get ready for bed."

He didn't miss Jessie's snort of laughter. "I'm looking forward to watching that," she said, quietly knocking as she pushed her way into his bedroom. "I'll bring our patient right out," she promised as she closed the door behind her with a quiet snick. She flipped the flimsy lock, although Malcolm knew Estelle would kick it down if she had the gumption.

Jessie padded into the room, a haggard expression crossing her lovely face. Her hair was loose and hung to her shoulders, and she was still in her cut-off overalls. She was adorable, and he cursed his broken body for not being able to pull her into bed with him. It could be the bandages and wraps, but his arms itched with the need to hold her, to cradle her against him. *But he would, in time ...*

"You're awake!" she exclaimed, jogging to his side of the bed and squatting down to be at eye level. "Did we wake you with all of our witty banter?" She pressed her cool hand to his forehead. The windows were closed and the ceiling fan was off, so he'd grown warm in the stifling room. "You're sweating to death in here. I'll turn down the AC." She began pulling back, but Malcolm stopped her progress with a gentle grip on her wrist.

"Wait," he croaked, throat dry and tender from sleep.

Jessie frowned. "What's the matter? Do you need more pain meds?"

Malcolm shook his head, although he didn't miss the stab of pain as he did so. His whole body revolted at his every move, but now he was more focused on his aching heart than his bones and joints. "Can we sit for a minute?"

Back when they began dating in high school, the pair would hang out all over Pinegrove. From their houses to the library to the creek to Hog Hollow, they always found a spot to call their own. During these moments, they would talk—and kiss—but also just be. Right now, as he started the long journey to recovery, the temporary loss of his job, and the invasion of his well-meaning but overbearing parents, all Malcolm wanted was Jessie.

Understanding exactly what he needed, Jessie kicked off her shoes and crawled next to him. She fluffed the pillows before sitting back, opening her arms so he could rest his head on her shoulder. Careful to avoid the bandages on his face, she kissed his temple. Malcolm felt a zing of awareness all the way down to his cast. *At least certain parts of him were in full working order…*

"Do you remember that one time out by the water tower?" she asked, her voice barely a whisper. If his mother was the queen of attention, Jessie was the princess of discretion.

Malcolm's chest rumbled as he stifled a laugh. "You'll have to be more specific. Do you mean the time in high school when we stole that bottle of schnaps from my grandma? Or the time you stole Trevor's high school yearbook with that girl's phone number in it?"

Jessie giggled, resting her head against his. "Actually, I meant that time a few years ago, when I was back home from Liberia and we stole the pie from Mrs. Watkins's windowsill." She snorted at the memory, and Malcolm could barely contain his mirth.

Mrs. Watkins was a sweet old woman known for her cartoonish lifestyle. She dressed in bright colors, always sang in public, and even left her prized pies to cool on the windowsill like she was living in a Looney Tunes episode. Much like Bugs Bunny, the pair of them had been walking by her house, debating where to stop for a snack. When they spotted the pie, Jessie got a wild hair to grab it and run … and that's what they did—all the way to the top of the town's water tower.

They hid up behind the ladders in the shadows, happily munching on the peach pie like it was their last meal. And knowing how connected to the local police department Mrs. Watkins was, it very well could have been.

"Wasn't that before the fireworks that year? I vaguely remember bumping into her while we still had evidence of the crime on our lips."

Without thinking, Malcolm latched onto Jessie's hand. He squeezed and she squeezed back harder. "Totally worth it. I'd do it again in a heartbeat, but I'd have to do some training first. My cardio skills aren't what they used to be," Jessie teased, waggling their joined hands.

For a few moments, they leaned against each other, the sound of Estelle's one-woman show seeping through the closed door. "I'm glad you're here," he said, tilting his head so his lips grazed her earlobe. After over a decade of off-again, on-again dating, Malcolm knew every inch of Jessie, every way to make her shudder.

Just as he'd hoped, a cluster of goosebumps erupted over the patch of freckles on her neck. Jessie turned toward him, licking her bottom lip. "I couldn't stay away, you know that." Her words escaped on an exhale, and Malcolm had to strain to hear her over his hammering heart.

Being mindful of his wrapped arm, he scooted over, tugging her against his side. Their lips were millimeters apart, closer than his favorite fireman's chair knot. This was it, he was finally going to kiss Jessie after ages apart.

Because his mother had the worst timing on the planet, she chose that exact moment to burst through the door, flimsy lock be damned. Jessie hadn't turned on his light, so the lights from the hallway had the same effect as a spotlight. Both of them shielded their eyes as Jessie hopped off the bed, nearly stumbling to the floor.

"What is taking so long? Are you okay, baby?"

Either oblivious or uncaring of the situation she interrupted, Estelle breezed in and turned on the bedside lamp. "You look flushed. Are you dehydrated?" Turning an accusing eye to Jessie, she added, "I thought you were going to bring him water?"

"I-I-I did. I mean, I will," Jessie stammered, smoothing her hands over the front of her overalls. Her cheeks were so rosy, they were brighter than her pink tank top. A flash of masculine pride washed over Malcolm, seeing her that flustered from his touch. He made a mental note—*Install deadbolt locks on his bedroom door… or enter witness protection.*

"Mom, for the love of God. We were just coming out for dinner." Malcolm sat up, pleased he didn't yelp out in pain. With Jessie's help, he swung his legs over the bed and made it to his walker. "Let me," he pleaded, desperate to keep some of his dignity.

Jessie nodded, but she stayed close to his side. "I'll get your pills ready. Did you want to stop by the bathroom on your way to the dining room?"

"Good idea." As he took a step closer, his mother rushed ahead and held the door open. Malcolm ground his teeth together. "Mom, please go help Dad with dinner. I'll be out in a minute, and I definitely don't need anyone's assistance in the next five minutes."

Craig shouted from the kitchen. "I could use help chopping this cilantro!"

Jessie jutted her thumb over her shoulder. "Do you mind helping Craig? I'll wait to make sure Malcolm gets to the table okay."

Estelle looked back and forth from her son to Jessie. "But I wanted to …"

Craig joined them in the hallway, a chef's knife in one hand and a bunch of herbs in the other. "Estelle, you know I'll likely chop my fingers off if you don't help. Then we'll have two Smith men down for the count, and I don't think your nursing skills are up for the task." He winked and headed back to the kitchen. "Jessie, I'll pour you a glass of caretaker juice."

Jessie wrinkled her brow. "Caretaker juice?"

"It's wine," Estelle said, finally allowing herself a smile. "I thought we could all use a little mood elevator."

Before Malcolm closed the door, he asked, "Can I have some? I feel like out of the four of us, my mood could use the most lifting."

"You can't drink on your medication," both Jessie and Estelle barked.

Malcolm pushed his walker into the bathroom and sighed. "Can't blame a guy for trying." He took longer than he needed, savoring a moment's peace.

Cracking the door open, Malcolm found Jessie leaning

against the far wall. "You okay?" she asked, stepping forward to help him get his walker over the seam in the floor.

"Yeah. You know how my mom is. I needed a minute of solitude."

"I made corn muffins!" Estelle shouted from the kitchen.

"Oooohhh," Jessie cooed as she steered them toward the dining room. The table was set for four, with Malcolm at the head closest to the doorway. Everyone had glasses of wine, except for Malcolm, who had apple juice.

"Really?" he scoffed, easing into his seat with a wince. "I'm surprised you didn't get me juice boxes, Mom," he snickered, raising an eyebrow.

Craig rubbed the back of his neck and sighed. "She did."

Jessie burst out laughing, recovering in time when Estelle sashayed to the table with a basket of corn muffins. "What did I miss?" she asked, placing two muffins on Malcolm's plate before settling into her own seat.

"Nothing, darling. Let's say grace and dig in."

Craig led a brief prayer before serving everyone hearty bowls of chili. True to form, Malcolm doused his in hot sauce until his eyes watered, but he could certainly take the heat.

Jessie was a different story. She put a dollop of sour cream on top and shook away any offers of jalapenos or hot sauce. The foursome ate and chatted about inane topics like the weather and happenings back in Tennessee. Malcolm considered the night to be a success, until his mother poked the bear.

"So, Jessie," she said, dabbing at her mouth with a cloth napkin Malcolm didn't know he owned. "Are you set to move back to Pinegrove full-time now?"

Jessie's spoon stalled on the way to her mouth, a bite of chili plopping back into her bowl with a sad splat. "Oh, urm," she muttered as she collected her thoughts.

Craig, always the peacekeeper, asked, "Did anyone see

the story in today's newspaper? They got one of the winners of American Idol to be the emcee of the Fourth of July parade."

Estelle flapped a manicured hand in the air. "We can discuss that later, honey. I'm curious what Jessie's plans are now that she's home."

Truth be told, Malcolm was as curious as his mother was—more so. Yet he knew how Jessie operated. The more you cornered her, the more she'd fight back. "Mom," Malcolm warned under his breath, but Jessie shook her head.

"I'm not sure, actually." Jessie squared her shoulders. "I'm up for a promotion in the Peace Corps, and I need to get back sooner rather than later. My boss, Noel, can only hold my application so long."

"Oh?" Estelle asked. "A promotion. Isn't that lovely." Her tone suggested otherwise. "I know your momma would love to have you home again. And we sure would like to …"

Jessie's spoon clattered to the table, and she hurried to catch it before it fell to the floor. "I know that, but there's a lot to consider."

"Such as?" Estelle pressed, and Malcolm couldn't bother to stop her. He tugged the napkin from his collar and balled it up, knuckles turning white as he waited.

Jessie blinked, as if surprised anyone was forcing the issue. "I've worked for the Peace Corps for nearly a decade. It's hard to walk away when I've done so much for them."

Craig nodded, draining the last of his wine. Judging from how he longingly looked at the empty bottle, Malcolm knew he wanted more liquid courage for this discussion. "You've done a lot of good things for the Corps, Jessie. They've been lucky to have you."

"We'd be lucky to have you, too," Malcolm said, instantly hating himself. Jessie's head whipped in his direction, her expression a mix of hope, confusion, and betrayal. "But congratulations on the promotion. That's very exciting, you earned it."

"I haven't gotten it yet." Jessie pushed to her feet. "I'll start cleaning up the dishes."

Malcolm's head fell back and he blinked rapidly up at the ceiling, willing the last five minutes to evaporate. They'd made such progress since she'd been back, tiptoeing around the elephant in the room. He'd been under the impression she was close to coming home for good, but apparently while he was mentally picking out engagement rings, she was renewing her work visa.

How did he get it so wrong again?

And would they ever get it right?

CHAPTER EIGHT

"Thank you for helping with the dishes, Craig," Jessie said, hoisting the stock pot back into the cabinet.

The older man chuckled. "Happy to help, Jessie." He leaned back to check the living room, where his wife was currently babying Malcolm to the point of insanity. "Although I should probably get back in there before Malcolm smothers his mother."

Jessie bit back a smile. "She's worried about him. We all are."

Craig nodded, putting a lot of focus into the wine glass he was drying. "I hope Estelle didn't upset you at dinner. We're grateful you're here, for as long as you can stay. We both understand the importance of a career."

It wasn't missed on Jessie that he didn't say the *three* of them understood. Malcolm was just as career-focused and driven, yet he never seemed to understand why Jessie did what she did.

"Speaking of," she said, trying to change the subject. "Malcolm said you're thinking of retiring next year."

Craig was an engineer, his job taking him and Estelle to Nashville after Malcolm graduated from the academy. He was meticulous, detailed, and incredibly bright, the perfect balance to his wife's sometimes emotional theatrics.

Putting the glass down, Craig leaned against the counter, his brow furrowed. "It's a possibility. The firm is looking at shifting departments around, and, frankly, I think I'm too old to start over with another team."

With a huff, Jessie shook her head. "My momma would spank me for calling out someone's age, but you're not even sixty, right?"

Craig's frown shifted into a grin. "Yes, young lady. You're correct." He tossed the tea towel over his shoulder, cocking his head to the side as he thought. "Estelle still gets her royalties from reruns of *Atlanta Hearts*, and I've saved up a little nest egg. While we love where we live in Tennessee, and we love still being fairly close to Pinegrove, we've always wanted to travel more. You know the retired cliché, go see the world."

Now that was something Jessie could relate to. "Granted, my travels take me to different places, but if y'all ever want suggestions on the best airports and travel tips, I'm your girl." She pointed to herself and beamed.

"You're our girl for what?" Malcolm asked behind her, practically scaring Jessie to death.

She gasped and whirled around. "How in blazes are you so quiet with that walker? I'll have to put on a bell or something."

Craig looked around, and asked, "Where's your mother? I'm surprised she let you sit up on the couch, let alone leave it."

Malcolm rolled his eyes, the effect slightly less impressive with the bandage on his face. "She's in the bathroom, and, to be honest, I think y'all can head back to the hotel for the night."

Father and son wore matching sour expressions, but Craig relented. "I'll ignore the lapse in manners since you're recuperating." His tone had a bite, but Malcolm didn't seem to care. "We'll come over for breakfast and relieve Jessie for the morning." Jessie opened her mouth to protest, to say that's why she was there, but all she got was a polite shake of the head. "We are grateful, but we're also here to help. Plus, I'm sure you'd like to see your family while you're here."

That was certainly true enough. "Makes sense to me."

"Malcolm! Baby, where are you?" Estelle cried from the living room.

Craig snorted. "Maybe the bell isn't a bad idea."

Ten minutes of tears and hugs later, Estelle and Craig finally bid them good night. Jessie put on the kettle to make tea before getting Malcolm's medications ready for bedtime.

Malcolm stood at the entry to the kitchen, leaning on his walker more than Jessie liked. "Why don't you take a seat while I fix us some tea and your nighttime cocktail of miracle meds?" He shuffled over without a word, unceremoniously plopping onto the chair with a wince. "Careful of your stitches!" Jessie warned.

"Oh, really? I totally forgot that I was incapacitated and useless." He attempted to cross his arms over his chest before realizing he couldn't. "And I don't want tea. I'm not an old lady in one of your British mysteries."

Gone was the jovial, carefree Malcolm she loved, replaced with a broken man with a bitter continence. It broke her heart. His curls were matted to his forehead, proof he was ready for a shower. His pajamas were rumpled, and his eyes were heavy. Although never considered a fashion plate, Malcolm always looked put together. He never missed a trip to the barber, he stayed in shape, and he liked to buy nice clothes.

The man sulking now looked like he'd been chewed up and spit out by life, and she hated that she couldn't snap her fingers and make it all better; couldn't carry the burden of recovery.

"Do you think you can handle a shower before bed? Maybe that'll help?"

Malcolm shook his head, his gaze laser focused on the

tabletop. He toyed with the salt and pepper shakers, the only sound in the room the kettle whistling. Jessie wordlessly poured two cups of water, dunking in the tea bags and sliding a mug in front of Malcolm.

No matter how much time passed in between her visits, Jessie could still read the man like a book. This was more than the pain of recovery and the frustration of a broken body; this ire was directed squarely at her.

"The way I see it, we have two choices." He didn't respond, but his fingers stilled over the shakers. Good, the goober was at least listening. "Option one, we focus on the here and now. I'm back in Pinegrove for a while, and I want to help you in your recovery. We can be the adults we are and save the future talk for the future." Taking a sip from her scalding tea, she flinched. "Option two is I call Estelle and make her wildest dreams come true by babying you to literal death. I spend a few days with Momma and Trevor and hit the road."

She let out a long sigh, willing Malcolm to engage with her. Granted, she didn't want another fight, but she certainly didn't want the silent treatment.

After another minute of quiet, Jessie pushed off her seat and collected his pill bottles, dutifully lining up his nightly regimen. "I'll get you some water," she said as she stalked to the fridge and poured a glass.

She slid it in front of Malcolm, and he stopped her by looping his arm around her waist. "Stay." The word came out as a whisper, a soft plea.

Jessie exhaled, not realizing how much she needed to hear that. "Okay." She covered his forearm with a splayed hand, hanging onto him like a life raft. She could have clung to him forever. "Time for pills, buster."

Malcolm took his pills with a trembling hand, downing all of them in one gulp of water. Finally he met her gaze before dropping his chin to his chest. "I'll try not to wallow about all this," he muttered, gesturing with his good hand to his air cast and bandages. "But what I'll really try is to not pressure you, JJ. I can't lie and say I'm not happy you're here. Hell, I'd gladly have another warehouse fall on me if it meant you'd be here in my kitchen having a nightly cup of tea."

She scoffed, swatting the back of his hand. "Hush up."

The corner of his lips quirked up, but he continued. "But you need to know, even if we're not talking about it, I want you here. Not just here in Pinegrove, but here, in this house with me." Jessie didn't miss the tear that slid down his cheek, her own eyes misting over. "You're still my best friend, JJ. You're the first person I think about when good things happen, and you're the only person I want by my side during the bad. I can't pretend that you leaving, even if it's for a wonderful opportunity, doesn't gut me." He swiped angrily at another tear and groaned. "I love you, okay? I'm simultaneously so proud of you, I want to rent a billboard and tell all of Pinegrove. But I know you could do amazing things anywhere, even here with our community. I wish you believed in yourself more."

He'd rendered her speechless, caught off guard by his observation. She did believe in herself, didn't she? Hell, wasn't that why she was obsessed with getting that promotion? She poured nearly a third of her life into this organization, into the field. It only made sense to want to move up the ranks, right?

"I love you, too," Jessie whispered, even though his words cut her.

Sensing their chat was over, Malcolm scooted his chair back, leaning on the walker as he found his footing. "Well, since we've confirmed option one, let's get ready for bed."

Jessie placed their mugs in the sink and turned off the kitchen lights. "Did you want to take a shower? It might feel nice."

Malcolm started to shake his head, but he stopped himself. "Yeah, why not."

"Good!" Jessie squeaked with a little too much enthusiasm. Despite all the roiling thoughts and feelings running through her head, the thought of seeing Malcolm naked brought the temperature up fifty degrees.

"I'll uh, get the medical tape and plastic sheets."

"This is going to be so relaxing, I can tell," Malcolm deadpanned, but he kept pace to the bathroom.

Before he was discharged from the hospital, the nurses gave Jessie a bag of accoutrements to help Malcolm settle in at home. Part of that goodie bag were the essentials for a shower, since he couldn't get his cuts wet yet.

By the time Jessie made it to the bathroom, Malcolm was doubled over the tub, one arm stuck in the hole of his shirt. "Little help," he said through clenched teeth.

Jessie bit back a smile, knowing even the tiniest giggle would land her in trouble. It wasn't that the scene was hilarious, but it was certainly novel. This was hardly their first shower together—but none of them started with him tangled in his clothes. Hell, if anything they usually couldn't get their clothes off fast enough.

"Hold still," she ordered, carefully peeling the shirt off his frame. She did her best not to touch any of his sore spots, but since half of his body was a walking bruise, that was impossible.

Malcolm hissed through his teeth, kneeling over to catch his breath. "Sweet Georgia Brown, JJ," he gasped. "These are your kid gloves?"

Jessie poked his side, the only square inch she could find that wasn't covered in bandages or welts. "Do you want me to call back Estelle? Because I know she'd be back here in a heartbeat with a rubber ducky and bubble bath."

Malcolm snorted, deflating slightly. "No, ma'am," he said on a sigh, easing down to the side of the bathtub.

Jessie ripped off a piece of tape and held a sheet of plastic against the biggest cluster of bandages. "Hold still now," she whispered, carefully covering the spot before moving onto the next.

For a moment, the bathroom was filled with the sounds of ripping tape and muttered curses when Jessie wasn't tender enough. When he was covered in more plastic sheeting than a Slip 'N Slide, Jessie clapped her hands together and beamed. "I think you're ready for a shower."

Malcolm held out his hand for her to assist him to his feet. "Make the water hot enough to melt this tape off my body," he begged.

"Aye aye, Lieutenant." Jessie saluted before turning on the water.

Behind her, the rustling of fabric alerted her that Malcolm was now in his birthday suit. She thought very unsexy thoughts as she turned to face him. Keeping her gaze locked over his shoulder, she gestured into the shower. "Ready." Her voice was as squeaky as a Smurf's.

Malcolm rolled his eyes, although he had cupped himself for the illusion of modesty. "JJ, I swear. This is probably the least sexy thing we've ever done. The least you can do is look at me."

"Nope, don't need to," she said, eyes squeezed shut as she pawed her way to the side of the bathroom. She kept one arm out so he could steady himself as he stepped under the jet.

He let go of her grip, sliding the curtain shut and leaving Jessie a moment to collect herself. Malcolm was naked, mere inches away, and she couldn't—and wouldn't—do anything about it.

"I can hear you thinking." He laughed from the shower. "Can you hand me a washcloth?"

"No," she blurted before recovering. "I mean, sure." She fumbled through his linen closet, retrieving a washcloth and clean set of towels. She neatly stacked the towels on the counter before pinching her eyes shut and thrusting the washcloth behind the curtain.

"Oof," Malcolm exhaled as she punched his chest. "Thanks, I think," he said, clearing his throat. "I appreciate you testing my balance, but maybe next time just hand it to me? The hit in the solar plexus wasn't required."

"Oh hell." She drew back the corner of the curtain and

winced. Malcolm leaned against the wall of the shower, rubbing at the spot where she'd punched him. "I'm really sorry. I wasn't thinking."

Malcolm snorted. "That actually makes me feel better."

"Ha ha." Jessie kept her gaze locked on his profile, temporarily mesmerized by the water running down his handsome face. He smiled, a real smile that popped his dimple and gave her butterflies. In that heartbeat, they were teenagers again.

"Room for one more if you're interested," he said with a wink, the glint in his eyes unmistakable. *Yeah, definitely teenagers* ...

At first, Jessie couldn't speak. Her tongue was glued to the roof of her mouth as if she'd devoured a peanut butter sandwich without milk. "Malcolm," she warned, voice low.

"JJ," he replied. His baritone sounded as rough as gravel. It could have been the smoke inhalation, or simply years of history and lust simmering between them. The shower wasn't the only thing steaming up the room.

"We can't, you're injured." It was a lame excuse, even to her own ears.

Malcolm cocked his head. "Not all of me."

Jessie couldn't say she wasn't tempted. Their chemistry always ran hotter than a five-alarm fire. Attraction had never been their problem. Their problem was all about timing, ambitions, and, on Jessie's part, a little fear. She could pull back that shower curtain and share a steamy moment with her ex. It would be easy, perfect even.

Yet when the bubbles rinsed away and she had to leave, the heartbreak cycle would continue. Right now that wasn't what Jessie wanted, and she knew it wasn't what Malcolm needed.

Yanking the shower curtain closed, Jessie braced herself on the edge of the sink. "Let me know when you're ready to come out," she said, shoulders sagging.

A moment later the shower turned off and Malcolm stuck his hand out for a towel. She handed it to him, careful not to touch him. Even if only one skin cell grazed him, Jessie would melt into a puddle of want.

"I'm decent," Malcolm said as he pulled back the curtain. "But I need a hand stepping over." Jessie put herself in nurse mode as she helped him out of the shower.

"I'll dry your back," she offered, picking up an extra towel and carefully patting the skin around the tape dry.

As she toweled him down, they faced the bathroom mirror, fogged up with steam. Jessie took her time making sure he was dry before carefully peeling away the tape and checking his bandages. By the time she was done, the mirror had cleared and she could see their reflections staring back at her.

Malcolm, damn him, looked incredible. He'd always been tall and lean, but years on the force had carved him into a walking marble statue. His dark skin glistened, and Jessie stood awe-struck as a single bead of water trailed from his collarbone down to his stomach. *Did he have eight abs now? What the hell was going on?!*

"I should …" Jessie dropped the towel, unable to breathe.

Malcolm spun around, bringing his good arm up to rest on her shoulder. "You should what?" he asked, angling his head so he could meet her blue gaze.

"I don't know," she said, a chuckle escaping on an exhale.

Bringing his hand up, he cupped her cheek. He swiped his thumb over her bottom lip, and Jessie shuddered. This was hardly their first time getting too close for caretaker comfort, but Jessie couldn't step away. Malcolm felt like a magnet, pulling her closer like a force of nature.

"JJ." He exhaled her nickname, his breath dancing across her lips. "Please."

That one word had maximum effect, chipping away any shred of resolve she had left. Jessie closed the distance between them, their lips crashing together. In a heartbeat, time stood still. Gone was the past, their worries of the future, all the words they should have said; they were just Jessie and Malcolm.

Malcolm angled her closer so he could deepen the kiss, and she felt him through his towel. All it would take was one little tug and he'd be standing there naked in front of her. God, she wanted that, more than her next breath. Yet common sense won out as soon as she leaned closer and pressed on one of his bandages.

"Oh!" he exclaimed, wincing in pain.

The mood shifted, desire evaporating. "Oh my God, what hurts?"

Malcolm gritted his teeth, flexing his hand over his side. "Nothing, I'm fine."

Jessie shook her head, angry with herself for prioritizing her libido over his injuries. "I'm so sorry, I shouldn't have—"

"Don't!" Malcolm's tone was sharp. "Don't you dare apologize for that. I would gladly kiss you until my limbs fell off, JJ."

"Graphic," she said, wincing at the visual.

Malcolm chuckled. "I thought it was sort of morbidly romantic."

Jessie tossed her head back. "Agree to disagree." She held out her hand and motioned toward the door. "Now, why don't we get you ready for bed?"

And with that, they shuffled off to the bedroom. Jessie got him a glass of water while Malcolm attempted to get redressed. When she came back and found him with his underwear on and a sock stuck on his toes, she bit back a smile.

"Little help again," he muttered, although this time there was no snark in his tone. He simply looked exhausted.

"Hold on," she replied, placing his water by the bed. In a deft motion, she had his socks on and helped him lie back on a stack of pillows. "Let me grab a pair of sleep shorts from your closet."

"No!" Malcolm shouted, so loudly, Jessie tripped over

her own feet. She whirled around, eyebrow arched in question. "I mean, the closet is a mess. I'll sleep in my boxers."

Jessie eyed the closet curiously, but did as she was told. "Okay, but no funny business, mister." She plopped down on the edge of the bed, sweeping a hand over his face. "How's the pain level?"

Malcolm flinched as he rested back on the pillows, but quickly enough found a comfortable position. "Not bad," he replied, wiggling back. "You're sleeping in here," he ordered, but Jessie wasn't about to disagree. Wild horses couldn't pull her from Malcolm's side.

"I will, but I meant what I said about funny business."

He closed his eyes and patted the mattress beside him. "I don't remember anything funny about the last ten minutes."

"No argument here," she teased, turning off the bedside lamp. "I'll be right back." She hurried down the hallway with her own pajamas, eager to get cleaned up before bed.

By the time she returned, Malcolm was already asleep. Carefully, she pulled back the covers and slid next to him. Resting her hand over his pecs, she finally relaxed when she felt the steady rhythm of his heart.

The kiss was a mistake, she knew that. And sharing a bed during his recovery was only muddying the waters of their relationship. Jessie didn't care. All she cared about was that Malcolm was safe, he was alive, and he was by her side. They could figure out the rest of it in the light of day.

LIBBY KAY

CHAPTER NINE

The sun peeked through the blinds, hitting Malcolm square in the face. He blinked a few times, attempting to roll over to check the time on the alarm clock before he remembered his body was broken and yelped out in pain.

Within five seconds the bedroom door flew open and his mother rushed in. "Malcolm, baby. Are you okay?"

Her shrill tone woke Jessie beside him, who bolted upright. Her brown hair was plastered to her cheek, her eyes crusted with sleep. "What?" she asked, pawing at her face as Estelle greeted them.

"Well, good morning, you two," she said with a wave of a spatula. "You better not be doing what I think you were doing. I asked the doctor about that, and he said no shenanigans until Malcolm gets the air cast off."

"Sweet Jesus, Mom," Malcolm chastised, praying for the ground to open up and swallow him whole. "We were sleeping, which the doctors said I need."

Jessie threw her legs over the side of the bed and stood, adjusting her tank top so as not to flash anyone. *Which was a real shame.*

"Good morning, Estelle. I'm sorry I didn't make coffee

yet." Jessie rubbed at the pillow creases on her face, unable to hold back a yawn. "What time is it?"

"Seven fifteen," Estelle said with more bite than Malcolm thought necessary.

"Why are you over her so early?" Malcolm didn't mean to be ungrateful. He understood how much his mother worried on a good day, and this was hardly a good day.

His father entered the room, dressed as if ready for the golf course in a polo shirt and colorful shorts. "Your mother wanted to make breakfast, which is almost ready." Turning to an embarrassed Jessie, he added, "Good morning, Jessie. How is our patient doing?"

Jessie opened her mouth to reply, but another visitor joined the fray. "I was wondering the same thing," Javi said, striding into the room like he owned the place.

"Ortiz, what the hell?" Malcolm pulled up the blankets to cover his bare chest.

As if reading his mind, Javi barked out a laugh. "Oh please, Smithy. Nothing I haven't seen in the showers." He raised his coffee mug in the air in greeting. "Hey, Jessie."

"Good Lord," Jessie muttered. "Is all of Pinegrove here?"

"Practically," Trevor said from the doorway. If his small bedroom wasn't already full with him, Jessie, his parents, and Javi, Malcolm would have invited his captain in. "How's everyone doing?"

"Really, Trev?" Jessie admonished, shoving her feet into her slippers and pushing past the crowd toward the bathroom.

When Malcolm dozed off last night, he envisioned a morning cuddling—as much as he could—with his girl. He wanted a few more stolen kisses before reality set back in. Apparently that was a pipedream, and he was about to have breakfast with half the fire station.

"Tell me, is Maxwell out there with the chief? Exactly how many of Pinegrove FD will be joining us for hotcakes?" Malcolm's question dripped with sarcasm.

Estelle perked up. "That's a good question, baby." She turned toward Trevor and asked, "Who else is joining us? I'd better get cracking."

Craig took that moment as an opportunity to take charge. "Okay, everyone out. Let's give Malcolm a moment." He strode to the closet and retrieved Malcolm's bathrobe. Tossing it onto the bed, he said, "Take your time, son. We'll see you when you're ready."

Malcolm highly doubted that. He knew his mother. He had two minutes at best before Estelle was back and hovering over him like a specimen in a Petri dish. "Uh-huh," Malcolm muttered, waiting as everyone filed out.

Before the door snicked shut, Jessie slid back inside. "I can safely say I could have lived another thirty years without your parents and Javi seeing me in my jimjams." She shuddered, but Malcolm chuckled.

"It's certainly not my preferred way to wake up."

Jessie closed the distance between them, resting her hand on his forehead. "I don't have a fever," he protested, but he still leaned into her touch.

"Just making sure," she said, placing a soft kiss on his temple.

His joints and muscles were stiff, but it had been wonderful sleeping in his own bed. The worst part of being in a hospital was the lack of privacy—which apparently carried over to his house as well—with nurses waking him to run tests or take blood. Not to mention the beeps and sounds of the hospital were hardly relaxing. Falling asleep to the gentle snores of Jessie Mays, however, was a welcome soundtrack for bedtime.

A few minutes later, Malcolm was at his walker, shuffling out to the dining room. While he understood Trevor and Javi wouldn't judge his current state, and total dependence on the walker, it still chafed to appear this helpless. "Is there coffee?" he asked as he plopped down in his seat.

Javi lifted his mug and jostled it. "I think I saved you a cup or two." Trevor rolled his eyes, muttering under his breath. As much as he wanted some peace this morning, Malcolm enjoyed seeing his buddies.

Craig slid a mug across the table, already with cream and sugar. "Thanks, Dad," he said, taking a long pull of the caffeine fix. "So what's the plan for today?" he asked, knowing full well he was experiencing it.

Estelle carried in a platter of pancakes, with Jessie following with a plate overflowing with bacon. Craig snatched two pieces before Jessie put the plate down, earning a scowl from Estelle.

"The doctor said you need to watch your fat intake. I can whip up some oatmeal." His dad chomped down on the bacon, raising a defiant eyebrow at his wife. "Fine, fine. Go ahead and have a heart attack." She turned to Jessie and Trevor and hastily added, "I'm sorry."

Trevor hid his smirk behind his napkin and shook his head. "No worries, Ms. Estelle. Our daddy didn't listen to Momma either."

Jessie stabbed a few pancakes and made up a plate for Malcolm. Despite wanting to feel independent again, Malcolm wouldn't stop Jessie from fixing his breakfast. Besides, she always remembered how he liked the pancakes in a puddle of syrup, not covered in the sticky stuff.

The six of them fell into comfortable, if albeit boring, conversation. Javi discussed the slew of women he'd recently dated, Craig nearly choking on his coffee when Javi mentioned a particular buxom redhead.

Malcolm balled up his napkin and tossed it at Javi. "Jesus, Ortiz. My parents are present."

Estelle flapped a hand. "Oh please, I starred in a soap opera, son. I'm aware of the shenanigans that happen in the world."

Javi splayed a hand over his heart and sighed. "Thank you for enjoying my storytelling, Estelle. It's not often I get to share a meal with such a lovely woman."

"Hey!" Jessie protested, a blob of syrup falling onto her shirt.

Trevor handed his sister a napkin, unable to stop a belly laugh from taking over. "As always, you're first class, Jessie."

Jessie stuck her tongue out and wiped away the mess. Malcolm tried really hard not to stare at her chest, especially with his mother watching and Trevor mere feet away. That was the thing about JJ, she was always herself. His mother could put on airs and be prim and proper, but JJ was always JJ.

Jessie started stacking plates, checking the time on her watch and completely ending his ogling. "We need to get ready. The nurse is coming in about fifteen minutes."

Trevor winced when he checked his own watch. "Javi, we gotta jet."

Javi helped Jessie carry the last of the dishes into the kitchen. "You mind if we swing by later with Maxwell and some pizzas?"

Estelle opened her mouth, but Craig was faster. "I think that's a great idea. Give you all a chance to talk shop, and Malcolm can see his friends."

"Who's Maxwell?" Jessie asked, doling out an array of pills for Malcolm to take.

"Thanks," he said, throwing them all in his mouth and swallowing them with the last of his coffee. "Maxwell is my partner."

Jessie gestured at Javi. "I thought Javi was your partner."

Trevor shrugged on his uniform jacket and shook his head. "Nah, we made some changes recently. I'll fill you in later."

"Can't wait until I can get back to work," Malcolm said on a sigh.

Javi clapped his shoulder, a little too hard, but Malcolm didn't react. "We'll get you back soon, buddy."

Trevor shook Malcolm's hand. "You want some company tonight?"

"Love some," Malcolm replied, meaning it. He wanted life to get back to normal, and he also wanted Jessie to be a part of his life, a part of his friend group.

Trevor pointed at Jessie and added, "You should probably swing by the house and see Momma if you have time. She misses you."

Jessie rolled her eyes but didn't argue. Turning to Estelle, she asked, "Would you mind doing nursing duty solo?"

Estelle pulled her into a hug and nodded, her blonde hair bobbing. "Of course not. It would be nice for the three of us to have some more quality time."

Over his mother's shoulder, Jessie mouthed *Sorry*, but he wasn't going to put up a fight. He understood his parents wanted to spend time with him, and he couldn't deny Daisy access to her wanderer daughter.

A loud knock at the door alerted the group that the nurse had arrived, and Malcolm braced himself for a day of suffocating parents, but at least he'd see his friends. He missed Maxwell, and hadn't seen her as much as the others. With a family of her own, her time was always full.

And then there was the fact that he needed a distraction from JJ. Their kiss, her reaction to him last night in the shower proved there was still something between them. The lady doth protest too much, or whatever the saying was. Malcolm knew Jessie was still attracted to him; now he needed to figure out what to do about it.

CHAPTER TEN

Jessie double-checked for the millionth time that Malcolm and his parents were set before excusing herself to visit her momma. Truth be told, she welcomed the change in scenery as her lips still burned from their kiss last night. What she needed was a distraction … a little space from a particular set of dark brown eyes that could stare into her soul.

"Momma?" Jessie called out as she entered her childhood house.

A warmth surged through her as she kicked off her shoes and took in the familiar sights and scents. Family photos greeted her in the entryway, gap-toothed grins from her and Trevor over the years mixed in with random snapshots of the four of them. Her father looking young and healthy, her mother's infectious grin nearly leaping out of the frame. The air smelled like coffee and cinnamon, cozy and inviting.

"In the kitchen, sugar!" Daisy called out.

Before Jessie could cross the threshold, Gus, the family basset hound, lumbered up to greet her. Jessie dropped to her knees and rubbed his belly and peppered his snout in kisses. "Who's a good boy? Who's a good boy?" she asked, eliciting NSFW sounds from the old hound dog.

When dog and owner had had enough, Jessie strode into the kitchen and found her mother and Chief Warren sharing a cup of coffee. "Hey, Chief!" Jessie greeted as she went in search of her own caffeine. After surviving a morning with Estelle, she needed another gallon to stay sharp.

"Good morning, Jessie. How are things going with Malcolm?" Chief rose to his feet and offered his chair to her, ever the gentleman.

Jessie added sugar to her cup before filling it to the brim with coffee. "Not too bad, actually. He slept through the night, is getting his appetite back, and Estelle hasn't smothered him to death yet."

He's also still the best kisser I've ever met ...

Shaking lustful thoughts away, Jessie took the proffered seat and slurped her coffee. "What brings you by this early?"

Her mother blinked, eyes hardly focusing, before turning back to the stove and asking, "You want some breakfast, sugar?"

"No, thanks. Estelle came over early to cook for her boy," Jessie explained, punctuating the statement with an eye roll. Her mother was well aware of how Estelle could get when Malcolm was fine, but when he was recovering, she was a woman on a mission. Yet despite her statement, Daisy didn't react at all.

Jessie cocked her head to study the chief a moment before offering, "If you're looking for my fool brother, you missed him. He stopped by Malcolm's with Javi on their way to the station."

The chief tapped his watch and grimaced. "Which is where I need to be." Jessie watched in fascination as her mother and Chief Warren stood and bumped into each other. He steadied Daisy by the shoulders before dropping his hands like they were on fire. "Um, y-y-yeah ..." he stuttered as he backed out of the room.

"I'll walk you out, Paul," Daisy said, her cheeks flushed. In her haste to follow him out, she nearly tripped over Gus.

The hairs on Jessie's neck rose as her mother and Paul shared a hushed goodbye. While hardly a stranger, it wasn't usual for the fire chief to make house calls before lunchtime. Chief Warren used to be Captain of the fire station, working under her father. A family friend for longer than Jessie had been alive, she was used to seeing him and his ex-wife during events and holidays.

Now though, this felt different. The sun still hung low in the sky, the birds in the middle of their morning song.

Daisy joined her daughter in the kitchen, fluffing her hair back into place. "Did you get breakfast at Malcolm's?" she asked, not quite meeting her daughter's gaze. She strode straight to the stove and started flipping on burners.

"Momma," Jessie called out, lips trembling with mirth. Daisy kept on pulling out pans like she was prepared to cook Thanksgiving dinner for all of Pinegrove. "Momma!" she shouted, finally earning her mother's attention.

"Yes, sugar?" She spun around, knocking a forgotten crust of toast onto the floor. Gus sauntered over and snarfed it up before either woman could move a muscle.

Jessie scooted to the edge of her chair, eyebrow raised. "I said Estelle cooked." Jessie watched her mother as she paced around the table before finally taking a seat.

"That's nice," Daisy said absentmindedly, toying with the corner of a placemat. She looked up and blinked before asking, "Did you get breakfast?"

And that's when Jessie knew, her mother was dating the fire chief. The woman couldn't keep a secret long, and she'd never had a poker face. Either she was in the middle of a medical episode, or she was dying of embarrassment. Jessie would bet her non-existent pension it was the latter.

"You're sleeping with Chief Warren, aren't you?" Jessie asked, although it was hardly a question. The color drained from her mother's face in record time.

"Jessica June Mays! I raised you to be a lady." Daisy's voice was indignant, but Jessie didn't miss her trembling fingers as she combed through her air.

Jessie tittered. "Says the woman who just said goodbye to her booty call."

Daisy's cheeks suddenly filled with color, and she covered her face. "My word, sugar. I think all your manners must still be south of the equator."

Jessie drained the last of her coffee and slid the cup away. "What's going on, Momma? Are you worried I won't approve?" Far be it for her to judge anyone on their dating situation. She was less than twenty-four hours removed from a scorching kiss with her ex, whom she was helping recover from a horrible fire. An ex who still made her stomach flip with merely a wink. An ex she shared a complicated past with. Yeah, she had no room to judge anyone.

"Yes. Paul and I are seeing each other." Daisy fiddled with her bracelet, unable to look up at her daughter. "Trevor knows, and truth be told, it took him a little while to calm down. I wanted to tell you sooner, but I hated the idea of telling you over the phone."

"Momma, I'm not mad," Jessie promised, resting her hand on top of her mother's. "Daddy would want you to be happy, and he loved Paul."

Incredulous, her mother scoffed. "You're not mad? Not even a little bit?"

Jessie lifted a shoulder. "Not really. I mean, should I be? You're a grown ass woman and poor Daddy wouldn't want you to wallow forever."

Daisy's worry melted away as she covered Jessie's hand with her own. "Thank you, sugar. I knew you'd understand."

Jessie blinked back tears, utterly delighted to see her mother so happy again after years of mourning. "I do, and I hope my goober brother got on board. Otherwise, I'd be happy to whip him into shape."

Her mother snorted. "He's been whipped into shape all right. Whitney is a Godsend."

"When do I get to meet this wonder woman?" Jessie

asked, intrigued and eager. Trevor and her mother spoke of nothing else since she landed in Atlanta.

"How about now?" Daisy suggested, pushing to her feet. "I thought we could do a little shopping before you're back on nursing duty."

Jessie wrinkled her nose. "Shopping?"

The "girl gene" skipped Jessie, leaving her poor mother without a daughter to take to manicures and hair appointments. Jessie was more likely to shave her head than get it styled. But every once in a while, Jessie was forced to follow her mother around town for a shopping excursion, mostly because she didn't want to wear rags. Fashion had never been her thing, and she was fine with that. Give her a pair of shorts or jeans, and she'd be happy as a pig in slop.

Daisy's gaze swept up and down her daughter's frame. "Yes, sugar. Shopping. For clothes that aren't overalls and cut-off shorts. If you're going to be in town for a bit, you should look like you belong."

Jessie looked down at her ensemble of denim and a tank top that had seen better days. There was still a mud stain at the hem from last month's trek into the jungle. Considering she was going to stay a little while longer *and* she wanted to meet Whitney, she gave in.

"Fine, Momma. You win. Let's go shopping." Daisy clapped her approval, and Gus barked from his spot under the table.

Twenty minutes later, they strode into Kim's Creations, a boutique in downtown Pinegrove that boasted the cutest clothes and was also the employer of her brother's girlfriend, Whitney.

A gorgeous, curvy woman with a shock of black curls squealed as soon as the door opened. "Oh my stars, you must be Jessie!" she ran over to Daisy and Jessie, pulling them both into a group hug that sucked the air from Jessie's lungs. "It's so nice to finally meet you."

"It's nice to meet you, too," Jessie said through a mouthful of Whitney's hair. Untangling herself, Jessie shoved her hands into her overalls and rocked back on her heels. "My fool brother has had nothing but wonderful things to say about you."

Whitney averted her gaze, but her cheeks pinked. "Oh, you're sweet."

"Jessica June Mays, as I live and breathe," Kim, the shop's owner, said as she joined the trio. She carried a tray of lemonade, her gray hair pulled back into a bun. With every step she took, she jingled from the array of bracelets running halfway up her forearm. "How ya been, girl?"

Daisy took two glasses, handing one to Jessie. "She's back helping Malcolm, and I thought we'd take advantage of her time in the states and get her some new clothes."

Whitney bounced on the balls of her feet. "Hooray! What are you looking for?" Her gaze swept up and down Jessie, cataloging every curve and angle. "With your cute frame, you're going to be a delight to style."

Although Jessie would rather be out in the fields of Costa Rica digging irrigation trenches, she couldn't help but be delighted by Whitney's enthusiasm. "Okay, but nothing too girly."

Waving off her concern, Whitney took Jessie's free hand and pulled her toward a display of shockingly pink dresses. "Don't you worry, honey. I've got ya."

Five minutes later, Jessie stood in a dressing room wearing a sundress the color of bubble gum. While she didn't mind the color, she certainly wasn't used to the flowy skirt and sweetheart neckline. "I don't know," she muttered, yanking on the fabric to try to cover her cleavage.

"Coming in!" Whitney announced two seconds before opening the door and gliding into the dressing room. She gasped when Jessie turned around, bringing her hands to her heart. "You're gorgeous, Jessie. Look how that color complements your skin tone, and I'd kill for your flat stomach." She rested her hands on her hips and waited for Jessie's opinion.

"It's very ..." Jessie looked back and forth between the

girliest dress she'd ever worn and Whitney's hopeful expression. She didn't want to be rude, but she also felt like this look wasn't *her*.

"What's the verdict?" Daisy shouted through the door.

Jessie opened her mouth to reply, but her mother was too fast. She and Kim barged into the cramped space. For the second time today, Jessie felt she was going to be smothered by the good folks of Pinegrove.

"Honey, you're a stunner," Kim said, dollar signs swimming in her eyes. "We've got a pair of kitten heel sandals that would go great with that dress."

Whitney agreed. "Oh, and what about that freshwater pearl necklace that just arrived? It would really tie the look together." She cocked her head, studying Jessie. "Or maybe the drop earrings and no necklace? It's Georgia in summer, no one wants too much going on around their neck."

Jessie turned to her mother, whose eyes were misting over. "Jessica June, I haven't seen you look like this since your confirmation."

Jessie wrinkled her nose. "That was like, twenty years ago."

Daisy dabbed at her eyes with a handkerchief. "So you can see why I'm overwhelmed."

Frowning, Jessie spun around and looked in the mirror. "I don't know, this really isn't me. I was hoping for some shorts and a tank top that wasn't caked in mud."

Whitney attempted to stifle a shudder. "We do have some more casual clothes. Let me see what I can find. I'll be right back." She held up a finger and disappeared, Kim on her heels.

"Spill it, sugar. You look like we're dressing you up for your execution." Daisy sat down on the stool in the dressing room, resting her purse on her lap.

Jessie crossed her arms and leaned against the wall, unsure how to move in this dress. The fabric was soft against her skin, and she couldn't deny it made her breasts look great. Idly, she wondered what Malcolm would think, but she shook that thought away. It didn't matter what he thought, and yet ...

"Momma, I don't see why I need to get all dolled up. This isn't exactly caretaker clothes, and when I leave again, this will hang in the closet at the house." She glanced down at the price tag and blanched. "Not to mention, I can't afford this."

"Pfft." Daisy flapped her hand, blowing raspberries. "Family discount, and I'm buying it anyway. Don't you think it'd be nice to have something to wear if Malcolm takes you out?"

"Takes me out? He's still shuffling around with a walker, and his parents are underfoot. I'm not here for date nights, Momma."

"Maybe you should be," Daisy mumbled.

Jessie shot daggers at her mother, throwing her hands in the air. "Momma, we're not having the Malcolm conversation." She lowered her voice and added, "Especially not in public."

Daisy was undeterred. "This is hardly public, and you knew this talk was coming, sugar."

"Malcolm and I are ..."

"Just friends, yeah yeah," Kim said, striding in and proving Jessie's point, although Daisy didn't appear bothered. "You kids and your labels and nonsense. If I was y'all's age, I'd be fooling around 'til the cows came home. Do you think hot firemen grow on trees?"

Jessie was dubious. "I am not having this conversation, Miss Kim."

Kim shrugged, thrusting a handful of clothes into Jessie's arms. "Fine, honey, but you'll be the only one."

She turned and left the dressing room, Jessie's jaw on the floor. "Why did I come back to Pinegrove?" she muttered, plopping the stack on her mother's lap.

Daisy didn't get a chance to answer, as Whitney returned with some capri pants and another dress. This dress was made of soft cotton and looked like a fitted, yet oversized, polo shirt. "These arrived last week, and I think you'll like it. It's breezy for summer, but also comfortable."

"I'm going to help Kim out front," Daisy said to no one in particular, leaving the stack of clothes on the stool. She squeezed both women's shoulders before making her exit.

Whitney turned to leave, but Jessie had already started to undress. "You don't have to go," she said as she tugged off the dress. She carefully hung it on the hanger before trying on the other frock. Whitney was right; it was comfortable and yet a little dressy.

"That really flatters your figure." Whitney nodded.

Jessie turned this way and that in the mirror, actually liking what she saw. "Thanks, I agree. I might actually buy this one." She winced. "Sorry, Whitney. I don't know what Momma and Trevor told you, but I'm not really that feminine. I've been a tomboy for as long as I've been dressing myself."

Whitney's smile was soft and warm, like the woman herself. "I'm sorry if I overstepped with the first dress. I get a little excited sometimes."

Jessie waved her off. "You're fine." Pointing to some of the shirts and capri pants, she asked, "Let's try some of these next."

Before her momma and Kim could invade again, Jessie had a selection of clothes that didn't annoy her. "I hope I didn't strongarm you into anything," Whitney said, chewing her bottom lip.

"Hush up now," Daisy admonished. "Jessie's a grown woman who needs to look the part. You styled her beautifully."

Jessie protested as her mother paid for everything, but she knew it was a useless fight. If Daisy Mays had it in her head to do something, she was going to do it. Also, it wasn't lost on Jessie that her mother had tucked that pink dress into the pile. *Clever girl.*

"Thanks, Momma."

"You're welcome. Now you and Whitney talk about the

plans for tonight, and I'll meet you in the car."

"Plans?" Jessie asked, turning to Whitney. "You're joining the firemen fray tonight?"

"Oh, I can't make it." Whitney tucked a lock of dark curls behind her ear. "Plus, it would be nice for everyone to have some guy time. Trevor said he had a nice time this morning, and I don't want to be in the way."

"Pfft, you'd hardly be in the way." Jessie flapped a hand in the air, dismissing the notion. "I hope we can see each other again soon though." She was eager to get to know this woman better, and not only because she was important to her brother.

Whitney beamed. "Wonderful. My sister lives in Savannah, and I miss sister time."

Jessie was charmed. "That sounds nice. Ask my goober brother for my number." She winked and headed for the exit, lighter on her feet after making a new friend.

"Did you know that Chief Warren is dating Momma?" Jessie asked as she strode into Malcolm's house.

Against all better judgment, she'd decided to wear her new polo dress to Malcolm's. She told herself she wanted to look nice for company later, but she also wanted to look nice for Malcolm. *Why lie to herself?* That kiss had turned her brain, and self-control, into creamed corn.

Estelle paused, shrugging on her cardigan at the sight of Jessie in real clothes. "Well, knock me over with a feather, Jessie. Aren't you a vision?" The older woman walked over, held both of Jessie's arms out to her sides, and took a long perusal before stepping back. "Adorable as anything, honey."

Jessie flushed at the praise, fidgeting with the neckline of her new dress. "Oh, thank you. I went to town with Momma and met Whitney. I thought I'd get a few things."

"Well, you're stunning." Estelle clasped her shoulders and squeezed. "And, honey, everyone knows your momma and Paul are bumpin' uglies. You need to stay longer."

Craig materialized at his wife's side, looping an arm around her waist and ushering her out, promising they'd return for breakfast at a reasonable hour. "Eloquent as always, darling. Call if you need anything, kids!" he ordered before yanking the door shut behind them.

Kids. That's what he used to say every time she'd visit the Smith household when they were dating. Estelle would bring them lemonade and cookies, gushing over how cute they were. Craig used to drive them to the movies and community events before Malcolm, the older of the pair, got his driver's license. As far as Jessie was concerned, the Smiths were family, and she'd missed them more than she'd acknowledged.

Malcolm shuffled up with his walker, looking tired but happy. "Mom is right, you are a vision, JJ." He took her hand and tugged her close, kissing her cheek. The sensation of his lips on her was a brand, heat searing into every pore. *Stay calm,* she chastised herself. No use getting worked up over a cheek kiss.

As if reading her mind, because the man always could, Malcolm eased back and leaned on his walker. "You didn't get this upset over last night's kiss," he mused, "maybe don't get yourself worked up over a peck on the cheek." He winked, turning and slowly walking to the couch where he fell back in an uncoordinated heap. Wincing slightly at the pain, he adjusted the pillows before Jessie could assist. "And in case you're wondering, Mom's right. Everyone knows Daisy and the chief are dating."

Jessie laughed. "Well, at least I'm on the same page now." She pressed her fingers to her cheek, still feeling the warmth of Malcolm's lips. Good Lord, she needed to pull herself together.

Striving to change topics, she asked, "I know you're more up on Pinegrove gossip than I am, but do you know when our guests are arriving?"

Malcolm smirked. "Yeah, Maxwell texted that Javi and

Trevor are grabbing the pizza. They should be here by six."

"Well then, I guess you know it all." Jessie stuck out her tongue, but she really didn't mind. It was good to see Malcolm smiling, and she was glad he had friends at the station. And, frankly, she needed more company in this house right now. Because despite his tired eyes and slouched posture, she desperately wanted a repeat of last night's kiss. *As well as other activities she shouldn't be considering ...*

Glancing at the time, Jessie asked, "What do you want to do with the next hour?" She took in the space around her, noticing how Estelle had already tidied up from the day's activities.

Malcolm yawned. "You mind if we sit for a spell?" Malcolm patted an empty cushion beside him.

"How was the nurse's visit?"

Malcom lifted a shoulder. "Not bad. She's pleased with how my wounds and burns are healing, and she only managed to annoy my mother once. Win-win."

Before Jessie joined him on the couch, she went to the kitchen to fetch a drink and his medications. "Be right back." She held up her hand as she darted away. Jessie rejoined him with a glass of sweet tea and a handful of pills a minute later. "I'd wager we'll have about an hour until the next invasion. Whitney said Trevor was stopping by the shop before coming over." She made a gagging sound, sticking her finger in her mouth.

"Knock it off," Malcolm teased. "Whitney is great. I think it's nice they found each other." His expression was soft. Malcolm was always a hopeless romantic. A tiny pang pulled in her ribcage that she'd missed her brother falling in love, but she didn't want to dwell on that. A happy ending was a happy ending, regardless of who was here to witness it.

Jessie was never a fan of her brother's ex-fiancée, Virginia. The woman was rude and stuck-up, the opposite of sweet-hearted Whitney. Trevor never seemed to relax around his ex, as if always waiting for the other shoe to drop. "I know, but he's my big brother. It's my job to knock him down a peg or two."

Malcolm reached for her as soon as she sat down, and she took his hand. She promised herself this was simply to comfort her patient while he recuperated. This didn't have to mean anything. It didn't mean she was still attracted to him, didn't mean she wanted to crawl into his lap and make out until her lips went numb. Nope, she was totally unaffected by Malcolm Smith's touch. *Yeah, right.*

The quiet of the house surrounded them, and before Jessie knew it, she was dozing right beside Malcolm. Their heads fell together, both exhausted from their days. Malcolm's hand was warm in hers, and every once in a while, he'd offer a gentle squeeze, almost to prove she was really by his side. Every time she'd squeeze back with all her might, eager to savor their time together.

Their bubble burst when the doorbell rang, and several annoying knocks, jolted them back to reality. Jessie scrambled to her feet. "Get ready for a Pinegrove FD invasion." She laughed as she strode forward, leaving Malcolm with his leg propped up on the coffee table, rubbing the sleep from his eyes.

"You can finally meet Maxwell," Malcolm said, his voice gruff from their impromptu nap.

Jessie flung open the door, expecting to see her brother, Javi, and a random guy. What she got instead was a view of a gorgeous blonde woman with a bright smile, stunning cheekbones, and curves she'd kill for. Despite being in her new dress, Jessie felt as frumpy as a sack of potatoes.

"Hi!" The other woman waved. "I'm Tiffany Maxwell, Smithy's partner." She took a step forward to come inside, but Jessie didn't budge. This might be the first time she was actually flabbergasted—her flabbers were literally gasted.

Holding up a covered dish, Maxwell added, "I brought my famous double chocolate brownies, Smithy's favorite." Jessie's lips pursed, her mouth as dry as sandpaper. Malcolm adored anything chocolate, and this bombshell made his favorite dessert. "Um, can I come in?" Maxwell asked, arching an eyebrow and jostling the plate.

Jessie shook her head, coming to terms with the fact that Malcolm had failed to share that this rookie was a woman—and a total smoke show. "Uh, sure," Jessie muttered, stepping back so Maxwell could enter. Before she could close the door, she heard the familiar voice of her brother.

"Hold the door, Jessie!" he ordered, carrying in a stack of pizza boxes, Javi hot on his heels with a couple six-packs.

"Jessie, how are you, girl? Nursing duty treating you well?" Javi pushed his way inside. His footfalls faltered at the sight of her in a dress. "You look nice. Dress up for me?" He made kissing noises before Jessie elbowed him in the ribs. "Oof. I guess not," he gasped, steadying the beers before they fell to the floor.

"Get everyone a beer, goober," her brother ordered, earning a lewd gesture from Javi before he joined Maxwell and Malcolm in the other room.

Trevor stayed back, already clocking his sister's weary expression. "What's wrong? Is it Smithy? Should we call the doctor again?" His voice was low, coated in worry.

"No, he's fine." Jessie craned her neck to ensure they were alone. "Why didn't you tell me that Maxwell was freaking hot?" She hissed, stabbing her brother in the chest with her pointer finger.

"Ow." He rubbed the spot with his free hand while he balanced the pizzas with the other. "What's the matter with you? I could have dropped these, and Buster put extra pepperoni on for free."

Without her permission, Jessie's mouth watered at the mention of pizza from The Pecan Pit, Pinegrove's favorite—and only—dive bar. Buster, the owner, was a grump with a heart of gold and a surprisingly good pizza recipe.

"Did you get one with mushrooms and hot peppers?"

"Does Momma read too many smutty romance novels?" Trevor deadpanned, rolling his eyes as he took a step forward.

Jessie stopped his progression by hooking her arm around his middle. "Answer my question."

Trevor scrunched up his nose. "I don't remember what it was."

Jessie swatted at his chest and swore under her breath. "Why didn't you tell me Maxwell was a girl *and* hot?"

Again, Trevor stared at his sister, his head cocked to the side. "Uh, what does it matter?"

Jessie glared, her hands on her hips. "It matters," she said through clenched teeth.

Trevor's posture slumped as he groaned, "Oh no." Head tipping back, he muttered something under his breath.

Jessie's heart rate spiked. "What?"

Shaking his head, her brother looked as disappointed as when she'd left the back gate open and their old hound dog Charlie snuck out. "Are you two back together again?"

Jessie's stomach plummeted at the mention, and she shoved Trevor two paces until his back hit the door. "No, we aren't. And even if we were, it's none of your business," she wheezed, swallowing past a lump in her throat. Ever since Maxwell entered this house, Jessie felt like she was going through a cardiac event.

"Um, do the Mays siblings want to join us?" Javi's question rang down the hallway, along with the sound of bottle tops clattering on the coffee table.

"Coming!" Jessie shouted, her eyes never leaving her brother's.

Trevor sucked his teeth. "It is my business if you start something and then leave again. You're not the one left picking up the pieces, Jessie. You can't keep jerking Smithy around, especially after all he's been through."

Jessie reeled back as if she'd been slapped. "Jerking him around? I don't do that!" She was appalled when all Trevor did was scowl. "Well, not intentionally anyway." The admission sat bitter on her tongue, and Jessie wanted the ground to open and swallow her up.

Her brother sighed, readjusting the pizza boxes in his grip. "Look, you're right. Technically, it's none of my business. Just don't leave him in worse shape than you found him, hmm?" Trevor side-stepped Jessie on his way to the living room. Before they reached the others, he tossed over his shoulder, "And Maxwell is happily married with two kids. Chill the hell out, please."

And just like that, Jessie deflated. "Oh," was the only response she could muster.

As she and the others dined on Pinegrove's best pizza, she tried not to overanalyze her relief at Maxwell not being interested in Malcolm, or the burning in her ribcage. It was likely heartburn from the pepperoni. Probably …

CHAPTER ELEVEN

One of the biggest benefits of being best friends with your ex is knowing what they're feeling. Malcolm would wager his collection of stargazing manuals that Jessie was jealous of Maxwell. This little development made him irrationally happy. Almost as happy as seeing Jessie all dolled up for pizza with the guys.

"When do the doctors think you'll be back for light duty?" Maxwell asked, helping Jessie serve up the pizza. She'd brought her famous double chocolate brownies, and Malcolm wanted to skip straight to dessert.

Javi popped the tops on the beers and handed them out. Unfortunately, Nurse Jessie stopped him from taking one. "Oh no, not on your medications." She handed the beer back to Javi, who gleefully double-fisted his beverages. Leaning in so only he could hear, Jessie whispered, "Be happy I didn't pull out one of those juice boxes." She slid a glass of sweet tea in front of him, a much better substitute.

"Sorry, Smithy." He didn't look sorry as he pulled from the first bottle. *Lucky bastard.*

At least the company was lifting his spirits. It was also the perfect distraction from thinking about Jessie and that kiss from last night. When he'd gone in for a peck on the cheek, he failed to fathom the magnetic pull to move his lips a few inches to the left.

"Not sure yet, I have an appointment at the end of the week to check on everything. The visiting nurse today was pleased with the progress on my wounds, so that's good. Considering I'm fairly mobile and not in a lot of pain, I hope next week." He held up his hand with the fingers crossed.

Maxwell smiled before taking a bite of her pizza. "Awesome. I need a break from my temporary partner." She tipped her head toward Javi, who gasped.

"Maxwell, I'm hurt. You don't like riding around with me? I got us to that scene this morning in record time."

"Record time?" She was incredulous, eyes bugging out of her head. "I'm surprised you passed the station's driver's exam. You nearly took out that mailbox on the corner of Carter and Peach Street." Swallowing a swig of beer, she added, "And I've never gotten car sick before teaming up with you."

Javi scoffed, folding his pizza in half before taking a massive bite. Through a mouthful of pepperoni, he said, "We were fine! I didn't realize they turned that yield into a *Stop* sign."

Trevor muttered under his breath, "It's always been a *Stop* sign." Javi didn't seem to notice, or care.

"Anyway," Javi said, drinking from his second beer, "when you get back, maybe you can help me with planning this year's fire station fundraiser? I'm officially in charge of the committee." Javi puffed out his chest with the announcement.

Jessie asked, "What was last year's?" Her attention was divided between catching a trail of cheese from her pizza slice and side-eyeing Maxwell. Malcolm could barely contain his smirk.

Maxwell covered her face and groaned. "A total disaster," she whined.

"Try not to remember it, Maxwell," Javi soothed, rolling

his eyes behind her back.

Sitting up, Maxwell scoffed. "Yeah right, Ortiz."

Jessie nibbled thoughtfully on the crust of her first slice of pizza. Her eyes darted between everyone, yet she was clearly focused on Maxwell. "What am I missing?"

"Being the rookie," Maxwell started, shaking herself back to the present, "they put me in charge. I planned a calendar."

Trevor choked on his beer, spluttering into his elbow as he caught his breath. "Ah, geez, here we go." He chuckled.

"Calendars are fun. What was wrong with it?" Jessie asked, slowly warming up to the other woman. Turning her attention back to Malcolm, Jessie topped off his glass of sweet tea without missing a beat in the conversation.

Malcolm chuckled, not wanting to upset his partner but unable to hold back his mirth. "They can be, but this one was a *cat* calendar."

Jessie raised an eyebrow, clearly intrigued. "And what, pray tell, is a cat calendar?" She wrinkled her nose in confusion, a gesture that never ceased to melt Malcolm's heart. JJ was always cute to him, but when she scrunched up her adorable face, her button nose popping, he was a goner. "Wasn't it cute pictures of fluffy cats?"

"No," Maxwell replied on a sigh. "It was pictures of cats we saved from trees over the last year, and unfortunately we didn't hire a professional photographer." She held up a hand. "That was on me."

Darting her gaze around the room, Jessie clocked everyone's sheepish expressions. "Well, how bad was it?"

Malcolm pointed with his pizza crust toward the kitchen. "Check the junk drawer. I think I still have mine."

Jessie hopped to her feet, nearly toppling his walker in her haste to see it. She returned a moment later, grimacing as she paged through the calendar. "Oh," she exhaled, stopping at a particularly sad cat in April. This one had gotten stuck during a rainstorm, its fur matted and its eyes wild. It was less "fluffy kitten" and more "drenched nightmare fuel." "I think it gets an A for effort."

Maxwell shrugged, wiping her hands on her napkin and collecting everyone's empty plates. "Well, I have officially taken myself off the planning committee. Now it's Ortiz and Smithy's problem." Jessie stood to help, but Maxwell politely declined. "Oh for heaven's sake. You're the one taking care of our guy here, putting a few plates in the dishwasher is the least I can do." As soon as she said it, her cell phone buzzed from her jeans pocket. "Shoot," she muttered, placing the dishes on the counter and frowning. "I gotta jet, Juniper and Jack are giving their daddy the runaround for bath time." She hurriedly put the plates away and gave Malcolm a fist bump. "Keep on recovering, Smithy. We need you back at the big house," lowering her voice, she added, "before I puke all over the truck."

He saluted and waved as she headed toward the door. "Take it easy, Maxwell."

"A mother's work is never done." She waved at Jessie and the others as she passed. "It was great meeting you, Jessie. I hope we can see each other again soon. It's nice to have a girl around this motley crew." Maxwell waved again, her smile infectious. "Oh, and report back on those brownies!"

Malcolm relaxed a little more when he saw Jessie return the gesture, her smile genuine. *That's his girl.*

Now it was the four of them, the pizza boxes empty and the beer supply dwindling. Javi leaned back in his chair, peeling the label off his empty bottle. "So I was thinking we could do another calendar, but maybe something a little, you know, sexy." He waggled his eyebrows, and Trevor tossed his balled-up napkin at his head.

"Wow, Ortiz. I think you went a whole five minutes without talking about sex. That might be a new record. I'll need to call the folks at Guinness to confirm."

"Haha, Trev. Just because I'm a ladies' man doesn't mean I don't have feelings." Javi frowned, theatrically throwing his head back in frustration.

"We know you have feelings, Ortiz." Malcolm came to his buddy's rescue. Javi might play the field, but he was a good friend and a hell of a fireman, even though his driving skills took years off Malcolm's—and apparently Maxwell's—life.

Javi splayed a hand over his chest. "Thanks, Smithy. I miss your compassion around the station. I'll talk to our new captain about sensitivity training." Trevor muttered something under his breath, but let Javi get away with the dig.

"So what's your calendar idea, Javi?" Jessie asked, adjusting the cushion behind Malcolm's back. He hadn't even realized how awkward he was sitting, but trust Jessie to pay attention.

Javi stuck his hands out and said, "Picture this"—he paused for effect, hands framing his face—"a sexy fireman calendar."

The room was silent, so he cleared his throat and tried again. "A *sexy* fireman calendar."

Trevor snorted. "We heard you the first time. We were expecting something different coming from you."

Jessie was incredulous. "Different? I would expect nothing else from Javi." She leaned forward and playfully pushed his shoulder. Javi pretended to fall off his seat, legs kicking in the air.

"What exactly are you suggesting? Hoses placed in suggestive ways?" Malcolm could barely hold back his smile.

Javi looked disappointed; his smile vanished. "No, man. Something tasteful, but sexily so."

"Sexily so?" Both Trevor and Jessie asked, unable to stop their laughter.

Javi pushed to his feet and groaned. "This is why Smithy needs to come back to work. He'll be able to help me without all the judgment."

"Suddenly I'm not too eager to return to duty," Malcolm said, unable to hold back his own amusement.

The foursome shared Maxwell's brownies and talked

about everything and nothing. This was usually how Malcolm spent his time off the clock, surrounded by friends and food, but it was so much better with Jessie.

Back when Malcolm was a kid, he'd gotten a horrible case of the flu that took away his appetite for over a month. His tastebuds had been soured, and even his favorite foods tasted like ash. He remembered the first day when he woke up and tasted his orange juice; it was like watching the sun rise for the first time. Malcolm begged his mother to take him to a farmer's market, where he ate strawberries that were bites of summertime, the sweet tang exploding on his tongue.

Tonight felt like that, strawberries savored after going so long without flavor. Jessie's delight brightened the room, her digs at Trevor and Javier pulling out belly laughs that stretched unused muscles. His girl belonged here, plain and simple.

The revelry of the moment was interrupted by Trevor's cell phone buzzing. He yanked the device from his pocket, face immediately splitting in two. "I'm guessing that's Whitney?" Jessie teased, collecting the last of their napkins and dishes.

Javi sighed. "You two are disgusting, but I'm happy for you."

Trevor typed away for a moment before tucking his phone away. "I should head out so I can see her before it's too late."

Jessie nudged her brother in the side. "Javi's right on both counts. I'm glad I finally got to meet her. Whitney is a doll."

"I can't disagree," Trevor said to his sister. He glanced around the room, a flush creeping up his neck. "I think she might be the one." The group was silent, and Malcolm couldn't decide if he should cheer or cry. He understood that certainly, that glint in Trevor's eye that hadn't disappeared since Whitney came to Pinegrove. Their captain was smitten, and it was obvious the feeling was mutual.

Snorting, Jessie shook her head. "Oh please, big brother. You've only been dating a few weeks."

"Yeah, but they've been good weeks." Trevor got the goofiest grin on his face, and Malcolm's heart ached. He was so happy for his friend, but he was simultaneously jealous the man was in love and able to parade around Pinegrove with his girl on his arm.

Malcolm was currently five inches away from the woman he loved, and he had no idea where they stood. That kiss last night had been the stuff of dreams. Hell, his lips still tingled from kissing her cheek this afternoon. Yet JJ had fled the house so fast this morning, he was surprised there weren't skid marks in his driveway. And then to have her return looking like a vision in this dress that hugged her hips and rode up her thighs when she sat. He was about to crawl out of his own skin.

Trevor strode ahead, clapping Malcolm on the shoulder. "It's good to see you looking like yourself, man."

Javi also rose, gathering their empty bottles and helping Jessie with the trash. They shared a fist bump and promised to see each other soon. "Think about my calendar idea!" he barked before the door slammed shut behind him.

Jessie flipped the deadbolt, turning off some of the lights, and rejoined Malcolm on the couch. His eyelids drooped, but all he wanted to do was spend more time with Jessie. Falling asleep on the couch was not how he wanted to spend their limited time. Every minute with JJ needed to be treasured, held close and relished.

Sensing his fading energy, Jessie tucked a curl behind his ear, letting her hand slide down his neck, checking one of the bandages. "These are still looking good. Have you had any new aches or pains today?"

Malcolm snorted. "You mean other than Mom babying me to death? No, I've got no complaints." He let out a slow exhale, feeling his muscles relax. "I'm good, JJ. Today was a good day."

Lips turning up in the corners, Jessie nodded. "It was."

Jessie stretched, the hem of her dress riding up her legs, exposing a fresh trail of freckles he'd forgotten about. Suddenly they were teenagers and Malcolm's pants were too tight. "I'm beat, too. It was a nice day, but a long one. I don't think I've done this much socializing in ages."

She held out her hands, assisting Malcolm as he clambered to his feet. They faced each other, hands still joined, and Malcolm couldn't stop himself. He leaned in, brushing his lips along Jessie's. She tasted faintly of chocolate and hops, and he could drink her up.

Jessie inhaled, but didn't pull back. Tentatively, he nipped at her bottom lip, earning a low moan he felt through his bandages. His tongue darted out, soothing over the bite, producing another NSFW sound.

"Malcolm," she warned, eyes unfocused, voice raspy.

"JJ," he said, dying to pull her close and devour her faster than a slice of Buster's pizza. "What's the big deal," he breathed against her parted lips. "This is hardly our first kiss."

Jessie shivered but didn't say anything right away. She traced the curve of his jaw until she ran her fingers through his hair. He purred like a cat, and she tugged him closer. "This is a very bad idea," she said before closing the distance and kissing him like her life depended on it.

Malcolm knew his certainly did.

That was the thing about him and JJ—they had the chemistry—hell, they were combustible.

Finding the spark was never their problem. Oh no, their problem was timing. Whenever he was ready for more, Jessie was the first to pull back and disappear. Very rarely had she been the one chasing him.

Malcolm tried not to let it bother him, but it was useless pretending he wasn't hurt. He had loved this woman all of his adult life, yet he sustained himself on the scraps she gave him. But she was here now, in his arms, their lips tangling in a kiss that brought him back to life faster than modern medicine ever could. He wasn't a fool; they needed to communicate and get on the same page before someone got hurt.

Correction, before *he* got hurt.

Jessie broke their kiss first, her lips red and swollen. "We should get you in bed."

"No arguments here," he whispered, keeping his hands on her hips, fingers digging into the fabric of her new dress.

Her blue gaze met his, and she sighed. "You know what I mean, Romeo. This is a bad idea."

"When hasn't it been?" he asked, trying not to start a fight that would ruin the moment.

"Malcolm, we can't do this now. You're recovering, and I don't know what I'm doing."

Finally, Malcolm stepped back. The moment was over, and he wasn't going to push it. "We could talk about it, you know. Like we used to."

Jessie's lips quirked. "You want me to get my car and drive us out to Hog Hollow? Lay in the meadow and count the stars?"

"We had some really great talks out there," he said, snaking her hand as she tried to walk away. "It doesn't have to be the farm, but maybe we can go outside, sit on the deck?"

Jessie nodded, holding up a finger. "Only if you have your helper." Despite his grumblings, she grabbed his walker. Malcolm shuffled toward the sliding glass door, needing her assistance to get him over the threshold. She waited patiently as he got settled on one of the loungers.

Malcolm's place was hardly fancy, but he'd bought two loungers when he moved in. He'd never admit this to Jessie, but he'd bought them with her in mind. Most of what he did was with Jessie in mind…

Once they were situated, they both lay on their backs staring up at the sky. It was July, and the heat of summer wasn't going anywhere. Malcolm's place was in the suburbs, so light pollution limited some of their viewing, but neither seemed to mind. The fireflies were out in force, peppering the sky with green sparkles. Malcolm linked his fingers and rested them on his belly, content with the silence, knowing his girl would speak when she was good and ready.

His eyes were gritty from a long day, but sleep wouldn't come when they were outside. His body was finely tuned to Jessie, and he could tell she wasn't anywhere near rest. She was pensive, holding on to something.

"I feel like I'm losing a race," she finally admitted.

Malcolm wasn't sure what he expected her to say, but that wasn't it. "What do you mean, JJ?" He turned his head to see her profile, his muscles protesting at the odd angle.

Jessie sighed, not quite meeting his eye, and he wasn't about to push. After a few heartbeats, she found her words. "I mean, look at everyone. You've got this lovely condo and a career. Trevor's practically engaged again, and even Momma is moving on with someone new."

"I thought you weren't upset with Chief and Daisy dating?"

Jessie flapped a hand in the air. "I'm not, truly. It's more that everyone has a life."

"You have a life." More words tripped on his tongue, words he feared would upset her, but he couldn't hold back. "It's a life I thought you wanted."

Malcolm held his breath, hopeful that maybe, just maybe, being back in Pinegrove and seeing everyone would show her what she was missing. *Show her she was missing him.*

"I know I do, and I love the Peace Corps." She shimmied on her lounge chair, unable to get comfortable. "I'm in my late twenties, and I guess I feel like I'm behind." She snorted at her realization, but Malcolm didn't see the joke. "That's it, isn't it?" she asked, blinking up at the sky.

"What's it?" Being with Jessie always felt like drinking truth serum. When they were alone and talking, it felt like anything was possible—which could be a good or bad thing.

"I always feel behind, from my school days to now. The trouble is, I don't know what I should do."

"What do you like most about the Peace Corps?"

Malcolm asked, genuinely curious at the answer. Over the years, Jessie had described a myriad of her favorite things, from the travel to the people to the challenge of helping folks from different cultures. The thing of it was, Malcolm thought all of those skills would translate nicely to Pinegrove.

"I'm really enjoying our current assignment," she admitted.

Malcolm carefully adjusted his position so as not to tweak one of his injuries. He'd noticed that it was harder in the evening, as if his body was too tired *not* to hurt. "That's the farming in the fire-ravaged areas?" he asked, although he knew the answer. Not only did he and Jessie send emails and letters to each other, but he soaked up every update Trevor or Ms. Daisy would give him.

"Yeah. There were fires there a couple years ago, and some of the farmers haven't been able to replant and start over. We're building irrigation systems and looking at options for crop rotation that should help."

Malcolm hummed. "Sounds like you're learning a lot out there ... and enjoying the challenge." He waited, hoping she'd acknowledge his observation. After a moment, he heard her sigh, so he soldiered on, "Don't sell yourself short, JJ. Not everyone's life looks the same." And even though he didn't want to draw more attention to her potential promotion, he added, "And it looks like all your hard work is going to pay off soon."

She reached out in the dark, grabbing his hand and squeezing it. As she loosened her grip, Malcolm held firm. Her voice barely audible over the chirping of crickets, she asked, "Why does talking to you always help?"

"Because we're best friends." He waggled their joined hands, earning a small giggle from his girl. "You feeling any better?"

That question earned Malcolm a real laugh. "Aren't I supposed to be asking you that?" She released his hand and swung her legs over her chair. Even in the dim light,

Malcolm didn't miss how her skirt rode up. He thought about baseball while he pulled himself together. Getting all hot and bothered wouldn't help either of them right now, at least not in the big picture.

"You want to start the nighttime routine?" she suggested, standing over him with her hands outstretched.

"Yeah, another shower might be nice." His voice was low, filled with need. Before she could pull away, he placed a soft kiss on her lips.

"We won't be repeating last night," she warned but didn't pull away. This time, she closed what little distance remained, the urgency of their kiss smothering any unsaid words.

Bracing her against him with his good arm, Malcolm nipped at her bottom lip before trailing his tongue up to her earlobe. He nuzzled the tender skin of her neck, then drew his lips back for more.

"What are we doing, Malcolm?" The question was a breath across his skin. "And don't be cute or funny, I'm serious." She took a tentative step back, eyes wild and mouth swollen.

"You want a real answer?" he asked, waiting until she nodded. "I haven't got a freaking clue, JJ. You're my best friend, my ex, and the girl I'm still in love with. I want to be everything for you, so the ball is in your court."

Malcolm had no clue what answer she expected, but for once, his girl was speechless. Finally, she opened her mouth to reply, but her cell phone blared in her pocket. It wasn't her usual ringtone, and she frantically pawed around the pockets of her dress until she retrieved it.

"It's Noel," she said, hands gripping the infernal device.

Deflated, Malcolm stepped back so she could take the call. "Go, I'm fine." He didn't watch her walk away, mostly because it was a sight he was used to. She closed the sliding door behind her, leaving Malcolm outside and alone.

They couldn't keep doing this, whatever it was. The back and forth was chipping away at Malcolm more than he'd realized. They'd become experts at this emotional chess game, their feelings never quite synching over the years.

Glaring at his reflection in the glass door, Malcolm saw the changes since his accident. There were fine lines around his eyes, his cheekbones were more prominent, and a certain edge bracketed his stare. Granted, he wasn't as stoic as his father, but he looked older, wiser—too smart to play this game again. Regardless of what her boss wanted, Malcolm was finally coming to his own realization.

Jessie might not be his girl anymore.

LIBBY KAY

CHAPTER TWELVE

Jessie clutched her still-ringing cell phone in her hand and darted into the kitchen. Lips still scorching from their kiss, she wasn't sure she'd be able to speak. She slid her finger over the screen and held her breath as she answered. "Noel?"

In the background, the din of their camp echoed through the line. Familiar voices mixed with tropical birdsong, the soundtrack of her professional life. "Jessie, hey! I don't mean to call so late, but I have some updates I wanted to share." He hesitated a moment and cleared his throat. "They're not great."

Her palms so slick with sweat, Jessie nearly dropped the phone in her haste to find a seat. She lowered herself on shaking legs and tried to remember to breathe. "No worries, s … Noel. I have a few minutes. What's up?"

The lie slid off her tongue so easily, Jessie winced. She certainly didn't have a few minutes; she was in the middle of an important conversation with the only person who made her feel alive.

The other thing that had come to life in the last few days—her libido. She hadn't been this turned on in far, far too long. Her belly was coiled tight, every nerve ending on fire. It almost felt inappropriate to take the call in her current state. If he weren't injured, she'd throw her career away in favor of climbing Malcolm like a tree. *It was all too much.*

Either unaware of her turmoil or uncaring, Noel continued, "Great! I spoke with some of the higher-ups about these promotions." Jessie made a noise, proving she was listening. "Unfortunately, due to budget concerns, the positions are on hold."

"On hold?" she parroted. "What does that mean?"

Noel huffed, sounding more tired than she'd ever heard him. "It means there aren't any promotional opportunities for the next budgeting cycle. You can either come back now and finish the last parts of this project, or you'll have to apply for another placement, at your current level."

At her current level—meaning nothing new. No new challenges, no more responsibility, and no pay raise. Jessie would be walking away from everything here for more of the same. Did she really want to do that?

Before she could overthink her next words, Jessie blurted, "I can't come back to finish the assignment. I know there's a lot to do, but there's a lot to do here as well." *Starting with finishing that lip lock from the deck ...*

"Oh, all right." Now Noel's tone was reminiscent of her father's when she did something naughty as a child. She heard the rustling of footsteps as the background din subsided. "Then there's something else we need to discuss."

Jessie's stomach plummeted. "What's that?"

Sighing, Noel said, "You're out of paid leave. When I thought we'd have a promotion opportunity, I was able to pull a few strings. But with these budget concerns, the head office isn't approving any unplanned PTO. I'm sorry."

He certainly didn't sound sorry. "What?" She wheezed. Her bank account was a barren wasteland on a good day, and after spending the money to fly home, it was hardly a good day.

The benefit of the Peace Corps is she rarely had the opportunity to spend a lot of her money. The downside was, the pay wasn't stellar. She did the work because she loved it, not because it made her a millionaire.

She pinched the bridge of her nose. "I thought I had a couple weeks banked up already."

"You did, last year before your other trip back to the states. Unfortunately, the PTO bank doesn't refill until the fall."

Jessie knew this, of course, but in her emotional rush to flee to Pinegrove, she'd forgotten these important details. In a pinch, she could ask her mother for help, but Jessie was too old for that routine.

"Thanks for the updates, Noel. I really appreciate it."

"I'm sure it's not the news you wanted, but please consider applying for your next placement now. Hopefully, if things calm down with the budgets, we can discuss more opportunities in a year or two."

In a year or two!?

Unable to think of anything else to say, Jessie thanked Noel for his time and disconnected. In this moment, she could not have cared less about professionalism.

No sooner had she tossed her phone onto the kitchen table, a sob bubbled up her throat. Not wanting Malcolm to hear, she turned on the faucet and splashed water on her face. Once she'd collected herself, she portioned out his pills and poured a glass of water. Arranging everything on a small tray, she headed toward the bedroom, ready to help him get ready for sleep. If she couldn't control her professional life, she could certainly work on repairing her personal life.

But she was too late.

Malcolm sat on the edge of his bed, clad in his sleep shorts. He was shirtless, his chest still glistening from the shower. A water droplet made the slow journey down to his stomach, and she wanted to fall to her knees and follow the trail with her tongue. History had proven they could get lost with each other's bodies, and that was the type of mindless bliss she craved now.

"Oh, look at you," she said, placing the tray on the nightstand and hurrying over to help him towel off. "You took your own shower."

As soon as the cotton fabric touched his skin, Malcolm flinched away. "I'm fine," he ground out. He scooted so far back, he risked teetering off the bed.

Jessie scoffed. "You don't look fine." Well, that wasn't true. He most certainly did look fine, muscles on display. If it weren't for his sour expression, she'd be begging him for more kisses, more moments in each other's arms. "Did you hurt yourself in the shower? How are your pain levels?" She gestured over her shoulder at the water and medications. "I brought your—"

"I'm fine," he snapped, causing them both to recoil. "Just want to go to sleep."

"What's the matter?" she asked, resting her hand on his forehead.

He reared back as if he'd been slapped. "I don't have a fever." Crawling backward, Malcolm fell onto his pillow and squeezed his eyes shut. "You can leave. I'll take my pills in a minute."

"Leave?" Jessie was incredulous. "What happened in the last twenty minutes, Malcolm?"

Well, other than her professional dreams and financial reality coming to a head—oh, and her pesky heart still burning—and lusting—for this stubborn man.

"Nothing happened," he said, turning his back to her in a position she knew would hurt.

"Nothing happened," she deadpanned, unable to catch up to his tantrum. "Is this about what we were talking about on the deck? I don't know what you want me to—"

"I don't want anything from you, Jessie. I want to sleep, okay?" His tone was icier than Alaskan igloos, and she shivered.

Jessie. He called her Jessie. It would have been less shocking if he'd called her every profanity in the book. But to not use her nickname? That hurt.

"Okay," she whispered. For a moment, she stayed cemented in place, willing him to face her and share the reasons for this complete one-eighty. But Malcolm didn't budge, so eventually she backed out of the room and turned off the light. "I'll check on you in a while."

Still, Malcolm didn't utter a single word, not even a grunt to prove he was paying her any attention. She closed the door, leaning against it while silent tears slid down her face.

Last week she was focused on her job and not much else. Jessie's schedule had been set, distractions limited. Now she'd been laughing with family and seeing old friends. She'd had the distinct pleasure of Malcolm's lips on her own, remembered what it felt like to lie in his strong arms. The notion of not being able to stare into his deep, soulful eyes wrenched open a pit of yearning in her chest.

Why did it suddenly feel like she was putting all her focus on the wrong path?

Jessie woke with a start at dawn when she heard a clatter in the kitchen. Shooting bolt upright, she knocked two cushions onto the floor. She'd fallen asleep on the couch after hours of pacing around Malcolm's place, unsure how to plan her next move. Unfortunately, Estelle had done a stellar job with keeping a tidy home, so she couldn't even stress clean.

"Malcolm?" she called out, rubbing sleep from her eyes. She'd slept in her new dress, the cotton now creased and sticking to her skin. She padded barefoot into the kitchen and found Malcolm scooping up coffee grounds from the counter, the canister overturned. "Here, let me help," she offered, grabbing a tea towel.

"I've got it," Malcolm snapped, his jaw so tense, she was shocked his molars didn't snap in half. "I need to take care of myself."

"Of course you do, when you're not bandaged up with a

busted leg." She swatted a towel over his hand like she was shooing away parrots in the jungle. Finally, he reluctantly pulled it back. "Take a seat. I've got coffee covered."

At first, Malcolm didn't budge. His gaze was zeroed in on the mess he'd made. "I can make coffee," he grumbled like a caveman, and Jessie didn't fight her answering scoff.

She took him by the shoulders and ushered him three steps back to a chair, nearly tripping over his boot. "Sit," she ordered.

Jessie busied herself with adding water to the carafe and pulling out the bowl of sugar. As soon as the coffee maker dinged, she filled a mug to the brim and slid it in front of Malcolm. "Drink up, grumpy." She poured her own cup and went in search of fixings for breakfast. "What time do you think your parents are coming for breakfast? I can't decide what to make." She nudged aside ingredients, willing Malcolm to say something.

"Dunno," he muttered, hunched over the table.

"I'll start with eggs and toast, I guess," she mused to herself, fluttering around Malcolm like a spinning top. "You still like grape jelly with extra butter?"

Silence hung heavy in the kitchen, nearly suffocating her. "What are you doing?" Malcolm asked, hands pressing into his temples.

Jessie whirled around, gut plummeting at his sullen expression. She dropped a stick of butter, which landed with a sad thud onto the tiled floor. "Jeepers creepers," she chastised, "what's the matter with you? Did you not sleep enough? I'm sorry I never made it to bed, I fell asleep on the—"

"I'm going to ask my parents to stay here with me." Malcolm's statement stopped Jessie short. He wouldn't meet her gaze, eyes trained on the tabletop.

"What do you mean?" Her voice shook, the question barely audible.

Malcolm wouldn't look up at her, his hands fiddling with his coffee cup. "I mean you don't have to give up your life to make me toast and watch me sleep. My parents are here, so I might as well have them stay."

"What did I do to piss you off?" He bristled, but didn't answer the question. "Am I not doing a good job with taking care of you?" She dipped her head lower, trying to snag his gaze. "Talk to me, please. I know we have a lot of stuff to figure out, but you know Estelle will …" Jessie's laundry list of reasons why Estelle would drive Malcolm crazy went unsaid.

"Jessie." He uttered her name on a sigh, and her heart shattered.

"JJ," she corrected. She got to her knees, taking his face in her hands until he was forced to see her. His trademark grin was gone, replaced with a frown that wrecked her. Dark circles marred his handsome face, and even his curls weren't as bouncy. This wasn't her Malcolm; it was a shell of the man she loved.

"You need to talk to me, okay? I can't read your mind, and I can't tell if you're in physical pain or emotional pain."

Malcolm squeezed his eyes shut, a single tear falling down his cheek. "It hurts, so much," he whispered. "I don't think I can do this."

Misunderstanding, she pulled him to her, cooing words of encouragement while he sobbed. "I know, baby. But you heard what the visiting nurse said. You're already making huge improvements. I mean, hell, you took a shower last night by yourself." Malcolm's shoulders shook as he sobbed into her rumpled dress, and Jessie fought her own emotions.

"It's not that," Malcolm admitted, leaning back from her embrace. "I can't pretend anymore, you know?" He swiped at his cheeks with the backs of his hands.

Jessie steadied herself for whatever he was about to say. The human brain was an amazing thing because it could sense when there was something wrong. Time slowed, her senses were all on alert, and her heart rate slowed. "What do you mean?"

"Us." The word landed like an atomic bomb between

them. "Every time you come back to Pinegrove, I tell myself that this is it. *This* is the time I convince you to stay, to give us another shot. Usually I rebound pretty quickly, but I'm getting too old for this, Jessie." He rubbed over his heart and sighed. "I'm thirty now. I want a family, a wife, a partner to live every day with."

Jessie opened her mouth to object, to promise she wanted those things, too. Yet the words didn't come, clogged in her throat like she'd swallowed a biscuit whole.

"You are who you are, and so am I. I'm going to stop trying to change that." Shoulders slumping, Malcolm looked down at his lap. His hands were balled up into fists, although he looked tired enough to pass out at any moment.

"Please." Jessie's voice came out as a sob. "Don't give up on us."

She reached for his hands, but he pulled them back. "It's been ten years. A freaking decade of toying with each other. I want you to get that promotion, Jessie. I want you to find what makes you happy."

An argument flared inside her, the truth of her call with Noel threatening to spill out. But she knew he wasn't wrong either. They had played this game before, and even though she wasn't ready to walk away, she couldn't deny she was tired.

Instead of fighting, she asked the easiest question racing through her head. "You're not shutting me out completely, are you?"

He huffed out a sad laugh. "I don't think I could if I wanted to, but we have to stop pretending we're more than friends. I need to have a little space and get my head on straight."

Before Jessie could reply, their emotional bubble burst.

"Yoohoo!" Estelle's voice rang through the house. Not bothering to knock, she let her and Craig in with the spare key. "Wakey, wakey, kids. We have breakfast!" The clicking of her heels alerted them that their private moment was over ... among other things.

Craig followed Estelle into the kitchen, two large pastry boxes in his hands. Once again, he looked ready for a day on the golf course, sunglasses tucked in the collar of his polo shirt. Estelle looked ready for her close-up, her blonde curls pinned off her face and clad in a matching capri and blouse set.

Jessie scurried to her feet like the floor was on fire, turning away so they couldn't see her swollen eyes.

"Good morning, son," Craig greeted with a gentle pat on the shoulder. Turning his attention to Jessie, he asked, "How is our patient today?"

Jessie was pleased her voice didn't waver as she replied, "Getting stronger every day." *So strong he doesn't need you anymore,* her traitorous brain reminded her.

"Let me get a look at you," Estelle clamped her manicured hands on his biceps and turned him this way and that until she was satisfied no bones protruded from his frame. "You look tired, but your coloring is better than yesterday."

Malcolm let his mother pepper his forehead with kisses before getting his father's attention. "What did you bring us?"

Craig beamed. "I went for a jog down Main Street this morning, and I bumped into Javi."

Jessie couldn't help herself. "This early?"

Chuckling, Craig nodded. "That's what I thought, too. He was headed toward that bakery near the library, and he kept talking about how good the pastries were."

Estelle interrupted him, flapping her arms in the air like she was doing the chicken dance, "And I knew we all could use a break from cooking."

"Exactly," her husband agreed, "so we swung by on our way here to grab a few things."

Estelle went to work plating a variety of donuts, Danishes, and sweet biscuits. "Javi even offered to pick you up today, if you're up for a little field trip."

Malcolm perked right up at that. "What do you mean?"

Craig held up his hand. "Now, son, this is only if you're feeling up for it. There's a meeting later today to discuss the fire station fundraiser. If you feel like an outing, he offered to pick you up."

Jessie didn't like the sounds of that. "I don't know," she said as Malcolm interjected, "That sounds perfect!"

"Well then, sounds like it's all settled. You can text Javi when you're ready, and he'll take care of it."

Malcolm smiled for the first time that morning, and Jessie's heart sank. "That'll give y'all time to move in while I'm out." Malcolm took a huge bite of a jelly donut, red jam sticking to the stubble on his chin.

"Move in?" Jessie and Estelle asked in unison.

"Jessie's going to go stay with her momma."

Estelle clutched her hands in prayer, her bottom lip trembling. "Oh, baby, that sounds delightful." Turning to her husband, she said, "Let's check out of the hotel before lunch, otherwise they'll charge us for the full day."

Already rummaging in his pocket for his cell phone, Craig nodded. "I'll take care of it."

And just like that, Jessie was dismissed.

"I'm going to start a load of laundry before I head out," Jessie said to no one in particular. It wasn't lost on her that both of the most important things in her life had vanished in the last ten hours. She'd gone from a tough decision to making an impossible one. Does she stay in Pinegrove even though Malcolm seemed done with their relationship? Was this the beginning of something new?

"Let me help," Estelle offered, looping an arm around Jessie's shoulders, bringing her back into the present. As they left the kitchen, she nearly stepped on the mess from earlier. "Is that a stick of butter on the floor?"

Estelle tugged Jessie into the guestroom on their way to the laundry room. Before Jessie could object, she closed the door and cornered her. "Now don't bother telling me it's fine, honey. What in blue blazes is going on with you and my son?"

Jessie looked down at her feet, hands flexing at her sides. "Nothing, Estelle. Malcolm wants some time with you and Craig."

"Hogwash," she spat. "I'm not a fool, although maybe my boy is." Jessie couldn't help herself, she snorted. "You two have been shooting heart eyes at each other since you arrived, and now you're headed home and he looks as surly as a longshoreman."

Jessie sighed. "It's complicated."

Estelle waved her off. "It always is with you two. Why are you leaving?"

Jessie didn't want to involve Estelle, but since she was currently locked in a room with the woman, she knew she had to give her something. "We're not exactly on the same page, and we've decided to be friends."

"Friends don't kick friends out of their houses."

"I'm not going to overstay my welcome," Jessie said, not adding the obvious: *More than I already have.*

Estelle tucked a lock of hair behind her ear. She let out a long exhale before meeting Jessie's eye. "This isn't over, young lady. I don't know much in his world, but you two are soulmates." Jessie wanted to both argue and agree with her next breath, but she held her tongue. "Go on home and see your momma, and I'll text you when my son gets his head on straight." Then she did the last thing Jessie expected: she pulled her into a hug that could crack every rib in her body. "I love you, Jessica. You've always been good to our son, and I know that won't change."

Jessie's bottom lip trembled, but she hugged Estelle back with everything she had. "Love you, too."

Jessie gathered what few belongings she'd brought with her and bid Malcolm and Craig goodbye. No one offered to walk her to the door. Malcolm looked defeated, resigned to their decision ... well, *his* decision.

As she swiped angrily at the tears that kept falling all the way to her mother's house, she told herself the emotions were due to exhaustion, not a broken heart. They'd broken up a million times before, and this was no different.

Well, that wasn't true. For the first time in a long time, Pinegrove felt more like home than anywhere ... even though she missed her other half.

CHAPTER THIRTEEN

Three Years Ago

Certain memories stick with you, no matter how much time had passed. Jessie could dissect every minuscule detail from the day she learned of her father's passing. She was stationed deep in the jungles of Ecuador, settled into the middle of her six-month stay. She was on a hike with some of the locals, staking out options for the best water stations for the village. Insects flitted around her face, her hair plastered to the nape of her neck. It was mid-summer, and the temperatures flirted with the hundreds, the humidity saturating the air.

One of her teammates, Jolene, was back at headquarters ... a.k.a. a collection of semi-permanent tents clustered together. There was a satellite phone and a shaky Wi-Fi connection they all shared to communicate with their supervisors, but also with family. After returning for the day, she saw a very worried Jolene pacing in front of their shared tent.

"Mays, thank the Lord," she exhaled, body deflating. Clutched in her hand was the phone, her knuckles white.

"You need to call home," she said, voice tinged with concern.

Jessie didn't understand how she knew it was something horrible, but her stomach bottomed out, all sounds around her turning to white noise. "Who called?" Her question evaporated on a whisper. Jolene chewed on her cheek, expression pinched. "Jolene," she barked. "Who called?"

Jolene closed the distance, thrusting the phone into Jessie's sweaty palm. "Your brother." Without knowing anything more, Jessie collapsed onto the ground, knees sinking into the dirt. It had to be one of her parents, she mused as Jolene shook her shoulders and struggled to get Jessie back on her feet. "Mays, Mays!" She kept repeating Jessie's name until they finally made eye contact. "Go to our tent, give him a call. Please, it could be nothing."

But it wasn't nothing; it was the worst news imaginable.

On shaking legs, Jessie stumbled and collapsed onto her cot. Without thinking, she dialed her brother's cell phone, simultaneously eager to hear his voice and utterly petrified.

After three rings, Trevor answered with a somber "Jessie?"

The tears already fell, her throat clogged as she choked out, "Trev?" Silence was all she heard for a moment, and she feared they'd already been disconnected. Jessie pulled the phone back, squinting at the tiny display to confirm he was still on the line. "Trevor?"

"It's Daddy," he finally croaked out.

Now, Jessie had seen and heard her brother be emotional before. As the little sister, it had been her job to taunt and harass him endlessly over the years. Yet they also shared a tight bond and often went to each other with their problems. This was new though. This level of tension and grief could only mean one thing.

"Was there a fire?" she asked, both hands pressing the phone to her ear.

Trevor cleared his throat and said, "No, Jessie. Daddy had a heart attack."

"A heart attack?" she repeated, inching forward on her cot. Heart attacks weren't bad, right? Millions of people had them and went on to live long, healthy lives … she bet. "Is he in the hospital?"

It could have been a split second or an eternity until Trevor finally spilled the news that cracked her world wide open. "No, Jessie. Daddy died." Then the only thing she heard was a sob as Trevor pulled the phone back and lost it again.

Jessie rocked herself back and forth, willing the words to be a lie, a cruel joke, anything but the painful truth it was. "No," she muttered. "Daddy's healthy as a horse. He can't have a heart attack."

Trevor sniffled. "I was there, Jessie."

"Oh my God!" She gasped, a fresh wave of pain washing over her at the news. Her brother, her strong, selfless brother had to witness the tragedy. "Are you okay?" For a moment, there was only silence. She heard muffled voices and Gus woofing in the background. Trevor was home, with poor Momma, and suddenly she couldn't stand the distance a moment longer. "I'm coming home, on the first flight out of Quito."

More snuffles filled her ear until Trevor said, "Good, that's good. I'll tell Momma. If Malcolm is up for it, he'll pick you up."

Jessie swiped at her cheeks, the thought of seeing Malcolm again a comfort she hadn't realized she needed. "Up for it?" she asked, dabbing at her eyes with the hem of her T-shirt.

"He was with me, Jessie. When it … " but that's all Trevor could get out before he started crying again.

"Oh no." She sighed, heart shattering at the fact that not only did her brother have to witness the event but also sweet-hearted Malcolm.

Malcolm, who gleefully followed her daddy and brother into service at the station. Malcolm, who still attended family dinners while she was gone, just because he loved her family as much as she did. Malcolm, who selflessly put himself in the way of danger.

Trevor replied, "We can talk about it all later. Email me your flight once you book it, and we'll see you soon. I love you, Jessie."

"Love you, too, Trev. Give Momma a hug for me."

Jessie ended the call, letting the satellite phone clatter to the ground. A million images of the man flashed through her head, tears falling silently down her face. Memories of her daddy during their most recent visit, the man had climbed the roof to fix a leak, hadn't even asked Trevor to help. Granted, he'd celebrated that task with a couple of hot dogs and a beer, but didn't all men eat like that?

A heart attack didn't seem real. Nick Mays's heart was as big as all outdoors—holding the love of his family and the whole damned fire department—it couldn't give out on him; it was too big and strong. *Too important* ...

The thought of her mother alone was the final straw. Jessie barely made it out of the tent before she lost her breakfast all over an ant hill. She retched until nothing came up, until her colleagues started to gather in the distance, dozens of insects skittering away at her feet. Her eyes stung, nose running down her face as she lifted her shirt and dabbed away the mix of vomit and snot.

Her daddy was dead. Her family was in mourning, and she was currently drenched in bodily fluids in the middle of a South American jungle. She'd never hated her job as much as she did in that moment.

She wasn't sure how she did it, but she managed to get with Jolene and Noel, to tell them the horrible news. They helped her book a flight, with a layover in Mexico City. She didn't want to have to stop, but she understood time and her budget were factors.

While she boarded the first plane to take her back to Pinegrove, take her back to a reality she didn't want to be a part of, Jessie thought of Malcolm. Trevor had mentioned in their last hurried phone call that Malcolm would meet her at the airport, and she was so relieved. For as much as she needed to see her mother, needed to hold Trevor tight, she also needed a moment with the person who understood her the most. She was also desperate to comfort Malcolm, to share the burden of losing her father.

Granted, her last visit home hadn't gone as she'd hoped. It was a year ago, and Malcolm and his parents had joined her family at her parents' anniversary party. All the talk of love and marriage had put him in a feisty mood, and he pleaded his case for her to stay—with him—for the umpteenth time.

Jessie had taken her star ring off, pressing it into his hand with a breaking heart. "Malcolm, I'm not ready," she'd said, despite the pain in her chest. "I've got a new assignment, this one in Kenya. You know I've always wanted to go there."

Malcolm had placed her ring on the table, stepping out of her hold. "JJ, I'm not going to wait anymore. Keep the ring or don't, but the next time you see me, it'll be as a family friend. My heart can't take anymore." *And now neither could her daddy's ...*

She'd called out his name, but it was no use. Every time she went back home, a part of her both clicked into place and ached to leave. It always felt impossible to find herself when everyone assumed she was Trevor's goofy sister, or Malcolm's flighty girlfriend.

When she was out on a job, she had a purpose, a plan, people to help. No one knew anything about her, beyond what she'd shared over campfire conversations or out in the field. She could be a woman of mystery, whoever the hell she wanted to be.

Of course now, as she stood outside the gate in the Mexico City airport, all she wanted to be was Nick May's daughter. She wrapped her arms around her middle, eager to get back to Georgia and see her family, to see Malcolm. Squeezing her eyes shut, she could almost hear him calling out for her.

"JJ! JJ, baby!"

Footfalls grew louder, and Jessie spun around, ponytail slapping her neck. She froze when she saw Malcolm, sprinting toward her. "Malcolm?" she asked, willing the sight to be more than a mirage.

Malcolm skittered to a halt in front of her, narrowly avoiding tripping over her duffle bag. "JJ," he said her name in greeting, carefully placing his hands on her hips. "JJ?" he asked, dipping his head low to meet her gaze.

The moment their eyes locked, Jessie couldn't hold her composure. She crumpled into his arms, wailing into his chest, soaking his shirt in seconds. "Malcolm." She kept repeating his name as he cooed and rubbed circles on her back. She was somewhat aware that people were watching, but she couldn't give a rip. "How are you here?" she asked when she'd caught her breath.

"I couldn't stay away," he admitted, holding her firm.

She inhaled his familiar citrus scent, the aroma instantly transporting her back home ... back to happier times. "How did you get here?"

Malcolm cupped her head, nestling as close as he could, given their surroundings. "When Trev shared your itinerary, I booked a flight. I didn't want you coming all the way home alone." He kissed her temple, and Jessie practically dissolved into a puddle of conflicting emotions. "I'm here, baby."

Jessie clung to him and that statement with all her might. "You're here," she said, savoring this bright moment in the middle of her grief.

Malcolm had flown down to find her, to comfort her in her darkest hour. If that wasn't love, she didn't know what was.

*

Everything was different; there was a new normal.
Frankly, Malcolm hated it.
His chief, mentor, and role model, was gone. Malcolm

knew he should stay and take advantage of the counseling sessions, help his team begin to heal. What he knew would really help get him through this shock and grief was seeing JJ as soon as humanly possible.

Due to transit limitations, Jessie couldn't simply hop in a rideshare and speed off to the airport like in the movies. It would take a few days to coordinate her journey, which left him plenty of time to burn his airline credit card miles on a ticket.

"Sugar, you don't need to do this. Picking Jessie up in Atlanta is more than helpful," Daisy had assured him that first night. He'd joined Trevor at the family home to pay his respects and offer his help, however that looked.

When he'd followed Trevor inside, the house already felt different. It had only been a few hours since the great man's heart stopped, but everything had changed. Daisy's eyes, which were usually bright as starlight, were dull and vacant. Her voice was weighed down with the loss of her partner; of her own heart.

"Ms. Daisy," he'd said, licking his lips to stop from crying himself, "I need to be there for JJ. I can't let her get on that plane alone." His bottom lip trembled, but he would not lose it in front of the widow. Chief wouldn't want that.

Covering her heart with her hand, Daisy nodded once before pulling herself to standing and plodding off toward her bedroom. "You're a good man, Malcolm," she offered over her shoulder before closing the door. A few seconds later, her sobs echoed throughout the house. Poor Gus had stayed by Daisy's side, a sad *woof* here or there to remind everyone he was mourning, too. Seeing the devastated basset hound was almost too much for Malcolm to bear.

"I'll walk you out," Trevor offered, clearing his throat and clapping a hand on Malcolm's shoulder.

As the pair headed into the sweltering summer sun, Malcolm let the first tear fall. He'd been to the Mays' house countless times over the years. First as a friend of Trevor's, then as Jessie's beau, and finally as a member of the force.

He could not fathom a life without the chief and his family in it, which is why he needed to get to Jessie.

"You're sure you want to fly halfway across the world, man? I'm with Momma, a ride from the Atlanta airport qualifies you for hero status." His lip quirked up for a millisecond before Trevor's somber expression took hold once more. Malcolm couldn't imagine what his buddy was going through, losing not only his father but his boss. There was no question he'd be chief one day, it just shouldn't be this soon.

"She's all alone," Malcolm admitted. His stomach clenched at thoughts of Jessie in the middle of nowhere, grieving this terrible loss. Nick and Jessie had been thick as thieves her whole life, and the heart attack had come far too suddenly.

Trevor coughed, clearly uncomfortable showing his emotions in the front yard. Neighbors had begun to hear the horrible news, and a slow procession of casseroles, punch, and cookies was about to commence.

"I'll bring her back as soon as I can." Malcolm shoved his hands in his shorts pockets, his palms slick with anxious sweat. With a simple nod, Trevor turned and headed back inside.

The journey was ridiculous, Malcolm would be the first to admit, but he almost enjoyed the flight. He'd brought a paperback crime novel he'd promised himself he'd read before the movie adaptation released, but despite the twisty plot, he couldn't pay attention. Instead, he thought about Jessie.

Whether they were friends, exes, or lovers, he loved Jessie more than ever. In his haste to hit the road, he wasn't sure if his messages would arrive to her Peace Corps office, but he knew from Daisy and Trevor that Jessie's flight out wouldn't leave until that evening. He would be there when she arrived.

Fortunately his flight was on time, which gave him an hour to find food and freshen up in the airport. While clearly not a romantic reunion, Malcolm still wanted to look good for his girl. She deserved nothing less.

After dusting sandwich crumbs from his hands, Malcolm checked the arrivals board and saw that Jessie should be arriving at her gate any minute. He quickly purchased her a bottle of water and a stack of magazines, in case she needed a distraction that didn't require Wi-Fi—or him.

Just as he reached the gate, he saw her approach down the concourse. Her hair was pulled haphazardly into a ponytail, swishing past her neck in time to her steps. She clutched her carry-on bag in one hand, her other dragging a duffle behind her. She was dressed for time in the jungle, hiking boots stomping as she trudged forward, her khakis worn yet comfortable.

Jessie paused at the board, checking on her flight time. Malcolm approached with caution. Her eyes were dry, but red-rimmed. Clearly exhausted, she dropped her bags and wrapped her arms around her middle.

"JJ!" He practically shouted her name. For a moment, she didn't look up, so he kept calling for her as he closed the distance.

Finally, she froze. "Malcolm?" Blinking, a single tear slid down her cheek. "What are you doing here?"

"I came to take you home," he said with a shrug. "I didn't want you flying alone."

Without a moment's hesitation, Jessie got on tiptoe and flung her arms around his neck, pulling him so close he could smell the faint hint of her shampoo. "You're here," she sighed into his chest, soaking the front of his T-shirt.

Malcolm cupped the back of her head, cradling her against him and away from prying eyes. "I'm here, baby. I'm here." Without thinking, he kissed the top of her head and held her while she wept, body shaking with every sob.

They stood like that, seized with grief. Malcolm bit his cheek, unwilling to show his own emotions. Pulling back slightly, Jessie covered her face and groaned. "I can't believe

..." but she didn't finish the thought. *She didn't need to.*

"Let's have a seat, hmm?"

Jessie collapsed beside him, reaching for his hand as soon as he deposited her bags at their feet. "Thank you," she breathed. "How did you get here?"

Malcolm lifted a shoulder, leaning down to retrieve the bottle of water for her. "Drink this, you need to stay hydrated."

She dutifully took the water and slugged back half of it before covering her mouth and belching. "That was ladylike." She huffed, a faint smile toying at her lips.

"JJ, you're first class." He winked and she snorted, the pair briefly falling back into their old rapport.

"But how did you get here?"

Malcolm tipped his head, tapping his chin as if he were deep in thought. "There's this crazy thing called an airplane. It literally flies through the air and can take you all over the world." He nudged her shoulder. "You're in the Peace Corps, I'm surprised you've never heard of this."

She chuckled, draining the other half of her water bottle and tossing it into the nearby trash can. "I'm aware of the wonders of aviation," she teased, exhaling until she folded into herself. "But why are you here?"

Malcolm didn't hesitate, snaking her hand in his. "Your daddy," his voice hitched, but he rallied, "he wouldn't want his best girl flying home alone. I couldn't stand the thought of you making this trip, JJ. Let me help you." He leaned down and placed a gentle kiss on her temple, savoring the moment of intimacy despite the situation.

"But after everything, I can't ..." He placed a finger over her lips, shaking his head.

"Let's not go there now, okay?"

Jessie nodded, dabbing at her damp cheeks with the hem of her shirt. "Thank you," she said on a shuddering breath. "This is the worst day of my life, but you made it better. I'm so glad you're here."

So was Malcolm. "You want anything to eat before we

board? That shop over there isn't half bad considering it's forty dollars per sandwich."

"I'm not really hungry, and you should save your money. How much was this flight?"

"Approximately a million airline miles, which I was never going to use anyway before you complain," he warned, reaching out to tuck a lock of hair behind her ear. "I want to be here, JJ. Let me be here for you."

Jessie nodded, nibbling her bottom lip as her eyes welled again. "You know what's funny?"

Malcolm huffed out a laugh. "In this moment? Absolutely nothing."

A smirk toyed with her mouth as Jessie sighed. "I was walking through customs, and all I thought was I was alone. I usually relish the chance to be by myself and do my own thing, but when I came through the gate, I wanted to collapse. And you know what else?" she asked, turning to face him.

"What?" Malcolm leaned closer, until there were mere inches between them.

"I wanted you to be with me," she said, closing the distance and resting her forehead on his. "When I felt your hands on my waist, I felt like I was home."

Malcolm enveloped Jessie in his arms, his own tears joining the party. "You are home," Malcolm promised, crushing her against his chest. "You're home, JJ."

He wasn't sure if Jessie realized it, but he would do anything for her until he took his last breath. She was endgame for him, and Malcolm wasn't going anywhere. He had the airline miles to burn.

LIBBY KAY

CHAPTER FOURTEEN

"Honey, you're not eating your salad," Estelle tutted, tapping her knife on Malcolm's plate. "I even added roasted beets. I know how much you love them." Her smile was filled with warmth and the love only a smothering mother could provide.

Malcolm stabbed a piece of the blasted vegetable with his fork. He held out his arm, making a show of how excited he was to put that piece of tasteless root tuber into his mouth. "Mmmm, delicious," he said through a mouthful, nearly gagging as he swallowed.

Here's a fun fact about the Smith men—they hate, loathe, and utterly detest beets. Estelle had read in a magazine back in the late '90s that they helped with weight loss, and ever since she'd been force-feeding them the magenta cubes on a weekly basis. During the height of *Atlanta Hearts*, Estelle had convinced all of her female costars of the miracles of the pesky vegetable. They'd eaten so many beets, Malcolm was surprised their skin hadn't turned pink.

Glancing over at his father's plate, Malcolm saw a pile of the squares hidden under his napkin. "Wonderful lunch, darling," Craig said, hurrying to his feet to clear his and Malcolm's plates.

Malcolm winked at his dad before turning to his mother. "Yeah, thanks, Mom. Lunch was great."

Estelle beamed, patting her son's arm. "Thanks, honey. Think of all the fun things we can cook together now that we're staying here." Malcolm could only hope his grin stayed fixed in place, otherwise it would break her heart.

Craig started loading the dishwasher, careful to dispose of the uneaten vegetables when his wife wasn't looking. "What time is Javi picking you up?"

Malcolm pulled his phone out of his pocket and checked the time. "Pretty soon, actually. I should get dressed." He pushed back his chair, ready to grab his cane.

The thought of shuffling into the station with his walker made Malcolm want to dive out of a plane without a parachute. Deep down he understood his colleagues wouldn't mock him, or even think less of him, but Malcolm needed his first time back at the station to not be a spectacle.

"Are you sure you shouldn't use your walker, baby?" His mother was by his side, a hand pressed firmly to his lower back as he struggled to stand upright.

In his haste to throw Jessie out of the house, he'd missed one of his virtual physical therapy sessions. Now he was paying the price with stiff muscles and an achy back. "I've got it," he said through gritted teeth. Patience was not a virtue that Malcolm possessed.

Apparently, his impatience included throwing the love of his life out of his home and inviting the chaos of his mother in instead. Yet he knew he was doing the right thing with Jessie. He'd seen the excitement when her boss called; knew her well enough to know she'd already begun mentally packing her bags.

These were the hardest times for him, when she was still there but not *really* there. Their kisses tasted different, the sparkle in her eyes was muted, and their embraces never lasted long enough. He was left with the husk of Jessie, and it always left him hollow and bitter.

Now Malcolm would go on record and admit he was no saint when they were on their "off" periods. He'd dated here and there, although never anyone serious. He always felt bad for these women, because while they were making plans for future trips and family gatherings, Malcolm was planning when they'd break up in time for Jessie's next visit. They were nice women whom he had fun with … but never as much fun as he'd had with Jessie. *Not even close…*

Pulling himself from his Jessie-induced funk, Malcolm took the handle of the cane and stood to his full height. He only winced a little when he heard his back pop. Estelle pulled out another chair, and even his dad looked a little green around the gills.

"You okay, son? That sounded painful."

Malcolm tapped his cane on the floor twice and nodded. "Totally fine. I'm going to change."

"I can help," his mother offered, already striding down the hallway.

Craig pushed to his feet and took his son's elbow. "Let's go make sure she doesn't try to actually dress you. Hmm?" Practically melting into his father's side, Malcolm shuffled down the hallway, grateful his dad understood the situation.

As they approached the bedroom, Craig held back. "You know," he said, voice low, "if at any point you want Jessie to come back, we can go back to the hotel like that." He snapped his fingers to punctuate his point.

Malcolm sagged against the wall. "Dad, not you, too. Mom's been on my case all morning."

His father held up his hands in surrender. "All right, never mind. I won't pretend to understand that song and dance you kids have perfected, but I know love. That girl will still move heaven and earth for you, and I don't want you to forget that."

Malcolm scoffed. He couldn't help himself. "She'd move half an earth away, you mean. C'mon, I need to get dressed before Javi gets here."

No sooner had the words left his mouth than the doorbell rang. Estelle popped her head out of the bedroom and gasped. "He's early! You're not ready yet."

"It's not a date, Estelle. The boy needs three minutes to brush his teeth and put on a clean shirt."

Judging from the once-over his mother gave him, Malcolm assumed she wanted him to have thirty minutes to get ready, not three. "Why don't you let Javi in, Mom? Dad's here if I need him."

Always the good Southern Belle hostess, Estelle flitted down the hall. Within twenty seconds, she and Javi could be heard laughing from the living room. "Javi's flirting should keep her busy for at least twenty minutes." Craig chuckled, opening the closet and pulling out a short-sleeved button-up shirt that was easy for Malcolm to put on and take off. "Here, how about this and those khaki shorts?"

"Thanks." Malcolm took his clothes and padded into the bathroom to freshen up.

He ran his hands through his hair, which was getting longer than he liked. His natural curls were starting to take over, and he already missed the no-nonsense prep that came with a buzz cut. It took longer than he wanted to get dressed, but Malcolm stepped out ready for public consumption.

Craig sat on the bed, scrolling through his phone absently. He looked up when Malcolm approached and offered a thumbs-up. "You look good." Waggling his phone toward the cane, he added, "And you're handling that thing like a pro."

Malcolm jostled the stick. "Oh yeah, this is quite the look for a thirty-year-old fireman." For a moment, the air in the room stilled. Malcolm rarely saw emotion on his father's face, but suddenly it looked like the old man might burst into tears. "You okay?"

Craig nodded, clearing his throat and standing up. He closed the distance to Malcolm, resting his hands on his shoulders. "You're a hero, Malcolm. What you did, that's bravery. I'm proud of you, son, and I don't want you beating yourself up over a stupid walking stick. Okay?" He patted Malcolm's shoulders twice before stepping back. "Now let's get out there before your mother runs off with Javi."

"Thanks," Malcolm said, unable to articulate more without bursting into tears.

When they made it to the living room, Javi and Estelle were seated on the couch. Clearly in the middle of a story, Javi waved his hands over his head, saying something that had her laughing so hard she almost fell off the sofa.

"Oh, Javi, you're a card!" Estelle gasped for breath, fanning herself with her manicured hand, her diamond bracelet catching the light.

Javi took a bow before he saw Malcolm and Craig enter the room. "Smithy, and Smithy Senior!" He clapped both men on the back. "How y'all doing?"

Craig's stern expression was all for show. "I'm fine, but I'll be better when you stop flirting with my wife."

Javi rocked back on his heels. "Flirting with the gorgeous, esteemed soap star Estelle Winters? Never!" He turned and winked at Estelle, who practically melted onto the floor.

"You really are trouble with a capital *T*," she cooed, preening at the attention.

Malcolm groaned. "No argument here."

Eager to change the subject, Javi gestured to the cane. "Look at you, Smithy! Already walker-free. The gang's gonna flip when they see you."

"Let's get me to the station then." Malcolm kissed his mother's cheek and waved to his dad as he followed Javi outside.

"Have fun!" Estelle clutched her hands in front of her as she watched her son get into Javi's truck with very little assistance.

Once the doors were closed and Javi pulled out of the driveway, he turned to Malcolm. "Real talk, man. How are you feeling? If this is too much, I'll drop you back right now."

"Ortiz, for the love of God. If you take me back home, I'll beat that pretty face of yours with this cane." He jostled the stick and glared.

Javi gulped, covering one of his cheeks. "Not my face! You wouldn't do that to the gorgeous women of Pinegrove, would you?"

Malcolm smirked. "Try me."

For the first ten minutes of the drive, they talked about the station. What was happening with Trevor's promotion, who was annoying whom, and even who had stolen the secret stash of peanut butter cups the chief hid in the garage behind the extra hose clamps. The banter washed over Malcolm like a balm, and he reveled at being able to feel like a fireman again ... even if temporarily.

As soon as Javi's truck crested the hill that led to the firehouse, he asked the question Malcolm waited for. "Couldn't help but notice Jessie wasn't there."

Malcolm's jaw tensed. "You're very observant."

Javi stopped at a stop sign, fingers drumming on the steering wheel. "Everything okay there?"

"Yup. She wanted to go home and see her momma."

"Uh-huh," Javi said, flicking his turn signal with a little too much gusto for Malcolm's liking. "You know what's crazy? She saw Daisy yesterday. Told us all about it over pizzas, if I remember correctly." He hummed to himself a moment, like he was a detective on the case.

Malcolm wiggled his cane, tapping it on the car door. "It sounds like you want me to rearrange your pretty face."

Javi chuckled, pulling into a parking space near the staff entrance to the fire station. "No, Smithy, I don't."

Malcolm shook away thoughts of Jessie, focusing instead on the station. Being back was a sensation that Malcolm wasn't prepared for. For years he'd come and gone with relative ease, never having to endure real hardships from the job. Hindsight reminded Malcolm how lucky he was to make it this far in his career without major injury.

After stepping onto the gravel parking lot, his feet were still a little unsteady. Clearing past the lump in his throat, Malcolm had to focus on breathing. Pain zipped up his legs, but it was more the emotions of coming back that did him in. And boy, he really didn't want to cry in front of Javi.

"You okay, man?" Javi was by his side, discreetly holding out an elbow to help steady his friend.

Malcolm leaned on him, grateful as he caught his breath. "Yeah, I'm fine. Just wasn't expecting to feel …" He paused, struggling to identify the emotions swirling through him. "Everything. I didn't expect to feel so much."

Always the jokester, Javi shrugged. "Meh, it'll be our little secret. Crybaby."

Malcolm nudged him in the ribs, but took a step toward the door. "Let's get back to work," he said, breathless as they stepped into the station.

Familiar sights, sounds, and smells assaulted Malcolm as soon as the door clicked shut behind them. The air was cold from the industrial AC, with the aroma of burnt coffee and rubber. Around them, his colleagues clicked away on their computers or gabbed by the water cooler. It was the most beautiful scene Malcolm had ever seen.

"Guess what time it is, boys!" Javi shouted as he entered the bullpen.

Maxwell jogged up to them, pulling Malcolm into a quick, careful hug. "And girls," she shouted at Javi, who smacked his forehead.

"And girls, Maxwell. My apologies. I'm so damned excited to have our boy back."

Everyone gathered around them, Trevor and Chief Warren included. "Welcome back, Smithy!" Trevor playfully shoved his shoulder. "It's great to see you here, man."

"Same, Captain."

Trevor beamed, clearly elated with his recent promotion. He knew Jessie was damn proud of her brother, too, but he pushed that thought aside. Now was not the time to be thinking about her.

"It's really good to see you standing, son," Chief said, blinking rapidly.

"Thanks, everyone. It's great to be back, even if it's just for a fundraising meeting." He turned and chuckled at Javi's sullen expression.

"This year's fundraiser is going to be amazing." Javi clapped his hands, getting everyone's attention. "Let's get to the conference room, because we have a special guest joining us and it's going to be fabulous."

Trevor rolled his eyes, pressing a coffee mug into Malcolm's waiting hand. "You'll need this, man."

Over his shoulder, Javi barked, "Yo, cap! I'll take my coffee black."

"You're a menace, Ortiz!" Turning back to Malcolm, he asked, "You sure you want to come back to this nut house?"

Malcolm nodded. "More than anything."

Trevor's expression turned serious. "We'll get you back here on desk duty as soon as my sister whips you into shape." He craned his neck and glanced around the station. "I'm actually surprised she didn't invite herself to this. You know Jessie. When she's on the job she'll stick to you like shit on a wool blanket."

Malcolm rubbed at the back of his neck, a headache blooming at the base of his skull. "She's, uh, gone back to stay with your momma for a bit." Trevor's eyes narrowed, but he didn't say a word. "You know my mom. If she doesn't get to smother me to death while she's here, I'll never hear the end of it."

Trevor smiled, but it didn't reach his eyes. Malcolm had made a rule to not discuss Jessie and him too much with her big brother. It wasn't because Malcom didn't trust the other man, but because Malcolm respected Trevor too much to pull him into their will-they-won't-they drama.

"Well, make sure Estelle doesn't coddle you to death. We need you back with Maxwell on the ambulance."

Malcolm stayed back a moment while everyone filed into

the conference room. He slurped his coffee, wincing at the familiar metallic burn. Maxwell must have made this batch, as it was thick as tar, the grounds barely filtered through. He loved it though—the coffee and being back.

Perhaps that was his problem. While he was happy where he was, content in his career and friends, Jessie still yearned for something else, something bigger than Pinegrove. *Why couldn't she see what was right in front of her?*

That realization burned almost as much as this horrible coffee, but Malcolm had to believe it would work out in the end. Because at the end of the day, he just wanted Jessie to be happy. Even if it wasn't with him …

LIBBY KAY

CHAPTER FIFTEEN

The biggest benefit of their pizza night, aside from seeing his friends and inhaling his favorite greasy comfort food, was that Malcolm knew exactly what was coming with this meeting. Every year, the Pinegrove Fire Department held some type of fundraising event or sold something to beef up their budget for the upcoming year. While City Hall supported PFD, their budgets only went so far.

Javi was a good fireman, a loyal friend, but also the biggest attention seeker to come out of Georgia since Estelle Winters. Taking his time to quiet the room, Javi stood with his hands out, gazing at the ceiling like he waited for the voice of God.

"Hurry up, Ortiz!" one of the guys from night shift yelled, clearly bored with his theatrics.

"I'm with Adams, get on with it!" Maxwell shouted beside Malcolm. She'd snagged him a chair at the front next to her so they could heckle their buddy unobstructed. "How's the coffee?" she asked, peering into his half-empty mug. "I added a pinch of cinnamon today." She grinned, and Malcolm didn't have the heart to tell her he'd rather drink the drainage water after a fire.

"It's perfect. Kick in the pants I needed today."

While the others continued to heckle Javi, Maxwell leaned closer. "How are you feeling, Smithy? I mean it. You seemed good at your place, but being back and everything ..." She trailed off. "I know it can be a lot."

Maxwell may have been relatively new to Pinegrove FD, but she wasn't new to being a firefighter. She'd worked in Atlanta for five years before marrying a small-town guy and settling in Pinegrove. She'd had her share of injuries in the field, but Malcolm hoped that trend ceased. She was mother to two kiddos under four, and he planned on keeping her safe and sound.

Patting her knee, Malcolm leaned back in his seat and kicked his feet out. "Thanks for worrying about me, Maxwell, but I really am fine. I need to keep up the PT and have some scans coming up next week, but all signs still point to a full recovery."

Her face lit up at the news. "I'm so glad. I still can't believe how everything went down, when we separated to check the perimeter, I should have ..." Her voice caught, and Malcolm shook his head.

"Don't," he warned. "It's part of the job, and we followed all the proper procedures. I won't have you beating yourself up over this."

Maxwell didn't look like she'd believed him, her eyes shimmering with tears. Malcolm understood that she needed to keep her emotions in check. Despite the fact that the crew was welcoming of their sole female colleague, she still didn't want to be known as emotional, or worse.

Maxwell gave a firm nod. "I know, but still."

"All right, goobers!" Trevor shouted from the back of the room, silencing the group and bringing Malcolm back to the moment. "Ortiz, get to the point, please. Your guest is here."

Javi's face lit up like a Christmas tree. "Excellent," he crowed. "Listen up, folks! It's time for our annual fundraiser, and this year I'm the chairman." The last stranglers arrived, filling the room to bursting ... and already looking bored.

"No more peanut brittle!" Chief Warren shouted from the back, earning chuckles from his crew.

A few years ago, the chief organized a county-wide peanut brittle sale from the local peanut farms. While a fine idea on paper, it was about as exciting as a tax return. Sales were moderate, and most of the force was still working through their own *cases* of the sugary, tooth-cracking sweets. Malcolm was pretty sure his stash was putting his dentist's kids through college.

Javi shot a grin at their fearless leader. "No offense, sir, but we can do better than that, boys." Wincing, he turned to Maxwell, and added, "And girl."

Maxwell raised a single eyebrow. "Thank you, Lieutenant."

Javi splayed a hand over his heart and sighed. "You know I will do anything for the ladies." There were murmurs echoing throughout the conference room until Javi snapped his fingers. "Actually, that's the perfect segway to my point."

"Oh, there's a point?" Trevor scoffed, earning a discreet middle finger from Javi.

"Yeah, Cap. My point is that this year's fundraiser is all for the ladies." He waggled his eyebrows suggestively, a move that HR would surely write him up for if they were in the building.

Maxwell frowned. "I have a feeling I'm going to hate this."

Javi shook his head. "I have a feeling you're going to *love* this. I'm all about gender equality."

Trevor gave up the pretense of not looking annoyed. "Just spit it out."

Malcolm couldn't disagree. "Ortiz?" He motioned for Javi to continue.

"Beefcake calendars!" Javi did jazz hands and beamed like he'd come up with a solution to world hunger. "Huh?!"

His voice went up an octave in anticipation.

"He's really going through with this?" Maxwell muttered in Malcolm's ear. She raised a hand, but asked her question before anyone could call on her. "Um, not to state the obvious, but how is a beefcake calendar highlighting gender equality?"

Trevor nodded, hitching his thumb in the direction of his new favorite employee. "I'm with Maxwell. I'm failing to see how us guys provocatively posing for a calendar is going to please our DEI Rep."

George Brock, their only openly gay teammate, turned a worrisome shade of scarlet as he cleared his throat. "I mean, I wouldn't say no to one of those calendars." After an awkward laugh, he added, "Calvin would probably buy one, too."

Malcolm met George's partner, Calvin, at the summer BBQ right after he joined the force. The pair were clearly smitten and had that air about them that only people truly in love share. Calvin, much like Javi, was also an incorrigible flirt. He had no doubt he'd buy enough calendars to paper their house.

Javi pumped his fist in the air and stalked over to George, clapping him on the shoulder. "That's the spirit, man." Dipping his head to his chest, George officially turned as red as their fire engine.

Trevor, ever the voice of reason, broke up the love fest with a round of very sensible questions. "First of all, Ortiz, have you run this idea past the chief?"

Javi smirked. "Yep, and he said that if the team is on board, he won't turn us down."

Every head in the room swung toward the chief, who was perched on a chair in the corner. "I'm not going to get in the way of a potentially successful fundraiser, but don't make me regret it."

Maxwell raised her hand again, and this time Trevor called on her. "Maxwell, please take the floor. We need to hear the other side of this insane idea."

"Well, not to brag, but I've had two kids in the last four years." The room erupted into whistles and cheers. "Thank you." She laughed. "The point is, I'm not sure how comfortable I am with posing nude with my colleagues."

Javi held up his hands. "Hear me out, it's not like that."

Malcolm snickered. "You mean you won't cover us in coconut oil and have us hold hoses in suggestive poses?" Despite his soreness, he splayed himself across his chair like he was posing for Leonardo DiCaprio in *Titanic*.

Everyone sniggered, but Javi wasn't deterred. "Okay, Smithy. You might have to show a little skin." He pinched his fingers together. "But it'll be tasteful, y'all. I promise." He held his hands together in prayer for a moment before turning to Maxwell. "And you can pose however you like."

Maxwell was skeptical. "You mean with rotary saws in front of my breasts?"

Malcolm choked on the last of his coffee, spluttering while his partner thwacked his back. "Damn, Maxwell. Thanks for that visual."

Javi snickered. "Not that I wouldn't be all about that, but I was thinking something different. Maybe you could bring the kids and have it be like a badass Momma shoot."

Her expression didn't give anything away, and Javi seemed bolstered by her lack of argument. "I've got the photographer coming in, and I think she can help share her vision. We've been chatting online, and her portfolio is killer. If you don't like her plan for the calendar, we'll do something different." He took a beat to glance around the room and joked, "But it won't be peanut brittle."

"I heard that," Chief Warren barked as he stomped out of the room to take a phone call. "It's all about community building, Ortiz." He didn't bother looking over his shoulder as he slammed the door.

"Ain't that the truth, Chief!" Javi agreed, turning to Trevor, he asked, "Cap, can you bring in our photographer?"

Trevor nodded, ducking out into the hallway and

returning a moment later with a tall, lithe woman with a shock of blonde hair, a camera bag thrown over her shoulder. She looked like she was made to be in front of the camera, not behind one.

For a moment, the whole room was silent as she strode up next to Javi and extended a hand. "You must be Javier. I'm Lola Peabody." Javi's jaw was unhinged, his eyes staring unblinkingly at her. He took Lola's hand, but he barely moved his arm. She cleared her throat and said, "Of Peabody Photography. We've been emailing for over a week."

Finally, Trevor nudged Javi out of the way. "Thanks so much for coming in to speak with us, Lola. I'm Trevor Mays, the captain here. My tongue-tied lieutenant was telling us about your thoughts on the calendar. Would you mind sharing your vision?" He gestured to the group, stepping back so Lola could have space.

Malcolm couldn't deny, she was gorgeous. He could understand why Javi was currently drowning in a pool of his own drool. While Jessie had unique features like a slightly crooked grin and wide-set eyes that made her beautiful, Lola was a stereotypical blonde bombshell beauty. She was on the taller side, with hair the color of sun-kissed straw. She commanded the room, which was no small feat when dealing with firefighters. They were a motley crew to say the least.

Lola smiled, a row of perfectly white teeth greeting the team. She had a confidence that came from knowing her business, shoulders squared, not a hitch in her voice. "Good afternoon, everyone. I'm Lola, and I've been a photographer for over ten years. I've done jobs varying from weddings and birthday parties to portraits and group photos at community events."

She pulled her camera bag off and fished out a flash drive, holding it out for Javi, who still looked like he'd been electrocuted. "You mind plugging this in?" she asked, eyebrow arched.

Javi nodded dumbly, walking backward to the laptop and projector until he nearly stumbled to the floor.

Maxwell snorted beside Malcolm, studying the silly scene. "I've never seen Ortiz like this around a woman before. Someone should be filming this."

Behind them, George whispered, "I'm on it." His phone was strategically placed between Malcolm and Maxwell, a shit-eating grin plastered on his face. "We can all enjoy this later."

Malcolm couldn't argue. He was torn between being entertained and horrified. "At least this meeting is more interesting than peanut brittle," he mused. Lowering his voice, he added, "And send me that when you're done, George."

After what felt like an eternity, Javi had Lola's presentation ready on the screen. It was a simple PowerPoint made to highlight her photography skills. For a few minutes she clicked through dozens of pictures featuring people of all shapes, ages, sizes, and backgrounds. There were laughing children, couples on their wedding day staring lovingly at each other, but it was her last few slides that got the room's attention.

"This is what I wanted to highlight," Lola said, stepping up to the screen and gesturing at an array of photos featuring police men and women. "Last year I took these snaps for the police station out in Peach Springs. They were doing something similar, a fundraiser, and wanted some fun shots to drive attendance to their policemen's ball."

She clicked through slides showing law enforcement in tasteful photos. There were no awkward poses, no scantily clad men draped in anything inappropriate, no women showing cleavage in their dress blues. Overall, it was classy and fun, exactly what Malcolm thought would work for Pinegrove. If the approving murmurs were any indication, he wasn't alone in his opinion.

When Lola finished her presentation, she asked Trevor to turn the lights back on as she addressed the group. "So, any questions on what I could do for Pinegrove FD?" Her blue gaze swept the room, finding only nods of encouragement. "I can make this calendar anyway you'd like it," she added, turning to Maxwell. "And I hope you don't mind me saying, but I overheard your suggestion for rotary saws. You only need to do that if you want to," she teased, winking at Maxwell.

"I like her," Maxwell said under her breath.

"Me, too," Javi agreed, hearts in his eyes.

Malcolm scoffed. "Is this the reason you hired Lola?"

Javi reared back, his voice low. "No, man, I swear. I saw her portfolio and thought it'd be nice to hire local."

Maxwell giggled. "Saw her portfolio, huh? Is that what the kids are calling it?"

Malcolm couldn't hold back his answering chortle, earning a glare from Javi. "Real mature, y'all. I'm trying to be the best fundraiser this station has ever seen, and you two have your heads in the gutter." He splayed his hand over his heart and sighed. "I'm being a professional." He pointed at George and sighed. "And don't think I didn't see you playing Spielberg. Delete it."

George tucked his phone away. "I don't know what you're talking about, Ortiz."

"Yeah, right." Javi left them to thank Lola, who was busy talking with Trevor.

Frowning, Maxwell studied their buddy. "Do you really think he's trying to be professional about this whole thing?"

Malcolm cocked his head, unsure what to make of his friend's transformation from ladies' man to fundraiser chair. "I mean, he seems genuine. I think he's telling the truth."

Lola answered questions as other teammates thanked her for her time. She strode up to Malcolm and Maxwell, extending her hand. "I'm Lola."

His partner beat him to the introductions, taking Lola's hand. "Tiffany Maxwell, and this is Malcolm Smith." She dipped her head toward Malcolm.

Lola took his hand, giving it a few shakes before

stepping back. "And judging from what I'm seeing, you two will be perfect for the calendar. I couldn't stop watching you laughing, and I think that playfulness will come through."

Maxwell preened at the compliment, but Malcolm suddenly felt uncomfortable. He wasn't sure he wanted to document his injuries with a calendar. For an entire year he'd be reminded that a warehouse fell on him, crushing his bones and nearly his spirit.

Rubbing the back of his neck, he exhaled. "Not sure I'll be camera-ready." He jostled his cane, praying she wouldn't ask follow-up questions. Human nature made folks curious, and he wouldn't fault her if she asked a few hurried, nervous questions. But he didn't like how her face fell. Ever the people pleaser, he rallied quickly. "Although I think it's a great idea. I love what you did with Peach Springs. There wasn't anything that looked meme-worthy." The trio chuckled, but Lola still appeared anxious, wringing her hands in front of her.

Lola leaned closer. "My job is to make people feel comfortable, so please don't worry about that. But I also don't pressure anyone into anything they don't want to do. Maybe we can talk about the process sometime?"

Malcolm flushed, hoping he misunderstood Lola's intentions. Granted, he was no saint and was used to women hitting on him in uniform. Although he was currently dressed more like an injured golfer than a fireman.

Javi joined them, breaking the spell. "Did I hear someone say we're talking shop? Lola, can my man and I take you out for drinks sometime?"

Lola turned to Javi and smiled. "Sure, that'd be nice. I'm new to Pinegrove and haven't met a lot of people yet."

"Then consider me your Pinegrove tour guide! I can show you all the sights," Javi exclaimed, causing poor Maxwell to choke on her gum.

"Like Javi's bedroom," she muttered, banging on her chest until she swallowed her gum.

Lola eyed the group and finally shrugged. "Sure. When's

a good time?"

"Now," Javi blurted before shaking his head. "I mean, what does your schedule look like?" He hesitated a moment and continued, "Do you need to check with your husband or anything?" He raised an eyebrow, and Malcolm nearly died from second-hand embarrassment.

"Smooth, Ortiz," he said behind his fist, coughing to clear the air.

Javi smacked his forehead and groaned. "I mean, I know your schedule must be hectic with all the events you handle."

Lola gave him a quizzical look, not bothering to answer his question on her single status. "If I have a little notice, I can usually find the time. This week is a little nuts. Maybe some night next week?" She pivoted to face their group. "Do you all have a night off in common?"

Javi's face fell. "Oh, um. All of us?" He rested his hands on his hips, head dipped down.

Maxwell chuckled. "We all usually have Thursday nights off in common. If I give my husband notice, he'll watch the kids."

Malcolm shifted his weight, his cane scratching across the polished concrete floors. "I'm not technically released to duty yet, so Lord knows I'm free." He hated that his words had a double meaning. Without Jessie in his life right now, he felt *too* free.

Now Javi looked truly despondent. "I can't next Thursday. It's book club night, and I don't want to miss it. We're discussing a hockey romance that nearly scorched my retinas." He blinked theatrically and added, "In a good way though."

Maxwell huffed a laugh, nudging Javi's side. "I still don't know how you got an invite to that club. I heard there's a wait list."

Blowing a breath on his hand, Javi made a show of polishing his knuckles on his uniform shirt. "I'm well connected, Maxwell."

"You're something," she pestered, sticking out her tongue.

Lola adjusted her bag, eyes dancing around their group. "A book club? That would be a great way to meet people." She shrugged and added, "I'd love to meet some new friends." She focused on Javi and asked, "Do you think you could get me an invite? Just to get the vibe?"

"Yes, absolutely!" Javi readily agreed. "I'll email you the details."

Maxwell poked Javi in the side. "You might as well get seats for Smithy and me. I want in."

Javi gasped, rubbing the spot and inching further away from Maxwell. "Ow, fine. I'll talk to Ms. Daisy."

Maxwell beamed. "Perfect! I can't wait."

Malcolm did not share his partner's enthusiasm. Plus, it was obvious Javi didn't want anyone else to join his outing with Lola. "I don't know, with my parents visiting, it might not be worth it."

Lola frowned. "Oh, that's too bad."

Javier's eyes darted back and forth between them, brow knitted in concentration. "Smithy will be there. I'll drive."

Maxwell draped an arm around Malcolm, anchoring him to her side. He wasn't sure if she'd noticed he was fading fast, or if it was moral support for these new plans. "I can always pick up Smithy. Let's make this happen."

Lola smiled at Malcolm, a warm expression that made her eyes sparkle. Malcolm returned the gesture, hoping he didn't look as drained as he felt. Between his recovery and missing Jessie, he was as wrung out as a sponge on engine washing day. And not for nothing, he didn't want to get involved with a woman who his buddy was clearly into. Bro code mattered.

"It was nice meeting you," Lola said.

"I'll email you," Javi promised, still drooling like a dog waiting on a treat.

Without another word, Lola waved goodbye and made her exit.

Javi watched her walk away, eyes nearly bugging out of his skull. "I'm a goner. That woman is incredible."

"Then maybe you two should go to book club on your own," Malcolm suggested, bone tired after being on his feet and out with people.

Javi scoffed. "Smithy, I need a wingman. My A-game did not make an appearance up there." He clasped his hands in front of him. "Please? You don't even have to read the book." Malcolm stalled, taking too long to form the perfect excuse. Javi continued his plea, "I'll have you home in time for *Wheel of Fortune*. It'll be like you never left your house."

Malcolm winced, not because he didn't like the game show but because it was accurate. Now that Jessie and he were ... whatever they were ... he knew his evenings were going to be lame as hell until his parents went back to Tennessee.

"Fine, but I might take up Maxwell on the offer of a ride."

Javi clapped Malcolm on the back, nearly knocking his cane to the floor. "You're the freaking best, Smithy."

"Yeah, yeah. You can show your thanks by getting me a ride home. I'm beat."

Maxwell checked her smartwatch. "I'm off in ten. Pop a squat, and I'll drop you off on my way to daycare pickup."

Javi pulled Maxwell into a quick hug. "That's perfect. I need to call Ms. Daisy and tell her about the updates to book club."

Both Malcolm and Maxwell snorted. "I can't believe you're taking this so seriously. Since when do you even read?"

"Javier can read," he said in a robotic tone. "Plus, these books are amazing. I didn't know what a book boyfriend was until Ms. Daisy showed me the light, and now I can't live without these guys." He made a heart gesture with his hands and nearly swooned like a Southern Belle. "These books are romantic and sexy, but you fall in love with the characters. You can relate to their heartbreak."

Maxwell bounced on her feet. "I'm actually really excited. An invite to a book club and the chance to watch Javi get tongue-tied around a girl? Yes, please!"

Malcolm shuffled toward Maxwell's desk, eager to get home. Hopefully this book would distract him from thoughts of Jessie—or it would drive him batty. Either way, he welcomed more distractions. Being at work had helped. Hell, watching Javi flounder with Lola worked wonders. Jessie wasn't far from his mind though, and he missed her. The missing her wasn't new, but knowing she was in town and could possibly show up hit him differently. Relaxing felt impossible when Jessie was breathing the same peach-scented air.

He envied Javi and his ability to play the field and date freely. Even when single, Malcolm never could commit to that lifestyle. Right now all he could commit to was his PT regimen. The trouble was, there weren't any exercises to fix his broken heart.

LIBBY KAY

CHAPTER SIXTEEN

Jessie lounged on the couch, the TV playing the third episode of *Law and Order* in a row. She'd seen this one, and the two before it, but she didn't care. Ever since Malcolm gave her the boot and Noel called, she'd fallen into emotional quicksand; listless and confused. Nothing excited her, not even the Hummingbird cake her mother made that afternoon. Although she did her level best to find enjoyment in the treat, having scarfed down half of it in thirty minutes … a choice she'd regret tomorrow.

Daisy emerged from her room dressed in a peach sundress. She'd done her makeup and nearly looked ready for church. "Where you off to all dolled up, Momma? Is the chief taking you out?"

Her mother walked over and nudged Jessie with her elbow. "No, not tonight. I'm meeting Kim and Javi to go over the plan for next week's Romance Book Club."

"That's nice," Jessie said, not really paying attention.

Daisy fixed an earring, frowning at the TV. "You're more than welcome to join us tonight, especially since you'll be attending the meeting."

Jessie rolled her eyes. "Momma, I'm not in the mood to be social. And from what Trev said, those books are sexy. I don't need to sit around listening to you talk about sex."

Daisy thrust her hands on her hips, exacerbated by her daughter's antics. "Jessica June, don't be such a prude. You don't think I know what sex is? Who do you think brought you and Trevor into the world? The stork?"

Jessie made a gagging sound. "Thank you for confirming why I have no desire to attend this book club."

"You have a week to get over yourself. And, honestly, I don't care if you don't. I will not stand by and watch my only daughter wither away on the couch eating her weight in cake."

Jessie lifted a shoulder, completely undeterred. "It's good cake," she explained, a blob of frosting stuck to her cheek.

Daisy beamed at the compliment but soldiered on. "Look, you haven't really gone out much since you got back home, and I think it'd be nice. Let people see you."

"Why?" Jessie wrinkled her nose. The very last thing on this earth she wanted was to be seen in her hometown. Even when they meant well, folks had questions ... nosy questions she didn't have answers to.

Despite knowing Estelle would likely keep Malcolm locked up at home, she still feared seeing him out in the wild. Hell, she could roam the African deserts or South American rainforests without fear of predators or the elements, but the notion of seeing Malcolm out on the town crippled her. Anxiety coursed through her, and Jessie considered another slice of cake as a source of distraction.

"Because I'm your momma, and I said so." Daisy raised an eyebrow at her daughter. "You'll have fun. And besides, we're at The Pecan Pit. You love The Pecan Pit."

That statement was accurate. In fact, that dingy dive bar was one of the major reasons Jessie gained weight whenever she was back in town, Hummingbird cake notwithstanding. Yet for all the promise of crunchy nachos and greasy burgers, she didn't feel like pretending her world wasn't imploding. For as long as she could remember, her life was either the Peace Corps or Malcolm Smith. Neither option was on the table, and she was listless.

"I dunno." She huffed, rubbing Gus's belly. While she'd been lying prone on the couch, the hound dog had been dozing on the floor, eagerly snarfing up scraps of cake that fell from her plate.

"You do know, and you have ten minutes to look presentable. Why don't you put on one of your new outfits that Whitney found for you?" Her mother swept her hand through the air, as if the dress would materialize on Jessie's frame.

Jessie scrambled for any logical reason to stay home. "I didn't read the book, and I don't need to help plan your meetings."

"Hogwash," Daisy spat. "We aren't discussing the book yet; it's more logistics for the meeting. Javi said he's invited some new faces, and we want to mix it up a little." She chuckled and said, "Sugar, this is basically just another excuse to gossip and drink wine. Get dressed."

Unable to hold back the whiny tone, Jessie argued, "Momma, I don't want to read kissing books right now. I'm not feeling very romantic." *Although the mention of wine was certainly tempting …*

Daisy huffed, but rallied. "Fine, don't read the book. Much like bad sex, you can fake it if you need to." She was undeterred by the horrified expression on Jessie's face. Daisy held up her fingers and tallied the key points. "Boy meets girl, girl kisses boy, boy does something stupid, they fight, and then they get back together." She clapped her hands. "There, now you're ready for book club."

Jessie was dubious. "Momma, please." Deep down, she understood that if she told her mother the full truth of what was happening with her career and Malcolm, she'd be allowed to wallow in peace. But she wasn't ready to admit anything to anyone right now. Except maybe Gus. He never judged, unless food was involved.

"You have eight minutes to get ready. I'll meet you

outside."

Without waiting for another argument, Daisy strode forward and turned off the TV. She whistled for Gus and let him out the back door, leaving Jessie without options. "Looks like I'm going," she muttered.

Their drive to The Pecan Pit was filled with her mother giving her the details on a hockey romance that frankly sounded a little too NSFW for Jessie's comfort. Not that she'd judge anyone's reading tastes, but her mother's descriptions of a scene in a locker room had Jessie fanning her face.

After pulling into a parking spot, Jessie flung the door open and hopped out onto the gravel lot. The rocks crunched under her sneakers, and Jessie inhaled a deep breath of the balmy Georgia air. It smelled like a mix of bacon, pine, and juniper. It smelled of home.

"Daisy, Jessie!" Hurried footsteps caught up to them as Javi sprinted over. "Glad I'm not late, work got a little wild." He ran his fingers through his unruly hair. "Thanks for meeting with me. The fundraiser planning went well, but I, uh, kind of need some help."

Daisy frowned, giving Javi a quick sweep of her gaze. "Sugar, take a deep breath. I've never seen you so frazzled." Jessie couldn't disagree; the man was a walking bundle of nerves.

"Nah, I'm okay."

Jessie huffed. "Yeah right. What's the matter? Didn't the crew like your plans for a slutty calendar?"

"Good Lord!" Daisy gasped, covering her mouth with her hand. "Javier Ortiz, what are you planning? Need I remind you that my partner and son are members of Engine 33? I don't need to see anyone's fannies in print," she admonished the younger man.

Jessie was impressed. She'd known Javi for years and had never seen him turn this particular shade of violet. "No, Ms. Daisy. It's not like that, I swear!"

Daisy raised an eyebrow, still unconvinced. "Uh-huh."

Before Javi could share more of his grand calendar plan, another pair of book clubbers joined the fray. Whitney strode up with her boss Kim, who also happened to be her momma's best friend. "Whitney, sugar! You made it." Daisy's smile grew at the sight of her new BFF. Idly, Jessie wondered what her brother thought of his girlfriend and mother being so close. Knowing her brother, he probably didn't even mind.

"When Kim said there was an emergency book club planning meeting, I knew I needed the dirt." Whitney cocked her hip and stared down Javi. "What are you up to?"

Kim waved to the trio, looping her arm around Whitney's. "And more importantly, what are y'all doing outside? Buster texted our table is ready, and he brought out the good Riesling."

Buster was both the owner of The Pecan Pit and Kim's nephew. He was a gruff yet sweet-hearted man who doted on his aunt and her friends. Jessie planned on soaking up the attention, and at least two glasses of vino. It had been a hell of a week, and she wanted to continue to eat—and drink—her feelings.

As if sensing her current mood, Whitney saddled up to her side. "Hey, Jessie." She motioned to the dress Jessie had thrown on at the last minute, although she'd hardly styled it properly. Her worn Chuck Taylors had seen better days and probably wasn't what Whitney had in mind when she said to make the outfit her own. "You look lovely in this."

Jessie pulled out the skirt, the cotton fabric sliding across her fingers. "Yes, thanks. It's simultaneously comfortable and cute."

"Like you," Daisy teased, stepping forward and yanking open the door to the bar. "All right, folks, let's pop a cork and get planning."

Javi clapped, leading the way inside. Kim couldn't hold back her snicker as they watched Javi take his seat at the table, lining up glasses and pouring some Riesling for everyone.

"Before we plan our next meeting, did anyone read that new book about the alien abduction?" Kim panted, reaching for her wine. Buster appeared at her side, pecking her cheek before sliding a tray of nachos to the middle of the table.

Jessie greedily took a handful of chips, eager for a distraction and more carbs. "Thanks, Buster," she muttered.

Buster dipped his head once. "Y'all enjoy." Coming from the stoic bartender, that was tantamount to a late-night talk show monologue.

Javi helped himself to some nachos. "Ms. Kim, you know I don't like the little green men. It gives me the ick."

"Oh, you kids, get with the times! Half the romance books I read now take place in fantasy worlds or involve a character with a horn and extra appendages." Kim wiggled in her seat, making an odd punching motion with her arms.

That got Javi's attention, and he opened the Notes app on his phone. "Hang on now, what was the name of that book?" he asked, thumbs flying over the screen.

"What are you taking notes for?" Jessie asked, craning her neck to see what he wrote.

Javi nudged her away carefully with his elbow. "Jessie, please. This is research."

Jessie was incredulous. "Don't take this the wrong way, Javi, but couldn't you write this stuff? I've never known you to have trouble with the ladies."

Falling back in his chair, Javi tucked his phone in his jeans pocket. "I'm losing my mojo." He sighed, and Jessie would have made fun of him if he didn't look so damn sad.

"I'm sorry?" she asked, leaning closer to hear over the din of the dining room. Buster had a full house tonight, a combination of locals and tourists passing through Pinegrove.

Javi drained the last of his wine, slamming the glass on the tabletop with more force than was necessary. "I think I'm in love," he said, exhaling so forcefully his napkin blew to the floor.

Jessie scrunched her nose, certain she'd misheard him.

"You're what?"

"You heard me," he said on a sigh, expression sullen. "Her name is Lola, and she's gorgeous and smart and so perfect." He waved his hands around the table as the other ladies finished their conversation. "She's the reason we're all here now. I invited her to book club."

"So what's the problem?" Jessie asked, stealing a forgotten chip from Javi's plate.

"I don't know what's happening, but I completely fumbled around her. It was wild," he observed, blinking rapidly as he spoke. "It's like I wasn't Javi. I was some tongue-tied goober. As soon as she walked into the station for the presentation, I was braindead." He took a breath, quickly slugging back a third of his wine. "She's new to town and wants to meet people. She only agreed to go out with me since I'm bringing Smithy. Then Maxwell invited herself to tag along."

"She's into Malcolm?" Her voice sounded foreign to her own ears; her brain was unwilling to allow Malcolm a future that didn't involve her by his side. But that wasn't fair, and she knew it. The hell of it was, she was wild with jealousy nonetheless.

And how could he have found a woman in less than a day? Jessie had been at his place, taking care of him … kissing him for Pete's sake! He went to work once and already had a crush. Meanwhile, Jessie had spent her time at home eating her weight in sugar and catching up on cable television.

Javi lifted a shoulder, his attention back on his plate. He trailed his fork through a puddle of salsa. "I dunno, but she definitely wasn't that into me." Usually the life of the party, it was jarring to see the man down on his luck.

After wiping his hands on his lap, Javi gave up on eating. He pushed his plate away, frowning at the remains of his dinner like they broke his heart.

Suddenly this book club planning meeting was the last place she wanted to be. In less than five minutes, everyone agreed that Maxwell, Malcolm, and this Lola woman could attend if they wanted. That decided, her mother and Whitney started discussing their own happily ever after, which ordinarily would make Jessie beam with pride. But she couldn't shake the feeling that this time with Malcolm was different—this time he might be ready to move on for good.

"Do you think you could take me home?" Jessie asked, already pulling out her wallet to pay. She had no desire to extend the evening another moment. She wanted to go home, hide under a pile of blankets, and figure out her next move ... or at least cuddle with Gussy.

Javi snorted. "Jessie, no offense, but I'm not interested." He balled his fists and carefully banged on his temples. "I can't get Lola out of my head!" He lowered his voice and added, "Plus, you know Trev would gladly kick my ass if I ever touched you."

That brought Jessie out of her funk long enough to throw a coaster at Javi's face. It was damp from her glass and landed like a wobbly frisbee on his cheek before fluttering to the table. "You idiot," she spat, "I meant take me back home since I didn't drive here. Gross."

Javi barked out a laugh, looking more like himself for a moment. "Oh, sure."

The pair bid farewell to the group, Javi holding the door open for her as they stepped into the muggy air. Jessie threw her head back, looking up at the night sky, a cluster of fireflies flitting around them. Nights like this were why she loved Pinegrove so much. It was peaceful, quaint, and felt like living in a dream.

Javi dropped Jessie off in the driveway, the house still quiet and dark. Gus barked, alerting Jessie that her dawdling could result in a mess to clean up.

"You need anything?" Javi asked, sticking his head out the driver's side window. It could have been his Southern charm or her anxious posture, but he didn't seem ready to leave her alone.

Jessie pursed her lips in what she hoped looked like a smile and not her swallowing her own tongue. "Nope. I'll take care of Gus and call it a night."

Javi shot her a thumbs-up, waiting until she unlocked before reversing toward home. No sooner had she opened the door did Gus push past her to mark his territory on the nearest shrub. She trusted the hound dog wouldn't run off, but she knew she had to stay close. Jessie stared up at the night sky, gaze unfocused as she blinked up at the stars.

Her ring finger remained bare, her promise ring from Malcolm still tucked safely in her wallet. It was a habit she'd started during their off times as a way to keep him close. That ring was sometimes all she had of Malcolm, regardless of the promises they'd broken over the years. Much like the ring, she couldn't stargaze and not think of him.

Was he looking at the stars tonight? Was he missing her as much as she missed him?

Gus finished his business and lumbered back into the house. From the kitchen, the clanging of his water dish echoed outside. Jessie chuckled, appreciating the distraction from her spiraling thoughts. "I'm coming, Gussy," she shouted, stepping away and closing the door on the stars.

She could only hope that, much like cycles of the moon, she and Malcolm could get in sync.

LIBBY KAY

CHAPTER SEVENTEEN

Day one without Jessie around went surprisingly well, if Malcolm said so himself.

Estelle had been called by her agent with rumors of an *Atlanta Hearts* reunion special, and he wanted to gauge her interest. Unsurprising to either of the Smith men, she was *very* interested—like embarrassingly so.

"They might not even want me back, you know?" Estelle had huffed and puffed as she paced around his house. "I'm so old now, practically a dinosaur." She patted down her frame as if inventorying everything that had aged, shifted, and sagged since the show went on hiatus.

"Darling, your agent wouldn't call if they weren't interested." Craig had looped his arm around her waist and planted a kiss on her cheek, adding, "And who are you calling a dinosaur?"

"Oh, Craig," she'd cooed, melting into his embrace and not panicking for ten whole minutes. Her two moods of the day were anxious over her career and anxious over her son. Fortunately for Malcolm, her career concerns took the brunt of her focus.

After lunch, when his nurse visit and PT exercises were complete, Malcolm and his dad sat out on the deck while

Estelle doom scrolled through social media, desperate for updates and public comment on anything *Atlanta Hearts* related.

Malcolm had managed to keep Jessie from his mind for a few hours when his dad asked, "You hear from Jessie today? Everything okay at her mom's place?"

"Can we not do this?" Malcolm sighed. He would rather sit through another Estelle Winters meltdown than tiptoe around feelings with his old man. Pushing himself off the lounge chair, he shuffled over to the railing and peered out into the pine trees. For a few minutes, his father let him ruminate.

"Have a seat," his father instructed, his tone leaving no room for argument. He dragged the lounger closer so all Malcolm had to do was plop down. "Oh boy," Malcolm muttered. His father crossed his arms, the furrow in his brow on full display.

When Malcolm was a kid, he could always tell how stressed or upset his father was based on how many lines creased his face. The first time Estelle had lost her daytime Emmy, those lines threatened to take over Craig's entire person. Then there was the time Malcolm had his first accident on the job. Granted, it had been minor, but his father had aged a decade when he saw Malcolm covered in gauze and burn salve.

Now though, these worry lines felt different. They felt weather-worn and tired—much like Malcolm's heart. "Spill it, Dad. In addition to a lower pain tolerance, I have very little patience."

Craig thrust his hands on his hips, his feet shoulder-width apart. "Easy now," he said, although his lips quirked with a smile. "I wanted to make sure you're doing okay."

Malcolm toyed with the handles of his walker, pushing the blasted device back and forth in front of him. "Peachy keen."

"This," his father said, pointing at the walker, "is temporary. But this," he said, pointing to his own chest, "is a more serious issue."

Another worry line appeared, and Malcolm had to look away. "We don't have to have this conversation."

Craig took a step closer, moving the walker aside so he could sit down next to his son. The chair creaked in protest, and Malcolm had to steady himself. "I won't pretend to be an expert on love or," he hesitated, flapping his hand in the air like love was all around them, "feelings. But I know that whatever you and Jessica have can be fixed. You two need to talk it out."

Malcolm's stomach roiled, the thought of rehashing his horrible love life with his father too much to bear. "I don't know. I feel like we've been talking it out forever. Maybe we're not meant to be together?" He asked it as a question, but Malcolm knew the truth. He and JJ were done, and he'd made the right decision. Much like his broken body, he needed to take care of his heart.

"Oh," Craig said, voice low and sad. "Then don't listen to me." He rested his hands on his knees, taking a moment to study his cuticles before offering more fatherly advice. "Just in case there's a sliver of hope, let me give you some advice."

Not wanting to be rude, Malcolm simply nodded, focusing on the fact that his father still cared about him to say his piece. He understood how much both Trevor and JJ mourned their daddy, and he wouldn't take these moments for granted. "Yeah?" he asked, voice barely a whisper.

"If you love someone," his father started, clearing his throat, "you need to love them with your whole heart. They should love you in return with such force that it knocks the wind out of your lungs. You might not always agree on things, but you should always crave the other. It's more than chemistry. Once you find that connection, you need to nurture it." For a moment, Craig's eyes lit up as he discussed love, and Malcolm barely recognized his stoic old man.

Malcolm playfully nudged his father's side, striving to lighten the mood. "Like you and Mom?"

Craig raised a hand and waffled it back and forth. "Well, yes and no. Estelle and I make no sense on paper. She's an extroverted actress who loves the attention." He pinched the bridge of his nose, chuckling softly. "I think we have a prime example of that happening right now." Malcolm couldn't hold back his own laughter. "While I'd rather work on planning cities and bridge expansions from the quiet of my office. Yet we balance each other out and complement each other. At the end of the day, I know your mother has my back, and she knows that I have hers."

"You make it sound so simple," Malcolm moaned. "This isn't Mom worrying about a part or your job moving you to Tennessee. JJ and I are complicated."

That got a true smile. "You can say that again, son. But be real. Have you seen your mother and me? It's hardly easy, but the effort is worth it. I can't imagine not having your mother in my life, and I have a feeling that's how you feel about JJ." He paused a moment, rubbing his hands together as he collected the rest of his wisdom. "And considering she flew halfway around the world to be at your bedside, then I'd say there's something to salvage."

Malcolm let his father's words wash over him, praying they'd buoy his hope at a reconciliation. But the sensation was fleeting, as reality hit him like a tidal wave. "She wants to leave Pinegrove, Dad. She has plans for a promotion, you heard her. JJ's done with Pinegrove."

Craig stood at the admission, his gaze not quite meeting Malcolm's. "Well, if that's the case, you have your answer. But there's something else you need to consider."

"What's that?" Malcolm was skeptical at best.

"Maybe you need to find out why Jessica is so hell-bent on leaving. What is keeping her away from here, from you? If you get to the bottom of that quagmire, you might have some answers and a path forward."

Sighing, Malcolm pressed the heels of his hands into his eyes, willing the tears not to fall. "And what happens if our paths don't go in the same direction?"

After walking to the screen door, Craig pulled it open slightly and sucked on his teeth. "Then at least you have your answer, and you can move forward."

Before Malcolm could absorb his dad's advice, Estelle swept onto the patio. "There you boys are!" She closed the distance and carefully hugged him, her Chanel No. 5 making him cough. "I think today we need to clean your wounds, but I wanted to see what you wanted for dinner." And with that, Malcolm fell back into the role of needy patient.

Estelle smoothed down the front of her shirt, pulling herself back to rights after cooking supper. "I was thinking about going to the farmer's market tomorrow."

Craig tossed the dirty placemats into the basket, narrowly avoiding toppling Malcolm's cup to the floor. "Is this the farmer's market on that old farm?" He nudged Malcolm carefully with his elbow. "You know what I mean? You used to go there with Jessie all the time."

Malcolm's dinner turned to cement in his gut, the sweet tea he'd finished threatening to revisit. "Hog Hollow?" he asked, voice tense.

Snapping her fingers, Estelle beamed. "That's the one. I thought it might be nice to buy some produce so I can make more salads." She turned her full attention on Malcolm, who squirmed uncomfortably. "You boys ate all the beets." Craig paled, and Malcolm crunched down on an ice cube.

"I'm happy to drive you, darling," Craig offered. "Son, if you're not feeling up for the trip, you can rest at home." Lowering his voice, he suggested, "You might even like the hour or two alone."

The last thing Malcolm wanted to do was walk—or in his case hobble—down memory lane. "I dunno," he muttered, suddenly very interested in the edges of his bandages. "That might be nice, a few hours alone."

Estelle brought her hand to her heart and frowned. "Will you be all right by yourself?"

Craig topped off Malcolm's glass of tea and patted Estelle's shoulder. "We'll wrap the boy in bubble wrap before we leave. He can't get into that much trouble."

Their planning was interrupted by the doorbell, and Malcolm's traitorous heart leapt at the thought that Jessie was mere feet away.

"I'll get it," Estelle announced, plodding over to the door in her slippers. A moment later, her squeal alerted the Smith men that it wasn't Jessie, but rather her new favorite person. "Oh, Javi, you're too kind. I happen to have some leftovers if you're hungry."

Malcolm scowled. He'd been looking forward to eating those leftovers later.

Javi strode into the kitchen wearing a shit-eating grin. "Hey, Smithy," he greeted, shaking Craig's hand before offering Malcolm a fist to bump. "Thought I'd swing by after work and make sure you're still living the dream."

Both his parents took the hint. Estelle portioned out some stew, while Craig poured him a glass of tea. He put everything on a tray and handed it to Javi. "Why don't you boys go out onto the deck? It's such a nice night."

"Thanks, Dad," Malcolm said, taking his cane instead of his walker. "C'mon, free loader."

Javi snorted, but he didn't disagree, clutching his meal close. The pair set up on the deck, Javi somehow finding a beer along the way. Malcolm asked how the day had gone at work, envious that he missed the arrival of some new equipment.

When he was finished eating, Javi stared down at his beer bottle, lips dipped down in a scowl. "Either you're really upset over the new axes, or something else is bugging you," Malcolm observed, hating that his buddy wasn't his usual jovial self. "What's up?"

Javi ran a hand down his face, muttering under his breath. "I can't explain it, man. You ever meet a girl and you feel that *zing*? Like an electrical charge or some shit?" He made explosion sounds and waved a hand in the air. "It's like that with Lola. I get, like, overwhelmed when she's around—or I'm even just thinking about her. It took me forty-five minutes to write an email to her this morning. I mean it—nearly a freaking hour to basically say hello."

Pursing his lips to smother a smile, Malcolm nodded. Unfortunately for him, he was very well acquainted with that electricity. It burned him every time he was with Jessie. "Uh, yeah. I'm familiar with the zing."

Javi's frown morphed into a sad smile. "I need your help."

"With Lola?" Malcolm blinked, unsure what he was supposed to do … other than stay the hell away from her. "How can I help?"

After draining the last of his beer, Javi placed the bottle on the deck. He swapped booze for his supper and shoveled in a few bites before continuing. "She's going to come to book club, and I need you to be my wingman. It's obvious she's into you, but I need you to be less charming and attractive." Javi held up a hand and said, "And don't be so nice and agreeable. It's hard to compete with you, but especially since you're rocking that whole 'fallen hero' vibe."

Malcolm was incredulous, motioning toward his air cast and fading bruises. "Oh yeah, the ladies are clamoring for this."

Javi playfully shoved Malcolm's good shoulder. "Dude, don't even. You saw how I was with Lola. I need help." There had been countless nights out in Pinegrove with Trevor, Javi, and himself, and Malcolm had never—not once—seen Javier flounder and fumble. He was always Mr. Cool, approaching any woman with the confidence of ten men.

"Javi, you've never needed a wingman. If you're this concerned, maybe Lola isn't the girl for you."

"Pfft, have you seen her? Malcolm, she's perfect for me." Javi let out a long groan, as if rejection was causing him physical pain.

"She's definitely your type." Although that was a

pointless observation. A vast majority of women between the ages of twenty and sixty-five were Javi's type. "So how can I help?"

For the first time since they came outside, Javi smiled. "Can you make sure I'm on my game? Maybe talk me up with Lola, see if Maxwell can stop bad-mouthing my driving skills and dating history? I want to look perfect."

Malcolm reared back in his seat. "Geez, man, I've never seen you like this."

"I've never felt like this!" Javi jumped to his feet, pacing back and forth across the deck. "I don't know why, but I really like Lola. Please, can you help? Jessie said she'll talk me up, too, so if Maxwell lets me down, I still have the female perspective."

"Jessie's going to be there?"

Javi's spiral paused long enough to register the fear in Malcolm's eyes. "Yeah? Why wouldn't she be? Her momma is the group leader, and, frankly, she's moping around town like someone stole her puppy." He snorted and said, "Which isn't true, because I saw Gus when I dropped her home last night."

Malcolm was on alert. "Why were you taking Jessie home last night?" Never would he think anything would happen between the two, but Malcolm hated having no contact with Jessie.

"Good Lord!" Javi threw his hands in the air. "Calm down, we went out with Whitney, Ms. Kim, and Ms. Daisy. If I knew you wanted to join the fun, I would have picked you up."

"What did Jessie say?"

Javi screwed up his nose. "About what? We're not chicks. She seemed a little off and asked for a ride home early. I wasn't exactly feeling like being social, so I dropped her off and went home to drown my sorrows in a tube of cookie dough." He flinched and admitted, "Maybe I am turning into a chick?" He tugged on the ends of his hair before rallying. "Will you help me?"

Malcolm relented. "Fine, fine. Only if you chill the hell out. I'm exhausted enough without watching you spiral. If I wanted that type of theatrics, I'd go talk to Mom about the potential *Atlanta Hearts* reunion."

"That's really happening?" And with that, Javi sprinted toward the house. "Estelle, is it true that—" His question cut off when the patio door slid shut.

Malcolm could have focused on any part of his conversation with Javi, but he couldn't let go of the little morsel that Jessie wasn't handling their breakup … if you could even call it that … well.

That shouldn't make Malcolm happy, but it did.

Parents and Javi distracted, Malcolm let his eyes go unfocused as he stared up at the stars. A streak of light dashed across the sky, and Malcolm made a wish.

He didn't ask for a speedy recovery, or even anything related to his friends and family. Nope, he was a simp and wished that Jessie was across town, head tilted toward the heavens, missing him as much as he missed her.

LIBBY KAY

CHAPTER EIGHTEEN

"Sugar," Daisy said over her shoulder, adding a spoonful of sweetener to her coffee. Jessie knew this tone. It was the tone her mother preferred when she was going to deliver bad news, or ask a question Jessie didn't have an answer to.

Jessie squared her shoulders, heaving a forkful of hotcakes in her mouth to stall for time. "Yesh?" she asked, her cheeks plumping like a chipmunk.

Daisy grimaced but rallied quickly. "Table manners are still a thing in Pinegrove," she said.

Ever the dutiful daughter, Jessie wiped her mouth with her napkin and stifled an eyeroll. "Yes, ma'am?"

Daisy smirked. "What I was going to ask," she said, dabbing at her lips. She took a moment to fold the napkin and place it on the table next to her empty plate. Jessie's pulse kicked up at the measured movements. "Did something happen with your job?"

Jessie's fork paused halfway to her mouth, a piece of pancake flopping back onto her plate with the saddest sound. Gus perked up, sauntering over and curling up at Jessie's feet, ready for a fallen treat. "What do you mean?"

Daisy arched an eyebrow. "That answers my question."

"No, it doesn't!" Jessie was too eager to correct herself,

but her mother saw through her like her favorite lace curtains.

"Jessica June, please. Not only am I your mother, but I ain't blind. You're usually on the phone or emailing until your fingers bleed to get back to your next assignment. Now Malcolm is settled and you should be halfway around the planet by now." She held up a hand to stop Jessie's interruption. "Obviously I don't want you to go anywhere, sugar, but something is up."

Jessie picked up a piece of bacon, tearing off half of it before tossing the rest to Gus, who woofed his appreciation before snarfing the treat down in one bite. "I don't want you to make this a whole thing," she started, willing her nerves to take a hike. "I, um, don't have a job right now."

To her credit, Daisy hardly reacted. She blinked a few times, the vein in her temple throbbing. "You don't have a job?"

Jessie scrubbed a hand down her face, her breakfast forgotten. "I spoke with Noel the other day, and that promotion I told you about fell through." She flapped a hand in the air, saying, "Budget cuts and such. I can apply for another placement elsewhere, at my level, but honestly ..." The truth tickled her tongue, begging to be released. "I don't think I want to go back."

Any restraint Daisy had melted faster than a pat of butter in a cast-iron pan. Her eyes welled, her smile grew, and she clasped her hands in front of her in prayer. "Lordy be, sugar. I never thought this day would come."

"I don't know what I'm going to do, Momma. This is hardly a time to celebrate. I'm nearing thirty, unemployed, single, and kind of broke."

Daisy jumped to her feet, retrieving her cell phone and a pad of paper from the counter. "I've got an idea," she said as she started clicking away and jotting down notes. Her mother's hand flew across the screen.

Jessie craned her neck to see what she was doing, but Daisy swatted her away. "What are you up to?"

"Hang on a second, I want to confirm something before I make any promises." Daisy squinted for another moment before adding a few more notes to the pad. She wrapped her knuckles on the table, clearly pleased with whatever she'd found.

"Anyway. I have a plan, or at least the beginnings of a plan." Daisy began collecting their dirty dishes, a silent invitation for Jessie to join her at the sink.

Jessie drained the last of her orange juice, wishing there had been a shot of vodka in it. "And I'm assuming I'm going to love this plan?" She followed her mother to the sink, already rolling up her sleeves. She pulled a tea towel from the hook on the wall and helped dry the dishes. Truthfully, Jessie loved this old routine. From as long as she could remember, this had been a bonding chore for the Mays women. While her father would show Trevor how to mow the lawn or trim the hedges, she and her mother would do the dishes, staring out through the picture window at the sun or the stars. There was something about not facing each other while talking and having their hands busy that allowed for honest conversations that didn't take as much of an emotional toll.

Her mother handed her a plate to dry. "Now I'm not saying my plan will make you a millionaire." She laughed to herself. "But I think I have the perfect job for you."

Jessie snorted. "Geez, Momma. I'm back home a few days and already you've solved all my problems." *Except for Malcolm, but a girl couldn't expect everything.*

Daisy sighed. "Hush up, I can't solve all your problems."

Unable to handle the suspense another moment, Jessie asked, "What do you have in mind?" Jessie's brain spun with potential suggestions.

Sell a kidney? Work with Whitney? Sell her other kidney?

"The Hansons need some help on the farm, and I thought you could swing by this afternoon."

"The Hanson farm? As in Hog Hollow?" A million and one memories with Malcolm rocked her back on her heels, knocking the air from her lungs. "What on earth do I know about farming?" Even as she asked, Jessie knew it was a useless question. Over her tenure with the Peace Corps, she'd learned a lot about farming. Hell, she was damn-near an expert on certain agricultural practices.

Daisy's grip loosened as a bowl clattered into the sink. "Heaven's above, I'm sure they have a training program. But I thought you'd like it. You said you were working on some farms out there." Her mother flipped her hand toward the window, as if Costa Rica was on the other side of Main Street.

Jessie chewed on the inside of her cheek. The Hanson farm, specifically Hog Hollow, held some of her favorite memories of not only her childhood, but her times with Malcolm. The meadows should probably be named in their honor for all the times they lay out stargazing ... and doing other things she wouldn't admit to her momma.

Daisy wiped down the counter and crossed her arms over her chest. "Sugar, listen. I won't pretend to know what you want to do. But you know what I do know?"

Now Jessie was intrigued. "No, what?"

"You aren't meant for a traditional job. No desks, no cubicles, nothing like that. You're good with your hands, you like working outdoors, and you love a challenge. Why not go over to the farm and see what they have available? The season's not done yet."

A smile tugged at Jessie's lips. "Those are all actually good reasons."

"Thank you. You know, I am due a victory." She winked and whistled for Gus. "While you're over there, why not pick up a few things for dinner?"

Jessie snickered. "So this trip has multiple purposes?"

Daisy pulled Gus's leash off the hook by the back door and tossed it to Jessie. "Technically, there's three reasons. You need a job, I'd like some tomatoes, and Gussy needs a W-A-L-K."

Not about to argue, Jessie bent down to clip on the leash.

Gus was already very excited for this plan and practically knocked Jessie to the floor. "What are you going to do while I'm running errands and filling out job applications?"

Plopping down on the couch, Daisy opened up a romance book and laughed. "Oh, I've got a full day planned. I need to finish this book and meet Paul for lunch. I'll be busy until dinner time."

Jessie schooled her features, always charmed by her mother's shenanigans. "Tell the chief I said hi."

"You can tell him yourself over dinner tonight. He'll be joining us, Trevor and Whitney too if I can swing it."

Jessie found a tote bag for the groceries and slapped a ballcap over her bedhead. She knew she should try harder since employment was involved, but she also thought there wasn't much point in fussing. If she got a job on the farm, she'd be no more dressed up than she was right now.

"Sounds good. See you later."

"Good luck, sugar!" Daisy said behind the cover of her latest book, which didn't fool Jessie. After their book club discussion, she knew that cutesy cover didn't change the fact that something smutty was going on. Oh well, at least it made her momma happy.

Enjoying the walk, Jessie steered Gus toward a walking trail that cut through the neighborhood and headed toward the outskirts of Pinegrove. When she'd meet Malcolm there in high school, she'd ridden her bike through these trails. By foot it would take her and the hound about thirty minutes, but she wasn't in a hurry.

With every step she took, Jessie thought about everything that was up in the air with her life. If this little sojourn led to meaningful employment, Jessie was all for it. This was the first time she'd have a choice to make that didn't involve a plane ride or leaving her friends and family behind. Yet for as much as she was excited to try something new, she feared that getting a job in Pinegrove was pointless if Malcolm wasn't her other half.

Was staying for a man who wasn't interested a fool's

errand? And if so, did Jessie really care?

Gus pulled on the leash as they approached the entrance to the farm. "All right, calm down, you crazy hound," she chastised Gus as he sniffed a questionable pile of dirt.

The Pinegrove Farmer's Market was held at the edge of the Hog Hollow farm. It was a farm and petting zoo that kept the locals fed and children entertained. Their petting zoo boasted some of the cutest animals this side of the Mississippi, especially their pigs. Jessie always had a soft spot for their curly tails and wide eyes.

They strode into the chaos, Gus's snout down and inhaling all the new and strange aromas of the farm. Jessie surveyed the crowd, seeing a lot of familiar faces but also some new ones. There were the standard vendors from the local farms and gardens selling everything from sunflowers and roses to jams and greens. A few tents even offered baked goods and doggie treats.

"Well, isn't this a small world?" a familiar voice asked behind her.

Spinning on her heel, she came face-to-face with Estelle. Her blonde hair was tucked into a straw hat, her lips painted a shade of purple that did not appear in nature.

"Hiya." Jessie's greeting felt lame, even to her own ears, but she raised a hand anyway. "Is, uh ..." She couldn't help it; her eyes scanned around Estelle for signs of Malcolm.

"Goodness, honey, my fool son isn't here."

Jessie's cheeks turned the same shade of violet as Estelle's lips as she stammered. "O-oh, n-no. I mean—" but her statement was cut short when Craig joined them. He wore a lavender shirt that almost matched his wife's makeup—something Jessie assumed wasn't a coincidence. His stern expression morphed into a grin when he saw her and Gus.

"Jessie, always a pleasure." She'd always liked Malcolm's parents, which made this tense interaction even worse.

Before Jessie could reply, Estelle pulled her into a hug. Jessie was assaulted by the aroma of Estelle's expensive department store perfume. She smelled like a mix of magnolias and apples. "I'm so glad to see you, honey. You've certainly been missed."

"Well, you know. My nursing skills are no longer required." She tried to smile, but it looked more like the grimace of someone sucking a lemon.

As if sensing her discomfort, Gus barked at a passing poodle. Craig chuckled, a deep laugh so reminiscent of his son that Jessie had to swallow a sob. "That dog is still a menace, I see."

"More of a goober than a menace," Jessie corrected. "But I should get what I need for Momma before Gus makes a scene."

Estelle frowned. "Will you stop by this week for supper?" She pouted, her purple lip jutting out at an alarming angle.

Craig linked his arm through his wife's and tugged her toward one of the bakery booths. "Let the poor girl go, Estelle. She has bigger things to do than hang out with us old folks."

"I beg your pardon!" Estelle thwacked her husband in the chest before splaying her hand over her heart. "I am not an old person. I'll have you know that *The View* said sixty is the new forty."

Craig cleared his throat and muttered, "If you say so," before his wife could react. "Jessie, excuse the bum's rush, but I'm desperate to get home and out of this heat. Plus, Malcolm is home alone."

"He's alone?" Jessie was incredulous. She was sure he was still making a fine recovery, but she couldn't help but worry.

"Just while we've been running errands. I believe he was going to check in with Javi on that calendar thing again." He paused his explanation to wave at someone passing by. "Anyway, hopefully we'll see you again soon. Send our best to Daisy." Craig steered Estelle toward the exit. She didn't miss how he winced at the tote bag brimming with beets hanging from his wife's elbow.

"Of course." Jessie smiled, but her heart wasn't in it. She loved these two, nearly as much as her own parents.

"Don't be a stranger!" Estelle begged as her husband tugged her back into the crowds.

Once they were out of sight, Jessie and Gus wandered out toward the barns. She needed to get things for her mother, but right now she needed the space to think and wrangle her feelings. Not since her father passed had she dealt with such a tangle of emotions.

Saying she missed Malcolm was a gross understatement. She wanted to hold his hand and trapse with him through town, through this market, anywhere he'd take her. She wanted countless nights of stargazing, days of laughter, and tender moments that stole her breath. She just wanted *him* …

Yet, here she stood. With Gus, the hound sniffing around her like he'd won the lottery. In his ten years on this planet, she'd rarely seen his tail move so fast. In the far end of the barn, she heard a snuffling sound. Holding firm to Gus's leash, Jessie strode further inside.

"Hello?" she called out, like one of the animals would answer her.

In the last pen, she stumbled upon a stall with a pig the size of a small golf cart. He was pink with black patches, his nose buried deep in a slop bucket. His belly was nestled in the dirt, his tail was as curly as an Arby's French fry. "Aren't you the sweetest thing?" she asked, bending her knee to lean in for a closer look.

With a tentative hand, she patted the pig's rump. "You might be the cutest pig I've ever seen."

At her praise, the pig lifted his head and met her gaze. One of his ears was bent, giving him an adorable lopsided appearance. Gus barked once, but the pig didn't seem to care. His eyes gazed back at her, little black orbs that gleamed in the dim light.

"I'm sorry, but the petting zoo isn't open for tours

today," a woman's voice echoed from the entrance.

Jessie whirled around, covering her heart with her hand. "I'm so sorry. I needed a break from those crowds." Raising her hand, she flapped it in the general direction of the market. "We'll leave. I didn't mean to trespass."

The older woman's head fell back as she laughed. She was clad in denim overalls, her graying hair pulled back in a bun. "Trespass? Calm down, child. I meant we weren't doing full tours today. That's about all this old hog is good for." Gesturing to the pig, he snorted before dipping his head back into his slop.

"He's adorable," Jessie said, watching his curly tail bounce as he inhaled his food.

"Who? Oinks? He's a mess, but he's our mess." The woman smiled fondly.

"Oinks?" Jessie's heart melted at the name. "I think I'm in love, what a great name!"

The older woman shoved her hands in her pockets, raising an eyebrow. "You look familiar." She took a step closer, her boots squelching in the mud. "Have we met?"

Now it was Jessie's turn to snort. "Probably. I'm Jessie Mays, Nick and Daisy's daughter." She waved, and Gus took the opportunity to mark his territory on a fence post. "And this rude fellow is Gus."

"I thought you had to be a Mays," the other woman said. She closed the distance between them and reached out to shake hands. "Gladys Hanson, owner of Hog Hollow. I haven't seen you in an age. I think the last time I saw you, you were knee-high to a grasshopper."

Jessie shrugged. "It's still a great space. I remember coming out here with my parents," her voice cracked slightly at the thought of her daddy, but Jessie was proud of herself for not bawling. *She'd also trespassed with Malcolm, but she wasn't going to admit that now …*

"It used to be." Gladys huffed. She rocked back, gaze drifting out the window toward the crowds. "I hate to say it, Jessie, but this farm is getting away from us. My husband,

Richard, and I can't handle some of the chores like we used to. I fear the place is starting to show it."

Jessie looked around her, taking in the stalls that needed a little cleaning, but otherwise not seeing an issue. "What's the matter with the farm?"

Gladys laughed. "Nothing really, but we're letting some things slide that I wish we had the energy for." She gestured toward Oinks and sighed. "Take this guy, for example. He should probably be a slab of bacon by now, but Richard and I don't have the energy or heart to move him off with the other swine."

Jessie's knees practically buckled at the mention of Oinks becoming her morning sausage. "No! You can't kill Oinks! Look at him." She hitched a thumb over her shoulder. "He's adorable."

Gladys really laughed now. "I won't argue with that logic, Jessie, but this is a business. We can't keep up with everything, and I think instead of offering the petting zoo, perhaps it's time to close up shop. We can butcher our lot and sell the place." She clasped her hands in front of her, gaze unfocused in the distance. "I've reached out to some friends in town, you know, to see if we could find qualified help."

Jessie bit back a smile, understanding Daisy's covert note-taking. "I'm guessing my momma heard about this," she offered.

Gladys giggled. "Oh, Daisy, she knows everything."

No argument here …

Despite only being back on the property for an hour, Jessie couldn't stand the thought of losing the place. The rolling hills, the adorable animals, it all combined to make a space that was too important for Pinegrove to lose. Where would the future generations of stargazers go if the meadow was turned into a housing development?

"Gladys, I'm going to be straight with you," Jessie said, licking her lips. "I came here for two reasons." She paused, jostling her tote bag that brimmed with tomatoes and peppers. "I came for vegetables, and to see if you had any job openings."

Gladys merely blinked at Jessie, jaw unhinged. "You ...you came here for a job?"

Holding up a hand, Jessie backpedaled. "I don't want to make assumptions that you're interested in interviewing me. I'm home for a while," she couldn't bring herself to admit it could be forever, "and, frankly, I need a job that doesn't require me to sit behind a desk all day. I've been working in the Peace Corps for nearly a decade, including some agriculture work, and I'd like to lend a hand if you have the need."

Again, all Gladys could do was blink. Jessie was starting to fear she'd stunned the poor woman into a catatonic state. "Miss Gladys? I know it's insane, me just wandering into your barn and asking for a job, but I want to help. I think I'd be good at it."

"You're hired!" Gladys practically shouted in Jessie's face.

Now it was Jessie's turn to blink. "I'm sorry?"

"I don't know what we have to pay you, but we can figure that out. If you're willing to work, Richard and I can find the scratch." Gladys wiped her hand on her overalls before thrusting it toward Jessie. "You're hired."

Jessie glanced down at Gus, just to see what he thought of this insane idea. Unfortunately, she'd have to get a second opinion elsewhere. The basset hound was asleep at her feet, his ears splayed out in the dirt.

Oinks made a snorting sound and knocked his slop bucket over with his nose. He looked up at Jessie, and she could swear he smiled at her. "One condition," she wagered, meeting the other woman's eye. "Oinks doesn't make it to the meat market."

Gladys chuckled. "You've got yourself a deal, Jessie. Welcome aboard!"

And with that, Jessie shook Gladys's hand.

She'd found a job. She found a new purpose ... and a

paycheck!
　　One small step for Oinks, one giant step for Jessie.

CHAPTER NINETEEN

"Y'all never guess who we saw at the farmer's market!" his mother exclaimed as she barged through the front door, his father on her heels.

And of course his mother was wearing actual heels. The woman strode through a farm in three-inch heels that had no business outside a fashion show. You can take the woman out of the soap opera …

Malcolm sat up from his blanket fort on the couch. His muscles ached, but he was pleased he could shuffle around his place without groaning in pain anymore. He'd been texting with his friends, doing his PT exercises, chatting with Javi about the calendar ideas, and watching a stupid amount of Netflix. Basically, anything he could think of doing without obsessing over a certain freckle-faced woman he loved more than life. You know, no biggie.

"I'm guessing half of Pinegrove?" Malcolm teased, taking his father's hand and pulling himself up to his feet.

"Jessie," Estelle said with a smile, completely unaware that even mentioning his ex's name had the same effect as stabbing him through the chest with a chef's knife. "And she looked so cute out with Gus. I invited her over for dinner one night. I hope she comes back." His mother's story faded as she marched into the kitchen. "I'm making supper. Are you okay with shrimp and grits?"

Craig stuck out his elbow so Malcolm could use the support as he walked into the kitchen. His legs had locked up from his time on the sofa, and he really didn't want to bother with his cane. By the time they'd made the short journey, Estelle had already dropped their farmer's market purchases on the counter, and she filled a pot with water for the grits.

"Easy on the chili flakes," his father warned, opening the fridge and retrieving a beer. He jostled one in Malcolm's direction, and he gratefully took it. Yes, the doctors said he needed to watch his alcohol intake, but when Jessie Mays was involved, he needed all the courage he could get.

"You invited Jessie over? Mom, I told you to leave that poor girl alone." Suddenly, Malcolm was a surly teenager whining to his parents.

Estelle sighed, washing her hands and carefully placing her rings in a dish on the windowsill. "Poor girl, my aunt Fannie. She's lovely, and I don't understand why you kids can't figure it out. Haven't you tried talking it out? Why, this reminds me of that one time, in season three of *Atlanta Hearts* when…." But her trip down memory lane was cut short by Craig's groan.

"Darling," his father warned, but there was no bark in his tone. He popped the top of his beer and slid a can across the table to Malcolm.

"Don't darling me." She huffed. "Jessie is a lovely girl, and I think she and Malcolm need to work through whatever is happening." She paused her onion chopping to wave a manicured hand through the air, as if that motion summed up years of heartache. "Maybe I should make some Jell-O for dessert, in case she shows up." She winced and muttered, "How that girl loves Jell-O so much is beyond me."

"Mom, you need to let this go." Malcolm felt the irony wash over him, as he certainly couldn't.

Craig sighed as he fell into a chair next to his son. "I hate to say it, but the boy's right. Let them figure it out."

"Figure it out? Craig, dear husband of mine, if these kids take too long, I'll be six feet under before my grandchildren are born."

Malcolm spluttered, beer shooting out of his mouth and all over his shirt. "Grandchildren? JJ and I aren't even dating." *Hell, they weren't even speaking.*

"Oh please," his mother said over her shoulder, gesturing wildly with a wooden spoon. "You kids are meant to be, like your father and me. Nothing stands in the way of true love."

Malcolm pinched the bridge of his nose, already pondering if chugging more beers on his meds would be a good thing or a *really* good thing. "Are you quoting *Atlanta Hearts*?"

Her husband interrupted before she could answer. "Maybe hold off on the love talk until we've had two beers, Estelle?" Craig snorted, downing his first beer in three more gulps. "My golf round today was abysmal, and you know traipsing through a farmer's market is hardly my idea of a swell time."

"Oh please. You had a lovely time. You got a little more exercise and …" She paused her rant to pour grits into the boiling water, whisking frantically for a moment before continuing, "We got to see Jessie and that ridiculous dog. I'm telling you, sometimes I think we should get a dog, Craig. Wouldn't that be fun?"

There was a better chance of Malcolm tapdancing out of this kitchen than his father agreeing to get a dog. "Mom, I love you, but can we please not bring JJ up for a few days?" He pleaded, adding under his breath, "Or years."

His mother had turned to the stove and angrily chopped a bunch of parsley. With her back to him, she asked, "So I should pretend that a family friend no longer exists? That certainly sounds healthy."

Family friend—ha! There was nothing friendly about his

feelings for Jessie. The more his mother droned on about seeing her at Hog Hollow, the more his brain provided helpful reminders of their times there. Stargazing, late-night chats, late-night something else that he wouldn't think about in the company of his folks. The Jessie in his mind's eye was more optimistic about her future, more willing to keep him in it.

Craig waved his empty beer in front of Malcolm, eyebrow raised. Malcolm nodded and was grateful his father wasn't badgering him about booze with his medications. "Malcolm, how was your afternoon? You didn't overdo it, did you?"

The distraction of other topics kept Estelle off the Jessie train for a whole ten minutes. "Javi and I chatted today about meeting with the photographer next week, so that'll be good. I like having stuff on my schedule." He stretched, savoring the sensation of his muscles moving with limited pain. "And I finished that documentary on Netflix and ran through my PT exercises twice."

"So long as you don't overdo it," Estelle warned, walking over and pressing a kiss to Malcolm's temple on her way back to her shopping bag. "Craig, can you dice those peppers?" Just as his father rose to his feet, she asked, "Are you sure we can't invite Jessie over tonight? Look at all these grits I'm making."

There was nothing Malcolm could do anymore; he'd reached the end of his rope. "We need to drop the Jessie topic, okay? We're done, and the sooner you get that, the sooner we'll all be happier."

In addition to bad lighting and critical reviews of her acting work, sass from her son was the only thing Estelle could not tolerate. "I see," she said, letting the wooden spoon fall to the floor with a clatter. She stalked off toward the guestroom, the stomping nearly leaving heel prints in his flooring.

The door slammed, alerting the men that their night would be anything but quiet.

Craig pulled himself to his feet and strode to the stove. He lifted the lid on the shrimp and sighed. "You mind grabbing a pepper for me? I'll finish dinner while your mother … gets ready."

Malcolm stood, retrieving a pepper from the bag and helping his father with dinner.

Breaking the silence, his father said, "I won't bother repeating my fatherly advice from our chat the other night. I'll talk to your mother."

Malcolm scoffed. "Really?"

Craig stirred the grits, not looking up to meet his son's gaze. A waft of steam gave them both a facial as their dinner simmered. "Yes, really. Son, we only want you to be happy." He clapped a hand on Malcolm's shoulder, squeezing a moment before letting his hand fall. "Go wash up and knock on the door for your mother. For all the drama, she'd never forgive us eating shrimp and grits without her." He winked, stirring the pot and sending the most heavenly aromas through the house.

Malcolm shuffled down the hall and knocked on the guestroom door. "Mom? Dinner's ready."

Through the closed door, he heard a muffled sniffle followed by, "C'mon in, baby."

The door was unlocked, so Malcolm slowly shuffled inside. His mother sat at the edge of the bed, dabbing at her eyes with a handkerchief. "I didn't want to make you cry. I'm sorry."

She flapped a hand in front of her face and tried to smile, but it didn't quite meet her blue eyes. "I know, and I'm sorry for being me." Malcolm opened his mouth to apologize, but she shook her head. "I understand you two are not very conventional, but this trip made me realize something."

Unable to stand for long periods of time, Malcolm left his cane by the door and joined his mom on the bed. "What's that?"

She covered his hand with hers. She squeezed it a few times before sighing. "Life is short, baby. We all make a million plans and think we have nothing but time, but life catches up to you. When *Atlanta Hearts* was canceled, I was devastated." She groaned and added, "Which I'm sure you remember well. But you know what got me through that time?"

Malcolm bit his lip, unsure where this conversation was going. "Your faith?"

Estelle snorted, then slapped a hand over her face as she laughed. "Oh heavens no! I wish I could say that it did, but what I meant was your father. Craig was my rock; he never let me doubt myself or my future. What I'm saying is, you two always gave me that feeling, like you're on this planet for each other. I know Jessie has her own plans and views on things, but I always assumed she'd come back and you two would find a way. But you know what, it's okay if that's not your path. You have every right to get out there and find the person who makes your heart sing, who holds you up and makes your days better." She took his hand and brought it to her mouth, kissing his knuckles and leaving a smear of purple lipstick. "I love you, baby. I'm sorry I can be ... well, me."

"Don't apologize, Mom. I love you, too."

"Good, now that that's settled, let's get some dinner. I'm starving to death."

As Malcolm joined his folks for dinner, he tried not to burst into tears. He was so lucky to have parents who cared, who were invested in his life. No matter what the future held for him and Jessie, he understood he was lucky to have had as many happy memories as they'd shared.

And he was able to hold on to those positive vibes until bedtime, when he rolled over and caught the faintest hint of Jessie's shampoo on the other pillow. Then his heart broke again, and he cursed this game they'd perfected over the years. That was the issue with off-again, on-again relationships: they never seemed to want to be on at the same time.

CHAPTER TWENTY

Jessie and Gus attempted the fastest land speed ever accomplished by an aging basset hound on the trek back home. There was a buzz surging through her every pore, an excitement over a new challenge. Granted, this wasn't the huge career opportunity she'd expected through the Peace Corps, but it was a good job. She would be helping around the farm, doing random social media posts, and whatever grunt work Gladys and Richard wanted to avoid. It meant a paycheck and a purpose, and right now she'd take it … gratefully!

And let's be honest, she wanted to spend more time with a few curly cuties—Malcolm and Oinks.

"Don't read too much into it," she told herself as she approached the house. Her brother's car was parked in the driveway, as was Javi's pickup truck. An old sedan was parked in the street, and Jessie recognized Chief Warren's car.

Gus barked, sauntering off to his favorite shrub to mark his territory before loping up to the front door. Jessie fumbled for her keys, but Trevor was too quick.

The door flung open and her brother stepped aside for Gus to get inside before ushering Jessie in. "'Bout time," he teased. "Momma's got dinner ready, and I don't think Javi will wait much longer."

"I heard that!" Javi shouted from inside. "I'm a perfect gentleman and will let Ms. Daisy work her magic as long as it takes."

Trevor pinched the bridge of his nose and sighed. "Please don't talk about my momma that way; it's creepy."

"Agreed." Came the chief's booming baritone. "Stand down, Lieutenant."

Javi simply laughed, and Jessie snorted as soon as she crossed the threshold. "I hope I'm not messing with your dinner plans too much," she said as she hurried into the kitchen with her bounty from the farmer's market. "I got a little distracted."

Daisy kissed her daughter's cheek as she took the tote, quickly pulling out the tomatoes for the salad. "No worries, sugar. Everything okay?"

Whitney emerged from the pantry, her hands full of bottles and cans. Trevor went over to lighten her load, placing a kiss on her temple. A sweet blush crept across Whitney's cheek, and Jessie felt a pang of loneliness. She wouldn't mind a certain fireman by her side to hear her news and share a meal with family.

Jessie's footfalls faltered at the realization that she'd made a major life decision without consulting Malcolm. Granted, their conversations in the past usually involved an argument and tears, but this choice meant staying in Pinegrove. This plan involved putting down roots. Her skin itched at the notion that Malcolm might not be thrilled with her choice.

She looked up to see Whitney staring at her, clearly having just said something. "Huh?" she articulately asked, tossing the empty tote bag under the sink.

Trevor rolled his eyes, pouring drinks for everyone. Muttering under his breath, he said, "Always a lady, Jessie."

Whitney's smile remained in place. "I asked, how was the market?" Whitney hip-checked Javi to get across the kitchen.

Nibbling on her bottom lip, Jessie considered saving her news until after everyone left. Her enthusiasm was fragile, and she feared a barrage of questions from well-meaning family would sour her joy. But looking into Whitney's eager eyes now, Jessie wanted to share her news. If she couldn't savor the moment with family, then what was the point of staying in Pinegrove?

"Well, um, the market was good." She shuffled her feet in place, leaving smudges of dirt on the floors. Fortunately, her mother was too distracted to notice the mess.

"Oh yeah?" Daisy asked, dicing the tomatoes into perfect cubes. She tossed them into the waiting salad bowl before drizzling vinaigrette over the top.

Whitney added a handful of homemade croutons and carried the bowl to the table. It was set for six, and Jessie rubbed at the knot in her belly that one of these chairs wasn't for Malcolm.

Daisy raised an eyebrow. "Did you get a chance to talk to the Hansons?"

Whitney, the newest resident of Pinegrove, asked, "Who are the Hansons?" She handed a bowl to Paul, who muttered his thanks before tucking a napkin into his collar. He was seated at her father's old seat, yet Jessie was pleased that she didn't feel anything other than relief at seeing her mother so happy, so cared for.

Trevor filled several glasses with sweet tea, sliding them across the table. "They own that farm up the road; we've driven past it before. It has the sign for the petting zoo."

Whitney nodded but looked to Jessie. "What were you doing at the farm?"

Although fearful of everyone's reactions, Jessie went for broke. "Well, I um, sort of got a job."

The room grew silent, save for Gus's snores from the corner of the room. Since food was involved, the basset hound preferred napping near the table in case anyone dropped anything.

Paul found his words first, wiping his mouth with a napkin. "What kind of job?"

"Working at the farm, Hog Hollow. I bumped into Gladys while Gus and I were walking the grounds, and she mentioned they were hiring." Raising an eyebrow at Daisy, she chuckled. "Plus, Momma's Pinegrove gossip radar alerted me they could use the help."

Daisy's manic expression should have scared Jessie, but she knew it was coming. "I know they could use more than a little help. What will you be doing?"

Jessie took a moment to chew her bite of salad before answering. This was hardly a job that would make her rich, but she was giddy with anticipation, with possibilities. "Well, it's mostly grunt work. I'll help with the animals and the grounds. Since I did a lot of that with my Peace Corps assignments, it shouldn't be too hard." She shoved another bite into her mouth and offered, "And Gladys said they need help with social media. I'll flex my baby millennial muscle."

Javi raised his fist in celebration, reaching across the table. "Congrats, Jessie. That sounds really cool."

Jessie hit his fist with her own and the pair made explosion noises. "Thanks, Javi." It *was* cool, and she was relieved everyone seemed to think so. Jessie liked knowing her days would vary on the farm, and she couldn't deny how excited she was to see Oinks again.

"So you're staying in Pinegrove then?" Her mother nearly vibrated off her chair. Paul leaned close and rested a hand on her shoulder, keeping her seated.

"Yes, Momma. For a while, at least. I don't know how long Gladys will need me. We're going to talk more specifics once I get started. Right now the only thing we confirmed is that Oinks is safe from the meat market."

The table grew silent, everyone sharing matching expressions of confusion. "Beg your pardon, Jessie, but who is Oinks?" Paul asked, mustache twitching.

"He's my right-hand man, Paul. Also known as a pig

who used to be the focus of the petting zoo. Gladys made a comment about how he wasn't as lively, and I told her I'd only take the job if they spared Oinks from the slaughter."

Trevor was incredulous. "You're rescuing pigs now? What is this, Jessie's Web?"

Javi chuckled, joining in the fun. "How are your web-slinging skills? Could you write *some pig* over his pen?" He fanned his hands out in front of him, earning a glare from the chief.

Their matriarch got them back on track. "Saving pigs or not, it's a big farm," Daisy mused, her fork piercing a cucumber wedge. "The Hansons could need you indefinitely. Maybe forever." Daisy's megawatt smile could melt the polar icecaps.

"Real subtle, Momma," Trevor muttered before clearing his throat. "That's awesome, Jessie. Glad you found something new."

Whitney nodded her agreement, her smile nearly as bright as Daisy's. "I'm so glad you'll be here longer. We can hang out more!"

"Hopefully not too much more," Trevor grunted, snaking Whitney's hand and kissing her palm.

"Calm down, Trev. Whitney is allowed to have friends, you know." Jessie rolled her eyes at her brother, then winked at Whitney. Jessie truly did love Whitney's company.

"Yeah, man, welcome to the twenty-first century. We've been waiting for you." Javi's comment earned him a crouton to the forehead, which clattered to the floor. Gus was on it in less than two seconds.

Paul snapped at Gus, who sat at his feet. He pulled off a piece of chicken and tossed it to him. "Good, boy," he said, earning a tail thwap against the floor.

"You're spoiling him," Daisy admonished. Her tone was serious, but she still pulled off a piece of her own dinner to share with Gus.

Javi's plate was already clean, so all he could offer the dog was a belly rub. "You need to come over faster for scraps from me, buddy," he cooed.

"Let me help clear the dishes," Whitney offered, collecting her and Trevor's empty plates.

"I can help," Jessie said, hopping to her feet and nearly tripping over Gus.

Daisy stood, dusting crumbs from her lap. "How would everyone like some pie out on the deck? It's such a lovely night."

She and Paul gathered plates and the pie pan, Trevor and Javi leading the way and holding the door.

When the door snicked shut, Whitney cornered Jessie by the coffee maker. "Okay, girl, spill it."

"Spill what?" Jessie asked, her hand trembling as she poured coffee grounds into the filter.

Whitney placed her hands on her ample hips, entirely focused on Jessie. "I know I'm the newbie here, but all I've heard since I met your brother is how much you want to travel and how much you and Malcolm mean to each other. Now he's not joining us at dinner *and* you're getting a job in town. What gives?"

"I'm taking pictures of pigs. It's not that deep." Jessie was proud of how casual she sounded. Hopefully Whitney didn't have x-ray vision to see how fast her heart raced.

"Uh-huh, and I'm the Magnolia Queen. Does this mean you're getting back with Malcolm? What does he think of your news?"

Jessie poked Whitney in the side with a spoon. "You've been hanging out with Momma too much. Me finding a job has nothing to do with Malcolm. There's been a few changes with my job with the Peace Corps, and I'm not in a hurry to leave. Nothing else is going on here."

Whitney's lips pursed together, but she didn't argue. "You realize I'm going to need more dirt than that if we're going to be besties."

"When I have dirt, you'll be the first to hear about it." Jessie raised a finger in warning. "But you better not say a word to Trev about this. He and Javi are the biggest chinwags in town. The fire station has turned into the gossip hub of Pinegrove."

"My ears are burning," Javi teased from the doorway.

Trevor came up behind him, putting him in a headlock. "Are you causing trouble with my girls?" His buddy pinwheeled his arms in the air like he was really gasping for breath. These two could start side hustles in the pro wrestling circuit …

Turning her attention to her brother, Jessie whined, "What are you goobers doing? You're interrupting my and Whitney's girl talk."

Javi broke free, arms crossed over his chest. "I can be one of the girls." He waggled his eyebrows. "Besides, you know I love gossip."

"At ease, Ortiz," Trevor said, opening the freezer and pulling out a tub of vanilla ice cream. "Save some of that charm for the photo shoot tomorrow."

Whitney perked up. "The photos are tomorrow? Can Jessie and I stop by?" Turning to Jessie, she added, "If you're not working?"

Jessie lifted a shoulder. "I told Gladys I'd stop by in the morning, but I can pick you up after lunch."

Bouncing on the balls of her feet, Whitney clapped. "Hooray! I get to see my boyfriend in a sexy photo shoot." She made camera clicking noises with her tongue.

"Tasteful photoshoot," Trevor corrected, shooting a scowl at Javi. "I'm serious, man. No strategically placed hoses."

Javi blew raspberries and snatched the ice cream from Trevor's grip. "You're literally no fun, man. That captain promotion went to your head."

From outside, Paul shouted, "This pie could really use some ice cream. On the double, men."

Whitney patted Trevor's butt and scooted past him outside. "Here we are," she said, handing out plates and forks.

As their little party of six ate dessert in the dwindling

twilight, Jessie couldn't help but look up at the stars. A few of the constellations she remembered flickered back at her, almost winking their ridicule. Tonight had been nearly perfect, from the food to the company, yet someone very important was missing.

Well, two people were missing, but her father wasn't coming back. As Jessie watched Paul and her momma giggle over slices of pie, she felt herself yearn for her next stage in life. Trevor had found his happily ever after, and Jessie wanted to find her own. She thought the time was finally right.

CHAPTER TWENTY-ONE

"A man of few words. I can respect that," Jessie said from her perch in Oinks' pen. She'd been clocked in for a whopping thirty minutes before she found herself face-to-face with the pig. She stared down at the hog, clocking how he blinked in time with his breaths, snout moving with each exhale.

"I think we'll have more fun together if you give me something here, Oinks." Jessie picked up the slop bucket she'd carried from the main house. Gladys had met her on the porch that morning with a travel mug of coffee, a slop bucket, and a list of instructions.

"We'll start you at five hours a day this week," Gladys had said, scratching her chin. "We'll get you up to full time, but Richard and I need to look at the books and our plans for next season."

Any income was better than no income, so Jessie merely nodded. "Sounds good to me."

Gladys waggled the list in front of Jessie. "This goes over the logistics of who needs what feed, but I also included our social media logins." She glanced over her shoulder and added, "I know this is hardly secure, but all our passwords are HogHollow123."

Jessie smothered her smirk with her fist as she coughed. "All right. What type of pictures do you want me to post?"

Head falling back as she cackled, it took Gladys nearly a full minute to catch her breath. "Bless your heart, Jessie. Feel free to look at our pages, but you'll see nothing but blurry photos and a few with Richard's thumb over half the frame. You could post a picture of your shoes in a pile of hog shit and it'd be an improvement."

This time Jessie couldn't contain her snort. "Noted." She took the paper, shoved it in her jean shorts pocket, and saluted her new boss. "I'll report back here in a few hours."

Gladys waved her off, the corner of her lips quirking. "I got a good feeling about you," she said before turning and walking back into the old farmhouse. Just as she crossed the threshold, she said, "You've come a long way since you used to fool around on my property."

Jessie's cheeks bloomed crimson at the mention of her old times with Malcolm. "How did you ...?" but she didn't get to finish her question, the old woman was already gone.

Deciding it was better to get to work instead of reminiscing about her trespassing days, she marched down to the barn to start her day with her new BFF, Oinks. Per Glady's instructions, Jessie would start her day feeding the pigs in the hog house, then she'd check on the gardens and take pictures for the website and social media. Jessie had already snapped a dozen pictures of Oinks and his colleagues around the pens, catching the morning sun as it reflected off their dark eyes and wet noses.

Finally, after the stare-down of the century, Oinks tilted his head and sneezed. Jessie took that as a greeting and emptied the slop bucket into the trough. "Bon Appétit!" she exclaimed as she hopped over the railing.

Once the pigs were fed, Jessie washed up in the outhouse by the barn and headed into the vegetable gardens. There was about an acre of grounds dedicated to the vegetables that were the staple of the Farmer's Market. Rows of carrots, beets, and other root vegetables took up the far side of the garden. Closest to Jessie stood stalks of asparagus, chard, and fennel. The lettuce patches were starting to fill out, turning the garden into nature's salad bar. As Jessie wound her way through the space, she checked on what items were ready to harvest and which needed more water.

Strolling through the garden, she stopped by a tomato plant nearly as big as Oinks. The plump orbs were as red as a fire engine and just as shiny. Jessie plucked one of the smaller tomatoes and took a bite, the warm juices sliding down her chin. The clean taste of summer exploded on her tongue, and Jessie bit back a groan.

"Maybe we should do harvest tours?" she asked herself, padding around in her pockets until she found her phone.

She took notes about where everything was, what looked ready to pull, and what processes could be part of events. Above her, the sun hung high and bright. The light was perfect for some close-ups, so Jessie squatted low and snapped a few more pictures in the noontime sun. She was midway through scrolling through her photos when a text came through from Whitney.

Want to pick me up at Kim's Creations after 1? We can check out this photoshoot.

Jessie grinned, loving that Whitney wanted to spend time with her. Jessie had never been popular like her brother, constantly surrounded by friends. She had her people, but the circle was small. Adding Whitney felt like a gift, especially as Jessie got reacquainted with Pinegrove.

Absolutely! I promised Momma I'd bring Gus along. I'll swing by after I clean up from the farm.

Whitney's response came almost instantly: *Can't wait!*

Jessie tucked her phone back into her pocket and retrieved a hair tie from her wrist. She tugged her chestnut hair up into a messy bun and surveyed the area. It was still hot, summer heat clinging to the Georgia soil. She made a mental note to check the watering schedule with Gladys for the gardens, because nothing would be sadder than watching these lettuces wilt before harvest time.

On her walk back toward the hog house, Gladys waved her down from the porch of her house. "Jessie! C'mon on up, girl! It's lunchtime."

There was a smushed PB&J Jessie had packed, and Gus had tried to steal, sitting in her car, likely melted from the heat. When she approached the porch steps, Jessie was delighted to find she wouldn't be needing that sandwich. "Oh wow"—she gasped—"I feel like I stumbled into a photoshoot for *House and Garden*."

Before Gladys disturbed the scene, Jessie took a few pictures. A glass pitcher of lemonade sat on a tray brimming with treats. There were cucumber sandwiches, an array of cheeses and sliced deli meats, and a bowl of fresh fruit that made Jessie's mouth water.

"Hope you're hungry," Gladys said, shrugging like this wasn't the most gorgeous sight to behold.

"I hope you aren't, Gladys. I don't plan on sharing." Jessie winked, popping a strawberry into her mouth. The fresh berry was still warm from the sun, with a sweetness that brought tears to her eyes. "I'll gladly take a cut in pay if lunch is part of my day on the farm." She was only half-kidding.

Gladys chuckled, gesturing to a rocking chair next to the table. "You're a card, Jessie." She eased down onto her chair as Jessie made a plate of food.

The pair settled into their rockers and munched away in companionable silence for a moment. In the distance, the chickens were clucking and running around each other in the coop. Far off in the pasture, a cow munched on grass as a few goats scampered nearby. A tabby cat strolled in front of the house, tail in the air and completely uninterested in the duo. Despite the temperatures, sitting out of the sun felt as refreshing as a dip in the creek. Jessie could get used to this.

"This place is gorgeous. More so than I remember."

Ice clinked in Gladys's glass as she refilled her lemonade. "Thank you. It's nice to share it with someone new. Richard and I sometimes get so bogged down with the day-to-day, we don't sit back and enjoy the splendor of this place." She swept her arm in front of her, as if capturing the moment.

"Thank you so much for giving me this job. I really appreciate it."

"Please, Jessie. You're the one saving me. Our son, Davey, keeps telling us to get the farm online and start drumming up business. But that's easier said than done when you're in your sixties. Frankly, I'd rather muck out the stalls five times a day than learn what a hashtag is." Jessie opened her mouth to explain, but Gladys waved her off. "And I don't need you to tell me. As long as you know what it is, I'm happy."

Jessie brandished her phone. "I've taken some gorgeous shots already. If you don't mind, I can get them up before I leave. What kind of business would you like me to focus on? The animals for the petting zoo, the gardens for the farmer's market, or something else?"

Gladys stabbed a cube of honeydew with her fork and chewed thoughtfully. "I'm embarrassed to say I haven't thought about it much. We'd like to increase foot traffic in general, so right now why don't you do a mix of everything?"

Nodding, Jessie dabbed at her lips with a gingham napkin. As she placed the fabric on the arm of her rocker, she had an idea. "Gladys?"

"Hmm?" Gladys asked, her attention focused on a rogue berry that kept rolling around her plate.

"Have you ever thought about hosting events here?"

Gladys raised an eyebrow. "At Hog Hollow?"

Jessie waffled her hand back and forth in front of her. "Sort of. Maybe station an area for events over by the pond. With the rolling hills and that willow tree, it'd make for some stunning pictures. The meadow is gorgeous any time of day." She leaned closer and added, "Which you already know."

Gladys snickered. "You and that Smith boy weren't the

only ones using our acreage for shenanigans. Lordy, if I had a nickel for every couple we had to shoo off our property"—she sighed, doing the math in her head—"well, we would have retired a decade ago." Lowering her voice, she teased, "I'm glad you two weren't troublemakers. A least not with our grounds."

For the first time since being back in Pinegrove, Jessie didn't bristle at the mention of her and Malcolm. Sitting here chatting with Gladys felt comfortable, felt right.

Turning to face the rear of the property, Gladys took in the space with fresh eyes. "You know, Richard and I were married by that pond nearly forty years ago. It's one of my favorite memories, yet I never thought about sharing the experience."

Jessie misunderstood, shooting her hands up in defense. "I'm sorry, I didn't mean to suggest you …"

But her apology fell on deaf ears. Gladys sprang to her feet and paced to the edge of the porch. "You're onto something," she exhaled, staring at something Jessie couldn't see. "That'd be a great way to bring in added revenue, and it wouldn't cost us much."

Jessie pulled her phone out again and opened the Notes app. She jotted down a few ideas before asking, "Do you mind if I do a mock-up of options for the land? I'll check out some local venues to see what they charge. I'll also reach out to City Hall and see what kind of permits we'd need. I can have a plan ready within a week." She hesitated, "And maybe we could look at tours or field trips for summer camps? There are so many things that are delicious and ready right off the vine." She gestured to the tomato juice stain on her T-shirt. "This could be a real experience."

"You can do all that in a week? And you thought all this up today?" Gladys was skeptical. "I'm definitely giving you daily lunches now."

Unable to hold back a laugh, Jessie cleared her throat. "I wore a lot of hats in the Peace Corps. Sometimes we had to get creative with space, and other times we needed to watch our pennies. It'll be nice to put these skills toward something fun and lighthearted."

Gladys rested her hands on her hips. "Jessie Mays, you're a miracle worker."

Jessie bid farewell to Oinks and the gang and sped back to her momma's house. Within fifteen minutes she'd showered, collected Gus, and was en route to Kim's Creations. Unsure if Malcolm would be there, she took a little care with her appearance. Jessie being Jessie, that added care was a swipe of mascara and twisting her hair into a bun at the nape of her neck. She put on one of her new outfits that Whitney had styled and hoped her new friend would approve.

Fortunately, she didn't have to wonder long. "Jessie, you're stunning!" Whitney exclaimed as she slid into the passenger's seat. Gus woofed and stuck his head in between the seats for a head scratch, which Whitney eagerly gave him.

"Oh, thanks," Jessie muttered, unfamiliar with folks praising her appearance. "Wasn't sure what to expect at the firehouse, and I spent all day in slop." She lifted a shoulder, but it belied how pleased she was with her new gig. She and Gladys really clicked, and she looked forward to going back tomorrow.

Jessie was also eager to go slow, not having to rush every interaction or catalog each memory. She could live in the moment, spend time with people she loved, and find a more permanent corner of the world just for her ... and maybe Oinks.

The thing of it was, Jessie didn't feel the itch in her heel anymore. She felt a deep burning in her heart for Malcolm, but she wasn't worried about him going away. She'd find time to tell him her news, and they could decide what that meant for them. *Wow, look at her getting all mature ...*

As her car crested the hill at the turn to the fire station, her palms grew slick with sweat. She hadn't seen Malcolm in nearly a week, and her belly roiled at the thought he wouldn't be happy to see her. Had he already heard her news? And what would he say?

"Earth to Jessie." Whitney laughed, flapping a hand in front of her face. "You want to get out of the car, or should we set up shop?"

Jessie blinked, realizing they were parked in front of the entrance. She spied Javi and Trevor's trucks nearby, as well as Paul's car. "Uh, yeah." On shaking legs, she got out. Happy for the distraction of Gus, she took her time getting him on his leash and out onto the gravel lot.

Gus sniffed around him, marking his territory on the front step of the firehouse. "Real nice, Gussy," Jessie said, steering him toward the door. Just when she was about to open it, Whitney covered her hand. "What's the matter?" Jessie asked, even more on edge at the sour expression on Whitney's face.

"I want to let you know," she said, licking her lips. "I texted Trevor, and Malcolm is here. Is that going to be a problem? You said last night it was complicated."

Complicated was the understatement of the century, but Jessie rallied. "Look, I really appreciate your concern. But I figured he might be here. This town is only so big, and I can't hide away forever. If things get uncomfortable, I'll take Gus for a walk while you hang out with Trev."

Whitney's gray eyes softened, and she pulled Jessie in for an awkward one-armed hug. "I know I keep saying it, but I'm so glad to know you, Jessie. I've got you, girl."

Jessie swallowed past the lump in her throat, desperate to get inside and see what awaited her. No matter what, it was comforting that Whitney cared this much. Her fool brother had really won the lottery.

Walking through the firehouse, Jessie waved at some familiar faces from her father's tenure as chief. There was

George, whom she and Malcolm had gone out with during one of her visits home. He and his partner had driven to Atlanta and invited the pair for a night on the town. They'd shared a fancy meal and even gone dancing at a club downtown. Seeing George now, Jessie felt silly for losing touch.

"Hey, George!" She waved as he closed the distance and wrapped her in a bear hug.

"Jessie, it's great to see you. Trev didn't say you were coming over." When he pulled back, he playfully swatted her arm. "Pick a night and come over for dinner. Calvin recently became obsessed with those decorative charcuterie boards, and you need to save me from the calories." He turned to Whitney and pecked her cheek. "You, too, Whitney. My sister hasn't shut up about how you dolled her up at the shop. Anyone that makes her that happy deserves a couple pounds of Gouda."

Both women laughed, charmed by the fireman. It was the perfect welcome as Jessie prepared to see Malcolm. While she'd considered what seeing him would be like, she hadn't planned for the sight that awaited her. A gorgeous blonde was draped around her ex-boyfriend, the pair laughing at a shared joke. The woman leaned on Malcolm, who only had his cane with him, their heads nearly touching.

Javi stood beside them, his laughter more forced, expression pinched. He lit up when he saw their trio saunter into the bull pen, Gus already yanking to explore the new space. "Hey, y'all made it!"

Before he could reach them, Trevor bounded out of his office, bee-lining right for Whitney. "Hey, darlin'." He greeted his girl with a loud smack on the lips and a few muttered words that caused Whitney to turn redder than her sundress. Gus, sensing there was more love to go around, sat back on his haunches and barked until Trevor gave him belly rubs.

The commotion drew the attention of Malcolm and the mystery woman, who joined their growing group. Malcolm took his time approaching, his face unreadable. "Who do we have here?" the woman asked, dropping down to pet the hound.

It took Herculean strength, but Jessie did not yank Gus away from her. Although she wasn't pleased with how much Gus enjoyed the attention. *Traitor.*

Trevor wrapped his arm around Whitney's shoulder. "This here is my girl, Whitney." He pointed at Jessie. "This is my sister, Jessie. And this fella here is Gus."

"You are too sweet; yes, you are," the other woman cooed, causing Gus's tale to thwap against the floor at an alarming rate. *Yeah, no treats for Gus...*

Javi motioned toward the blonde. "This is Lola; she's helping us with the calendar. Best photographer in the state." He shoved his hands in his pockets and rocked back on his heels. Beads of sweat peppered his temples, and Jessie felt pity for the flustered fireman.

Finally, Lola stood to her full height and extended a hand to both women. Whitney was quick to reach out, pumping her arm a few times and sharing a hello. Jessie reluctantly threw her hand out, although it was limper than a dead fish. "Hi," she muttered, not caring if she looked surly. Besides, Whitney had enough grace and charm for both of them.

"Are y'all here for the photoshoot? My guy Malcolm and I were getting ready to start." She hitched a thumb over her shoulder, and Malcolm's smile didn't quite meet his eyes, while Javi flinched at the comment like it caused him physical pain. Jessie had no idea what to make of this scene, but she felt Javi was her ally.

Javi lamely added, "And me!" He raised his hand like he was waiting on the teacher to call on him in class. "Like I said, Lola's the best."

Jessie scrunched her nose. Unable to stop herself, she hazarded a glance to Malcolm. He wore a similar baffled expression, and her heart ached to share one of their private moments. Even a little laughter would nourish her soul.

Malcolm finally caught her eye, blinking as if he'd

forgotten she was there. "Hey," she whispered, inching closer. "How are you feeling?" She gave him a head-to-toe once-over, powerless to stop herself from inventorying his entire body. *And not strictly in the medical sense.*

He hadn't shaved in a few days, and his jawline was speckled in dark stubble. His eyes were bright and clear, proving he was sleeping fine without her. He was clad in a Pinegrove FD T-shirt, which even after nearly a month out of the gym still hugged his pecs and shoulders. Instead of his dress uniform pants, he wore cargo shorts in favor of his walking cast. She wanted to pull him close, kiss him senseless, and make sure he was healing—in every sense of the word.

"Fine," he said, lifting a shoulder. "You?"

Great, a decade together and they were reduced to one-word conversations. She wanted to filet herself right here in the middle of the firehouse. Instead, she straightened, ready to share her news about Hog Hollow. If talk of their favorite spot and her new employment didn't garner a reaction from the man, she knew she was truly in deep trouble.

Jessie opened her mouth to say something, but Lola interrupted them. "Y'all ready to start?" She brandished her camera, clearly eager to get clicking, regardless of Jessie's splintered heart.

Everyone headed toward the garage, laughing and talking animatedly like Jessie wasn't going through a crisis of the heart. Couldn't they feel the tension? Couldn't they tell that she was dying inside, desperate for even the smallest hint of the old Malcolm?

Regardless of their relationship status, Malcolm had never been so cold. Sure, he could be surly or ill-tempered, but nothing like this. He'd never flaunt someone in front of her, would never shut her out like this.

Suddenly her plans of staying in Pinegrove seemed as flimsy and useless as a Kleenex.

CHAPTER TWENTY-TWO

Malcolm felt like he was playing a game of emotional tug-of-war. His day started with his mother hovering over him, his father trying to distract her, and his mind racing with nothing but thoughts of Jessie. By the time Javi had picked him up, he was desperate for a distraction. Yet when he found one, he realized he didn't want it.

Lola was a nice woman; there was no point denying that. They'd shared a few jokes while she got set up, and he liked chatting with her. She knew her stuff with photography—from her cameras and lighting to the props and locations they could use for the calendar—but watching Javi fumble his way around her was growing tedious. The humor of the situation evaporated about ten minutes into their session, when Javi almost twisted an ankle on a rogue length of hose.

And the hell of it was, Javi wasn't making an impression on the blonde. He was throwing out compliments, jokes, and witty remarks like his life depended on it. Yet she seemed immune to all of it, even the stumbles.

As Javi continued his tap dance and Lola got others in place for their photos, Malcolm sat down and thought about what his dad had said the other day—about craving someone. That notion was confirmed the millisecond Jessie entered the fire station. Whitney may have been a vision in red, but his eyes were locked on Jessie. She wore a pair of hip-hugging shorts that highlighted her toned legs. Her tank top had a neckline that showed the perfect amount of cleavage, her hair was pulled back to highlight the kissable curve of her neck. If he wasn't careful, he'd throw his cane to the floor and crawl on hands and knees to get to her.

And after all that ogling and pining, how did he greet the love of his life? By being cold and offering one-word answers, like an asshole. "Pull yourself together, man," Malcolm groaned, running a hand down his face. He was starting to sweat in the crowded room, fatigue only weighing him down further. He'd never admit this to anyone, but he was already pushing his strength for the day. What was worse, he knew Jessie had noticed before she'd even said hello.

Javi saddled up beside him, his usual careful demeanor muted. "Hey, that's my line." He sighed, shoulders slumping forward. "I don't know how much more of this I can take."

Misunderstanding, Malcolm promised, "It's going well, man. Lola has some great ideas, and everything will be tasteful and fun."

"I don't give a shit about the calendar, Smithy. My heart is breaking over here." Javi punched his own chest to punctuate his point. "Lola doesn't even know I exist. It's killing me."

Malcolm scoffed, but he couldn't really argue. Lola was putting out some very clear signals that even a blind man could see. "I dunno," he wagered, hoping his buddy would come around. "I mean, she's on the clock right now. It's probably not the best time to be laying down your A game." *Or F game if he were being honest ...*

Javi crossed his arms over his chest. "Huh, I never thought of that."

"Think about it." Malcolm cleared his throat. "You've only ever seen her on the job. Maybe chill a bit before we all go out to book club? Then you can gauge how she's reacting?"

"That's a good point. Thanks, Smithy. I actually feel better." Slowly, his signature grin slid back in place, his eyes recovering their twinkle.

Malcolm relaxed, sensing he was telling the truth. "Good, now let's get ready."

They followed the group into the garage, where half of the team was already dressed in their uniforms or bunker gear for the shoot. After a few days of emails, Lola, Javi, and Malcolm decided that each firefighter could pick their own theme. Trevor had decided to pose with Gus in his dress blues, while Malcolm and Javi would do a "buddy shot" of them laughing in their Pinegrove FD T-shirts—which would conveniently be available for sale. Maxwell was due any minute with her kids, opting for a family-style photo by one of the engines. George had chosen an action shot of him sliding down the pole, which Calvin enthusiastically approved. The latter was at the station before Lola even arrived, and it wasn't lost on Malcolm that he'd taken just as many photos as Lola had.

Lola set up a tripod and a lighting stand in the corner, walking Chief through his photo. He'd decided to sit behind the wheel of their biggest truck, a stern expression on his face. Or, as stern as the sweetheart man could look.

Jessie stood in the far corner of the garage, talking with Whitney. Malcolm didn't miss the way her gaze kept darting around them, ping-ponging between Malcolm and Lola. He knew his girl; she was jealous. This was the same pout she wore before she realized Maxwell was his partner.

A tiny flame of hope took hold in his gut, and Malcolm prayed he could rally and approach her without being gruff. Sometimes though, it was hard to separate the past from the present. There had been so much happening lately, and Malcolm feared his heart couldn't handle the yoyo roller coaster ride.

Trevor finished his photos first, quickly dashing over to spend time with Whitney. The pair fussed over Gus until

Trevor turned his attention to his sister. He said something that got Jessie talking, her hands waving as she spoke. She was clearly excited, and that flame of desire burned out when he assumed she was talking about her promotion. Lord, he couldn't go through this anymore.

Forcing himself to turn around, he walked over to Lola, who was setting up his and Javi's shot. "All right, boys," she said, pointing at a stack of helmets, rolls of hoses, a few axes, and an array of fire extinguishers. "Why don't you each put on a helmet, and maybe a hose?" She cocked her head, deep in thought. "On second thought, the hose might be too suggestive. Let's start with the helmets and maybe an ax?"

Once Malcolm pulled his helmet on, Lola frowned. "What's the matter?" he asked, adjusting the chin strap so it fit snugly.

She clicked a few photos and shook her head. "I guess the flaw in this plan is that no one will see your gorgeous curls."

Javi yanked his helmet off and fluffed his own hair, a rogue curl falling perfectly down the center of his forehead. "How about we try a few like this?" He winked, leaning closer. Malcolm didn't miss the heated look the pair exchanged, but it was gone in a blink.

Lola shook herself and gestured toward the tailgate of their ambulance. "Yeah, um. Let's try over here in this lighting." She headed toward the vehicle, only to stumble over a traffic cone. Javi was at her side in a heartbeat, carefully steadying her by the shoulders. "Thanks," she breathed, and Malcolm took her reaction as a good sign.

For the next ten minutes, she had Javi and Malcom try various positions and expressions. By the time they were done, both men were holding their sides as they burst out laughing. It felt amazing to be back at the station, and even better to be laughing again.

Maxwell and her children bounded in through the back door, Juniper running circles around Gus. "Doggie!" she cried, clapping her hands until Maxwell put little Jack down.

She blew a lock of hair off her face and sighed. "Yes, Junie. It's a doggie." She turned to Lola and circled a finger around her face. "Please tell me I have time for makeup. Our day got away from us, and I refuse to look as tired as I feel."

Whitney materialized at her side, hoisting her purse in the air. "I've got you, girl. I'm unofficially here for hair and makeup."

Maxwell covered her heart and choked up. "I love you, thank you. I spent the whole drive here peeling paste out of my hair." She looked at Trevor and teased, "Sorry, Cap. I think I'm stealing your girl."

Trevor smirked. "I'll allow it for a few minutes." He blew a kiss to Whitney, and Jessie made a snarky retort.

Lola chuckled, checking a few settings on her camera. "I get it. I'm a single mom, and I know sometimes the smallest things feel like a chore."

Beaming, Maxwell asked, "How many kids do you have?"

Lola returned the smile and said, "Only the one. Katie just turned nine, and she's really enjoying getting settled into our new home." She opened her mouth to continue, but the chief hollered her name. "I'll get some shots with a few others while you prep. Holler when you're ready."

Maxwell shot a thumbs-up and then took Whitney's hand and dragged her to the ladies' room.

Malcolm looked for Jessie again, finding her deep in conversation with Trevor. He understood they hadn't seen each other as much since she'd been home. Yet they spoke in hushed tones that made the hairs on Malcolm's neck stand on end.

He took the opportunity to find a seat, easing back so he could eavesdrop like the creep he was apparently becoming.

"I think that's great," Trevor said, his smile broad. "This job will be a perfect fit for you, Jessie. I'm proud of you."

Jessie tucked a lock of hair behind her ear. Malcolm's fingers itched with the need to touch her, even if it was just for a second. "You don't think it's ridiculous? I mean, is it a good gig?"

Trevor rested his hands on her shoulders. He dipped his head so they were eye-level. "Don't be a fool, go with it!"

Jessie's bottom lip trembled as she pulled her brother in for a hug. Malcolm had to look away, already feeling guilty for sticking his nose where it didn't belong. They were clearly discussing her promotion, and a tiny part of him was happy for her.

"You suck a lemon?" Lola asked, startling Malcolm back to the moment. She gently tapped his good foot. "I've never seen anyone this upset during a photo shoot. I'm tempted to take a picture and promote funeral packages."

Malcolm snorted. "Sorry, long day. I guess I zoned out."

Lola kicked out a chair and sat beside him. "Y'all are great." She swept a hand around at the crew he loved like family. "I've done a variety of shoots over the years, but I can tell you're a tight group."

"We are," Malcolm agreed. "Thanks for reminding me of that. Since the accident"—he waggled his walking cast—"it's easy for me to forget that."

Lola nodded, her eyes locked on Javi as he and George ran around with cones on their heads, earning belly laughs from Maxwell's kids. Javi paused their shenanigans long enough to catch his breath, then hoisted little Jack onto his shoulders and dodged Gus as he woofed and played along. "Sometimes we don't let ourselves see what's right in front of us." Her voice was almost wistful as she watched Javi a moment longer. Their moment of solitude came to an end when Lola slapped her knees and stood. "Looks like I better get snapping. Kids can't keep their energy levels this high forever." Before she left, she said, "Thanks for inviting me to your book club. It's nice to meet people while I get settled."

"It's our pleasure," Malcolm replied, pleased to be able to help.

While he and Lola had been talking, Whitney and Jessie

had made their exit with a very exhausted Gus. Trevor came up, hands brimming with candy from the vending machines. "Knock it off, Ortiz and Brock! We don't need to document your hijinks on film."

Both men grumbled, but they took the cones off and sauntered over to where Trevor had dropped his bounty. "I snagged you the last peanut butter cup, Smithy, but you better hurry."

Malcolm didn't need to be told twice. He grabbed the packet and ripped it open with his teeth. Peanut butter and chocolate were his favorite combination, and in this moment the perfect distraction.

George joined them, hair mussed from his time as a Conehead. "Sorry, Cap. I'll go help Chief with those budget reports." He took a bag of M&Ms and jogged back toward the bull pen.

Javi flopped down next to Malcolm, clapping him on the shoulder. "Oh, snacks!" He took a Snickers bar, not bothering to rub the smudge from the cone off his forehead.

Malcolm enjoyed the brief snack break, his grumbling stomach reminding him he'd missed lunch in his haste to leave his house. Lord, he craved his own space again, but he didn't know how to get his parents to agree to go back to Tennessee. Naturally, he'd miss them, but he felt like they'd had enough family togetherness to last the year ... and maybe the next.

His captain rudely brought him back to the present. "Whitney and Jessie are doing a girls' night Friday, so I thought us guys could do something."

Javi rubbed his hands together. "I'm in. I need to get out there, man. I'm going crazy."

Trevor scoffed. "We're not trolling for girls, goober. I thought we could order pizza and watch the Braves or something."

"C'mon, man! Some of us need to get out there and get laid. Help a guy out," Javi pleaded, cheeks full of candy. He hitched a thumb over his shoulder and sighed. "I'm getting nowhere with Lola, and it's killing me."

Trevor turned to Malcolm. "Smithy, what do you want to do?"

Malcolm cupped the back of his neck. Truthfully, grabbing pizza with the guys sounded ideal. "I mean, I wouldn't mind a night in. It'd be nice to relax and not have my parents underfoot."

Javi stole one of Malcolm's peanut butter cups. "Fine, we can stay in. I don't want to wear you out, man."

Malcolm thwapped Javi on the bicep. "Aww, thanks. That was almost heartfelt."

Changing the conversation back to his favorite topic, Malcolm asked, "So Jessie and Whitney have hit it off?" He liked the idea of Jessie having more connections to Pinegrove, and not only for his own selfish reasons. She deserved to have friends and family to lean on.

Trevor grinned, his dimple popping. "Yeah, they are. Whit's charmed by Jessie, and vice versa. Although obviously it's easy to be charmed by Whitney." Lord, his buddy was smitten. "Plus, it's getting Jessie out of the house and socializing with humans."

That little comment got Malcolm's attention. Javi's observations after seeing Jessie were one thing, but Trevor knew more of the full story. "What's going on with Jessie?"

"She didn't tell you? Her first day at work went great, and she's thinking Gladys will get her on full time." Trevor wiped at his mouth with the back of his hand before throwing out the candy wrappers. "She won't stop talking about that damned pig though."

Malcolm was totally lost. "Huh?"

Javi whooped and clapped, clearly already in the know. "That's awesome. I knew she'd love it." He muttered under his breath, "And she thought she'd be terrible at it. Pfft, please."

"Love what?" Malcolm asked, his tone a little sharper than was necessary. This was a new sensation, this debilitating sense of missing out. Never had he been the last to learn of something in Jessie's life, and suddenly he wanted to toss his chair and throw a toddler-style tantrum ... much like Maxwell's son Jack was doing across the garage.

Trevor raised an eyebrow. "I'm sorry, Smithy. I assumed she told you." Trevor paused his explanation as Jack let out a wail and threw a traffic cone under the engine. Lola took Juniper's hand as Maxwell ran circles around the truck, chasing her giggling toddler. "Anyway," he continued, finally putting Malcolm out of his misery. "Jessie got a job at Hog Hollow. She's helping Gladys out with some of the farm work, but also something with events. Sounds right up her alley."

Malcolm felt the color drain from his face as his stomach swooped. "Huh?"

Javi chortled. "You deaf, man? Jessie got a job."

"JJ's working here? In Pinegrove?" Hopefully if he kept repeating the news it would finally stick ... finally be real.

"I'm as shocked as you are, but she seems really into it. In fact, she hasn't mentioned the Peace Corps in days. She was bummed she'd lost the opportunity for promotion, but I won't lie that I'm happy she's sticking around. Hopefully she's lost that itch in her heel." Trevor held up his hand, which had all the fingers crossed.

Suddenly the room spun around Malcolm, his body trembling from nose to toes. Jessie had started working locally, at Hog Hollow?! And the promotion was gone? When did that happen? And more importantly, why didn't she tell him?

Lola joined them, tossing her camera bag over her shoulder. "All right, y'all, I got what I needed for today. I'll come back tomorrow to shoot the B-shift crew."

Javi stood so fast, his chair fell backward and skittered across the floor. "I'll walk you out," he said, tripping over his own feet.

And with that, Malcolm collapsed back into his chair, staring at the ceiling. Jessie got a job in town, at a place that meant so much to them. Was she thinking about him while she was there? Was she strolling the meadow that held some of their favorite memories?

These were just some of the questions swirling around his brain as he waited for his dad to pick him up from work. Malcolm sat on the stairs of the entrance, his heart in his hands as he prayed he could figure out this quagmire. This time felt different; he needed to find Jessie and get to the bottom of this. Because if she meant to stay in Pinegrove, he'd be damned if it wasn't with him.

CHAPTER TWENTY-THREE

Jessie helped her mother clean up their breakfast dishes. She was about to leave for her morning on the farm when Paul and Trevor strode into the house, causing Gus to yelp excitedly. The old hound bounded around for rubs until he got bored and went back to his doggie bed. Daisy hugged both men as Jessie made her excuse to prep for her day.

While she hardly needed a lot of time to get ready, she wasn't in the mood for the current love fest happening in the kitchen. She had no trouble with Paul and her mother, but she still felt off about how things were going with Malcolm.

And by things, she meant that they still hadn't talked to each other. Her phone remained void of any contact, and it was starting to piss her off. He kicked her out of his place, he should make the first move. *Right??*

After throwing on her sneakers and her favorite pair of overalls, she headed to the kitchen. "Morning," she greeted the clan with a wave as she poured orange juice.

Trevor snorted at her ensemble as only an older brother could do. "Good morning, Farmer Jessie. You excited to see your new boyfriend today?" He made obnoxious kissy noises, egging her on.

"How dare you speak ill of Oinks." When their mother had her back turned, Jessie flipped him the bird. "Are you going to make fun of me every day you see me in overalls, or just today?"

Daisy tipped a pan of scrambled eggs into a bowl and placed them in front of her children. "Trevor, be nice. We're all thrilled that Jessie found a job she loves." Before stepping back, she nudged Jessie with the blunt end of her spatula, "and I saw that middle finger, sugar. Watch your table manners."

Jessie was incredulous. "How did you …?" but her question died as Paul chuckled, tucking his napkin into his collar. Both siblings muttered apologies as Daisy joined them at the table. "Trevor's sore that he won't get Friday night with his girl." She scraped some butter on her toast, waiting for her brother to take the bait.

"Whit's allowed to have a social life," he said primly before muttering, "although I like it when her social life involves me."

Paul passed Trevor the hot sauce, a smirk fixed on his face. "Son, you've hitched your wagon to a good woman, but she's also a popular woman. Get ready to share." He winked, turning his attention to Daisy, who flushed as red as the strawberry jam on their toast.

Jessie slurped from her coffee, anxious to get out to work and away from all this romance. "Face it, big brother, Whitney likes both the Mays siblings." Despite all her teasing, Jessie truly was thrilled to have a girls' night out with Whitney.

Firehouse chatter quickly took over the conversation as Paul said, "Couldn't help but sneak a peek at the photos so far for this calendar. I have to give it to Ortiz, he chose a great photographer. Everything is tasteful and professional."

Trevor nodded his agreement, dabbing at his mouth with a napkin. "You're right. Javi knocked it out of the park. He even got Smithy to finally relax for the pictures. I think it's going to be real hoot."

Daisy stood, pulling a tray of turkey sausage patties from the oven. "Almost forgot these," she said. Not only were they healthier, but since Jessie had started at the farm, she couldn't stomach pork products.

Paul pierced a sausage patty and dropped it on his plate with a thud. He took a bite and met Daisy's gaze. "These are new," he surmised, drenching it in syrup when no one was looking.

Daisy shrugged, distracted by sneaking Gus a few pieces. "It's turkey. It's probably better for all of us anyway." She looked up and smirked at Jessie, who took a patty of her own. No offense to the poultry on the farm, but Jessie didn't love them enough to go full vegetarian. She mouthed *thank you* after taking a big bite.

Trevor, clearly bored with the topic of breakfast meats, changed the subject. "So while you're out with Whit, I'm having the guys over for pizza and the Braves game." He pointed his fork at Paul. "You wanna join us?"

"Thanks for the invite, son, but I'll have to decline." Paul tugged his napkin free, wiped his hands, and stood to collect his and Daisy's dishes. "I'm taking your momma out to dinner."

Daisy beamed. "Paul's taking me to that new seafood restaurant just out of town." There were limited dining options in Pinegrove. While they were all delicious, there were only so many low country boils and BBQ a person could handle before they needed something more refined. Jessie was well aware of the restaurant; it was the type of romantic place you went to with your sweetheart. It warmed her to see Paul doting on her momma so much. The woman deserved nothing less.

"What guys are joining you?" Jessie asked, mostly to keep the conversation going.

She'd assumed Malcolm would stay with his parents, so she nearly dropped her mug when Trevor said, "Likely just Javi and Smithy. I invited George, Calvin, and Maxwell, but they all have plans."

"That's good that Malcolm's up for coming out. Is he driving yet?" Jessie asked, hating that she didn't already have the answer. Hating that she didn't have the *right* to have that answer.

Trevor lifted a shoulder, helping Paul with the dishes. "Don't know, but I'll confirm the details later." He was quiet for a moment as he collected the condiments and stashed them in the fridge. "I will say, he was surprised to learn you had a job at Hog Hollow. I can't believe you didn't tell him."

Daisy's head whipped up so fast, she nearly lost an earring. "You didn't tell Malcolm you're staying?"

Jessie held her hands up in defense, backing away slowly. "We haven't exactly been on speaking terms since he threw me out. I figured when he wanted to talk, he'd reach out."

Trevor moaned, covering his face. "Jesus Christ, Jessie. No wonder he seemed bothered by the news."

"Language," Daisy warned, swatting Trevor with a tea towel. The commotion woke Gus, who slowly sniffed around the table until giving up on the hopes of more scraps. He sauntered over to the patio door, collapsing into a beam of sunlight.

A new question hit Jessie square in the gut. "When did you tell him?"

Trevor cocked his head. "I dunno, yesterday I guess?"

Yesterday. Malcolm had known for twenty-four hours that she took a job not only in Pinegrove but in their favorite place and he hadn't called. No text. Not even a carrier pigeon. What did that mean? Was he angry? Excited?

The questions threatened to choke her, so Jessie made a hasty retreat and ran out the door for work. "Tell Whitney I'll see her tonight!" she shouted to no one in particular as she snatched her purse off the hook by the door and sprinted outside.

She needed to clear her head, and she knew work would be the perfect distraction. Jessie sped through the backroads until she reached the entrance to Hog Hollow. Now that she was an employee, she got to drive around the back of the property and park by the farmhouse.

Once the car was off, she fumbled in her purse for a stick of gum. She knocked her purse off her lap, scattering the contents all over the floor. "For the love of Pete," she mumbled, collecting her belongings. Her wallet had opened in the fall, and mixed in with a cluster of coins was Malcolm's promise ring. She picked it up, the metal cool in her palm. She thought of tucking it away again, hiding it with the rest of her feelings, but instead she slid it on her finger. It felt like playing pretend when she was a girl, and right now it's just the talisman she needed.

After taking a long breath, Jessie walked up the stone path, finding Gladys and Richard on the porch with a few notebooks, animatedly discussing something.

"Good morning, y'all," Jessie greeted as she took the porch stairs two at a time, her sneakers squeaking with each step. "What's the plan for today?"

"Right on time, Jessie." Gladys shook her notebook in front of her, the pages rustling like leaves. "Richard and I had dinner with our son, Davey, last night."

"Okay?"

Richard gestured to a vacant rocking chair for Jessie to sit. She hadn't had as many interactions with the other half of the farm, but he'd always been sweet, if not a little stoic. *Kind of like a certain man she was trying to forget ...*

"Have a seat, Jessie. Gladys and I want to talk a few things over with you."

"Okay?" Jessie collapsed into the rocking chair, her breakfast turning to cement in her belly. They were going to lay her off, right after she'd made plans. Now that would be ironic, she mused.

Gladys smiled, taking the seat next to Jessie. "Honey, we're not about to send you to the electric chair." She patted Jessie's knee. "You look like you sucked a lemon."

Going for broke, Jessie exclaimed, "I know it's only been

a week, but I've enjoyed working here. I love the gardens and the grounds, and I think Oinks and I have bonded, and I know it's just a few Facebook posts, but Hog Hollow has gained a hundred followers this week. This is Pinegrove, so that's basically going viral."

The longer she babbled, the more confused Richard looked. "Viral? Has one of the hogs gotten sick?" He shot a worried look to Gladys, who waved him off.

"Jessie, I mean this with all due respect, but please hush up."

Jessie clamped her mouth shut, sitting on her hands to stop fidgeting. So much for playing it cool … "Okay," she mumbled.

"We spoke to Davey," Gladys continued, "and he thinks your idea is brilliant." Her smile was so wide, the skin around her eyes crinkled.

"My idea?" Jessie pointed to herself.

Richard chuckled. "Yes. Your idea for events, for doing more with the land. If you're interested, we'd like to bring you on full-time. You can help us get the events started, including expanding the petting zoo. Oinks isn't the only draw; we have a barn full of animals that we could show off." He puffed out his chest, nodding at the idea. "But we need someone who has a little more …" He trailed off, waffling his hand back and forth.

"Energy," Gladys supplied. "Neither one of us has the vigor to do this, but we think you're the woman for the job."

It took less than a heartbeat for Jessie to nod enthusiastically, her excitement palpable. "Holy shit, yes!" She clapped a hand over her mouth and winced. "Sorry, sorry! I'll join Momma at church on Sunday," she promised, causing Richard to snicker.

"Don't worry about the language. We've heard it all."

The trio talked about their ideas, sharing notes until the sun hung directly overhead. "My stars"—Gladys gasped—"we need to feed the hogs."

Jessie shot to her feet, helping her bosses collect their

notes. "I'm on it," Jessie said, bounding down the steps.

Richard cupped his hand over his mouth and shouted as she descended the hill. "You want those full-time hours to start today? I could use some help in the meadows after lunch."

"Good luck getting rid of me now!" Jessie laughed as she spun to face the house. "Thank you!"

The pair waved from their perch, their grins matching her own. This felt right, this felt like something worth savoring.

By the time she reached the hog barn, Jessie was giddy to see Oinks. Over the last few days, this silly swine had turned into her favorite being. She'd swapped Malcolm's curls for a curly tail, and she wasn't complaining. Quickly, she filled the other pigs' buckets with slop before getting to Oinks' pen.

"Hey, buddy," she cooed as she carefully slid through the gate. Oinks seemed as excited as usual to see Jessie—which meant he wasn't excited at all. He lifted his snout, sniffed twice, and then relieved himself by her shoes. Jessie jumped out of the way just in time, laughing as she filled his bucket and climbed onto the top of the pen.

Feet hanging over the side, she listened to her surroundings. The other animals were eating their late breakfast, the tabby cat even making an appearance with a mouse in her teeth. Jessie shuddered, but turned her attention back to Oinks. He'd already demolished his meal, snuffling through hay for any lost treats.

"Well, now that I have your undivided attention," Jessie said, toying with the straps of her overalls. "I get to share the great news that I'll be working full time here. You won't be able to get rid of me." Oinks sneezed, and Jessie took that as permission to keep talking. "I'm excited, really." She let out a long exhale. "I'm still a little worked up over the whole Malcolm thing. I miss him, Oinks. I miss him so much it physically hurts. But do you know what's funny?" She hesitated, as if she were Cinderella and the animals would start talking back. "Good things are still happening. I had a nice breakfast with my family, and then I saw Gladys and Richard, and boom." She clapped her hands, the sound echoing through the stalls. "I got a job offer that gives me goosebumps. I get to work here, with you and this motley crew, and I'm excited. We're going to get events going, the petting zoo back, grow more flowers, and who knows what else."

Behind her, one of the goats bleated. "Thanks, pal!" she yelled over her shoulder. "I really appreciate the support."

Realizing she'd spent ten minutes pouring her heart out to farm animals, Jessie collected her things and headed toward the outbuilding to grab her gardening supplies. She had a little time to kill before lunch. The sun peeked through the grove of pecan trees, the light casting streaks across the grass. It looked like something out of a movie, and she quickly grabbed her cell phone and took pictures for social media.

When she was done taking photos, she opened the Notes app on her phone. This vantage point would be lovely for event pictures, whether they be for wedding albums or graduation photos. The space between the groves and the meadow was perfectly flat, ideal for tents and tables … maybe even a dance floor.

The more her mind wandered, the more notes she took. Jessie envisioned small, intimate weddings being held at sunset, the grounds cast in moody purples. Or maybe family reunions in the middle of a sunny Saturday afternoon, the kids running away to play with the animals … with Oinks holding court by the barn.

As she strode up to the house for lunch, she had a desire to text Malcolm one of the pictures. Not only did she feel a deep sense of pride for what she was doing, but she'd been flooded with happy memories with her favorite person. Many late-night rendezvous on Hog Hollow had been spent dashing through the pecan groves on their way to stargaze. Jessie was pleased to discover these memories didn't hurt as much; she was able to look back with fondness and not bitterness. Some relationships last the test of time, like Gladys and Richard or her momma and daddy, while others aren't meant to burn bright forever.

Perhaps that was where she and Malcolm had ended up, safely in the burned-out category. Since she was staying in Pinegrove, she wanted to take a step toward friendship; toward having him in her life. Choosing the best picture, she sent it to Malcolm with a note:

It's a beautiful day here, and I couldn't help but think of you.

Jessie hit *Send* before she could talk herself out of it. The text was a test, an olive branch to see if Malcolm felt the same way about her as she did him. They'd hardly talked earlier at the firehouse, and she wasn't about to walk on eggshells anytime their paths crossed. This was Pinegrove; they'd be bumping into each other all the time. Hell, they were going to the same blasted book club next week.

After her first full day on the farm, Jessie bid farewell to her bosses and hopped behind the wheel. She hummed to herself the whole way back home, eager to get ready for her night with Whitney. Jessie had finally realized that Pinegrove was where she belonged, and she tried not to let it bother her that Malcolm hadn't responded to her text.

LIBBY KAY

CHAPTER TWENTY-FOUR

Malcolm spent his day doing PT exercises and having a productive meeting with his visiting nurse. She was pleased with his wounds and even suggested he'd be able to go back to light duty full time within a week or two. Granted, he wouldn't be speeding to scenes and putting out fires right away, but he'd be able to drive himself to the station. That small hint of freedom gave him purpose.

More importantly, his parents could head back to Tennessee. He was grateful they'd done everything they had, but he was a grown man who wanted his house back. Well, that wasn't true. He wanted his house back, plus Jessie.

"What time am I dropping you at Trevor's?" his dad asked, sticking his head in the doorway to Malcolm's bedroom.

"Six, if that's okay. We're gonna watch the game and order pizza."

Craig smiled, leaning on the doorjamb. "I'm glad you're getting back out with your friends, especially after such a productive nursing visit. You must feel like a million bucks."

"Not gonna lie, it's pretty sweet." Malcolm ran his fingers through his hair, struggling to keep his curls in check. He pawed around his pockets for his phone, muttering when he couldn't find it.

"Oh." Craig snapped his fingers and pulled Malcolm's phone from his shirt pocket. "You left this charging in the kitchen."

"Thanks," Malcolm said, already planning on turning off the infernal device so he wasn't more distracted than he already was. As he was about to shove his phone in his pocket, he noticed a text from Jessie. His eyes widened, and he fumbled to unlock the screen. He saw the picture first, a familiar scene he'd thought about often. It was the groves near the meadow, right in the middle of Hog Hollow. Jessie had taken this shot at work, and she'd thought enough to include him in the moment, despite his ghosting her.

"Everything okay?" Craig asked, leaning forward to see what had Malcolm so enraptured.

Her message had his heart racing more than it already was. *It's a beautiful day here, and I couldn't help but think of you.*

What the hell did that mean? Did she wish he was there with her? Did that mean she was really staying?

"Son?" Craig asked, standing directly in front of Malcolm. So lost in his own musings, he hadn't even heard his father approach. "You look like you've seen a ghost."

Yeah, the ghost of ex-girlfriends.

"It's nothing. We should go."

Malcolm and Craig walked into the living room, where Estelle lounged on the couch watching a YouTube interview with one of her former *Atlanta Hearts* costars. She was hinting at a reunion show, and Estelle nervously picked at her cuticles.

"You all right, darling?" Craig asked, walking over to peck her on the cheek.

Estelle sighed, falling further back in the couch cushions. "I don't know. Ever since Netflix got the show, everyone is talking reunion. But my agent hasn't confirmed my contract, including how many episodes I'll be in. My word, they could use that AI mumbo jumbo and have me be a ghost or something!" she whined, covering her face with her hands.

Through her fingers, she asked, "Do you think they've changed their minds?"

She looked to her husband and son expectantly, and Malcolm suddenly wanted to evaporate. He loved his mother, dearly, but when she got these episodes of self-doubt, it was crippling. "How about you join me and Malcolm? We'll drop the boy off at Trevor's, then I'll take you out for dinner. We can go to Cajun Carl's. You love it there."

Estelle glanced back and forth at the screen and her husband. Chewing on the inside of her cheek, she took a moment to decide. "Do you mind if we swing by that little ice cream shop on the way out of town? I could go for a little sweet."

Craig held his hand out, easing Estelle to her feet. "Anything you want." They kissed chastely on the lips, causing Malcolm's already muddled brain to turn into rice pudding.

For his whole life, he'd watched his parents' relationship ebb and flow, like most couples. The big difference was, they always complemented each other—they always knew what the other needed. He had that with Jessie, from knowing how she liked her coffee and evening tea, to why she favored overalls to shorts. The woman was a part of him, heart and soul, and he needed to figure this out.

Malcolm shuffled out with his dad, Estelle clacking behind in her favorite pair of heels. He slid with relative ease into the backseat, eager to get to Trevor's for some guy time. "Just text when you need a lift home," Craig said, catching Malcolm's eye in the rearview mirror.

Estelle turned back and smiled, although she looked nervous. "Have fun, but not too much fun. I know the nurse released more restrictions, but you don't want to—"

Malcolm silenced her rant with a pat on the shoulder. He felt like a parent placating a child. "I'll be careful, Mom. We're ordering pizza, not flying to Italy."

"Oh hush," his mother admonished him. "Have fun. If

Jessie's there, tell her we said hello."

Craig's head fell back as he ground out, "Estelle, we talked about this."

Malcolm's hand froze over the door handle. "Talked about what?"

Craig said, "Nothing," as Estelle said, "Jessie."

"All right." Malcolm huffed, shoving the door open. "It's guys' night; JJ won't be there." He didn't think … *No.* His stomach roiled with possibilities. If she were there, it would certainly make things easier. That text was burning a virtual hole in his pocket, and he didn't know how to respond. *Didn't know how he wanted to respond.* "That's my cue to exit. Have fun at Carl's. I'll text you." And with that, he slid out of the car and shambled up to Trevor's place.

Malcolm didn't get a chance to knock, as Javi threw the front door open with a theatrical "Thank God, you're here. Trev refused to order food until we knew what pizza toppings you wanted." He stepped back so Malcolm could enter, before letting the door slam shut.

"Were you raised in a barn, Ortiz?" Trevor joined them in the living room, handing out beers. "You're okay with one?" he asked, not releasing the bottle neck until Malcolm groaned.

"Please, not you, too, Trev. I'm about to go insane. I'm a grown ass man, and I'm allowed a drink." He tugged until Trevor released his grip, nearly spilling beer on himself and the couch.

Trevor backed away, arms in the air. "Sorry, didn't realize that was a touchy subject."

Javi rolled his eyes, flipping through channels until he found the baseball game. "Smithy's been as much fun as a wet mop lately. I thought you'd get happier the more you healed."

Malcolm reared back. "I'm happy," he lied.

Javi's head fell back as he cackled. "Oh yeah, you're a regular laugh riot." He nudged Malcolm in the ribs. "C'mon, man, you're allowed to be upset. A freaking building fell on you last month. I guess I miss my happy-go-lucky friend."

Trevor joined them, tossing his phone on the coffee table. "Pizza will be here in thirty." He eyed them on the couch and sighed. "What did I miss?"

"Nothing," Javi said, glugging back his beer.

Malcolm scrubbed a hand down his face and sighed. "Javi's on my case since I'm not my normal, smiley self."

Now it was Trevor's turn to sigh. "I'm guessing this has to do with my sister."

That got Javi's attention. He slapped the remote to mute the TV and gawked at Malcolm. "What does that mean?"

Trevor snorted, nearly sending beer through his nose. "Javier Ortiz! You're one of our best friends, and you didn't realize that Malcolm and my sister have history?"

Javi was dubious. "I mean, I listen. I know y'all dated, like, what, a million years ago?"

"That timeline seems accurate," Trevor mumbled, his attention fixed on the muted TV screen. "Oh, look, the Braves are up five runs already."

Malcolm placed his beer on the coffee table and offered Javi the abbreviated history of Jessie and him. "JJ and I were high school sweethearts," he started.

Javi interrupted him with a raised hand. "I knew that already!"

"Gold star for Ortiz," Trevor groaned. "You've mastered level one of Pinegrove history."

Malcolm soldiered on, hoping that talking it out would make him feel better. "To make a long story short, mostly because her brother is sitting right here"—Malcolm gestured with his beer bottle—"JJ and I have been dating on and off again since we officially broke up after high school."

"Dude!" Javi was aghast, mouth hanging open as he pivoted to face Malcolm. "How in the hell did I not know this?" He looked down at his hands like they held the answers. "Have I been this oblivious?"

Trevor said, "Yes," while Malcolm tried a more tactful

"No."

Javi was dumbfounded, jumping to his feet so he could pace the length of the living room. Trevor kept craning his neck to see the TV, but Malcolm was too entertained to stop him. It took a lot to rattle Javi, and this news apparently was a bridge too far. "So is that why she wanted to go home with me the other night?"

That question sucked the air from the room, and both men glared at him. Malcolm knew the story, but clearly Trevor was pissed. "What did you just say?" Trevor asked, his expression murderous.

"That's not what I meant," Javi backpedaled. "When we were at book club planning meeting, she was upset and asked to go home. I teased her that Trevor would kick my ass"—he flapped a hand toward a very irate Trevor to highlight his point—"but apparently I should have included Smithy in the list of men who would gladly tear me limb from limb."

Trevor held up a finger. "Please tell me you didn't try anything with my sister. I might have to kill you."

"Eww, no man," Javi quickly agreed, only to realize his folly and moan. "Poor choice of words. Jessie's great, but she's not my type."

"No shit," Trevor argued, clearly not done being pissed. Only the knock at the door from the pizza delivery driver stopped his tantrum. He stomped off to get their dinner, leaving Javi and Malcolm alone for a few minutes.

Javi rubbed the back of his neck. "So you're still into Jessie?"

That question seemed too simple. Of course he was still into Jessie. Their situation was far more complicated than feelings. No, their problem was all about timing. But if Jessie was staying in Pinegrove, did that mean the timing was finally right?

Trevor joined them with three plates of pizza. He held one out for Malcolm, but he hesitated to share with Javi. "I promise I've never done anything with your sister," Javi assured him, pulling the plate from Trevor's hand. "If anything, you should probably be pissed at Smithy. Sounds like he's stringing her along."

Great, now Trevor's death stare was focused solely on Malcolm.

Trevor took a big bite off his slice, a piece of pepperoni falling onto his plate. His eyes narrowed as he chewed. Finally, he asked, "What are your intentions now that Jessie's staying in town? Can you two manage to be friends, or do I need to threaten you with bodily harm?"

Javi reached out, patting Trevor's knee. "Cap, the man's already had a building fall on him. Maybe give him a break?"

"Aww, thanks, Javi," Malcolm tutted, "I appreciate that."

Trevor dropped his plate on the cushion beside him, still not smiling. "I'm not going to actually break anything, but I want to know what to expect. Are you back on, or still off?"

That was the million-dollar question. Malcolm opened his mouth to reply, but Trevor's phone went off, distracting everyone. "Excuse me," he muttered, snatching his phone and striding into the kitchen. "Momma, is everything okay?" he asked, voice getting quieter as he turned a corner.

Javi shrugged, stealing another piece of pizza and focusing on the game. "For what it's worth," he said, folding his slice in half, "I hope you and Jessie can figure it out, if you want to. Before meeting Lola, I'd never understood the frustration of crushing after a woman who doesn't want to talk to you. It freaking sucks, man."

Malcolm opened his mouth to reassure Javi, to tell him that if it was meant to be with Lola, it would work out. But he didn't have a chance, as Trevor joined them, his nose wrinkled in confusion.

"What's up?" Malcolm asked, suddenly more concerned over Trevor's worrying expression than his pizza and love life.

"Momma asked if I could come by real quick, said it's important." He still clutched his phone in his hand, lips dipped down in a frown. The background din of the baseball announcers added an odd soundtrack to the moment.

Javi turned off the game and wiped his hands down the front of his jeans. "Is Ms. Daisy okay?"

Trevor's head dipped in a nod, but he didn't look convinced. "She said she's fine, but had something important to tell me."

Malcolm cursed the fact that he still couldn't drive. He felt so helpless. Javi must have sensed the same thing. "Can I drive you over there? You look shaken up."

"I'm coming, too," Malcolm said, deciding he didn't want to be far away in case it was bad news. Jessie would need a shoulder, and he'd be damned if she cried on anyone else's.

The trio piled into Javi's truck and headed toward Daisy's house. When they pulled into the driveway a few minutes later—hooray for Pinegrove's small size—they all hopped out as fast as they could and barged into the living room.

Gus barked excitedly, and Malcolm took the opportunity to pet the hound dog. Glancing around, he only saw Paul and Daisy. They strolled in from the kitchen, both wearing megawatt smiles that could be seen from the international space station.

"Oh, wonderful, you're all here," Daisy said, rushing over to hug both Javi and Malcolm before pulling Trevor close and pecking his cheek. "I'm sorry to interrupt boys' night."

"Is everything okay?" Trevor looked around frantically, eyes wild. "Where's Jessie and Whitney?"

"Right here," Whitney announced, closing the distance to Trevor and kissing him like they didn't have an audience. "We got here as soon as Daisy texted."

Jessie hung back in the doorway, clad in a dress that Malcolm wanted to pull off with his teeth. It was another pink number that hugged her curves and made her glow.

Her hair was loose, hanging in waves down to her shoulders. She'd even put on a little makeup, and Malcolm silently cursed any man who got to see her looking so fine. Their eyes locked, and her cheeks flushed a matching rosy hue.

Despite being in a crowded room, they ogled each other for an eternity. "Hey," she breathed, stepping closer. She may have been dolled up, but he was still his JJ. A pair of worn sneakers were on her feet, and Malcolm couldn't stand the distance. This was his girl, standing mere feet away, and he couldn't do anything about it.

"Hi," he said, lips quirking up.

Javi threw his hands in the air. "How the hell did I ever miss this?" He pointed to Paul and asked, "Chief, were you aware these two had a history?"

Daisy snorted, covering her mouth as she laughed. Whitney pulled back from Trevor's embrace long enough to join in the laughter, Trevor finally looking more relaxed. "Oh, Javi, you must be blind."

"Apparently," he agreed, falling back onto the recliner, legs splayed.

"Now that you're all here," Paul said, his voice booming and demanding everyone's attention. "Daisy and I have something to say."

"Oh Jesus, did someone die?" Jessie asked, collapsing onto the empty chair by the television. Her hands twitched, already anxious at the news.

After muttering something under her breath, her mother rallied. "Sugar, you really do have a flair for the dramatic. If your current career doesn't work out, maybe you can join Estelle on the *Atlanta Hearts* reunion tour."

"You wanted to have a family meeting to discuss my ex's mother's soap opera?" Jessie was incredulous, shooting a glance to Malcolm.

At her question, Whitney gasped. "Wait!" She whirled around, mouth agape at the news. "Your momma is *the* Estelle Winters? How have I not made the connection?"

Trevor shrugged, taking her hand. "Darlin', how would

you know? She uses a stage name and ..."

Paul cleared his throat. "As much as this is fascinating, Daisy and I wanted to talk with you kids." He draped his arm around Daisy's shoulders, pulling her close.

Daisy looked at him like he hung the moon. Malcolm wasn't too proud to say he envied the older couple. He burned for those moments of closeness, of being on the same page with everything. And Lord, he missed that with Jessie. He craved it more than his next breath ...

"So what's going on?" Trevor asked, ready to get to business.

Paul looked to Daisy, who beamed. "Well, I'll just come out with it," he started, licking his lips. But he didn't get the chance to share the news, because Daisy jumped up, punching the air with her left hand.

"Paul and I are getting married!" Her outburst startled poor Gus, and he piddled in his doggie bed.

Whitney was the first to react, sprinting to Daisy and pulling her into a bone-crushing hug. "This is amazing! Congratulations!"

Trevor needed a moment to absorb the news, but when he did, he strode up to Paul and pulled him in for a man-hug. "Congratulations, Chief. You know you're marrying the greatest woman in the world. Well, maybe second greatest." He winked at Whitney, who rolled her eyes.

Daisy broke free from Whitney's embrace and walked over to Jessie. "Sugar? You're awfully quiet."

Jessie clasped her mother's hands. "I'm so happy for you both," she said as she squeezed her. "I know Daddy would be thrilled, too. He loved you both so much." She pulled back and hugged Paul quickly before dabbing at her damp eyes. "This is wonderful."

For a few moments, the seven of them were all hugs, kisses, and happy tears. Malcolm shared his regards in between Javi's whoops and shouts. "This is amazing news! I freaking love it!" Javi blinked back tears and said, "This is just like that book with the duke when he proposed to the housekeeper after years of being in love with her."

"You remember the details of these romance books, but you didn't know that Malcolm and Jessie are in love with each other?" Trevor scoffed, punching Javi in the shoulder.

That statement stopped the celebrating cold, and all eyes turned to Malcolm and Jessie. He was desperate to say something, anything to get her to join him out on the deck for a moment of privacy.

Yet he didn't get the chance to say anything, as Jessie clapped her hands, keeping them clasped in front of her. "Well, since we're all here, I have an announcement to make as well."

Malcolm put all his weight on his cane, fearing his knees would buckle at the determination in her voice. He had no idea what she was going to say, but he couldn't look away.

LIBBY KAY

CHAPTER TWENTY-FIVE

Jessie rubbed her sweaty palms on the front of her dress, carefully not to wrinkle it too badly. She had a very lovely plan on how to share this news with her family and friends, and in particular Malcolm. That plan did not involve stealing the thunder of her mother and Paul's announcement, but here she was.

"I, um, got a full-time job today at Hog Hollow. Richard and Gladys are liking what I've accomplished, and they'd like to expand."

Daisy nibbled her lip and asked, "Expand what, sugar?"

Jessie swept her arms out, encompassing the whole room. "Everything. They want to start events, get the petting zoo back up and running, and I'll still tend to the gardens and my buddy Oinks."

Malcolm interrupted with, "Oinks?"

Jessie's grin took over her face. "He's a pig, and—" but her annoying brother cut her off.

"He's basically Jessie's best friend. It's become ridiculous," Trevor replied, rolling his eyes.

Paul smirked, but chastised Trevor. "Now, son, it's good Jessie found a job she likes."

Jessie blew a kiss to Paul, causing the older man to flush.

"Thank you, Paul. You're officially allowed to marry Momma if you keep this goober in check."

"Real nice, Jessie," Trevor groaned, until Whitney nudged him and pursed her lips.

"So no more Peace Corps?" Malcolm asked, his voice barely a whisper. "What happened with your promotion?"

Jessie hazarded a glance around at everyone, but she wasn't going to get into the details with an audience. "I'll fill you in later, but long story short," she exhaled, still disbelieving what she was about to admit, "I've left the Peace Corps."

Whitney took the opportunity to squeal and yank Jessie into an embrace. "I'm so glad we'll get to see each other more." Whitney sighed into her hair. "More girls' nights out."

Trevor joined their huddle to pat her head like a dog. "That's freaking amazing, Jessie. I mean it."

Paul nodded his approval as well. "You did good, kiddo."

Jessie was never one to savor being the center of attention, so she gestured toward the rear of the house. "Can I, um, borrow Malcolm for a minute?"

"Oh man," Javi whined. "I don't want to miss this. I'm invested now."

"Stand down, Ortiz," Paul ordered, although there was no bite in his tone. "Help me find a bottle of champagne in this house. We need to celebrate."

Javi followed the older man into the kitchen, and Jessie snatched Malcolm's hand and tugged him toward freedom ... also known as the deck. Gus followed them out, curious about all the excitement.

When the trio was on the deck, Jessie kept hold of Malcolm's hand and led him toward a pair of chairs on the fair side. She was no fool, knowing full well her brother and the rest of the house would be looking out the window, but she wanted the illusion of privacy. She loosened her grip, and all too soon Malcolm's hand dropped away, and Jessie nearly wept with the loss.

This last week had been hell, plain and simple. She'd missed him more than all the years combined on the road. All of their goodbyes were nothing like this now, stilted and awkward. It wasn't how they operated, and she couldn't take much more. She needed answers, and this was as good a time as any to start asking questions.

"You never responded to my text," she blurted, squeezing her eyes shut so she couldn't see his reaction. Of course, that plan melted faster than a snow cone during the Fourth of July fireworks festival. She couldn't not see him, couldn't not see his reaction to her question.

"I know." He sighed. "I ... I ..." His words faltered, but he refused to sit in one of the chairs. Jessie couldn't move, couldn't breathe, until he gave her an answer. Malcolm closed the distance between them. His head dipped low, their foreheads touching. She smelled his familiar citrus scent, and she could have whimpered at his proximity. "JJ." Her nickname was a whisper on her skin, her hands came up to cup his face, his whiskers tickling her fingertips.

"Malcolm." She swiped along his bottom lip, earning a low grumble for her efforts. She knew that sound, intimately, had it memorized along with all the other details that made Malcolm hers.

His fingers tensed on her hips, her belly warming the longer they embraced. "JJ," he repeated, nuzzling her ear with his nose, sending goosebumps cascading over her. "When I saw your text, you know what I did?"

"No." Her response was so quiet, she feared he didn't hear her.

"I smiled," he said plainly, and Jessie deflated.

"That's nice," she said, not meaning it. She wanted more than smiles and simple reactions; she wanted passion, grand declarations ... a future. She'd reopened communication with the man she loved, and he cracked a smile?

Malcolm pressed closer still, steadying himself in her arms. "Do you know how freaking good that smile felt? It was the first time a text from you floored me, JJ. I saw that text just as I was leaving for Trevor's, and I didn't know what to do with myself. I couldn't tell. Did you want to prove a point? Were you inviting me to join you in those pecan groves? Regardless, I felt like it was something real; a sign you weren't done with me."

Reluctantly, Jessie pulled back enough to catch his eyes. "I was never done with you, Malcolm. I may not have known what I wanted, but I sure as hell was never done with you."

"I'm never done with you, JJ."

Malcolm traced over her mouth, sending shivers from her spine to her toes. His touch was tantamount to lighting a stick of dynamite, and she was about to combust. Even though all she wanted was to kiss this man, she had so much she needed to say, to confess, to apologize for.

"The promotion fell through, on that phone call our last night together." Her admission caused Malcolm to tense, but she continued, "I wanted to say something that night, but I didn't know how to articulate everything I was thinking. I wasn't sure how I felt, and suddenly one of my options was gone. I never thought I'd fall into this job at Hog Hollow, but I'm loving it. I wanted to tell you, really I did, but I was afraid you'd think I was settling for you."

"Settling?" he scoffed. "How could that be?"

Jessie's voice was small, but she forced herself to explain. "Because I was out of options. The Peace Corps had always been there, always been a gateway to the world and adventure. I didn't want you to think I was only staying because I was out of options."

"Did it ever occur to you that maybe we could have our own adventures? I'd love to travel with you, JJ. I want to have a life with you. How would that not be an adventure?"

Jessie hadn't realized she'd started crying until a breeze ghosted over her damp cheeks. "I want that, too."

Malcolm's hold tightened, and she was ready to kiss him when another thought intruded on their moment. "What about Lola?"

"Huh?" Malcolm pursed his lips. "What about her?"

"I saw you two at the station, and she seems really into you." Jealousy flared in her belly, and she hated that it took from the heat of their moment.

Instead of reassuring her with words, Malcolm snorted and shook with mirth. "JJ, are you kidding me? First, you're the only girl for me. And second, Javi is so into her, it's embarrassing. She's a nice person, and I enjoyed chatting with her. But we're not dating, and I don't want to."

"Oh," was all Jessie could muster. They were the words she wanted to hear, but now that she had the truth, she had no idea what to do with it.

Malcolm inched closer. "Oh? That's all I get?"

She lifted her chin. "You still didn't return my text."

"Ha! We're back to that. Because I didn't know what to say." He sighed, but it wasn't a sad sound. He collected himself. "The second I saw that picture, my whole body lit up. It was like hopping in a time machine and waking up in my favorite place, with my favorite person. I can't keep pretending anymore, JJ. I love you, okay?"

Jessie smiled so hard her face hurt, cheeks nearly seizing. "Okay."

"Can I please kiss you now?" Malcolm begged, hovering his lips over hers. "You're not staying in Pinegrove as my friend, JJ. You're staying as my girl. I'm sorry I pushed you away, but I thought I was doing the right thing for both of us."

"I think the right thing for both of us is you kissing me."

Malcolm carefully cupped her face, gently squeezing the apples of her cheeks before finally kissing her.

The last thing Jessie thought before Malcolm's lips crashed against hers was there was no point fighting fate. They were two magnets, the pull toward each other constant. This was the first kiss of many, and Jessie could not wait to start her new life in Pinegrove … with a certain fireman by her side.

*

Malcolm might as well be in a dream, because nothing had ever felt so right. He was kissing Jessie, *and* she was staying in Pinegrove for good. Lord, nothing could beat this feeling.

He angled Jessie's head so he could deepen the kiss, and she made an animalistic sound that had Gus barking from the far side of the desk. "Shut up, please," Jessie scolded the dog in between kisses. She clung to Malcolm from the front of his shirt, fabric straining in her grasp.

Unfortunately, Gus wasn't the only one making noise. A cacophony of chaos erupted behind them. "Oh my heavens, it's happening!" Estelle shrieked as she joined them, tears spilling in perfect lines down her cheeks.

"Estelle, for the love of ..." but his father's voice hitched at the sight of Jessie in his arms. "Oh, hello, Jessie."

"Hi, Craig, Estelle," Jessie greeted as she stepped back and tugged her dress back into place.

Malcolm wasn't feeling as welcoming. "What are you doing here?"

Instead of answering his question, his mother plowed forward with her own. "Does this mean what I think it does?" she gasped.

Malcolm rubbed the back of his neck, wishing more than anything for working legs so he and Jessie could run away. "Mom, we're kind of figuring that out."

"Yes," Jessie interrupted. "We're back together." She snaked Malcolm's hand, keeping him by her side. *Like he'd want to be anywhere else ...*

"Ahhhh!!!" Daisy screamed as she paraded out onto the desk, arms full of wine glasses. Paul was right behind her, with a bottle of champagne, Javi, Trevor, and Whitney bringing up the rear. "Does this mean?" Her eyes darted back and forth between Malcolm and Jessie, bottom lip trembling.

Estelle stole the moment, shouting, "They're back together!"

Daisy thrust the glasses to a confused Trevor and then leapt into Estelle's embrace. "It's finally happening. I can't believe it."

"Praise the Lord," Estelle chanted, causing Craig and Malcolm to both roll their eyes. His mother hadn't been to a church since it was a set on *Atlanta Hearts*.

Paul and Javi went to work popping the cork and pouring glasses. Whitney approached and giggled. "I knew this would happen."

"How?" Jessie had to raise her voice to be heard over the mothers' squeals of delight.

Whitney cocked a hip, raising an eyebrow. "Well, aside from the fact that your momma never shuts up about you two, and I saw the looks you're always throwing back and forth, it was only a matter of time."

Javi joined them, pressing chilled glasses into their hands. "How the hell did I miss this?" he marveled, shaking his head. "I'm almost embarrassed."

"You should be," Trevor tormented Javi. "I mean, part of your job is being observant, and you ignored the signs for years." He smirked at Jessie and Malcolm before offering his own congratulations. "Seriously, I'm glad this is finally settled. It was getting tedious, y'all. I'm just sayin'."

"*You* thought it was tedious?" Malcolm admonished, earning a playful nudge from Jessie. "But you're worth the wait, JJ." He pressed a soft kiss to her cheek, simultaneously loving and hating that their families were here.

Estelle yelped, "They're kissing again! Craig, where's my purse? I need to find my cell phone. We need to be documenting the moment."

"Mom," Malcolm ground out while Javi saved the day.

"Estelle, there's actually two reasons we're celebrating." He tipped his head toward Daisy and Paul, who were huddled in the corner, giving heart eyes to each other.

"Oh?" she asked, already on the verge of another

reaction.

Daisy held up her left hand, the new diamond sparkling in the twilight. "Paul and I got engaged tonight."

That did it. There was no point trying to harness Estelle when there were things to celebrate. She practically teetered out of her heels as she skittered over to the couple, enveloping them so tightly Paul had to gasp for air. "Craig, camera!" she ordered in between sobbing her congratulations.

And so their evening continued with tears, joy, laughter, and a little too much enthusiasm from their favorite soap star. Gus even hopped around, clearly thrilled that everyone was excited. He tripped over his own ears and rolled off the deck, but he'd found a forgotten hot dog from the night before and happily munched away. All was right with the world ...

Craig joined his son, cuffing his shoulder as his eyes glistened. He rested his other hand on Jessie's arm and squeezed. "I'm very excited for you kids, and I want to say ..." His voice hitched, and Malcolm feared he'd burst into tears with his old man. "You're both going to be very happy. I know it. You've been in each other's orbit for your whole adult life, and I've watched you both grow, mature, and excel. I'm glad we can share in this moment with you."

"Thanks, Craig," Jessie said, tears already falling. She tugged his dad close for a hug, and Malcolm used the moment to gather his own whirling emotions. Even though they were good feelings, they were a lot to handle. After years of starving for more of JJ, he'd been offered everything and more on a silver platter. He still couldn't believe it.

As Craig stepped back, Malcolm asked the question that he'd had since their arrival. "How did you know to come here?"

Craig looked embarrassed. "Trevor texted that y'all were coming over here for news. We weren't sure if it was good or bad, but your mother and I ..." He waved helplessly toward the group. "Well, you know how she is."

"Sure do," both Malcolm and Jessie said in unison.

Whitney joined them, her cheeks flushed. She chewed on her finger nails for a moment before nudging Malcolm. "Um," she whispered. "I'm totally embarrassed that I'm even asking, but do you think your momma would …"

Craig saved her from further awkwardness by reaching out to shake Whitney's hand. "I'm sorry, darling, we haven't met. I'm Craig, Estelle's husband and Malcolm's father. And I can promise you, my wife will appreciate whatever you want to ask her." He lowered his voice and added, "As long as it's remotely related to *Atlanta Hearts* and isn't illegal, it'll make her day."

That was all the confirmation Whitney needed before she darted over to Estelle. Malcolm heard, "I'm so sorry, Ms. Winters, but I'm your biggest fan."

And that was the story of how Whitney and Estelle became BFFs.

Not for the first time, Malcolm chafed at not having a space for Jessie and him to escape to. He still couldn't drive, his parents were staying at his house, and Jessie was currently shacking up at her mother's place, where his boss was also staying. What a quagmire.

Jessie gripped his elbow, scooting them a few paces away from the chaos. Javi had started arguing with Whitney and Estelle on the best season of *Atlanta Hearts* while Daisy and Paul cuddled on a lounge chair, Gus dozing at their feet. Trevor was busy tidying up the empty glasses, clearly trying to get his girlfriend's attention so they could leave.

"Can I just say?" he asked, nuzzling Jessie's neck.

She angled herself so he had better access, and he felt himself react to her moans as he peppered her with kisses. "That we're still basically teenagers without any privacy?" she supplied.

"Yeah, pretty much. I'd suggest we trespass again, but I won't jeopardize the job that's keeping you here."

He meant it as a joke, but Jessie stiffened in his hold. She pivoted so their eyes locked, and she shot him a stern look. "You're keeping me here, Malcolm. Full stop. The job is a financial motivator, but not the reason I'm staying."

"I didn't mean to—" but she cut him off with a hand over his mouth.

She leaned into him, and he almost licked her palm so he could explain. The juvenile action wouldn't win him any favors, so he stilled and listened. "I'm sorry, for all the running away, for the doubt over our future, for all of it." She squared her shoulders, which provided the perfect view of her cleavage in this dress. Being a man, his gaze swept down, but Jessie caught him. "Eyes up here, mister. I'm pouring my heart out, okay?"

"Mmmkay," he mumbled through her hand.

"I've never felt like I belonged anywhere," she started, licking her lips. "I grew up in this perfect family with a dad and brother who always knew what they wanted to do. Momma's always been supportive, but she couldn't understand why I didn't want to follow in her footsteps and become super wife and mom." This wasn't news to Malcolm, that Jessie felt this way, but hearing her be so vulnerable stole his breath. Sensing he wasn't going to stop her explanation, Jessie's hand fell away. "When I left for that first tour, right after high school, I'd never been more terrified or excited. I found something that was only for me, not connected to my family or any expectations. And you know what? I still couldn't get you out of my head. I was so happy to see you over the holidays, even though I knew we'd break each other's hearts again." A long shuddering breath escaped as the tears finally dried. "But I realized something when you picked me up at the airport after Daddy ..." Her voice caught, and Malcolm cradled her close.

"Shhh, you don't have to do this now, JJ," he promised, meaning every word. The end result is what mattered to him. Jessie wanted to be here, with him; the explanations could wait.

Jessie shook her head. "No, I do. You need to understand that you're where I belong, Malcolm. All of my doubts, my insecurities, my fears melt away when I'm with you. You're where I belong, you're my home, and I'm only sorry it took me years to figure that out."

There was no stopping his waterworks at Jessie's admission. He was certainly doing his mother proud with the spectacle as Jessie's words sank in.

"You're my home, too, JJ. I'm here, and I hate to say that you're not allowed to leave without me. The next time you hop on a plane, it'll be for vacation with me." *A honeymoon sounded nice, but he wouldn't press his luck.*

Javi noticed their combined sobbing and came over to investigate. "Oh hell, Smithy. Did you muck this up already?" He thrust his hands on his hips and sighed. "I'm going to watch you two like a hawk from now on. I'm not missing a thing." He made a V with his fingers and pointed at them.

"Shut up, Javi." Jessie stuck out her tongue.

Trevor came up from behind and pulled him into a headlock. "I swear to God, Ortiz." He gave him a noogie before Javi broke free.

Daisy sighed, clearly exhausted from the busy night. "All right, children, everyone calm down."

Whitney followed Estelle and Craig inside, whistling for Gus to join them. Once everyone was in the living room, Javi announced he was leaving. "Anyone need a ride?" He jangled his keys.

Trevor took Whitney's hand, already backing away to the door. "We're going to head out. Congratulations to the happy couples."

Estelle retrieved her purse, looping it through her arm. "I guess we'll take you kids back to Malcolm's place."

Even though they were nearing thirty years old, neither one wanted to state the obvious—that they'd very much like to spend the night together *alone*.

"Actually," Jessie said. "I was thinking Malcolm and I

could go for a quick drive."

Trevor made a gagging sound, tugging Whitney out after him. "That's our cue to exit."

While her brother was grossed out at the prospect of his sister's love life, Whitney was a walking pair of heart eyes. "Love y'all. Have a wonderful night." She admonished Trevor with a poke to his tummy. "You hush up, this is lovely."

Javi followed them, playfully punching Malcolm in the shoulder. "I'm serious. I'll pay more attention, Smithy," he promised.

"Not too much." Malcolm winked and Javi smiled.

"See y'all at book club! It's going to be a blast. And maybe it'll involve more than one happy ending." He crossed his fingers.

"Ortiz!" Chief choked out, eyes wide.

Javi stuttered, "N-no! I meant, never mind. Good night, y'all."

"See you at book club, Javi." Once he's stepped outside, Daisy took her car keys and shoved them in Jessie's bag. "Think fast!" she ordered as she threw Jessie's purse. "We'll see you when we see you."

"Subtle as a freight train, Momma," Jessie replied, catching the jangling bag in the nick of time before it clattered to the floor. All teasing aside, she wasn't the least bit bothered by the dismissal. She turned to Malcolm and asked, "You ready?"

The look she flashed him was mischievous, and for a moment, Malcolm thought they were back in time. This was the Jessie of high school, smirk in place and a sparkle in her eye. That was what felt different now. This was truly *his* JJ. She wasn't looking for an exit, wasn't building walls between them.

Yet the biggest difference was in Malcolm. He was listening to her, to what she needed and wanted. He wasn't lost in the idealized version of his girl; he wanted Jessie, however she was in that moment.

And in that moment, she was perfect and *his*.

"Ready for anything, JJ."

Unable to be apart from her, he wrapped an arm around her waist and followed her to Daisy's car. "You want to go on a mini road trip to the opposite side of town?"

Malcolm pressed a soft kiss to her lips, savoring the freedom to kiss her whenever. "JJ, I'll go anywhere with you."

LIBBY KAY

CHAPTER TWENTY-SIX

This was happening ... This was *happening*!

The chant rang through Jessie's head as they strode to the car. Clearly, Malcolm's recovery had been trucking along without her, as he had no issue keeping pace down the driveway.

Jessie's pulse hitched as she slid behind the wheel. Waiting until Malcolm was inside, cane tucked next to the door, she pushed the button and waited for the car to roar to life. Driving Malcolm wasn't new, and hell, she'd driven him to this particular destination more times than she could count. But this was the first moment alone since reconciling—for good—and she wanted to savor it.

She drove a block until the first *Stop* sign and threw the car in park. Not bothering to see if anyone was looking, she lunged across the center console, gripped his shoulders, and tugged him in for a real kiss—without an audience. Since their last lip-lock, he'd lost the bandages on his face, one step closer to being his old self. They took their time exploring each other, tiny moans echoing through the car.

Malcolm kicked his cane as he unbuckled and tugged on Jessie's arm. "I'm not ..." he breathed in between kisses, "complaining." He nipped at her bottom lip and gasped as she slid a hand down his chest. "But is this"—gasp—"the plan?"

"The plan?"

Jessie attempted to shake her head without breaking contact, but she only managed to bump their noses. She giggled as Malcolm rubbed his face. "Careful, JJ, that's basically the only part of me that wasn't injured."

Jessie pecked the tip of his nose. "Sorry, but I couldn't help myself." Lips traveling south, she nipped at his bottom lip, and Malcolm growled, trying to haul her closer in the tight quarters. Their efforts managed to bump the car horn, essentially popping the passion bubble. Chest heaving, Malcolm reluctantly pulled back from their embrace. His lips were swollen, dark eyes wild. He was perfect—and he was hers.

Malcolm sat up straight, putting his shirt back to rights. "Sweet Georgia Brown, JJ." He sighed, running a hand through his hair. "I can't stop, but maybe in the middle of your momma's neighborhood isn't the best place for this." He hitched a thumb toward the window, where a pair of dog walkers had stopped their late evening stroll to gawk.

"Good evening, ladies," Jessie greeted, throwing in a polite finger waggle. After waiting for them to cross the street, Jessie sped through the intersection. "Well, good thing we already told our families. That's Mrs. Murphy and Mrs. Brock. I love those women, but they're the biggest gossips in Pinegrove. Tongues will be wagging in approximately ten seconds."

Jessie waited for the cloying feeling of her life being everyone's business to return, but she was delighted to feel nothing at all. Not even a pang of worry prickled her skin; it was refreshing and kind of nice.

"Wait? Malcolm asked, craning his neck to look out the rearview mirror. "Mrs. Brock, as in George's momma? All of Engine 33 will know before we make it to your mystery destination."

No sooner had they crested the hill out of the

neighborhood than Malcolm's phone buzzed in his pocket. He fished it out and guffawed. "Wow, I underestimated George's passion for gossip."

Jessie bit back a laugh. "What did he say?"

Malcolm swiped on his screen, voice tinged with mirth. "He said, *'Just heard from my mom, she said you and Jessie need to get a room.'*"

Jessie joined Malcolm in cackling, clutching the steering wheel while she caught her breath.

They settled into a companionable silence as they drove through the winding roads headed toward their not-so-mysterious destination. Jessie quickly glanced over to Malcolm, whose eyes grew misty as he recognized a familiar turn.

"Where are we going, JJ?" Gone was the laughter and lightness of a few moments ago. In its place was a quiet hope she hadn't heard in far, far too long.

"I thought we'd go stargazing," Jessie said plainly, as if she hadn't uttered the words she'd been dying to say. When she was out of the country, sleeping in cramped tents or soggy sleeping bags, this was the place she'd picture when she wanted good dreams. Clear skies, warm air, and fireflies keeping them—and the stars—company. Nights like this, alone with Malcolm, were her favorite. Striving to keep the moment light, she added, "And this time, we won't be trespassing." She giggled. "I'm kind of a big deal at Hog Hollow."

Malcolm took her free hand and pressed a kiss into her palm. "You're always a big deal to me."

A few minutes later, Jessie parked on the outskirts, leading Malcolm into the rear of the old barn. Before they went inside, she spread her arms wide, encompassing everything they could see. "This is my office," she bragged. "I help with the gardens and grounds, but I've also made some friends."

Malcolm offered an indulgent smile. "You're a popular gal."

Jessie fluttered her eyelashes, smile still fixed in place. "Thank you." She took a few paces until she reached the barn door. "I want you to meet someone very important to me," she teased.

Incredulous, Malcolm asked, "Should I be jealous of a pig?"

"No, of course not ... much." She opened the door. The space was dark, save for a few lightbulbs hanging from the ceiling. Jessie strode ahead, stopping at the rear where the biggest pig lounged on a pile of hay. "Gentlemen, can I have your attention?" she asked, darting her eyes between Malcolm and Oinks."

"Are you serious?" Malcolm chuckled. He leaned against one of the pens, cane forgotten in the car.

Jessie shook her head. "You love me, so you have to deal with my insanity." She stuck her tongue out and gave a quick whistle. The pig looked up, blinking at Malcolm. Jessie squealed, bouncing on her feet as she clapped. "I knew he'd love you." She took Malcolm's hand and reached into the pen. "You can pet him, he's very sweet."

"He'd be sweeter as a rack of ribs," Malcolm muttered, only slightly jealous of the swine.

Jessie gasped, clamping her hands over her ears. "I will not listen to such nonsense. Oinks is amazing, and I'm almost a vegetarian now."

Malcolm did as he was told and gently patted the pig's head. To his credit, Oinks tolerated the praise before flopping back down in his hay bed. "There, we've met. Can we please get out of here before my allergies act up?" Jessie understood he was only half kidding.

"Fine." She sighed, holding the door for him. "I guess we'll go lie under the stars and make out or something." She tossed a flirty look over her shoulder. "We do have a lot of lost time to make up for."

Malcolm grabbed her hand, linking their fingers together. Jessie pushed her shoulder against him, turning into an impromptu walking stick as they ambled through the groves of pecan trees. Leaves rustled around them, the only sound heard over their raising hearts. Jessie's palm grew slick in Malcolm's grip, but she never let go.

He swept his thumb over her knuckles, meeting resistance. He nearly toppled onto the ground when he saw her promise ring. "JJ?" he asked, holding her hand up. "When did you start wearing this again?" His voice was wistful, full of hope.

"Right around the time I came to my damn senses," she admitted. For a moment, they didn't speak, merely stared at the other like they couldn't believe their reality. Jessie tugged on their hands and ordered, "Let's go take a load off."

When they made it to the meadow clearing, Jessie found a spot that was flat and eased down onto the ground. Malcolm joined her, and once he was seated, she laid her head in his lap. The sun was finally asleep, turning the sky a stunning purple reminiscent of blackberry jam. Above them, a million stars sparkled, winking their approval at their reunion. Or at least that's what Jessie told herself.

Jessie pointed up at a cluster of stars. "What's that one?" she asked, lowering her hand and resting it on his thigh.

Malcolm shook beneath her. "We're getting right down to the important stuff, huh?"

Hand flexing on Malcolm's warm skin, Jessie hummed. "Yeah, why not? You've already met Oinks, might as well get to the good stuff."

He wiggled a little, jostling Jessie's head. "I can think of other good stuff we could be doing."

Thankful for the darkness, Jessie's cheeks turned a violent shade of red. Oh boy, she wanted to do everything with Malcolm, but not out here. Their first time since reuniting deserved a little more pomp than this ... although she'd be lying if she said she wasn't tempted.

"As soon as we kick your parents out, we'll get to the *great* stuff," she promised.

Placated, if even for the moment, Malcolm trailed his hand up and down Jessie's neck. His touch was slow, methodical, a lovely change from how frantic things had been when they were under a deadline. She shivered against him. "What's one over there?" she asked.

"I think that's the Spangled Star," Malcolm said, voice dripping with certainty.

Jessie wrinkled her nose. "The Spangled Star?"

"Yeah. You know, like the national anthem. How unpatriotic of you not to know that."

"Okay, Copernicus. What's that bunch over there by the North Star?"

Malcolm snorted. "Easy peasy. That's the Pop Starlet Party." Forgetting they were supposed to be quiet, Jessie laughed so hard it echoed across the meadow. "Shhh, JJ. You're going to get us kicked out and yourself fired."

Jessie tilted her head back so their eyes met. "It's your fault. Now tell me who the Pop Starlet Party is."

"That one is Sabrina, and there's Chappell. That pair over there is Britney and Taylor."

She nestled closer and teased, "You're ridiculous."

"Never said I wasn't," he agreed. "But I'm ridiculously in love with you, so you'll have to get used to it. You are best friends with a pig, and I am a master astronomer."

"We're quite the pair," she mused, swiveling around and pressing a tender kiss to his lips. The weight of the moment, of the change in their relationship, hit Jessie right in the chest. She couldn't run away from that sweet smile, or that warm chocolate stare anymore.

"You okay?" Malcolm asked, sensing a shift.

Jessie swallowed past a lump in her throat and said, "I'm so sorry you had to get injured for me to come back to you."

Malcolm exhaled, his body quaking with need and raw emotions. "JJ, I would gladly fight a million fires for one chance at forever with you."

"That's the most romantic thing I've ever heard," she whispered as she closed the distance and kissed him hungrily. She melted into Malcolm's hold, his arms cradling her close like she was a precious treasure.

The world was no longer calling, only Malcolm was. Jessie had never been happier to be home.

*

Malcolm savored every press of Jessie's lips, every swipe of her tongue. The longer he held Jessie, the more alive he felt. He wasn't kidding. There wasn't anything he wouldn't do for JJ. As they sat there in the meadow, the insects buzzing and the sky turning an inky black, Malcolm knew this was everything he'd ever wanted.

They likely would have fooled around like teenagers until the sun came up, but Malcolm's phone vibrated from the depths of his shorts pocket. Seeing as how his favorite girl was on top of him, he was in no hurry to move her so he could see what all the fuss was about.

Unfortunately, curiosity caught hold of Jessie. "You should probably check that," she breathed, resting on her elbows.

"Says you," he scoffed. "Get back over here." His phone whirred again, and Jessie took control of the situation. She nudged him to his side and pulled out his phone, snorting when she saw a series of texts from his parents. "Do I want to know?" He sighed, scrubbing a hand down his face.

Jessie nodded, mussed hair falling around her face as she leaned closer with his phone. "Oh yeah." She laughed.

The first text was from his dad.

Got a hotel room. Hope you and Jessie have a good night. We'll call for breakfast in the morning.

The next slew of messages was from Estelle.

We got a hotel.

Have fun with Jessie.

I'm so happy you're back together! Do you think you'll get married soon?

Jessie wants babies, right?

Tell Jessie we're happy for you both!

Oh, and tell Jessie we love her, too.

Maybe we should leave Georgia now, give you kids more privacy?

Jessie rested her head on his shoulder, reading the messages as he scrolled. She covered her mouth as she shook with laughter. "Your momma thinks they need to leave the state now that we're back together?"

Malcolm tossed his phone a few feet away and groaned. "It's not a bad idea," he mused, toying with the hem of her dress. "There are a lot of things I'd like to do with you, JJ. And none of them involve my parents." He swatted at a mosquito that landed on his neck. "Or involve insects."

"Want to get out of here?" she asked, already pushing to her feet. She held out a hand and helped Malcolm up. He wobbled slightly, but thanks to his PT exercises, he understood how to balance and steady himself better. He still had a ways to go with recovery, but knowing that JJ was back for good took away the sting of healing.

On the drive back to his place, Jessie kept the radio off, and they chatted about everything and nothing. Malcolm kept his hand on Jessie's leg, squeezing it every few minutes to remind himself that this was all real. When she pulled up to his place, he had a thought.

"When we get inside, I want to show you something."

She waggled her eyebrows. "Is that a euphemism?"

He pecked her cheek and chuckled. "All right, I'd like to show you two things." Jessie playfully punched his shoulder before hopping out of the car and scurrying around to his side. "I can handle the walk to the door."

Jessie leaned into him, mouth set in a frown. "Never said you can't, but I'm here and I like helping." She swatted his backside and added, "And I like touching you."

"In that case, I think I need help getting to the door." He spun her around to face him, leaning down to pepper kisses from her neck to her lips. "And help getting to the bedroom," he purred, sending goosebumps all over her exposed skin.

Jessie's head dipped back, exposing more of her neck for his consumption. "You know what," she breathed, fingers digging into his biceps, "I think we should skip right to the sex. You can show me that other thing later."

Her comment stalled his progress, and Malcolm reluctantly backed up. "No, first things first." He dug in his pockets for his keys, letting them inside and turning on the lights. His place was spotless, his parents having cleaned up everything from their lunch dishes to the pile of laundry on the couch. Even his mother's celebrity and gossip magazines were gone, in their place a sparkling clean coffee table.

Malcolm didn't let himself be distracted by anything though, because he was a man on a mission. "Have a seat, I'll be right back."

For once, Jessie didn't ask questions, plopping down on the sofa with an unceremonious *thud*. Malcolm walked as fast as he could to his closet, rummaging around until he found what he was looking for. It was nothing of monetary value, but he hoped Jessie would appreciate the effort … the thought he put into documenting their love story.

When he emerged from the bedroom, he spied Jessie on the couch, tapping her fingers on her knees. "You nervous?" he teased, not used to seeing his girl antsy in his home.

She shot him a sheepish grin. "Not really, but it still feels surreal, you know? Usually this is the part of our relationship where one of us picks a fight and the other storms out."

"You want me to start something for old time's sake. I'll be happy to throw you out." He winked, and she giggled. Now was the perfect time for this.

"I've been working on something," he said, clutching the frame in his hands, the front facing him.

Jessie inched toward the edge of her seat. "Oohhh. What is it?"

Malcolm exhaled, suddenly terrified she'd find this lame … or worse, embarrassing. "Let me say that if you hate it, we can pretend it doesn't exist."

Blowing raspberries, Jessie flapped her hands in front of

her. "Let me see already. I'll be the judge." She arched an eyebrow, but he wasn't quite ready yet.

"I started this when we were still in high school," he said, voice low. "I'd collect little trinkets or tokens from our times together, and I'd throw them in this old shoe box." She tilted her head, clearly hanging on to every word. "Then as the years went on, the shoe box wasn't big enough to hold all our keepsakes, so I started a real-life Pinterest board, I guess." He lifted a shoulder, sweat pooling under his arms. *What if she hates this?*

Jessie's eyes glimmered with tears, as if already knowing what he'd done. "A Pinterest board, huh?" The question sounded like it had been run through a sander.

"But I didn't know how to organize it, so I thought I'd make a constellation." He swallowed, slowly turning the frame around to face her.

With a gasp, Jessie covered her mouth with a trembling hand. "Oh my God."

The board had a black matte finish, and Malcolm had pinned everything from tickets from their first fireworks festival and flowers from their prom corsage and boutonniere to photos of them through the years. The images spanned brace-filled smiles and lanky limbs to Malcolm at his academy graduation, Jessie proudly hanging from his arm. He'd even saved the corks from some of their awful Moscato binges in the meadow, a receipt from Bojangles, and most recently Jessie's visitor's badge to the hospital.

"I made this," he started, clearing his throat, "because I wanted to document us. No matter what happened, or wasn't happening, with us, I knew we'd get here, JJ. I know we're meant to be together."

Slowly, she rose, closing the distance in a few paces. Her fingers traced through the constellation of their memories together, the black barren space a placeholder for their times apart. "This is beautiful, Malcolm." Their eyes finally met, and Malcolm watched a single tear slide down Jessie's cheek.

He swiped it wordlessly away, never blinking for fear he'd miss something. Carefully, she took the board from his grasp and placed it next to the couch. "I love that, and I love you, and I love your patience most of all. I don't think most men would have waited for me, let alone kept our memories so close."

"I was simply keeping them warm for you, JJ." He brought his hands up, resting them on her shoulder while she collected herself. "I didn't do this to make you sad. I'm sorry."

Jessie sniffed, taking his hand and looping them around her neck. She walked into his embrace, breathing him in and letting out a contented sigh. "I'm not sad. I'm happy that I'm finally here. We're finally getting our happily ever after."

"I love you," he breathed, pulling her as close as he could. He kissed her, sweetly and with all the time in the world. Because that's what they finally had now—time.

"I love you more," she replied.

Malcolm chuckled. "And they say high school romances don't last."

LIBBY KAY

EPILOGUE

Eighteen months later

"Momma, I love you," Jessie said through clenched teeth. "But if you don't stop fussing with my veil, I'm going to throw you in the pond."

Daisy's hands faltered on the lace, but she finally stepped back. "I'm sorry, sugar, but I wanted to help."

"You are helping, but you're also fidgeting." Turning her attention to her matron of honor, she asked, "Whit, be honest. How do I look?"

Whitney dabbed at her eyes for the third time in as many minutes. "Y'all look perfect. Thank you so much for letting me style the wedding." She blew her nose, the sound echoing throughout the room.

Gladys had given them full rein of the farmhouse and grounds, saying it was the least she could do for bringing Hog Hollow back to life. Truth be told, the farm brought Jessie back to life. She'd found a purpose she'd been searching for, and it had been right under her nose this whole time.

Jessie savored this sense of accomplishment, of belonging, but today was about more than work and finding herself. She'd found Malcolm, permanently. Even more importantly—today she was *finally* marrying Malcolm. No more games, no more yo-yoing; they were putting rings on it and making it legal. And right where it all started, Jessie couldn't imagine a better location to say *I do!*

"Room for one more?" Estelle said from the doorway. She was dressed in a dusty pink gown that brought out the hue of her cheeks, her blonde hair styled in an updo that looked more complicated than her Momma's recipe for Hummingbird cake.

"Of course, Estelle." Daisy tugged her future in-law into the room. "We were just talking about how we're not going to cry anymore, because it ruins our makeup."

Estelle's bottom lip trembled, but the tears didn't fall. "Oh goodness, I've been a mess all morning. Craig can attest to that, but I won't ruin my makeup for anything. Not even my baby boy finally putting a ring on it." She clutched her hands in front of her and gushed, "You look gorgeous, Jessie. I've never seen a more beautiful bride."

"Thanks, Estelle. I appreciate everything you and Craig did to help."

Her future in-laws had pulled out all the stops, from hosting the rehearsal dinner to paying for more flowers than the state of Georgia had ever seen. Every type of bloom imaginable was shoved in bouquets, tucked into tuxedo jackets, or strewn across tables. Trevor had warned the station to double up on their allergy medications, which, in hindsight, was smart thinking.

Craig and Estelle had also made scarce so Malcolm and Jessie could enjoy a little time together before the festivities got insane, which Jessie knew was not easy for her almost mother-in-law to do. In the lead-up to the big day, both bride and groom had been working hard so they could enjoy their vacation time and honeymoon. Malcolm had been back to full service at the station, which meant he pulled a few double shifts here and there. Jessie had morphed into a full-on farmer, lovingly obsessing over every animal and plant that graced Hog Hollow. In short, life was busy, but damn was it good.

"Oh hush now, it's our pleasure." Estelle preened at the praise.

Whitney dabbed at her eyes again before checking her reflection and sighing. "Are y'all sure I don't look too bloated in this? I've put on a few pounds since our final fittings." She frowned, her hand resting on her growing baby bump.

Daisy was incredulous. "Now it's your turn to hush, sugar. You're glowing and growing my first grandchild. I won't hear such nonsense."

"And neither will I," Estelle agreed, gently patting Whitney's bump. "You're gorgeous any day of the week." Lowering her voice, she added, "And I'm not saying it has to be tomorrow, Jessie. But if you and Malcolm wanted to make me a grandmother sooner rather than later, I wouldn't say no. We start filming for the *Atlanta Hearts* spin-off next month, but I'd be back here by the holidays."

Daisy laughed, but Jessie blanched. "Um ..." She opened and closed her mouth like a goldfish while she struggled to find her words.

There was a knock at the door as Trevor joined the fray. "Well, I'd love to know what's being discussed that got my dear sister tongue-tied." He mimicked her expression, earning a not-so-discreet middle finger from Jessie.

Whitney closed the distance to her husband and kissed his cheek, hastily wiping the lipstick smear with her damp tissue. "Be nice, it's girl talk. Is everyone ready?"

Trevor nodded, draping his arm around his wife. Jessie felt herself well up at the sight of them. Her brother had been through a lot, and seeing him this happy still made her want to weep with relief. It also made her want to be with her own man.

"Tell me it's showtime," Jessie pleaded. "I'm ready to get out there and become Mrs. Smith."

Now Estelle couldn't keep her tears at bay. "Oh, I love

the sound of that," she blubbered, snatching a wad of tissues from Daisy's hand. "We're finally family!" If the *Atlanta Hearts* reboot didn't garner the woman a daytime Emmy award, this performance surely could.

Whitney squared her shoulders and whistled, silencing the sobs of joy. "All right, ladies! Let's get to our places so Jessie and Malcolm can get hitched." Turning to her husband, she asked, "Are the boys in place?" She raised an eyebrow and added, "All the boys?"

"Yes, ma'am," Trevor promised, kissing her cheek before stepping back. "Momma, Paul is waiting to take you to your seat. Jessie and I will be there in a minute."

Daisy, Whitney, and Estelle all left, leaving the siblings alone for a moment.

"Y'all know I'm not one for speeches," Trevor said, sitting down on the edge of the bed.

Jessie's eyes misted at her brother, knowing whatever he was about to say was coming from the depths of his heart. "I know that," she whispered.

"We both know it should be Daddy walking you down that aisle." Trevor's voice caught, and he cleared his throat twice before he found his words. "But since he can't be here, I'm truly honored that you asked me to give you away."

Makeup be damned, Jessie couldn't hold back her tears. "You're the only person I want giving me away, Trev." She stepped closer, taking his hand in hers and squeezing with everything she had. "He would be so proud of you, you know that, right?"

Trevor snorted. "Jessie, I'm supposed to be saying that to you. You're stealing my speech!"

"Well, it's my wedding day, so I can do what I like." Jessie wrinkled her nose, not through with her argument. "You're captain of the greatest fire station in the great state of Georgia, you married the greatest woman alive, save for me and Momma of course." She laughed, watching Trevor's frown turn into a megawatt grin. "And you're going to be a daddy yourself soon. He would be so proud and thrilled for you."

Trevor stood, letting out a breath before carefully resting his hands on Jessie's shoulders. "You're the one he'd be proud of, going around the world to help people. Then you came home and shared your love and hard work with the people of Pinegrove. And I won't even waste my breath on how much Daddy loved Smithy. He's doing cartwheels in Heaven watching you two today. I know it in my bones."

"And now Whitney is going to be furious for me ruining my makeup." Jessie dabbed uselessly at her eyes, but she didn't care. "I love you, big brother."

"Love you, too. Now let's get out there. I'm already sweating in this monkey suit."

"You fight fires for a living, and a tuxedo is what pushes you over the edge?" She thwacked his arm. "Some captain you are."

Trevor hugged her, careful of her veil and dress. "Let's get you hitched, brat."

"Deal." Jessie took her brother's hand, gleefully walking out into the sunshine to marry her favorite person in her favorite place.

*

Malcolm's face hurt from how hard he was smiling. Not even his mother's theatrics or Javi's shameless flirting with the photographer could dampen his spirits. He was about to marry JJ, the love of his life.

"I've got something you can take a picture of," Javi whispered from the far side of the barn.

"Javi, knock it off. I'm on the clock," Lola protested, batting away Javi's hand as he attempted to grope her bottom. "Now get over there with the groom or I'll have to Photoshop you into the pictures."

"That sounds like a better idea, especially if I get to keep touching your ..."

"Good Lord, Ortiz! Can you do as the woman says?" Malcolm threw his arms in the air and sighed.

"You two are ridiculous, you know that? Here I am, expressing love for my girlfriend on a very romantic day, and you're squashing my joy." He patted Lola's butt again to punctuate his point.

Lola playfully pushed him aside. "And I said I would only be the photographer and your date if you behaved. And here you are, causing trouble before they even make it down the aisle."

"I never really promised anything, and it makes sense you're here. You're my girlfriend and the best photographer in Pinegrove."

Lola thrust her hands on her hips, staring down at her boyfriend. "Enough flattery, mister. Now, go out there and make sure Katie and Oinks haven't gotten into trouble. I won't have her ruining her dress before she's performed her flower girl duties."

Malcolm, Jessie, Lola, and Javi had gotten closer over the last year, and that included spending more time with Katie. She felt like part of their group from the moment Lola and Javi started dating, and having her as part of their special day made perfect sense. For once, Malcolm had been proud of Javi's determination on the dating front. Lola was a breath of fresh air, and he'd truly never seen his friend this smitten.

Javi looked chastened, pulling Lola close to peck her lips. "Fine, you're right. I'll make sure she stays out of the pig pens until after the reception. I want a dance with both my girls, and being covered in mud won't do." He pinched her hip and sauntered off to find Katie.

"And just when I thought I made the wrong choice, the man does something like that." Lola huffed out a laugh.

"He's an idiot, but he's our idiot," Malcolm agreed, reaching out and giving Lola a side hug. "Thank you."

"For what?"

"Everything. Being our photographer, being such a good friend, and obviously putting up with Ortiz. I know he's no picnic." He waggled his eyebrows.

Lola blinked a few times, finding her voice. "You're welcome, but you know I should be thanking you. You're part of the reason Katie and I have settled in as well as we have, and I mean more than the Javi thing. You welcomed me into your circle, and I really appreciate that." Clearly on the verge of more tears, Malcolm cleared his throat. "Having said all that, you're still paying me for this gig." She let out a watery laugh, and Malcolm gave her another quick hug.

"Yeah, but payment doesn't include loving my friend."

"It should. I think I deserve hazard pay."

Malcolm's head fell back as he laughed, and Lola took a quick picture of the carefree moment. "Let's get you out there. Your girl is waiting. Besides, I don't trust Katie and Javi not to let that damn pig out before it's time."

"Excellent point, let's roll." Malcolm and Lola exited the barn and headed toward the pond.

Dozens of white chairs were lined up in rows facing the water, the sun just starting to dip to the horizon. They were approaching the magic hour, when the farm transformed into a wonderland bathed in purples and pinks. If he had a dime for every time he and Jessie watched fireflies and stars on this land, he'd be a rich man. But that wasn't fair, he mused as he collected himself. He was richer than any man here, because he finally had his girl.

Malcolm joined Javi at the front of the scene, hugging his parents on his walk to the altar. He was proud of his mother, as ridiculous as that was to say. She'd kept her theatrics mostly private, letting the bride shine like the diamond she was.

A moment later the string quartet started, the familiar wedding march floating around the guests. The air smelled like juniper and a mix of perfumes and colognes from their guests. A sea of happy faces beamed back at Malcolm, and he nearly pinched himself. Everything was perfect; it was almost a dream.

He saw everyone from town whom he loved and respected, from his brothers—and sister—from the fire station to his friends and neighbors. The chief was seated with Daisy, Gus at their feet. His ears were splayed out, snout sniffing the grass. He and Jessie had discussed which animals in their lives would help on their special day. Since Gus had stolen the show at Trevor and Whitney's wedding, it only seemed fair to give him the night off.

As the music grew louder, Whitney walked down the aisle, slowly in her heels and growing frame. When he and Jessie had picked the date, they never imagined Whitney and Trevor would be weeks from their due date.

Next he spied Katie, who held a leash for Oinks and had the biggest smile on her face. Oinks had a harness on, topped with the box of rings. As she walked down the aisle, Katie tossed rose petals on the ground, all the while keeping the pig from eating them. If he wasn't so eager to see JJ, he would have laughed at the adorable scene. Judging from the sniffles beside him, Javi was losing the battle to stay composed.

Then the music changed, and he spied his captain and his girl at the end of the aisle. It was all he could do not to sprint to her—because he could thankfully do that now—but he stayed put. He wouldn't do anything to ruin this perfect moment.

Jessie and Trevor walked toward him, her gaze never leaving Malcolm's. She was a vision in white, her eyes welling with tears. It was only when she reached him at the altar that he realized his cheeks were damp. She yanked a handkerchief from around her bouquet and patted his cheeks. "Don't cry," she cooed. "I've already bawled enough for the both of us," she teased, a tear escaping.

Malcolm snatched her hand before she could pull away, gently kissing her palm. "I love you, JJ."

"I love you, too," Jessie said, lip trembling.

Trevor leaned forward and said, "Can you two keep it together, please? My wife can't stand in these heels for long."

"Shh." Whitney *tsked* behind him, and everyone laughed.

"If we can get started." The pastor chuckled. "I think these two would like to get married." Under his breath, he muttered, "And I wouldn't mind a seat, too."

Malcolm would love to say he remembered every moment after that, but he didn't. What he remembered, what he would cherish until his dying day, was the feeling of committing to not only Jessie, but to their life together. He remembered the sensation of her hand in his as she slipped a ring onto his finger. He remembered the feel of her in his arms as they twirled under the fairy lights to their song, the taste of the sweet sparkling Moscato as they toasted their nuptials. He remembered their first moment alone after the wedding was over, the sight of her in her lingerie that will live rent-free in his mind.

Malcolm will remember the feeling of so much love from all the people he cared for, together to celebrate him and JJ.

As he rolled over in bed, cuddling his wife against him. He traced a finger over the cluster of stars she'd had tattooed after their engagement, right on the tender skin of her wrist. Malcolm had a matching set of his own, their own permanent constellation.

Malcolm whispered, "Good night, Mrs. Smith."

"Good night, Mr. Smith," JJ hummed. "Today was perfect."

And Malcolm couldn't agree more.

LIBBY KAY

ACKNOWLEDGEMENTS

I've said it before, and I'll say it again—writing can be a solitary endeavor. But the following people's support and love make it a whole lot less lonely ...

First, my thanks to the team at Inkspell Publishing, especially Melissa and Yeza. This book would not be what it is without you. Thank you for your patience and support while we crafted Malcolm and Jessie's happily ever after.

Thank you to Emily at Emily's World of Design for making a stunning cover ... and allowing me to request a few dozen changes to make it perfect. You're a rock star.

I want to thank Liz Donatelli for being my fearless podcast cohost on Romance Roundup. You promote my work without hesitation and are one of my biggest champions. Thank you for making the romance industry a better place. Here's to another round of adventures—giddy up!

To the authors who share in this journey, at Inkspell and beyond. A special shout out to Logan Sage Adams, who navigates the indie publishing scene with me and keeps me motivated ... not always an easy task.

To my friends and family, who listen to me vent and support my insanity during the writing process. Mom, Dad, Kathleen, Carri, Thelma, Ernie, and the Jets—you're my heart.

The world's biggest thank you to my husband for filling my life with so much love, laughter, and support. It's easy to write romance books with you by my side. Love you to pieces, Curly!

Last, but certainly not least, to the readers who have found joy in Pinegrove, and Buckeye Falls before, and follow me on this crazy journey. Your support is magic, and I appreciate it more than you know! Thank you for loving these characters as much as I do.

Happy reading!

Sneak Peek at a Holiday Novella- Coming Soon!

Thanksgiving Overruled

Winnie Kerr stretched in her seat, neck popping as she flexed. Her phone was cradled against her shoulder, the angle doing nothing to soothe her frazzled nerves. Outside her office window, Savannah was getting into the holiday spirit. Thanksgiving hadn't happened, but already the streets were lined with twinkle lights, garland, and holly. Her office building hadn't gotten the memo—there wasn't a garland or candy cane to be found.

Despite her neighbors and colleagues buying turkeys and packing for road trips, Winnie was firmly planted in her office chair. The holiday didn't call to her, and frankly, if it did, she wouldn't answer. Gravy and dressing were the furthest thing from her mind...

"You cannot have Chinese takeout for Thanksgiving, Win." The sweet, well-meaning nagging of her baby sister, Whitney, brought a smile to her face. It was a nice, considering she hadn't cracked a grin all day. Smiling is frowned upon when negotiating and arguing with opposing counsel. A toothy grin can kill reputations faster than a series of lost cases.

"Thanks for your concern, Whit," Winnie chuckled. "I'll have you know, this is a victimless crime, skipping turkey day."

There was a pause on the other end while her sister presumably wrangled in her retort. Whitney lived her life based on her heart, an organ that, up until recently, hadn't been getting a lot of action. In stark contrast, Winnie let her brain do the talking. She was an attorney after all, it suited her well.

"Win, what does Mari want to do?"

And that's how her sister got her to finally put down the brief she was working on and listen. "Wow, way to bring my girlfriend into this," Winnie sighed. "I don't think Mari minds. We've both been so busy with work these last couple months."

Whitney was incredulous. "You're both workaholics, but that doesn't mean you couldn't take a couple days to stop and smell the cranberry sauce."

Pursing her lips, Winnie pushed off her seat and stalked around her desk. She cupped the back of her neck, willing her traitorous heart to slow. "Mari's fine with it. We agreed we'll order takeout and just lay low for a couple days."

A loud snort echoed through the phone. "Ha! Give me a freaking break, Win. Granted I don't know Mari well—yet—but I'd wager y'all will be working within five minutes of eating your Kung Pao Chicken."

Winnie opened her mouth to argue, to tell Whitney that her and Mari could enjoy a few days without being glued to their laptops, phone ringers set so they wouldn't miss a single notification. But the words wouldn't come; she'd never lie to her sister.

She imagined it clearly, her apartment cluttered with files, empty takeout containers, open laptops, and a very surly Xena strutting around waiting for extra kibble. Her cat could always tell when it was a special occasion, and she'd set up shop next to her food bowl with a smirk on her face. If cats could smirk, that is…

Whitney gave up waiting for a response and said, "Come to Pinegrove. Daisy is making a whole feast, and we certainly have room for two more."

Pinegrove, Georgia was a picturesque small town where her sister had moved that summer. After falling in love with a hot fireman and finding her dream job, she had never been happier. Winnie had met Daisy, Trevor's momma, a couple months ago during a rare visit. The woman was sweeter than her favorite pralines, and Winnie had no doubt she and Mari would be welcomed with open arms.

OLD FLAMES

"We don't want to impose, and besides. I don't even know if Mari and I could get off work."

LIBBY KAY

Don't Miss the First Book in the Pinegrove FD Series

When Sparks Fly

Two broken hearts, one charming small town, and a few sparks may be the recipe for love...

Whitney Kerr is at a crossroads—literally. After jumping behind the wheel to flee Savannah, and a bad breakup, this Southern Belle is in search of a fresh start. Stopping in a charming smalltown seems like the perfect place to catch her breath and find herself. It's too bad a certain fireman with a crooked grin and kind eyes could have her plans of self-discovery going up in a puff of smoke.

Trevor Mays is at a crossroads—figuratively. Still grieving the loss of his father, he was unceremoniously dumped by his fiancée, who quickly rebounded with his work rival. Just as he thinks things can't get worse, he loses the captain's promotion—to the man who stole his ex. He's about to give up on ever smiling again when a curly-haired beauty with curves for days stumbles into his hometown.

With some help from the residents of Pinegrove, this pair will discover that much like the perfect fireworks show, love only needs a spark.

Fans of Sherryl Woods' <u>Sweet Magnolias</u> series and Sarah Adams's <u>When in Rome</u> series will fall in love with Libby Kay's sweet fireman romance. Ms. Kay's engaging, cozy stories fill your heart and head with possibilities and will quickly become your new favorite!

EXCERPT

"Thanks for dinner and the walk and the talk." Whitney seemed flustered, and she couldn't keep her mouth shut. "I know it was a rough day, but hopefully it ended on a high note."

Trevor closed the distance in two strides. Reaching up, he tucked a curl behind her ear. His finger grazed her ear lobe as he pulled back, and she shivered. Every cell in his body was on alert at Whitney's proximity. "Tonight was perfect. I can hardly remember why my day sucked."

The admission came easily, and he was incredibly grateful at his mother's matchmaking skills. "I'm glad." Whitney breathed, goosebumps erupting down her neck.

"Good night, darlin'. I'll see you soon."

"See you," she agreed.

Trevor strode to his car and got behind the wheel with a lightness in his step. When the day had started, he'd been certain it would end in disaster. Yet now, with Whitney in town, things just felt better … more hopeful. He hadn't realized until he parked his car that he'd been singing along to the radio the whole drive home. Yeah, Trevor was going to be all right.

Available Now in Ebook and Print!

ABOUT THE AUTHOR

Libby Kay lives in the city in the heart of the Midwest with her husband. When she's not writing, Libby loves reading romance novels of any kind. Stories of people falling in love nourish her soul. Contemporary or Regency, sweet or hot, as long as there is a happily ever after—she's in love!

When not surrounded by books, Libby can be found baking in her kitchen, binging true crime shows, or on the road with her husband, traveling as far as their bank account will allow.

Libby cohosts the Romance Roundup podcast with Liz Donatelli where they recommend romance books and interview authors, influencers, and publishers. Check it out for your weekly dose of romance!

Website: https://www.libbykayauthor.com/
Instagram and Facebook: @LibbyKayAuthor
Goodreads and Bookbub: @LibbyKayAuthor

LIBBY KAY

Made in the USA
Middletown, DE
14 September 2025